"Answer me this," she said. "Do you ever want to be loved? Like your next heartbeat depends on it?"

He chuckled. "Yeah, but I focus on something else, like sailing in the regatta with a pina colata."

"Admit it, Patrick, you're as hopelessly in love with me as I am with you. My vulnerable side draws you to me."

Vulnerable? If she only knew. Even now his heart seemed to recognize that. Intimacy felt more meaningful with her than with any other woman. Somehow she had touched him with a deeper tenderness and caring.

"Actually," he said, "love has that unforgettable face and seductive voice, a certain lolling of the head, and eyes so brown they melt this man's heart."

"Hmmm, so you do love me in that same special way I love you."

"Does thinking about you day and night count? I'm so into you, I never want out."

"Are those your real thoughts, baby? And don't say it unless you mean it."

"Genes don't lie and neither do I," he said.

"I need to ask you something," she said. "Do you ever imagine me being pregnant?"

ONE

Anxiety knotted his gut as Patrick Murph paced the floor of the studio greenroom. What if his standup routine flopped? His talent agent said this appearance on America's top-rated talk show—a weeknight production in New York City—would be his one big chance at stardom.

Only a few minutes remained before he would be signaled to appear onstage. Even in the cool room, beads of sweat formed on his forehead as he vocalized his lines.

Interrupting him, two young women appeared in the greenroom doorway. They applauded his vocal rendition while sashaying to sit in studio chairs. Custom-fit blouses and designer jeans revealed the contours of each one's physique.

He feigned shock. "Aha! Central casting sent you here to upstage me, didn't they?"

The tall strawberry blonde, her voice steeped in Southern sweetness, spoke after a closer look at his toned body. "We're here to support Dr. Ronofski. And who are you?"

"I'm the scheduled comedy act, a buffoon with a tune." He adjusted a strap on bib overalls worn over his bare torso. "What brings you girls to the Big Apple, besides a telegenic tune-up?"

The blonde eyed him closely. "Tele-what?"

Her shorter companion raked back her chestnut-brown hair and stood to offer her hand. "We're on a lifesaving mission," she said. Her voice, a sultry contralto, matched the allure of her honey-brown eyes. She was maybe three inches shorter than Patrick's five-foot-nine.

He bowed low as a sly grin curled his lips. "Pat McGroin at your service. Just kidding. That's my stage name. I portray a macho guy who flubs his pickup lines."

She lolled her head back. "Really?"

"Yeah, I'm in a bar and I say to a pretty woman, 'Is this seat shaved for me?'" He grinned. "So how's that for a quickie?"

She hinted at a smile while shaking his hand. "I'm really not into bars or quickies but please, call me Easter."

"Easter?" he said. "Okay, like the Babylonian goddess?" Her firm handshake surprised him. "All jokes aside, I'm Patrick Murph. It rhymes with...." The thought hung in limbo as he nodded at Easter's companion.

"Smurf!" the blonde answered. "I'm Vanessa. It rhymes with, well, nothing really." She stood tall as Patrick, her eyes translucent green crystals, hypnotic in their beauty. "We're putting together an entertainment group. To us it's spiritual, sort of."

He toasted her with an imaginary drink. "Spiritual, huh? As in Twenty-Three and *Thee*? Get it?"

"Yes, it's a pun. We're hiring for the Sweethearts of America Show —the SAS."

"SAS?" he said to Easter. "Sounds almost sassy."

Multi-colored charms jangled on her bracelet as Easter snapped her fingers and directed attention to a television monitor braced on a stanchion. "We'll have lots of skits, all purposed to save the human race from deeper devolution."

"And you'll perform entertainment gigs?"

Easter's earnest demeanor made her seem older than her companion. Endowed with an olive skin tone, her eyes showed the steely resolve of a leader who could light a fire under recruits without making their blood boil.

Returning to her seat, she said, "The idea is to educate audiences. Comedy can do that."

"Got it," he said.

"But there's more. Major changes have to take place. Now!"

Perplexed but intrigued by the urgency in her voice, he plopped down on a studio chair next to them and focused on the television monitor.

"Look, there's our mentor," Easter said. "Listen and learn how we'll save humanity."

Hosting *The Hotz Show,* Wynn Traynor introduced his primary guest, Dr. Henry Ronofski. A world-renowned geneticist, Ronofski's high forehead seemed to exaggerate his gaunt features. Thick eyebrows hooded his intense gaze. He spoke in a graveled drawl, strong and authoritative.

"It's all about choices," Ronofski said. "Regenerative matching versus degenerative luck. One is essential to our survival. That is why, based on genetic testing, we do it for the greater good. You might call it genetic mating."

Seated next to Ronofski, a sports icon known as Dan the Man DiNago to American football fans, nodded in agreement.

Patrick leaned forward, eager to hear how genetic choices might be used as a survival technique.

The host snorted in his typical scoffing tone, "Dr. Ronofski, surely you must know those master race protocols ended with Hitler's downfall."

"That's not what I propose," Ronofski said. "We favor science without Hitler."

Wynn indicated Danny DiNago whose height and broad shoulders bolstered his iconic status. "So why a super jock?"

Ronofski deep-frowned as his voice growled out an answer. "Do you realize how costly genetic diseases are to society? Look at the talent being wasted when gifted people die with no hope of a cure. It may sound strange but Danny here never gets sick, and that's why he's my donor of choice to sire the privileged; those whose genes are not corrupted."

Danny spoke with the confidence of a superstar. "I've got the bloodline to offset bad mutations, Wynn. You know, those people with genes gone wild."

As though at his wit's end, Wynn raised his arms skyward. "Lord help us."

"Wait," Danny said. "Think, man. A hemophiliac doesn't choose a free-bleeder mate, does he?"

Amused, Patrick shook his head. *Genetic matching prevents hemophilia? News to me. What else will it prevent? Tooth decay? Bed wetting? Stuttering?*

Wynn Traynor grinned. "So you're saying we should match the best and discard the rest? I can imagine your come-on line—your egg, my sperm, let's boogie, baby." As the audience laughed, he said, "Where do you guys get off trying to boost some elitist icon's genetic status?"

"Why not?" Danny said. "Boosting isn't boasting."

The slope-shouldered scientist stared into the camera. "Genetic matching is no joke. As a matter of fact, in my new book, *Pedigree Promise*, I remind people that the few have sabotaged the many. And mismatching genes leads to genetic implosion, which is another big step toward Armageddon."

Wynn pounded the desk, his tone mocking. "Yes-yes, frickin' shameful, yada-yada-yada."

Ronofski's voice thundered, "But we can help! And despite junk genes that predispose some to deadly flaws. Take emblot. It's a heritable disease. It mutates like a stealth virus, a glitch in DNA."

Wynn scratched his head. "So you're telling us that victims of emblot should stop reproducing?"

"It's their choice, Wynn, but regenerative matching is the only answer to prevent it."

Facing the camera, Wynn said, "So says the wizard. Do we have volunteers out there who want to avoid this color-me-dead pestilence while at the same time approving Black genocide?"

The scientist's eyebrows met at the bridge of his nose. "Dammit, you're skewing my message. Emblot is not their fault. Some Blacks never get sick, so they have genes well worth matching."

"Some? How many? Fifteen, twenty percent?" He hammered the desk. "This sounds like racial inequity masquerading in pedigree garb. No sex. No offspring. No hope."

"You're distorting the science of gene matching, young man, and ignoring our secret weapon."

Wynn knuckle-rapped the surface of his desk. "Really? Is racial purity your secret weapon?"

In the wake of derisive boos from the audience, Ronofski shook his head. "Would you rather match diseased genes, Mr. Traynor? That, sir, should be taboo, like suicide and incest."

His eyes wide in surprise, Wynn looked at the professor. "What? Explain yourself."

"I'm saying far too many retrogressive misfits are breeding. Their effect on the gene pool causes out-of-control genetic maladies. Again, genetic matching will help."

The host peered hard at Danny. "How were you suckered into this breeding thing, pray tell?"

"One in six males in America have severely flawed sperm," Danny said. "We have to right the inherited wrongs."

Wynn chuckled. "Really? Ha! So your group will prevent Spermageddon."

"Of course," Danny answered without blinking. "The hi-tech medical industry with their gene editing and big-money backers don't like us because genetic matching is natural, and it's free."

Wynn palmed his face momentarily. "Mother of God! Seriously, are any Black people—*any*—allowed in this elitist mating club?"

Before he could answer, a chorus of shouts rumbled from the studio audience as cameras panned a cluster of Black activists. Their leader, Spence Lovejoy, stood with fists raised and voice booming. "I know y'all hiding something behind all that razz talk, fooling us, like we're too gone to mix with all you blue bloods." An All-Pro linebacker, recently retired and destined for the NFL Hall of Fame, Lovejoy had always been a formidable foe on and off the gridiron.

In the greenroom, Patrick understood Wynn was framing the debate to incite adverse reactions from the audience. The chaos could only worsen by bringing the Black leader onstage.

"Uh-oh, girls," Patrick said. "This can't be good. Spence's nickname is Hush Yo' Mouth and he has a reputation for making people do just that."

"It's just a ratings ploy," Easter said. "Wynn likes to rile audiences and stir things up."

Patrick paced the floor. "My act will be hijacked if Wynn keeps up his showboating."

Easter pointed at the television. "Oops! What's going on out there?"

A flurry of movement on the monitor caught Patrick's eye. Wynn Traynor gestured like a referee as Spence smacked Dr. Ronofski upside the head. The scientist's glasses sat lopsided on his pale face. As he righted himself, he blinked rapidly, disoriented by the sudden jolt.

From the greenroom Easter and Vanessa bolted down the straightaway and across the stage to the scientist.

Danny DiNago sprang to his feet, his muscular physique a wedge protecting the scientist from Spence. Guards rushed onto the stage but kept a respectful distance from the Black behemoth. Patrick reached in his pocket and retrieved a small flask as he followed close on the girls' heels, all the while hoping to defuse the on-camera standoff.

Within reach of Spence, the comic drew himself up to his full height, his smaller size at odds with the linebacker's bulk—a badger confronting a cougar. Patrick swigged a mouthful of lighter fluid from the flask and spewed it over a butane flame. The flame billowed larger but quickly disappeared.

"Don't make me do my burning bush routine, Spence. Stage hands are union and all they know are thunder farts."

An amused gleam showed in Spence's eyes. "You firing up that flame thang for show, Bozo?" He nodded at Vanessa. "I say you hinting for some chick to lick your Bic."

"Dr. Ronofski, come with us." Easter steered the scientist beyond Spence's reach with Vanessa following her.

Studio lights faded to semi-darkness and silence replaced the clamor. Guards quickly escorted Patrick Murph and Spence Lovejoy away from the set. As the lighting returned to normal, Dan the Man DiNago, America's most vaunted football icon, remained as the show's only guest.

Patrick knew the drill. Confrontation and drama were standard for the show. With his last chance at fame now in jeopardy, disappointment eroded his hopes for national recognition. Rescheduling him for the show would be a long shot. As anger seared into his sense of fairness, he wanted to drive his fist through the studio wall.

At the far end of the stage, Easter slowed to gaze at him. On the chance that his own gaze would excite her curiosity, he stared back at her. As she hesitated before departing the stage, a nimbus of light glowed momentarily around her face.

Though her smile radiated genuine warmth, he wondered about the aura.

"So, Miss Irresistible, why do I suspect we're the perfect match?" he mumbled before shaking his head. "No, not again. I'm done with fantasies."

But she turned again, sending him a quick finger-roll wave before easing down the hall.

Transfixed, he relished the kindness in her eyes. "Here we go again. Can I afford to fall in love? No, it's definitely not my gig."

He considered calling Liz to report his routine had been hijacked. *Not now, maybe later. After all, my longtime enemy may revive its interest in whatever fame comes my way.*

Easter's smile seemed to linger, as if chiseling a message into Patrick's mind and heart. He could not deny the feeling, illogical as it might be, that he belonged in her future.

Two

S till vexed by Wynn's antics on *The Hotz Show*, Patrick changed into street clothes and stuffed his wig, brogans, and bib overalls into a gym tote. Within minutes he rode an elevator from the studio inside the Waldorf Astoria down to the art deco lobby.

Embarrassed to call his talent agent, he knew it had to be done.

She answered on the first ring. "Liz? Did you see me get hijacked on the *Hotz*? The breakout performance I wanted went sideways. Am I snakebit?"

A long sigh released into the phone. "Sorry, but with Wynn you never know."

"One other thing; hillbilly wit works for most audiences but I'm ready for a change, Liz, like create a new persona. What do you think?"

"Stick with what works, Pat. I gotta take this other call. Sorry. Bye."

Chimes reverberating from a bronze clock in the lobby distracted him. More distracting was the reappearance of Easter and Vanessa standing only twenty yards away. The young women seemed intent on studying a glass-encased exhibit.

He wondered if Easter's flirtations earlier on the set had been sincere. He considered a follow-up introduction. Perplexed, he shifted the tote to his right hand and back to his left. How easy it would be to toss comedy and return to a life in sales. But then he realized it would not lessen the pain of having his performance hijacked on Wynn's show.

What other antic in his repertoire could he have used to steal the show?

If his great-grandfather were present, he would have a trope ready to comfort a struggling comic. Landon Murph's vaudevillian one-liners was the stuff of legend.

He glanced at Easter again before facing the hotel's revolving doors. *I can't appear too anxious to meet her. Besides, I have a comedy tour ahead of me.*

He pondered walking the distance to Grand Central. From there he could easily take a transit to the airport at LaGuardia. But heavy sleet on this day in January could mean flight cancellations.

He trudged toward the doors.

A feminine voice rose above the noise in the lobby. "Where ya' going, comedy man?"

As Easter and Vanessa appeared in his peripheral vision, he angled his head to observe their strides toward him.

Drawing closer, Easter held his gaze. "Hi there. Got a minute?"

"Sure thing. What's up?"

"You're not easy to recognize without your costume." She flashed a megawatt smile. "You were quick to improvise on Wynn's show, so being curious I peeked at the reel on your website. You're really hilarious. Why not join us for a faster ride to success?"

A quick reading of her eyes revealed no hint of guile. In their mesmerizing sparkle he almost lost track of the topic. "Why should a mere mortal like me share the spotlight with two glamour goddesses?"

She nudged Vanessa. "See? What did I tell you? This man has Casanova written all over him. I like the sound of Casanova Comic; it'll be good branding for our road show."

"Roadies, huh?" He admired the tilt of her head and her assertive voice. Her darkish skin tone suggested Black ancestry. "So how many performers will be going on tour with you?"

"Twenty, plus me. It'll be similar to a concert tour. First, I'll hold auditions and qualify dozens of women like Vanessa. But our recruits have to be true believers in our cause. How do you feel about compatibility matching? Like not only personality but genes, too."

"I'm intrigued. But how does the genetic breeding part figure in?"

"Genetic *matching*," she corrected. "Don't say breeding. But I'm glad you asked. We want to teach audiences about gene matching while entertaining them. Know what I'm saying?"

He gave her a wary look. "Okay, but how would I fit in?"

Easter poked his arm. "You'll write comedy sketches for us and direct them. But I'd like to see your genetic profile." She mimed a mouth swab with her finger. "Your DNA will tell us everything we need to know about your pedigree."

"Are you funning me? So far, Miss uh...."

"Beaulieu," she said. "Easter Beaulieu. It's French. Beaulieu was Priscilla Presley's maiden name. You know, before she married Elvis. Just call me Easter."

"Right. Well, Easter, I've managed to be funny without a DNA test for ten years. If comedy was a felony, I'd get life without parole."

"Love it, love it, love it!" Easter said. "With your wit, that voice, and those gemstone-blue eyes, I'm sure you'll be more useful than just creating skits."

"More? Like more of what?"

"Well, I need someone to train and direct my entertainers. They're novices."

"Whoa!" he said. "I've never teamed with a troupe of entertainers, nor directed them. I suspect gene matching isn't wildly popular, so who's backing you? Dan the Man DiNago? And what all's at stake besides genetic breeding? I mean, uh...matching."

"You'll find out soon enough," Easter said. "Our skits will emphasize how we can help get rid of all—and I do mean *all*—inherited defects among humans."

"What defects?" he said. "Pimples and warts? Ingrown toenails? Cowlicks? To hear Ronofski tell it, we're all flies flitting about in a world of cobwebs, like our GPS steered us off course to a trap in some Jurassic nightmare."

Vanessa's spontaneous giggle reminded him of a teenage neophyte. "You're so funny!" she said. "And unique, like someone who's never existed and never will."

Noting her quirky reply, he couldn't resist a rejoinder. "I can see teaming up with you, girl. You the ditz, me the straight man onstage."

"Good, visualize it," Easter said. "And try to see regenerative matching in a better light. It's a lot more than trivial cures. Think hemophilia, diabetes, or autism. Like if your mom were schizoid, you'd be about thirteen times more likely to have it. Do you realize we're facing a genetic meltdown?"

A skeptical grin curled a corner of his lip upward. "Genetic meltdown?"

"It's a fact, Patrick. We humans are plagued with over six-thousand heritable diseases."

Impressed by the number, he wondered what else motivated her activist stance.

"Our program will attract millions of wellborn applicants," she added.

"Wellborn? Do all the girls in this movement turn pro, as in *pro*creating?"

"Let's just say good genes work and bad genes don't, Patrick. Simple as that."

"You eliminate genetic junk, huh?"

Easter squeezed his firm bicep. "With a strict program of quality control, bods like yours will soon be the norm. Life forms don't have to be grotesque, but we see evidence of it everywhere. People have become so desensitized to it, they think it's the norm."

He gave her a mischievous smile. "So to deed my seed, I have to breed?"

"Well, that's sort of the idea." She smiled. "But perhaps artificially."

"Believe me, hon, I know a better way." He snapped his fingers, his rhythmic song in sync with his swaying hips. "Bees build a hive to thrive but their surplus has a purpose not so rare we can't learn to share when hormones beckon egg and sperm to pair."

Easter crossed her arms. "Nice, but Dan the Man is our poster boy."

Voice low, he growled. "Does he have an exclusive on reproduction?"

"No, but he *is* America's most popular jock," she said. "Dr.

Ronofski thinks Danny's profile may rank in the top one percent. We'll know for sure when all the genetic data are in. That should mean our gene matching efforts will pioneer the twenty-first century. Ta-da!"

"So you figure everybody wants a kid who's a duplicate of Dan the Man DiNago."

"Well, he's led the Mobile Marauders to four Super Bowl wins in a row. In—a—row. Seriously, Patrick, I need your expertise in comedy." She spread her arms wing-like. "Think what you could do to jazz up our appeal as entertainers."

"Impromptu is what I do best. Think Globe Trotters. Sight gags, slapstick, and snappy antics like icing...." He gave Vanessa a nod to complete its ending.

"On a cake!" she said as the pendant of a double helix dangled over her cleavage.

He raised his hand for a high-five palm slap. "In a blink we're in sync."

Easter poked Patrick's shoulder. "You'll have Cheryl Decairo to help write the skits. She's a wit. I can't wait for Princess Cheryl to meet our Prince Patrick."

"Okay, let's say I accept your offer—" he stalled for effect "—will I be paid in gold or silver?"

"Let's discuss it over drinks next week at Ellie's," Easter said. "It's in Sanctuary Beach near—"

"I know, just east of Mobile, Alabama, at Gulf Shores," he said. "My old stomping grounds."

"Really? By the way, you can help us recruit, too. It'll take maybe five months but Cheryl will assist, too. Women are naturally drawn to a smart, good-looking man."

Though wise to her strategy, the compliment, along with her dazzling smile, caught his defenses at rest. "So you'll screen my genes, test my best, and let this showman do the rest?"

The strawberry blonde smiled. With fingers snapping, she swayed to a rhythmic beat. "We're all into the gene scene now. Hey, it rhymes. I have a way with words, too, but you should teach me how to limber up my language so my lines flow like yours. I want to be impromptu, too, like you."

"You can," he said. "Just lose your inhibitions."

"How?"

"Easy. I'll teach you how to make the most of your natural spontaneity."

Vanessa clapped her hands. "Please say you're on board with us."

He grinned. "Well, I'd have to cancel my standup tour and I'll need to sharpen my act spoofing a bumbling Romeo. Imagine that in a skit with you as my foil. I'd be using this pickup line in a bar; 'Are you seating that save for me? Good, drink up, the house is on me.' It's a new one I was working on for my standup act."

Vanessa's emerald eyes widened. "Ha! House is on me. Such clever jig-jagging you do."

He gave the pair a thumbs-up. "No second-rate skits. Y'all with me?"

"You're in for a surprise," Easter said. "We're not only with you, we're *wayyy* ahead of you. I've been working on this pedigree idea for a long time."

"Good, then your cause is no fluke, is it?" he said. "We can make it happen in record time."

Easter pecked him on the cheek. "You're a real treasure, Patrick."

SIX MONTHS LATER, on the Fourth of July, a pro huckster named Raul "Goat" Goodnowe celebrated the nation's freedom by driving a preacher from Tampa International Airport to a hotel where dark loquat trees contrasted with its pink exterior.

The televangelist preferred his entertainment uncensored, reason enough to visit a club later on the causeway near Clearwater. A big man at six-five, Luther T. Moreau opened the sliding glass door of the hotel room and breathed deep. In the distance, gulls hovered above a shrimp boat on Tampa Bay. The clinking of ice cubes behind the preacher signaled cocktails.

Goat approached him with the drinks. "Glad you're ready to make a comeback, L.T. As they all say, timing is everything."

Moreau shucked his suitcoat and removed his red bowtie. "You better believe it. Oh, yeah, my theological clock is ticking. Ohhh the vexation they heaped upon me. Next time I won't be so careless. Like the young doe said when she came out of the woods, 'I'll never do that for two bucks again.'"

Unsmiling, Goat proposed a toast. "Here's to the ingénues who never see it coming."

THREE

Antigua.

A cabal of fifty men, all billionaire members of the Central Order, viewed the pictorial of a grotesque human face. The image lit up a flat-screen television as Chairman Samuel Crown emptied a jigger of whiskey into his mug of coffee.

As Imperial Master, Crown thumbed toward the imagery. "What you're seeing is degeneration. Fact is, some think half the human race has devolved so far that it's doomed."

Seated among the elite at the conference table, a tall Brit—Reggie Torgenthal—shifted uneasily in his chair. "Genetic engineering is the answer, Sam. Wall Street agrees, ol' chap."

The elderly chairman glared at the Brit. "Editing genes is a quick fix, Reggie, not the long-term solution." He nodded at his son. "Let's hear from the younger set. Tell him, Teddy."

Though in his late twenties, Teddy spoke with authority to the senior audience. "We all know scientists can replace faulty genes, but it weakens the cell line. We have an alternative. It allows us to exploit genetics for bigger dividends. Eugenics—reprogenetics in polite company—is a gold mine."

"Sounds like selective breeding," the Brit said. "Does Cupid not have a say in choosing a mate, or doesn't love matter anymore?"

"Love is for losers," the younger Crown said.

A sly grin creased the chairman's face. "Can't trust love, Reggie."

He thumbed at the television screen where an adult male's face appeared, the eyes narrow and dull, mouth droopy. "There's the proof. Imagine how this mongrel, and millions more like him, have adversely affected our bottom line."

"So the money game tops love," the Brit said.

"Absolutely," the chairman said. "It always has."

Reggie shook his head. "Fine, but what's the game plan for this windfall of profits?"

Samuel Crown squinted. "We exploit the gene matching industry."

"How's that done?"

"We dramatize decrepit retrogrades," Crown said. "Think of the shock value. Optics matter, so we expose the worst, the most degraded. Illustrate genetic mismatches. But we also glamorize pedigrees to show the better bloodlines."

"Really?" Reggie said. "Isn't a pedigree movement already underway?"

"Yes, but trust me, that group is into socialism," the young man said, his gaze roaming over the faces of the wealthy attendees.

"But don't most people think love matters?"

"That'll change, Reggie." The chairman grinned. "We target impressionable people and show them how romantic myths have always been a disaster."

Reggie shifted impatiently in his chair. "I'm listening, Sam."

"Good, then consider the kind of radiant beauty and good health never before seen. Nature, to its credit, has programmed humanity for a surprise. And what better time for eugenics to honor our elevated status, now that a pariah disease dominates the daily news?"

Reggie Torgenthal squared to face the chairman. "You mean emblot? True, it's the most hideous disease ever, but—"

"It's very special to us." Crown's lofty gaze favored his son again. "Teddy, explain."

Teddy aimed a remote at the television. "Emblot lurks in defective genes, dormant but waiting to ambush its host." A Black man's face appeared on the screen with bloodshot eyes. "Their genome lacks the necessary inhibitors to suppress an emblot mutation." His gaze drifted to the sliding glass doors and a view of turquoise waters gently rolling from Deep Bay onto the beach outside Villa Champagne.

"If you don't mind my referencing Holy Writ, they're genetically cursed," Crown said.

Reggie glanced at his colleagues, a cadre of financial giants who studied the onscreen image of the emblot victim. "It's now rather common. Right?"

"Not been keeping up, have you?" Teddy said. "Because it's been neglected, it's now become a surreal plague—" he bounced in celebratory fashion "—at last."

True to his adversarial habit, Reggie vocalized his doubts. "Why neglect emblot? Our blatant indifference to it smacks of racism. We could take heat for that."

Teddy's voice mimicked his father's. "Hello! We're blaming emblot on natural cause and effect. Those people are predisposed to their fate. It's their genes, remember. How hard is it to understand that emblot is the most convenient artifice in achieving our goal?"

Reggie frowned. "But isn't that like endorsing genocide?"

The younger man raised his voice, mimicking Reggie's British accent. "Do you have a bloody way that's better to stop them from overpopulating the land, old chap?"

The Brit smoothed down a mustache grown to conceal his cleft lip. "Shameless, aren't we? But just how, may I ask, is the money made?"

The chairman sipped coffee from his mug as all eyes rested on him. "For us, it's simple. All we need are pedigrees whose genes we can monetize to the max."

Again he nodded at his understudy. "Tell him, son."

Teddy pointed the remote to onscreen images. Among the lineup, an adult male stood with face bloated, eyes goblin, and lips ashen. By contrast, the other man stood robust with a twinkle in his eyes. "Surprise! A registry of individuals with superior genes has existed for many years."

The elder Crown folded his hands. "Fact is, most humans harbor a secret desire for offspring that not only look better than average but live better, too. In all parts of the world, status matters. The idea is to exploit that concept among the affluent."

"Ah, yes, status," the Brit said. "Why am I not surprised? In addition to good health, now we're throwing in aesthetics, and there you go with the vanity factor. Sell the sizzle, then the steak."

Teddy poured coffee from a carafe and stirred packets of sugar into his cup. "In the abstract, it's good breeding that prevents heritable diseases. It also suggests utopia. Are you surprised?"

Reggie sighed. "Breeding for superior offspring has been done before. Today's geneticists won't fall for a failed Aryan thing again."

Samuel Crown snuffed deep in his throat. "It's not the scientists we want to convince."

Teddy sneered. "We monetize genetic assets by dramatizing a certain group of humans who are destined to fail. We show it round the clock. That's how this damn thing works, Reggie."

Reggie propped his elbow on the table and planted his chin into the heel of his palm. "Let's not forget the Nazi regime left a lasting stigma on genetic breeding."

The chairman gave his colleague a pitying look, as if assessing his intrinsic value. "But it was an undeserved stigma, Reggie." He cleared his throat. "We now have new methods."

Teddy followed his father's answer with a sardonic laugh. "Devious methods. Supergenes is our most valuable commodity, all the more reason for the masses to envy our power and wealth. We look to our lobbyists to pressure focus groups. Everyone knows bad breeding is a security risk."

Bemused, Reggie said, "This program will take more than a few quid to pull it off."

"Of course," the elder Crown said. "But we'll need a facilitator, a veteran huckster who can stage a scam on a grand scale." He chuckled. "We know a man like that, don't we, Reggie?"

The Brit nodded. "Yes. He has an uncanny talent for convincing skeptics."

"Since I've flown the man to Tampa, you can handle the particulars," Crown said. "By the way, it's a perfect day for golf. Seems I hear the siren call of the Jolly Harbour fairway."

Reggie Torgenthal pondered the terrain he would have to traverse alongside the elderly chairman. "Tallyho," he said. "We all love a challenge."

Teddy unbuttoned the coat of his pinstriped suit, a contrast with his colleagues' casual attire, and adjusted the knot in his tie to hide his turnip-sized Adam's apple. "You and Dad won't last long on that rumpled course, Reggie. I'm betting you'll be back in our villa for a stiff drink within ten minutes of the turn on the back nine."

A spate of chuckles followed the comment.

Teddy pointed the remote at the television screen where three attractive couples embraced, males with female companions, all super-imposed on a digital chart to show pedigree matchmaking. "Nothing there that Reggie or Dad could handle," he said before blanking the screen.

Silence followed Teddy's awkward attempt at humor.

Samuel Crown's supinating gesture indicated it was time for the recitation. He rose, tottering and stiff, his eyes trancelike as he leaned upon a teakwood walking stick. Following his example, the men stood and faced eastward with their right hands raised. Fifty voices droned in a solemn chant that might have been recited by ancient Druids at another place, another time. Eyes closed, they honored their spirit leader with a pledge.

"Oh Divine One, we pledge the Central Order will cloud the vision of its foes. By divine right we are empowered to conquer the opposition. Our sovereign rule must exercise dominion over all the things entrusted to our care. Guided by the sacred vision handed down to us by Solomon the Wise, we dedicate this mission to those who follow the celestial light."

After the recitation, Teddy slipped behind the departing group and pointed a finger at the Brit's head. He cocked his thumb and let the hammer down on a make-believe bullet. His lips popped softly to mimic a kill shot while making a wish.

Here's to you, Reggie. Hope you burn in hell.

FOUR

Nestled near the end of the peninsula on Alabama's Gulf Coast, Sanctuary Beach was now home to the Sweethearts of America Show. For years the coastal fishing and tourism industries had suffered from oil slicks and tar balls caused by the Deepwater Horizon oil spill, but a reclamation project convinced locals that their ecosystem had been restored.

But the Sweethearts' arrival was a week too early.

Listed as a beach cottage on steroids in the bi-weekly *Buttcrack Beacon*, their two-story house was not ready for occupancy. But Patrick found life aboard the Silver Eagle luxury bus was better than bearable with his twenty-one trainees. For comedy practice, he had decided to use a sandlot close behind the Sanctuary Research Institute next door to the big house.

But today on the peninsula, his job became a challenge in the sweltering July heat.

The research institute faced Mobile Bay and, like the antebellum house adjacent to it, failed to benefit from the shade of pines, wind-blown oaks, and cabbage palm. Its sandlot afforded only enough space for a softball diamond's infield. Two pathways, one from the big house and one from the institute, merged at the shoreline where a long pier led to a yellow boathouse at its far end.

Both structures lay four miles east of Fort Morgan where saltwater from the Gulf merged with the tawny Mobile Bay at its ship channel.

The brackish waters of the bay continued thirty miles north to the Causeway, a land bridge. From there, the picturesque Mobile Delta stretched northward to embrace a vast maze of freshwater bayous, rivers, and creeks.

Ecotourism in the Delta employed several of Patrick's kin.

Today, one of Patrick's skits had Easter and her actresses reacting to the famous conquistador Hernando DeSoto's eye-opening visit to America. In his search for gold, DeSoto discovered Maubilla where 10,000 Native Americans were led by Chief Tuscaloosa. Most striking were the natives' robust health and generous spirit, along with women of incomparable beauty. But such was his greed that the Spaniard failed to recognize their genetic assets. Thus the real treasure was forever lost to him.

Hours later, with a series of satirical acts completed, Easter signaled a midday break. The girls hydrated with bottled water and ignored a light rain sweeping over Mobile Bay.

A flotilla of skiffs docked at Gulf Shores Marina on the bay where anglers dined at Tacky Jacks or sipped 150-proof bushwackers—milkshakes with attitude. On the Gulf side of the 22-mile peninsula, local volunteers monitored sea turtle nests.

Patrick mopped his sweaty brow, relieved that today's coaching session had reached a halfway point. Also glad the girls followed team videographer Larry Lemoyne. With dark hair flicked stylishly up in gelled spikes, Larry captured their antics with his video camera.

Gulls circled overhead as Easter, in a reflective mood, wandered to a nearby inlet where she watched dolphins herding a school of mullet.

He shadowed her as she suddenly reversed course and strolled toward her troupe of actresses. Sensing her melancholy mood, he guessed she needed a confidant. Again he would listen, as he had listened since meeting her and Vanessa Wynley on the set of *The Hotz Show* months earlier. After the national search for candidates ended, his trainees now included young women like Freckles Lambert, Peaches McCollough, and Cassandra Wellington—a nucleus talented enough to justify a comedy tour.

He wondered if, given more time, their comedy routines might transition into something truly spectacular. Easter had blunted his question, borne of curiosity, about a financial backer. But since his own pay was adequate, why complain?

He also wondered what Easter's silence at the moment meant. Was she daydreaming? Perhaps he would cajole her. "Speaking of Danny, is Peaches his favorite masseuse?"

Easter offered no answer.

He chuckled. "Atlanta, her hometown, is a hotbed of talent." He suppressed another comment and studied the big house, regarded by the girls as a mansion with its fluted columns glistening white in the sunlight. The two-story wooden structure stood on concrete support pillars. Fronted by a flagstone yard, it provided a distant view of Sanctuary Beach.

On its west side, tall palm trees provided shade for the idling tour bus. Along the side panels of the Silver Eagle, a sign read *Hooter Commuter*.

"Guess what?" he said. "Yesterday I jokingly informed Danny if his grandmother couldn't have children, the laws of heredity dictate *he'd* have none either. He didn't get it, just walked away."

"Forget Danny," she said. "Stick with coaching."

He kept pace with her stride. "But what am I missing here?"

"He's sensitive about his family, okay? The big plus for us is his status." Stopping beneath a canopy of palm trees, she parked her visor high on her forehead and sat on a wooden bench at an oval table. "Sports fans buy whatever he endorses. Did you know him?"

"No, I'm ten years his senior but I knew him by reputation. After all, he's our Heisman winner. Long before he arrived, I played tailback at Tech."

"Bayou Tech? It's my alma mater, too," she said. "Golf scholarship. I trained with a nice young man who was biracial, so we had that in common. He wanted to marry me."

"And you dropped the guy for Danny?"

"It was sudden, yes. Danny was quarterbacking the Marauders. I asked for his autograph." She smiled. "He said I dazzled him. I ranked in the top fifty on the LPGA Tour and I thought we were the ideal match." Her voice turned wistful. "No wedding ring, though."

"But you're still hoping for one, right?"

She raked her chestnut-brown hair away from her face, yanked her visor off, and closed her eyes momentarily. "Not really. I even offered to sign a prenup. His business managers demanded my medical history and my genetic profile. And that's when—ta-da!—don't you know I was in the top percentile of pedigrees? I mean, jeez! What more could a man ask for in a woman?"

Patrick smiled. "Never known a woman who'd sign a prenup. Soon after I turned pro, a stripper in Miami ripped off my football sign-up bonus."

Easter finger-combed her hair. "Scammed you, eh?"

"Yep. It was a set-up. Her attorney was in on it. After that, I avoid devious divas."

"Danny will never marry," she said. "His manager is too possessive."

"Possessive? Why?"

"She stupidly pushes him into B-grade flicks, yet she wouldn't dare be seen in one herself. A big part of my plan is stopping Sorelle from obsessing over him."

Patrick's heart fluttered at the mere mention of the model's name. "*The* Sorelle?"

"Yes. Sorelle Ebanetti. She's about twenty years his senior."

"Right. And she's ten years older than me. Must be quite a story behind their matchup."

"You bet there is. There were scandalous stories before he joined my genetic matching network. Sorelle still controls his money, but I'll keep trying. Her Zipit Talent firm complements her Zipit Beauty Fest. Its ratings are in the pageant stratosphere. Pedigree is a priority in that system, too."

"Oh, then that explains—"

"Yes, some of our girls were finalists in her shindig. Peaches was first alternate and second only to Cheryl Decairo, the grand winner. You might say I raided her talent pool."

"As the pedigree network's owner, do you captain this boat alone?"

"Boat? How about ship? Yeah, I'm at the helm but nobody can own a cause. I need Ronofski's expertise when the seas get rough. Of course, I need you, too."

He snapped a quick salute to her. "Aye, aye, captain, your first mate reporting for duty. But why wasn't I told about the pedigree requiem before we held talent auditions?"

"Patrick, you must have known about their special status."

"Well, I submitted to a DNA test, too, but it wasn't the whole deal."

"Okay, but your need to know everything at the time was not my priority."

"Priority? Hey, it might have made a difference as to which girls I helped you choose. And this thing about pedigrees saving the human species still escapes me."

"You'll understand soon enough. I also introduced Danny to Dr. Ronofski. Sorelle is chafed that I didn't consult her."

"Can you blame her?" he said. "He's her best client—worth billions."

"Well, anyway, she's kept Danny on a short leash way too long. She fawns over him like he's her long-lost child. I'm not done with him. I need to repurpose him for our program."

He glanced at the girls as they mingled only ten yards away. "What does repurposing involve?"

"I'm steering him deeper into my pedigree program," she said. "But his Marauder contract is up for renewal in September. That means I have less than sixty days to counter their offer. Sorelle must not be told Danny is traveling full time with our road show. Okay?"

He sat beside her. "Trust me, I'm zipped but your relationship with Danny strikes me as a bit off kilter. Aren't you bothered about him being on the bus alone with Peaches?"

"Oh please, I just feel bad for him, that's all. And never mind why." A smile erased her frown as she elbowed him. "But they're not as close as you and Freckles Lambert are."

"Freckles? Yeah, we worked together a short while. Anyway, I view her as a good friend."

Easter grinned. "Uh-huh." She slapped his knee. "Don't get any romantic ideas about my girls. Keep it professional. No hanky-panky. Respect the boundaries. It's my team rule."

"No problem." He grinned. "Working with the girls is heightened by your approval, which could explain why I like staying high on heightened."

She gave him a dubious look. "You'll bear watching, Romeo. Like I said, we have rules."

"Don't tell me, tell the Sweethearts. They're the ones who do the flirting. Me, I just smile, but it's hard to focus on coaching when they hug me...accidentally."

"Yeah, right. Do you happen to know Slack Creel?"

"No, but I've heard he's a golf pro. By the way, are we moving the girls into his house over the weekend? It'll be a welcome change from sleeping on the bus."

She shook her bracelet so the charms tinkled. "The big house is what I call it, but sure."

"What about Slack? Where will he stay?"

"He lives near Pensacola." She shook her head. "He's very generous, but what a lush."

"What does he drink, craft brews in a local taproom?"

"Brandy, rum, vodka, the works. Says his friend has Hollywood connections. The guy wants to shoot one of our performances and help us land a TV series."

"What's his take?"

"Don't know but Slack says it's a deal we can't refuse. It's guaranteed."

"Can't refuse? Sounds bogus to me, especially if he's scouting for naive young women."

Easter thumbed her chest. "At twenty-six, I'm anything but naive, Patrick."

"At thirty-eight myself, I'm not either." He winced in pain as he stood. "Yow!"

She gripped his arm, steadying him. "Are you hurt?"

He braced against her, the snug feel of her body exhilarating. "Yep, my knee has been sore more than a year. Can't make any tricky moves. The pain comes and goes."

"Football injury?"

"Nope, last year I got in the way of Sledgehammer, a rodeo bull."

"Really?" She offered a wry grin. "Must be a gory story behind that one."

"There is." He grinned crooked. "No gory, no glory, they say."

Playful, she pushed him away but held his gaze.

"What?" he said. "You're smiling like you might know something I don't."

"When you get that look, I can't help myself."

"Look? What look?"

"It's like the surprise of a child, a little-boy shyness, innocent but sexy."

He chuckled. "Your words, my ears. Keep talking."

"Jeez! I sound infatuated. Oh, well, think nothing of it. Cupid makes people stupid."

"Yeah, I've had a few run-ins with that little imp. He needs a few archery lessons if you want my take on it."

She gawked as Danny emerged from the bus. "Look! Peaches is walking behind him."

"Hmmm, so she is."

"I wonder if they...." She let the thought drift.

"Made out?" he said. "If so, your super jock must have pulled up short today. Are they in love or is it just a fling thing?"

"No, massages are about therapy, not flings. All celebrities like him get daily massages."

"Yeah? She ought to get one, too. She would if I was in charge of her, um...therapy. I have a masters in *masseuring*, so if the girls need—"

"That does it." She slapped her thigh. "First thing tomorrow, I'm taking him to see Reverend Moreau in Pensacola."

"Moreau? Why would you want him to see that charlatan?"

"Charlatan? Have you not seen the famous Reverend L.T. Moreau on TV?"

He frowned. "Who hasn't? Staged miracles are his thing. You know what they say, 'It's the rush, not the riches.' He's in the pen for fraud."

"Not any more. Last week a news anchor said he's out with time served."

"What? That scoundrel is out after only two years?"

She looked a question at him. "You know him?"

"Know him? I worked for the rascal. We sold condos on spec."

"Say no more," Easter said as she sauntered away. "Let's get back to work."

Patrick studied her gait and the snug fit of her white jean-shorts. What secret had she refused to share about the football jock's family? Would Dan the Man's image as a pedigree poster boy change if she revealed his past? Something was amiss and Patrick was too curious to let it go.

Sorelle Ebanetti might know the answer. He wondered if his romance with the world-famous model could be rekindled. How long had it been—twenty years?

———

FROM THE PIER behind the mansion, Cheryl Decairo studied the bay through her binocs. A variety of flora came into focus along its periphery—sawgrass, swamp holly, saw palmetto, bracken fern. And, courtesy of a Bon Secour Wildlife Refuge flyer, she identified gopher apple, a red cedar, and dwarf live oaks.

She withdrew a diary from her shoulder purse and sat on the ground. Dare she enter her musings about the script writer who doubled as the Sweethearts trainer?

Thursday: Patrick is training us to be entertainers. I've never met a man who is so motivated. He calls me the team scribe, says he admires smart women. I hope he doesn't see our road show as a pit stop to his personal quest for fame. We need his coaching expertise. Easter says our troupe is destined for fame. Intuition tells me she's preparing us for more than a road show. Much more. I want to expand on the skit about Maubilla. The word was also used as a modified language for trade between tribes.

FIVE

Goat Goodnowe and his friend, Luther T. Moreau, sat comfortably in the upper level of the famed Tropix Gentlemen's Club, their gazes fixed on the carousel platforms where women gyrated topless to a jazzy rendition of *Bad to the Bone*. Though his past was aligned with charismatic religious fame, Moreau easily adopted a Saturday night persona.

"How's your wife, L.T.?" Goat asked.

"Life, did you say?"

"No, I said how's your wife—your ex?"

Moreau grinned. "Compared to what?"

"Prison didn't dampen your sense of humor, I see."

"TV reporter Ada Golden sure did, though." Moreau eyed the bare breasts of the female server who set a hot dish of shrimp fettuccine on the table in front of him. "She made a name for herself when she broke the story about the rehab center."

Goat ran a hand over the gloss of his slicked-back hair, its blond fix fading between treatments. Sporting the deep tan of a lifeguard, his eyes shone gunmetal gray as he flicked a gold-plated lighter on and off. "How long did you run the rehab scam?"

"The rehab was not mine to run," the preacher said. "It was like a fortress—guards, Dobermans, razor wire. My outreach ministry found runaway teens for the place. They gave me a fair price for each gal, though."

"Anyone else besides the reporter turn the tables on you?"

"I did most of the table-turning," Moreau said. He forked pasta into his gaping maw, chewing as he spoke. "Medics there had a secret lab. I swear it was unbeknownst to me."

"Are you saying they carved up runaway teenagers?"

No. Castaways Rehab was a breeder farm. Every nine months they got a new crop. At toddler age, a kid's kidney, heart, whatever was took and flown to a transplant center."

Goat's eyes betrayed no emotion.

Moreau speared a hot garlic roll from a basket on the table. "I was at odds with them cartel bastards. Naomi Savoie and her boyfriend gave that bitch reporter the inside scoop. She and her friend—I forget the name—yeah, Murph it was. He pushed the rescue because he had a daughter in there, so they all bunched up to find her."

Goat's eyes narrowed. "Just a streak of bad luck got you, eh?"

Bombastic, the preacher bellowed, "I'm not playing martyr for nobody. Feds or not, them's the ones gonna get their comeuppance for framing me." His large ears twitched. "But right now, partner, I'm primed about this new deal you got cooked up for us."

"It's not that new." Goat dragged on his cheroot and blew the smoke upward. "Senator Blockton lobbied Congress for me. Grant money was finally approved for our clinic but bureaucrats need reports, so he runs interference."

Using a wet napkin, Moreau wiped his sauce-stained shirt from belt to bowtie. "Just how did you come by that kind of leverage with a U.S. Senator?"

"The people I work for called in a few favors," Goat said. "I added a twist that made it a lot more fundable, though. Are you familiar with genetic mating?"

"Something to do with animal breeding?"

"Superior humans in this case." He paused to blow cigar smoke again. "Dr. Ronofski sells the idea that we're all on a downhill slide, like we've shit in our gene pool so long that we're looking at dooms-day. Says it's time to breed out all the crud we've inherited."

The preacher's head rocked side to side. "Breed in, breed out, breed in, breed out."

Goat leaned back in his chair. "Ronofski was laughed off Wynn Traynor's TV show."

"Sorry to hear that," Moreau said.

Goat coughed into his hands. "He's hyping pedigrees as a way to battle a disease called emblot." He plucked a sprig of tobacco off his tongue. "The disease distorts a patient's facial features and lesions in the skin bleed. It's more common among Blacks. Imagine how it reinforces their victim mentality. So with Senator Blockton's help, we can divert money from minority rescue programs to our clinic."

"How do we get away with that?"

"Easy. We have ways to neutralize the opposition and extort megabucks, all the while cashing in with Ronofski's name on it." He opened the lighter and clicked it shut. "Within a few months I can trade my yacht for a bigger one."

Moreau smiled at the server who plopped a ticket on the table. "What I wanna do is resurrect my Gospel Galaxy TV empire." He passed the check to Goat, dipped the end of his napkin in ice water and wiped his chin and sideburns.

The girl ignored his pretentions and scooted away with Goat's platinum card.

"How do we know people will buy into this thing?" Moreau asked.

"Because we'll sell it as a fountain of youth and promise to stop inherited crap."

"Now you're talking, man, but how do we launch it?"

"First, we create a demand for it. It's what Socrates would call the noble lie. We present the program in a religious context. It puts you in the limelight. Then, for more appeal, we use a celebrity with demigod status. I have one in mind who may help our cause."

"I get the religion part, but who's the celebrity?"

"I'll let you know." Goat donned his hat. "We have an appointment at Sanctuary Beach with Dr. Ronofski tomorrow."

The preacher slapped his huge palms together, grinding them. "Is that where the gene mating thing is gonna happen?"

"Yes. And I'm staffing my clinic there."

"It's a mighty fine place," the preacher said.

"Here's the deal, man. A cabal of financial giants are limiting access to biotech solutions. And they're allowing emblot, as nature intended, to pretty much wipe out the unfit, those who can't control their appetites."

"That's a big order, Goat. How would anybody limit access to solutions?"

"I'm sworn to secrecy on that, but the clinic is the ideal front for our plan."

"Speaking of fronts," Moreau said, "I've got access to some documents. They're stories written by an Israeli, like fantasy stuff about a genetic messiah who's into polygamy."

"Does this messiah have kids?"

"Yep. And his dozens o' young'uns turn out to be just like him."

"You mean genetically flawless?"

"You know it. Least they do in fantasy. I'll make it a doctrine. The Israeli's agent is a rich Jew in Paris. I'm the only one he trusts with an advance copy before we push the English version. It just might fit your plan."

Goat nodded. "Yes, it might. In fact, eugenics had a spiritual component back in the day."

"And the Bible speaks about New Scrolls," Moreau said. "We might as well call 'em that. Yeah, believers want a better future. Who knows? Maybe life gets gooder with good mating. God's children love life. Love life. Hey, it's a great buzzword, ain't it? Love life."

"Yeah, that it is. Beneficent mating could begin with a divine mandate."

The topless server returned Goat's card. Slightly rising on tiptoes, she bounced in sync with a popular surfer song, repeating its lyrics. "If it swells, baby, ride it, ride it, ride it."

Moreau ogled the server's departure. "Wait'll I show you what all's in them Scrolls. Yep, chock full o' promises 'bout celestial marriages."

"Celestial has a nice ring to it," Goat said. "It'll fit nicely with down-home genutopia."

The preacher's voice boomed. "Gimme five, man. I like the way you think."

Six

Soon after Goat Goodnowe moored his yacht, *LoveLord*, at the far end of Sanctuary Marina, he stood with L.T. Moreau and hailed Dr. Henry Ronofski to their meeting on a pier.

The preacher's ears protruded like sails in a headwind as he propped his bulk against a guardrail. He glanced at the geneticist before addressing Goat. "You got a market for this thing?" he said. "I'm just wondering how it's different from what most folks find at sperm banks."

Goat backed up to the rail beside his friend. "It's all about presentation, L.T. The sperm we take has to be from a gifted celebrity."

"Gifted?" the preacher said. "You mean, like them genius types?"

"Geniuses don't have kids named for them," Goat said. He tossed minnows from a bait bucket to a lone blue heron on the pier. "They're fireflies, give off light but no heat. Come on, think. We all know a super jock who's a household name, the lead in a buffet of B-movies. He's often cast as a Romeo and women flock to him like pigs to a peanut field."

Moreau bumped his forehead with his fist. "Yeah, kid has a sling-shot arm."

"More like a cannon," Goat said. "Does the name DiNago ring a bell?"

"That's it, yeah, Dan the Man DiNago."

Dr. Ronofski cleared his throat. The pale-faced geneticist wore scuffed wingtips with no socks, corduroy pants with no belt. "Could we continue with our meeting, gentlemen?"

"Yes, we'll discuss business," Goat answered. "But I hope you understand that selling the idea of pedigrees is not for lightweights. It requires finesse." An expensive cigar never far from his lips, Goat lit a slender cascada and held it up at eye level. "Margaret Sanger made birth control popular. Eugenicists sided with her cause. Easter Beaulieu is a parallel of Sanger's legacy, but she has to distinguish herself beyond her obvious beauty."

"Regenerative mating is a noble cause," Ronofski said.

"So?" Goat said.

Ronofski stared into space. "It safeguards people against dreaded diseases, like spinal muscular atrophy, the leading cause of death in infants. One year's treatment by injection is cost-prohibitive, so people should accept my program based on its economic benefits, not just its humanitarian merits."

Goat pushed away from the guardrail. "You can forget merits. Only two things will move people to accept it. Greed and vanity. We have to put a pretty face on a supergenes deal to make it palatable." He nodded at Moreau. "The Reverend is our salesman and a pedigree society is our deal. Next we'll set up a plan to push it."

"Would you care to explain how?" Ronofski said.

"Doc, I've rented space for a clinic but we'll need to buy enough sperm from DiNago to make us legit. With a hundred grand set aside, we offer Susie-Q Volunteer twenty grand. All she has to do is sign up and have an intern force-feed her womb."

Ronofski frowned. "How much of the money goes to my pedigree program?"

"All of it," Goat said, "except operating expenses, and the money we pay the women fertilized by DiNago's sperm, plus eighteen-grand to DiNago. That leaves you forty-grand for biotech research. The grant is ninety million, so we treat nine-hundred volunteers. But then we reapply for another grant, only more next time. It'll soon turn into billions. That's how a genutopia becomes a grand reality."

Moreau, his large feet in leather house slippers, shuffled over the rough-hewn planks of the pier, pacing back and forth. "How do we get supergenes DiNago to cooperate?"

Goat tossed more minnows to the heron. "He's in the bag, thanks to Miss Beaulieu. She's our inside manipulator, though she doesn't know it yet."

Ronofski began swaying side to side, hands in his pants pockets. "We'll need to meet with Mr. DiNago's attorneys and make it legal."

Goat waved him off. "I'll take care of the legal end, so leave the sharks to me."

"Are you a lawyer?" the geneticist said.

"No, but I know contract legalese."

Ronofski squinted. "I beg your pardon?"

Dismissing the question, Goat said, "My staff will interview applicants at my clinic. Roughly nine months later and each Suzie-Q receives a final payment. Meanwhile, they can all expect a big tax break. The feds won't question a non-profit clinic."

The scientist's eyes peeked up from his bent position. "How long will funding take?"

"It's as good as done," Goat said. "Federal agencies depend on Blockton's committee to finance them. Need I say more?" He glanced at his diamond-studded watch. "Let's get rolling. I have to visit Slack Creel, the golf pro, for seed money." Turning, Goat waved over his shoulder as if giving Henry Ronofski, the esteemed geneticist, a parting adieu. "Later, Doc."

"Good luck," Ronofski called from the pier as they strode toward a Lincoln Navigator.

With twenty yards soon between himself and Ronofski, Goat blurted, "Fuck luck."

Moreau shook in silent mirth. "You figure the feds won't come snooping, eh?"

"I won't sugarcoat it, L.T. Our investors pull the strings. You do know multinationals run the world of commerce, don't you? These guys you don't cross."

"Ahhh, sounds like corporate power brokers to me."

"Ruthless too. Our non-profit is legal, by the way. We're properly registered."

"Sounds like you've got everything figured out," Moreau said. "But other than the twenty-grand, what will move people to go for this supergenes plan?"

"It's about a sweepstakes mentality, L.T. But it's also about status. Pretend for a moment that you're sterile as a gelding, or you carry genetic flaws and you don't want them passed along to your kids. You want lots of money, a son who plays in the Super Bowl, and gifted daughters who bear cute rug rats. Suddenly, your dreams appear attainable. It's just a matter of us knowing how to toot the loot."

"I gotta hand it to you, Goat, you cover the bases better'n anybody I ever knowed."

"It's a gift, man, but it's why billionaire sponsors give me a free hand." Goat relit his cigar as he trudged along the sandy path. "I'll pay a kickback to Senator Blockton and to hell with the rest of them."

"How do we get away with that?"

"Timing. Eight months and I'm done. No up-front payments until each volunteer tests pregnant. They won't, of course. We tell the feisty ones it's due to government red tape. Stall when they call. And they all sign a nondisclosure agreement."

"What if Doc starts bitching about his forty percent?"

"We'll keep Ronofski busy speaking at symposiums. Studies say heritable diseases have reached critical mass. Infertility is a biggie, too. The Prez may sign an executive order and push our deal faster."

"Yeah, I follow you."

"Bet your ass you will." Goat pointed at the horizon with his sunglasses to indicate the gathering clouds. "If the feds put two and two together, I'll be gone, basking in Brazil or any country that ignores their extradition treaty with Uncle Sam."

"Does Danny get shafted, too?"

"Yes, but I have a more interesting plan for DiNago and his glam slam entourage. I know how to milk that cash cow, too. Easter Beaulieu is key to it all. Rest assured, it'll put your Gospel Galaxy show on top again. L.T., this is my finest hour, my grandest scam yet."

DRY PALM FRONDS rattled in a stiff breeze along Bon View Boulevard, the seashell path that began at the mansion. It intersected Peninsula Road and ended at the boardwalk next to Ellie's Restaurant on the beach. Patrick stood in the mansion yard and watched the girls milling around the Silver Eagle. On each side of the bus a large inscription read, Sweethearts of America Show.

Larry Lemoyne aimed his camera at the girls as each posed in iridescent gold uniforms, then swung the camera to focus on Patrick whose garb consisted of ripped jeans, a red bandana, western-themed shirt, and Stetson hat set at a jaunty angle.

Patrick shrugged in response. "How am I going to fit in with all these gorgeous girls?"

Larry answered with a slight lisp. "You'll pose as the misfit. Audiences will view you as the troublemaking foil, the guy who gives the team a reason to kick his pestering ass."

"But I'll be as conspicuous as an albino rhino."

He snapped a picture. "By the way, the girls think you are one fine hunk." He patted the air with a flourish of his hand. "So, Danny had better be on guard or they could *ssstrayyy* your way."

Patrick tested the bicycle horn at his side, squeezing its bulbous end and forcing a *tootle toot* blast. "Trust me, Larry, they won't stray. With my directions, they'll stampede my way."

"Oh? Since when does a Casanova Comic have a death wish?" Larry said.

Ignoring the repartee, Patrick marveled at Easter who coordinated the Sweethearts for a group photo by placing the shortest girls up front. Her sensuous tone when alone with him stirred something profound in his psyche. An intimate connection with her seemed entirely possible.

Professional distance. How could he honor the hands-off rule when his daily visual of her stirred libidinal longings?

Behind him a sonorous voice bellowed. "Picture day never looked this good on the PGA tour." Slack Creel introduced himself with a handshake. "Who takes credit for these babes?"

"You really don't know?" Patrick said. "We toured almost every college from kudzu to cactus to find the best, but Sorelle Ebanetti's beauty gig yielded the finest. All pedigrees, you know."

"Yeah, I'm counting on Sorelle loaning me a few," Slack said.

"That would be Easter's call, Mr. Creel, not Sorelle's."

Slack removed his fedora and wiped its sweatband with the tail of his celebrity signature shirt. The gum in his mouth smelled of lemon.

"Vanessa Wynley and a few others would be great decoration for my Celebrity Shootout."

"Shootout? A golf biggie, right?"

"Yeah, it's where Easter introduced me to Danny. Our winnings go to the Paladin Charity to help victims of child abuse." Slack set the fedora far back on his head. "I'll give her gals all the comforts of home at my mansion. Better be some perks in this for me, though."

Given the man's retro sunshades, Slack's voice yielded the only clues to his meaning but Patrick had learned to listen like a blind man. The man obviously had a lustful agenda.

A protective urge welled inside him. "Well, if you have any ideas about these girls, you'd better be up to date on your tetanus shots. Come nighttime, they turn into vampires."

"Worry not," Slack said. "Turning vamps into tramps is my specialty."

Patrick cringed. "They're still south of twenty-one so I doubt they play in that league."

The Sweethearts formed a double line, using the silver-hued bus as a backdrop. At every nip and tuck the outfits resembled the dazzle of pro football cheerleaders, the clinging fabric of their shorts cut in a deep inverted V along the hip.

Slack shifted his big frame and leaned toward Patrick. "What I'd like to do is rig that bus with cameras—spy cameras—and catch Danny in the act with them. Look at their moves. Every day they jog the beach at sunup, like they're in some jiggle contest." Slack sucked in his gut. "Nobody used to come out at daybreak. Now geezers hang around Ellie's, sipping coffee and gawkin' and tawkin' and gettin' their eye-candy fix. I ought to charge a gawker fee."

As he spoke, Gertrude the security chief ambled closer, a handgun holstered on her hip. Her uniform fit snug against her beefy arms and wide hips. She nodded in passing and moved on, voiceless but alert to anyone who might try to approach Danny DiNago without her scrutiny.

Slack's laughter rang with cynicism. "Know what these gals need? Recognition."

"I agree," Patrick said. "But that takes years."

"Not if my friend signs them on. I'll introduce y'all to him at the pool party tonight. He'll put these beauts on TV in no time flat."

"He wouldn't be the first to make that offer," Patrick said.

"Maybe not, but this man's a cinematographer. Easter owes me. And she owes it to the girls to meet him and listen to his pitch. He's got gobs of Hollywood connections."

Patrick caught Easter's signal, summoning him to the lineup. "Gotta go," he said while moving away from Slack, relieved to end the conversation.

"Six o'clock tonight," Slack called after him.

"Got it," Patrick answered.

"And if you want to know what's going down, talk to Easter. We go way back."

"Got it."

"A gal like her makes your work seem like play." Less jocular, he added, "Don't take her on as a business partner, though, or it'll cost you plenty."

Patrick drew close to Easter and posed for the group photo. "Slack is expecting us at a pool party at his mansion," he said, low-voiced. "What's up with that?"

Easter sighed. "Just business. Now smile till your face hurts."

"Launching a showbiz career is a tricky thing." He waited out a five-count. "Lots of pitfalls can trip up a novice."

"I heard you the first time." She pulled him closer for the photo, her arm encircling his waist, her breast snugging his ribcage.

He raised his hands in surrender. "Hey, I think out loud when stimulated."

"Think all you want." Her fingernails clawed into his side. "My word is final, so look around you. To be a Casanova, you have to *feel* like one."

He squeezed the bicycle horn in answer. "Okay, okay, I'm feeling it," he said. He told himself the first rule in life was simple—disarm with humor. "Like my great-grandpa says, to open their minds to learn, you first gotta open their hearts to laugh."

As the truism hung in the air unchallenged, he doubted that a new angle offered by a man with Hollywood connections would speed up the Sweethearts' career as entertainers.

SEVEN

Wispy clouds ribbed the late afternoon sky as Patrick joined the 21 Sweethearts on Sanctuary Beach for refreshments at Ellie's. A hefty woman with a nametag reading *Birdie Mae* assisted him in sliding a few tables together before she poured a round of iced tea.

"Got a goodly selection of pastries and what-not," she said, her pen and order pad ready. "If y'all are real hungry, we got tuna. It's fresh-caught out around Beer Can."

Vanessa Wynley cocked her head and laughed. "Tuna with a hangover, eh? Fun-neee!"

Patrick made a snicking sound in his cheek. "Beer Can is an offshore oilrig," he said. "You get there on a charter boat that takes you on an overnight trip. You'll catch lots of king mackerel."

Birdie Mae chuckled. "Looks like you already caught your limit of ladyfish right here."

"Yep, I like fishing for ladies," he said. "Years ago I hooked a narcissist here. You might say she couldn't get enough of herself."

Birdie flopped her order pad against his head. "Still talking in riddles, ain't 'ya?"

The girls laughed as she walked away. "The narcissist was a famous model," he said. "Ten years my senior, though. My great-grandma Eugenia said it was scandalous. End of story."

Twenty minutes later, Patrick and Easter accompanied the girls on their stroll to Slack Creel's mansion. At the peak of physical prowess, the excitable girls viewed the two-hundred-yard trek as an opportunity for horseplay. Patrick kept pace with Easter as she took the lead.

"The girls are sporting short-shorts and halter tops," he said. "Your idea?"

"I told them to go casual," Easter said. "Underneath, they're wearing bikinis."

"That's a switch," he said. "Moving into Slack's house will be a welcome change from sharing space on the tour bus." Nearing the big house, he slowed his pace beside her. "But speaking of housing, Slack says he's expecting a few perks. Any idea what he's talking about?"

Interrupting, Peaches swatted his head and sprinted away to climb the steps and cross the marble porch. She pressed the doorbell and stepped back as the door chimes played Dixie. "Glad he didn't place a bunch of Confederate icons in the yard," she said.

"Slack wanted to capture the charm of his hometown in Natchez, Mississippi," Easter said. "I toured the grounds earlier. No Rebel flags anywhere. And I have a door key here in my...." She fished in her handbag as her eyes clouded with concern. "Did I give the door key to you, Patrick?"

The large door, accented with beveled glass, suddenly opened. A diminutive Asian, his squinty eyes showing amusement, appeared and greeted the bevy of guests. "Come in, come in," he gushed, his smile wide. "I'm Stu Watanabe, manager of Mr. Creel's estate."

Patrick followed the girls inside the foyer. A large Persian rug accentuated hardwood floors in the parlor, which abutted a broad staircase. Narrow rectangles of light, cast by the afternoon sun and filtered through folds of sheer drapes, lay in long muted strips along the floor. A staircase of polished mahogany swept to a mezzanine fronting a row of bedroom suites on the uppermost floor.

With a prim gesture, Stu Watanabe pointed eastward. "This way to the patio," he said. "Mr. Creel and his guest will be here shortly. I trust you ladies came prepared for a dip in the pool."

"You bet," Easter said. She introduced the girls, then Patrick and herself.

The Sweethearts seemed awed by large murals covering the upper reaches of the walls. Each one depicted the epic Battle of Mobile Bay —a turning point in the American Civil War. Suspended from the center of the parlor, a quartz-spangled chandelier with hundreds of crystals captured the rays of sunlight in a myriad of prismatic colors.

The women sashayed toward double French doors that opened to the patio before Stu's frozen smile settled back on Patrick. "I'm also in charge of Ellie's and the kitchen here. Grapevine gossip says these lovely ladies entertain."

"Yup, and I train them," Patrick said. "In some arenas we'll even stage a softball game."

The chef's eyebrows formed a curiosity arc. "*Stage* a game? Why not play it?"

"Well, Stu, we're about mimicking for amusement, like the Globe Trotters do."

"So you play for laughs?"

"Sure do. Directing these girls is the difficult part but I'm learning."

A few seconds behind the girls, Patrick admired the kidney-shaped swimming pool and big hot-tub bookends. Encased within the patio's low-slung walls, semi-tropical plants allowed a distant view of the beach where sea oats topped sand dunes. Contrasting with the gulf, the north view revealed the bay and a trail leading to it through saw palmetto. At the far reaches of a long pier, yellow caution lights at a boathouse helped vessels navigate through early-morning fogs.

On the patio near the shallow end of the pool, Patrick settled across from Danny DiNago. Both sat in rattan chairs beside a glass-topped table. A canopy provided an oasis of shade. A petite Asian, no doubt Stu's wife, helped him grill shrimp. The aroma of steamy-hot coconut lime rice in large wooden bowls awakened Patrick's taste buds.

Slack Creel and his shorter companion soon appeared from the patio entrance. Slack, attired in a maroon blazer, also wore a white golf shirt stretched over his gut. His companion's swagger reminded Patrick of a cocky bantam rooster. The stranger wore sneakers, knee-length pants, and a blue-and-yellow Hawaiian shirt open at the front revealing gold chains nestled in chest hair that glistened with body oil.

Patrick wore a black T-shirt with Pony Xpress imprinted in gold-embossed lettering, an easy contrast with his tan cargo shorts.

Danny DiNago, bare-chested and wearing walking shorts and sandals, slumped in his cushioned chair and raised a big hand with all the fanfare of a sleep-deprived sloth hailing the new arrivals.

"I'd like you folks to meet Raul Goodnowe," Slack said too loud, his face an alcoholic flush, his shuffling gait unsteady. "Just call him Goat." His gesture floated from Goat to Danny. "This is my pal, Dan the Man DiNago. Or *the* Danny, as football fans call him."

Danny opted not to stand and greet them with a customary hand-shake. "Take a load off and drink till you sink," he said.

Patrick stood and shook each man's hand without an introduction by Slack. "I'm Patrick Murph, point man for the world's most beautiful road show."

A Rolex encircled Goat's wrist and diamond rings sparkled on his fingers. He nodded toward the pool. "What have we here, angels trying to keep their halos dry?"

The Sweethearts had shed their outerwear to reveal thong bikinis: two tiny triangles at the top with strings around the neck and back; the bottom, narrow spandex peeking out from the tight crease of buttocks, but then snaking high over hips and gliding snug in front.

Ten yards away at the pool, Easter's olive hue contrasted with Vanessa's lighter tone. Cheryl Decairo, Cassandra Wellington, and Anastasia Andrews—all blondes—stood tall and statuesque. Some of the girls lingered in the shallow end of the pool. Others leisurely applied sunscreen or tossed a beach ball a few yards from the patio's tiki bar.

Goat, not yet seated, studied Vanessa whose retrieval of a beach ball brought her within a few feet of the men. "That one could be in one of my movies," Goat said. "She's ripe for Hollywood. They all are. On second thought, why not put them in a TV show?"

"We're more into roadshows," Patrick said. "Live audiences give us the rush we need. Think slapstick. Comic shenanigans. Sight gags. Fine-tuned antics."

"Think trouble if you do that," Goat said as he settled into a chair. "I can guarantee big bucks on the Funtasy TV Channel. It's only the beginning, though."

"Guaranteed?" Danny said, his legs bouncing like pistons on the balls of his feet.

Goat nodded. "Yes, guaranteed. Cable TV and streaming platforms are hungry for all kinds of entertainment, even your point man's silly monkeyshines."

Silly? The snarky remark caught Patrick off guard. Why upstage the Sweethearts' comedy coach or question the entertainment value of their antics?

Unsmiling, Goat fished a slender cigar from the pocket of his shirt. "With TV you'll get more exposure at less cost. Syndication is the way to go. If you can get past the tour mindset, I have the ideal trade-off for you."

His voice boisterous, Slack Creel slapped Danny's knee. "Man, y'all are gonna love this one!"

Goat chewed the unlit cigar. "It starts with a promo video to sell producers on a deal."

"What does the deal mean for them?" Danny said.

"A top-of-the-line TV pilot," Goat said. "In exchange, I'll ask that they also allow me a video in trade for a client, a company known for marketing the world's best-selling lingerie."

Lingerie? Patrick recoiled in suspicion at the idea. Designers of couture from New York to Milan recognized some lines of lingerie as more diaphanous than others. Sheer peignoirs in fashion shows had been usurped by mesh bodysuits—some flesh-toned with no undergarments.

Danny's face registered no surprise.

A shriek from Vanessa Wynley turned the men's attention toward the pool. Goat pointed his cigar toward her. "I would imagine that strawberry blonde could be habit forming."

Patrick grinned. "She comes with a warning label," he said. "Just kidding. In our recruiting, we opted for the girl-next-door look. No tattoos. And we wanted talented girls with a measurable IQ." He wanted to add, *And we usually don't showcase their nearly-nude bods.*

From poolside, Easter Beaulieu grinned while strolling to their oasis. She eased into a chair next to Patrick and nudged him with her sandaled foot. "You boys hung over yet?"

Patrick glanced poolside. "Yesterday I was hung over," he said. "Today I'm just hung."

Easter ignored the hackneyed line by rolling her eyes and fixing her gaze on Slack. "Good to see you again, Mr. Creel."

"Same here." Slack pointed toward his guest. "Mr. Goodnowe here would like to work with us on the clean genes deal." The bourbon sloshed over its rim as he set the drink on the table. "By deal I mean gene mating. We'll promote the gals on TV, too."

Easter looked at Danny whose gaze had drifted beyond her to the pool. "What do you guys have in mind?" A twisty grin broke her serious composure. "Or should I ask?"

"By all means," Goat said. "If all your girls are as talented as they are gorgeous, I can open doors for you. As always, it's about knowing the right people, and I know all the Hollywood kingpins."

"Let's hear it," she said, as if unaware her bikini-clad body was a distraction.

"My interests are twofold." Goat stifled a cough, gripped his fingers, and released each while making his point. "First, we work a deal on a promo video for your girls. It involves a lingerie tradeoff. More about that in a minute. Next, I like your matchmaking idea. Your pedigree program interests me, but only if I'm guaranteed a steady supply of product."

Easter crossed her legs; their deep tan worthy of a Coppertone display ad. "It'll cost you."

"Cost is relative," he said. "I manage a genetics clinic here and I don't mind paying market value for Danny's sperm, provided I have no competition."

"Exclusive rights?" Easter gripped the arms of the wicker chair midway back, elbows out like a bird drying its wings. "That's different. And more costly, too. What am I bid, Mr. Goodnowe? Going once, going twice...."

Goat remained stoic. "No doubt you have an idea of its worth, so let's start there."

"Priceless." She snarled. "We're talking liquid gold. I may consider five-hundred-grand per straw. Cash only."

Goat peered skyward, his thumb clicking a gold, flip-top lighter as if pondering his next move. "Your quote, Miss Beaulieu, is no doubt based on its romanticized value. I'm offering ten-thousand per straw —final."

Easter hissed and shook her head. "That's not a bid, Mr. Good-nowe, it's an insult. Surely you know about the high fees for sperm from a Triple Crown stud. Ask any Saudi prince or U.S. breeder what they pay in thoroughbred fees. It runs in the millions."

Grinning, Patrick stole a glance at Danny. Still slouching in his chair, the super jock seemed not to be fazed by the indiscreet bidding for his personal commodity. Stu Watanabe broke the group's focus with an offer of lemongrass steeped in green tea.

Easter placed the icy glass against her chest. Moisture soon ran in rivulets over the swells of her bosom and into her cleavage before vanishing inside the bikini top.

Patrick knew such a ploy often skewed an adversary's traction in buying situations.

Goat's tone remained dispassionate. "I suggest you show more charity, Miss Beaulieu. Humans are facing a rather dismal future. The line at the bottom is important but not to the exclusion of those in distress."

Patrick's thoughts tumbled into place. *The man knows how to play hardball.*

"Who's in distress, Mr. Goodnowe?" she asked.

Goat shifted in his chair. "Men of a certain color, for sure."

She sipped the tea and tossed her hair back off her shoulders. "So what's your point?"

"Ethnic cleansing, dear, has never had a better ally than emblot," he said. "It would seem no cure is in the offing for a heritable disease that bad, but genocide is unacceptable."

Patrick realized emblot, like sickle cell disease, affected mostly Blacks. But with a difference. It had become a moral issue due to lack of a medical cure. With Goat now taking the high road, Easter's response needed to be sensitive but sensible, perhaps even scripted.

"Why offer a weak argument?" she said. "Genetics allows for only two options. The degenerate genes weaken our gene pool, generation after generation, yet uncaring people insist on playing Russian roulette—potluck versus pedigree—as if gambling on romance by chance is somehow okay. It's time we did the right thing and give voice to a better choice. Regenerative matching is not only about surviving. It's also about thriving."

She flashed a quick smile at Danny. "Hon, after you've duplicated yourself with so many cookie-cutter kids, Father's Day will never be the same." She lobbed an ice cube to bounce off his bare midriff. "Your kids, the ones who hit the genetic jackpot, could hire an agent. Your duplicates would need the International Genetic Registry to track them."

Danny managed a grin. "Your game, your rules."

Patrick studied the icon's demeanor. For a renowned athlete, Dan the Man DiNago seemed the least concerned about making a difference in the world's gene pool.

Easter's outstretched arms attended her dreamy gaze into the distance. "Imagine the sky-high fees that seeders would charge for their pedigree lineage."

Though Easter's words gushed forth like a tsunami, Patrick detected sarcasm in her tone. "Think about the ripple effect our class-A pedigrees may have on the world economy." She lobbed another ice cube that bounced off Danny's knee. "You're a national resource, sport. If you retire from football, I'll keep you busy with this new genetic matching venture. You might control the future of all humanity."

"Fifty thousand per vial," Goat said. "Paid out over twelve-months with most of the funds held in escrow. Deal?"

"Is that your honest-to-god final offer?" She drained her glass, plucked a wedge of lemon from its bed of ice, and chewed its pulp without making a face.

"Indeed it is," he said.

"I'll think about it," she countered.

Her reasoning took a moment for Patrick to dissect. How far-reaching would Danny's impact on the gene pool become? If Dan the Man's genes were viewed as a commodity by opportunists, someone stood to make astronomical sums of money. But what if he simply shared his sperm cost-free instead? Would the supply and demand be controlled by hucksters such as Goat Goodnowe? Goat would never hesitate to profit from the football icon's sperm.

Goat leaned toward her. "First, I'll need to view the girls' showbiz antics."

"I'll have to think about that too," she said.

He glanced toward the pool. "Only those who prove to be telegenic get a shot at stardom, so I'll shoot a video of them tomorrow, like a screen test, but using only the most telegenic. And ten girls max. I'll choose the best, only the best."

Easter rose to leave. "My girls were born for stardom, Mr. Goodnowe. Of all the pedigrees, and thousands auditioned, these few were chosen. I'll see you guys later."

"It's been a pleasure." Goat watched her stroll toward the girls at poolside.

In Patrick's estimation, Easter should receive high marks for negotiating. Leaving the bidder in cold suspense—a takeaway move—would make him want the product even more. Her misdirection ploy had thrown Goat off guard by implying Danny's vast posterity would impact the worldwide economy beyond measure.

The men's gaze followed Easter's departure as Slack whistled low. "If that ain't a classy chassis, there ain't no sweet in sugar."

Patrick spurned Slack's comment but wondered about Goat Goodnowe's motives. The man had more going on behind those steely gray eyes than working a deal for DiNago's sperm. Victims of that look wished they were armed with a handgun and a silver bullet. The man would bear watching, but who had time to surveil him?

He had known that teaching Easter's world-class beauties to act would be a challenge. Tailoring skits for each dance performance had tested his ingenuity. Cheryl Decairo wrote skits but they required editing. He imagined Sorelle Ebanetti would arrive any day. Vanessa Wynley insisted on being cast as a partner in over half his skits. And Freckles, basking at poolside, finger-waved to signal her readiness for their overdue chat.

Patrick's introduction to genetic matching as a panacea made him realize how much Easter had influenced him. He had come full-circle from solo gigs to coaching actresses whose very existence seemed geared not only to performing, but to some type of regenerative philosophy. It seemed impossible for him to achieve fame without them. A loaded name like Casanova Comic had little or no meaning apart from the Sweethearts. That symbiosis struck him as a necessity, not only to achieve fame but for happiness itself. Easter's words seemed significant: *Give voice to a better choice*.

He sensed fame was not beyond his grasp. But, like happiness, it was often fleeting and could not be taken for granted. He also felt the troupe's momentum toward fame had slowed. To speed it up, he would have to avoid distractions.

EIGHT

Patrick refused to answer a call from Liz Osborne, his agent. In the entertainment business, agents expected their clients to produce an income. She was no different. Perhaps he owed her an explanation, but perhaps not. She had clients to book who ranked higher.

The slogan—*give voice to a better choice*—resounded in his mind.

With a gentle breeze drifting off the Gulf of Mexico a half-hour before sundown, he rested in a glider love seat on the veranda with her. The expanse of water on Mobile Bay, now calm amid a daily tidal change, provided the tranquil setting to discuss the Sweethearts' change of venue.

"If we do a variety show on a comedy channel, we'll need to dazzle viewers," Easter said.

He sighed. "I understand, but I've been thinking Goodnowe will go beyond risqué and opt for, well...raunchy. I mean, you had them in thongs at poolside. It looked like a setup. Goat's tradeoff also presents a big distraction. I fail to see how it's compatibile with the Sweethearts' good girl image."

"Why? Because they model lingerie?"

He inhaled the briny aroma drifting from the bay. "Goat's idea of a tradeoff may be, well—" he hesitated "—shady. I can't see how the girls you choose will have time for his lingerie video. Those TV deadlines could be hard to meet. The girls will focus on lingerie modeling and that's a huge distraction. We'll lag behind and—"

"No problem," she said. "We'll work around the lingerie shoot. Our show comes first."

"Okay, but still our goal is to educate viewers about genetic matching. How can we leap from his lingerie project back to a comedy show? And his proposed tradeoff, well, I think the girls flaunting their physiques gave him the wrong idea."

"Sorry, but I don't think the transition will be a challenge."

"Again, consider the imagery. It's your project but we agreed on training neophytes."

Looking away, she gestured toward the bay and the golden rays streaming toward it. "Don't you just love beautiful sunsets like this?"

"Yes, and the Sweethearts are just as spectacular as a sunset, but sheer lingerie sounds cheap."

"You worry too much, sport. Look at today's fashion mags and you'll see nude bodysuits with mesh panels." Her quick finger-snapping resounded like a rifle shot. "Chainmail bikinis, too. Besides, people today aren't that prudish."

"Okay, but I've seen my share of men like Goat." Distracted, he admired the subtle colors in the sunset. Its afterglow melded into a burnished orb and spread wide in soft pearl hues as the horizon threatened to swallow the rare display.

Easter gasped. "Look how it's changing, Patrick. It's like the bay is painted with fire."

"So it is. By the way, is your professional distance rule still in effect?"

"You know it is. Why?"

"Then you need to inform Vanessa."

"Look, if she flirts too much, it's just her persona bonding with your persona."

"Yeah, but it's too much persona for my wanna-wanna. Like when I took a short break; the girls were moving their gear from the bus into their bedrooms when Vanessa and Freckles came strolling into the den in sheer tops. They asked me to critique a new cheer —'More quake to the shake, take one guess, we're the S-A-S'—that sort of thing."

"Clever," Easter said. "Provocative, yes, but clever."

"Yeah, right, clever. But then in no time flat they lunge, uh-huh, tried to strip me bare."

"Don't tell me you let them."

"No, I escaped, but while I'm running away, Freckles is yelling 'Payback is hell' and Vanessa screams out 'We know where you live.' Yeah, it was done in fun, but it could have been embarrassing. Word gets around, you know. Now I'm fair game for all kinds of pranks."

"Sounds like they're competing for your attention. I don't think it was a payback, or...wait a sec. Did you do something to provoke them?"

"Me? Provoke them?"

"Yes, you, mischievous you."

"Well...."

"Out with it, Patrick. Now!"

He cupped his hands as if concealing an object. "Um, I had captured a chameleon just to show them. I hid it, but as I opened my hands it leaped on Vanessa's arm." He chuckled. "How could I know it'd do that? Vanessa jumped, screaming, slapping her arm. Freckles wasn't prepared for her leap. They fell all over each other. I'd sure make a great slapstick scene. I should have caught Vanessa's reaction on a video camera, one with a slo-mo feature. Nobody could possibly replicate that look—ever."

Easter poked his arm. "So who was the real provocateur? Sounds like *you* were. And we know—yes they all know—you were once a dancer with the Pony Xpress."

"Well, yeah, I needed the work. This one night I was performing for all these sorority sisters on Scream Nite when things got way out of hand. The cops showed up. I skedaddled."

"Okay, work up a skit," she said. "We'll spoof a bachelorette party onstage during our tour. You can come dressed as a beat cop. But the girls will suddenly disarm you, blindfold you, strip-search you and then—"

"No-no-no," he said. "No way."

"But audiences will love it, and it's the Sweethearts chance to shine. After all, you do encourage them to be spontaneous. Yeah, that skit will work just fine."

"I get it," he said. "You'd conspire with them against me." He breathed deep. "I don't want them doing exploratory stuff on me."

"Look, I'm collaborating with you, not them. Okay?"

"Yeah, right."

"Okay, let's brainstorm the idea with Cheryl and get her take on it."

"I don't think so," he said. "Too many things could go wrong with that act." He had begun to see another side of Easter, one that didn't coincide with her attitude over the last several months of working closely with her.

A half-hour later they said goodnight outside her upstairs bedroom. But once aboard the luxury tour bus, he couldn't shake Goodnowe's naughty plan.

How could he offset Easter's acceptance of the man's deal? He must find a way.

DURING REHEARSALS behind the college gymnasium, Easter and her recruits performed on a sandy, makeshift softball diamond. One of Easter's favorite comedy acts had Patrick playing an umpire with Vanessa as his scene partner.

"Play ball!" she shouted as Vanessa, acting her part as the team ditz —dubbed Squeaky for this skit—stepped up to home plate. In the crook of her neck she held a plastic bat, its color matching her roseate fingernail polish. The pose freed her hands to unwrap a block of pink bubblegum, which she fed into her mouth and, with eyes closed, emitted exaggerated moans of pleasure.

On the pitcher's mound, a tall blonde lobbed a whiffle ball over home plate where Vanessa failed to swing at the pitch.

"Strike *un!*" Patrick jabbed a finger skyward as he portrayed a French-speaking umpire in a tux with a red cummerbund about his waist.

Vanessa removed a lint roller from her back pocket and worked it along her legs. "Got a spot on my jeans," she said. A second ball crossed the strike zone. She ignored it.

"Strike *deux!*" Patrick gingerly placed his headgear on the ground.

"What might you be doing, mademoiselle? I suggest you swing at *le objet*, foul it, or try some other—" he stuttered "—mimiiiiii-mimiii-mimicry?"

Vanessa shrugged. "Okay, but you said I must have clean jeans to participate." She blew a pink bubble that grew larger until it popped and masked the lower half of her face.

Feigning exasperation, he sidled up to her. "Pardon, *Cherie*. I speak of your comely DNA and those genes—g-e-n-e-s—inside your *manifique* body. Thus the *la raison* for recruiting you. It is also to advance *la* matching."

"*Mashing*?" she said, her voice high-pitched as she stressed his clumsy French.

"*Nada!*" he said. "We mean to jettison the detritus inside us and mate for better traits."

She giggled. "Why not just tell people to never mate for less than the best? You and I could give it a go, maybe win a special appearance on *The Hotz Show*"

"Cut." Easter stepped forward. "The nasal twang is good, girl, but open those big doe eyes wider and blink faster. Only you can do the ditz. Play it to the hilt, okay?"

Larry Lemoyne lowered his camera. "It's getting hot out here. What's next?"

"The suspenders scene," Easter said. "Go easy on him, Vanessa. No blister marks."

Patrick flinched as he realized she would stretch his suspenders two feet before releasing them.

On the sidelines, Danny DiNago stood with Sandy and Mandy Dupleiss, identical twins from Canada who chatted with him.

Easter blew her whistle, signaling each team to regroup at the shade-tree tables. "You gotta show more pizazz, girls, but take a break and get with Patrick later. If a TV show doesn't accept us, we'll be a road show and perform slapstick and sight gags."

As the Sweethearts sauntered toward the shade to review their scripts, Patrick noted Easter was too preoccupied as skit director to notice Danny's departure with the Dupleiss twins, beauties who stood five-seven and excelled as singers. They quickly boarded the bus with Danny.

He decided not to question Danny's daily need for a massage. Nowhere in Patrick's résumé was snitch listed in his comedy repertoire.

Always eager to talk, Vanessa moved into his peripheral vision. "Why not use me more in your skits?" she said. "Back home I have a roomful of dance trophies."

He wanted to say she also was the most willing to break Easter's professional distance rule. Instead he said, "I agree you're the most talented in the group. I mean, what's a train without a caboose?" He winked at her. "We'll discuss it later." The delay allowed him to ponder why Danny took exception to Easter's rules. For the rich, it seemed status had its privileges.

———

LINGERING with Slack Creel in the shade of palm trees behind the backstop, Goat nodded toward the tour bus after the Canadian pair entered it with Danny.

"Check out the gals," Goat said. "You have to wonder which one's his favorite."

"Vanessa Wynley of course," Slack said.

Goat fanned a fly away from his face. "Excellent choice. I'm betting Danny won't object to a video keepsake with her. It could be an erotic tribute to his expertise with women like Vanessa."

"Okay, you're already doing a lingerie shoot, so why do a video when he's got the real thing?"

"Because he has a certain grandeur about him. Besides, to become a legend, a man of Danny's caliber must secure his status as a demigod, an immortal one."

"Huh? What's with the demigod stuff?"

Goat tilted his Panama hat. "Humans erect statues and build halls of fame, don't they? In much the same way, a video preserves a legacy in the context of its history. You see, we know Danny is sure to become a legend. But legends fade with time unless—" he raised a finger "—worshippers have access to tangible evidence of their hero's superior status. With that in mind, he could rise above every legend who's ever lived."

"Like a superhero?"

"Exactly. We humans idolize fantasy heroes—sports, military, religious. I want to sell Danny on being immortal. This lingerie video, if enhanced, will also give you leverage with Vanessa."

"Leverage?"

"Yes, guaranteed. It will prompt her to put out, or else." Goat lowered his voice. "I'll expand the lingerie shoot to include an intimate session between her and Dan the Man. A keepsake. Get it? Chances are she wouldn't want to risk something like that going viral. Get it?"

"Yeah, now you're talking. Uh...ain't that blackmail?"

"Happens every day. Once we shoot them together, she'll have no choice."

Slack chuckled. "Man, that's devious as hell."

"Machiavellian, to be sure." Goat slapped his neck and a yellow fly spiraled downward. "I'll be producing a cult masterpiece, and a half-million dollars is what I need to do a first-rate production. It'll generate that much in video rentals and downloads alone. It'll mean megabucks for us. Are you in for a fifty-fifty split?"

"Maybe, but what's my obligation in this deal, besides money?"

"Depends. Can I count on you to get Easter's approval for it?"

"Uh...okay, but how will I do that?"

"She was your business partner, remember? You know what makes her tick."

"Yeah. We had us a sports agency but she bailed. She owes me plenty. I could call in the debt, or threaten to, but she might lean on Danny to pay it."

"Not a chance. Sorelle Ebanetti holds the purse strings and Easter is her nemesis, so it's an open-ended contest. But no need to mention Vanessa's sex tape with Danny."

"Okay, but Easter has a stubborn streak," Slack said. "This'll take some thinking."

"Thinking is for sissies, Slack. Easter's vulnerable. Creating leverage, my friend, is an art. Thing is, without it Sebastian won't approve this gang's show on the Funtasy Channel."

On the infield, Easter's demeanor resembled an irate mother hen as she approached Danny and the twins. Sandy and Mandy peeled away like jets on a precision flying team.

"Are we having fun yet?" Easter said, her sarcastic tone hinting of a reprimand.

Danny shrugged. "Just another morning massage."

Easter's voice rose in a harsh pitch. "Here we are trying to impress our guest...." She shook her head as the tempo of her voice regained its momentum. "Do you not realize the twins are more than just a novelty act? But did Mr. Goodnowe see them perform? No. Why not? Because they were on the bus with an impulsive jock whose goal is to pamper his supersized ego."

"But I thought the twins were up later. I mean, doing a skit later."

Her hand skimmed the top of her head. "Sheeew-zoop! What time warp are you in? Don't you realize we worked up a special just for the twins? Where's your mind? Not on the script, is it?"

He shrugged. "But this was just a screening, right?"

"Wrong!" Easter slammed her clipboard on the ground. "Have you no sense of timing?"

Patrick lingered yards away, curious about Easter's harsh reaction. Apparently, she had not yet become desensitized to Danny's morning massage routine.

Nonchalant, Danny hailed Goat and Slack as they strolled toward him. "Come on over, guys. We're fine-tuning some details in the skits. Scolding is part of Easter's act."

Easter stalked away, leaving her clipboard behind.

Patrick could almost feel the steam of her frustration as she brushed past him. Her anger was no act. He hoisted an equipment bag onto his shoulder. Gathering softball gear left behind on the infield became his cover to discreetly eavesdrop on Goat and his friend.

Slack Creel, keeping pace with Goat, whistled low as he drew close to Danny. "Say, big Dan, have you ever thought about making a bare-ass video of you with your women?"

Danny's outstretched arms rose and fell at his side, as if limbering up for a game. "No, can't say that I have. Why do you ask?"

Goat held up a hand as if to throttle Slack's obtuse approach. "I'm curious about something," he said. "Nigel Pregnor says you're the world's most overrated lover. Even more insulting, that celebrity sleuth is writing an unauthorized biography about you."

Danny's trademark demeanor remained cool and unruffled. "Oh yeah? Why should I care?"

Goat scratched his goatee. "Nigel claims your romancing women is more myth than fact. His book is certain to disappoint your fan base. You owe it to them, legion that they are, to defend yourself and your macho image. I propose that we do a sensual video and set the record straight for them."

Danny rocked back on his heels like a batter taking an inside pitch. He lowered his voice. "We should talk about this later, in private."

Patrick positioned the duffle bag higher on his shoulder and eased away, though he imagined Goat's stare burning laser-like into his back.

NINE

Patrick chose the parlor to show the Sweethearts how to visually synchronize body language with vocal expressions. He selected Cheryl Decairo as his dance partner before playing a recording of *Killing Me Softly With His Song*. By interpreting the poignant words with each turn of his body, he led her into the song's romantic finale with a cradling embrace while looking deep into her eyes.

Each of the girls took turns dancing with him. The session concluded with Cheryl, along with Vanessa Wynley and Peaches McCollough, showing the most versatility.

Larry Lemoyne and his assistant, a twenty-something cameraman, captured multiple angles that helped Patrick to review the videos later. At sundown Easter ushered the Sweethearts to Ellie's where its large windows allowed a panoramic view of the Gulf of Mexico. The dining menu offered a buffet that drew beachcombers and assorted jetsetters.

In a private banquet area with the girls, Patrick waited for his order of an Asian dish while the girls chatted nonstop.

Easter interrupted their chatter with knuckle-raps on the tabletop. After a request for a few girls to stay behind, she lifted a DVD from her handbag and waggled it. "Allow me to explain why only ten of us girls are meeting. Here's the screen test we shot yesterday. Ta-da! We— yes we only—qualify for something special by Mr. Raul Goodnowe."

She waited a moment for their excited chatter to subside. "We have a chance to model a lingerie brand. Their slogan is, *Impress the best with Nothing Less*. It's the rage of Fashion Week." She rapped the disc like a judge's gavel on the table. "And the sole distributor for that collection is Kluuge of New York City."

Patrick finished eating his bok choy, pocketed a fortune cookie to read later, and glanced about at the girls. They seemed to be impressed by the announcement.

Easter grinned. "Kluuge operates the largest franchise for intimate apparel."

Cheryl Decairo frowned. "Nothing Less?" The girls paid little attention to her until she spoke more assertively. "Kluuge is also known for racy videos. They sponsor a pageant with a million-dollar award to the winner."

"Really?" Vanessa said. "That's a lot of moolah."

"Yes," Cheryl said. "The winner's sash reads *Miss Nude Kluuge*. Believe me, that's not where we want lingerie modeling to take us. Posing in microkinis is exhibitionism."

The girls looked around, their eyes showing disenchantment, but Freckles broke the brief silence. "A million bucks, eh? One question. Does the winner get to keep the crown?"

"Yeah, like it matters," Cheryl said. "Sorelle says models who do that are desperate."

Easter palm-slapped the table. "The pageant has nothing to do with us. We'll model the best negligees, peignoirs, teddies—all in good taste." She studied each face as if the challenge was to explain peek-aboo cleavage to tribal women in some Middle East desert.

Amused by the exchange, Patrick knew Cheryl kept a daily log and a diary. *Yes, she ought to glean plenty from this meeting.*

Goat Goodnowe approached from Easter's blindside. He moved to join the gathering with a tan satchel at his side. "You're all headed for stardom. I guarantee it."

"There you are...finally." Easter rose to jab him on the shoulder as if his machismo merited the sporting gesture. "My, but you look suave in a white shirt and bolo tie. I was telling the girls about—"

"Sorry I'm late," he said, interrupting. "We have a lot to cover in this star-maker project."

Easter offered Goat a chair next to her. "We're excited to hear your proposal, Mr. Goodnowe, and we thank you for selecting the ten of us—the ten most telegenic."

Patrick marveled at her conciliatory tone; such a contrast after her first meeting with Goat on the patio. He wondered what had changed.

"Something to drink?" she asked.

Goat seated himself next to her. "No thank you. I'm content to drink in the beauty of my elite selection." He gave Patrick a passing glance. "Absent rejected comedians, of course."

"Ahhh, ain't life hard," Patrick retorted. No doubt the man knew about his snafu on the *Hotz.*

"Life is easy," Goat said. "Comedy is hard."

Patrick's eyes lost their gleam. "Says the man who thinks deep-fried is a suntan lotion." Some men could upstage a rival with a smile and not seem rude. Patrick wasn't smiling.

"A little background regarding my personal profile might be in order," Goat said. "Years ago the Godinho patriarch changed his name to Goodnowe. He was a pirate. Unlike him, I was a respected bush pilot in Brazil. I flew directors to exotic locales for movie shoots. I also shot a docudrama. It was about the *Biaune*, legendary princess of the ancient Sea People who followed the green turtle migrations. That tradition was matriarchal, so women ruled. They paddled from the Amazon, topless, to the ocean and up to Cuba."

"In boats?" Vanessa asked as if to clarify a significant point for her companions.

Patrick stifled a laugh. Her quirky habit of inserting humor into dry conversations still endeared her to him since their first meeting at *The Hotz Show.*

Ignoring her, Goat continued. "In Rio de Janeiro I acquired a partner, a renowned videographer. We made a lot of movies. Trust me, I know the real dealmakers, men like Sebastian Rubleau, owner of Rubleau Entertainment."

He stroked his whiskered chin. "I also know the pitfalls and how to avoid scammers who make promises they can't keep. With me you'll be headliners within weeks, not years, and at no cost...if you agree to a tradeoff."

Patrick tensed. A tradeoff in the hands of a huckster was never an even swap. Even the most profitable Hollywood studios could not guarantee success for their own films.

From his satchel Goat pulled color brochures. "These are the latest styles from Nothing Less. A few decades ago, models would blush to wear such lingerie, but—"

"It's the nipple craze," Vanessa deadpanned as she helped pass his literature to the girls.

As if the pictorials were radioactive, Cheryl Decairo pushed the brochures away.

Sensing a kindred spirit in her attitude, Patrick twisted in his chair, eager to find a fissure in Goat Goodnowe's armor.

"What you're doing is riding the coattails of a trend, not a fad," Goat said. "It's a great success already." He glanced at Easter. "We'll do two shoots. The first is lingerie on Wednesday, followed by your own promo video that'll run as a teaser on TV. Sebastian, my friend, will view the promo. He can make a decision within a few days based on one episode."

He struggled to contain a cough. "But we have to work fast so he can hype it with a video trailer on Funtasy, the comedy channel."

Easter nodded. "I did my homework. Rubleau Entertainment is a prestigious company and its TV and video streaming welcomes new productions. So our Sweethearts of America Show will be a big hit."

Goat offered additional documents to pass around the table. "I'll need your signatures on these model's release forms. There's one for each of you."

Patrick considered cautioning them not to sign, but Easter had endorsed the project. A protest at this juncture would appear subversive. His best option seemed obvious—a private discussion with her after the meeting, but only after Goat had gone.

Despite Goat's redoubtable stare, Cheryl slid the release back toward him, unsigned.

"Is there a problem, Miss Decairo?" Goat said. "It's a standard agreement."

Cheryl stabbed the contract with a finger. "I've never heard of Orgo Cinematic."

"It's a Rubleau offshoot." His cavalier manner suggested his statement was more than sufficient. "Any other questions? If not, then—"

"Yes!" Cheryl crisscrossed her arms. "Is Orgo listed with any credible guilds?"

"Like SAG, the Screen Actors Guild?" he said. "Check it out." He pulled a thick folder from his satchel. "Or save yourself the effort. I have all the documentation needed."

He held the folder at eye level. "You'll need a more ingenious stalling technique than that, young lady. Paralysis by analysis, I call it. Of all the vices, nothing stings like ingratitude. Shakespeare, as you may recall, spoke that truth centuries ago. Surely you can appreciate this once-in-a-lifetime opportunity to achieve the fame you girls want."

Goat's wilting stare, aimed at Cheryl, lingered a moment before he placed the documents back inside the satchel. He made no move to gather the signed modeling agreements, but his tone threatened finality. "Funny how we don't lose our balance when we have no place to fall. When there's no one to catch us, we seem to move ahead. Question is, ladies, do you have the courage to do just that?"

His gaze turned on Easter as he spoke. "It's your show, your future, your move. But bear this in mind; a lost opportunity is just that. Lost."

Easter gathered the modeling forms, her eyes downcast. "I'll need a few minutes alone with both Cheryl and Danny."

Patrick wanted to say, *And me, dammit!* Disturbed that Easter was so easily swayed, he tried in vain to make eye contact with her. Why had she not invited him to join the tribunal? Was it his lack of status? If he were taller, would it make a difference? Any demand to be heard now might mean the loss of what little clout he had.

"I understand your high regard for Miss Decairo," Goat said. "But dare I suggest you spend your valuable time alone with me and Danny first? And may I also ask, is there anyone else other than her —" he indicated Cheryl with a thumb "—who'll question your decision?"

Patrick's jaw muscles flexed as he tried to restrain the fury welling inside him. "What an insult," he blurted. "Shysters are always long on promise and short on delivery."

Easter's eyes reflected her chagrin as her hands fluttered like a wounded dove. "Patrick! It's my decision, my call...and Danny's."

Patrick rolled his shoulders and forced himself to bridle his temper.

Goat gripped his knees to rise. "That being the case, if we three agree—you, Danny and me—do we have a deal?" He raised his hands at half-mast, freezing any objection. "Otherwise, we're all wasting each other's time. I have other projects in the works, all awaiting my professional expertise."

The Brazilian's hand waved off potential retorts. "Not that I would weasel out at the last minute. To be candid, other offers mean more money, short term, but the Sweethearts' charm and sex appeal far exceeds anything I've seen elsewhere—ever. I'll do the lingerie shoot on Wednesday."

Unspeaking, Easter summoned Danny with a head-jerk to follow her outside.

Patrick glanced at Cheryl, wishing the remaining girls would side with her, yet he understood their dilemma. They wanted fame. After all, they were actresses. None had signed on to be wallflowers.

A wise truism, spoken long ago by his great-grandfather, sprang from his subconscious. *On the Serengeti the lame are left behind. The pride moves on.*

With Goat joining Easter's confab, Patrick descended the steps and strolled along the boardwalk to the moonlit beach. He sought the solace of the gulf tide to soothe his troubled thoughts. Would Easter cooperate with a potential scam? How could he not have seen a turn-about coming? He recalled she had been famous on the golf circuit, but he doubted her business skills.

Something had gone sideways and he sensed it would not end well.

Would the Sweethearts' sensuality be flaunted on a sex video? Vanessa and eight colleagues—Anastasia Andrews, Cassie Wellington, Peaches McCollough, Dodie Appling, Freckles Lambert, the Dupleiss twins, and Easter Beaulieu herself—could become victims.

Only one holdout, Cheryl Decairo, would be spared the humiliation.

Undulating waves broke along the shoreline. If only they would break the logjam of his thoughts.

A savvy woman he knew in Dewberry, Georgia, might have a solution to the dilemma. Naomi Savoie's genius and courage had helped him rescue his teenage daughter only two years ago from a donor organ cartel fronting as a rehab center for runaway girls.

Why am I delaying a call to her?

Like a rip current, anxiety engulfed him. After years of living close to the beach, he knew that fighting a rip current was useless. A strong swimmer could swim parallel to the shore, go with the flow, and keep his head above water. Surviving strong currents in life called for similar ingenuity.

Yet an enemy inside him—panic—worked contrary to rational thought.

He recalled his great-grandfather's words: *If a man can't control his emotions, what else can't he control?*

Even if not fully convinced the pedigree cause was all it claimed to be, he decided his girls—the lovely and talented Sweethearts—had to be saved from Goat Goodnowe.

TEN

Turning back from the shoreline, Patrick strolled along Ellie's boardwalk. The journey took him across Peninsula Road and up Bon View Boulevard where he veered across the mansion frontage. It occurred to him that he could abandon the tour bus and sleep in the unoccupied den, uninvited.

It might refresh his mind and fire up his creative juices to write humor.

True, the Sweethearts welcomed his repertoire of scripts, but to adapt each one's personality to a particular skit pleased him. Tapping into each of his protégé's reservoir of talent and seeing it expressed in a scene was its own reward.

Vanessa, the most demonstrative, often clung tight to him as if hugging was a competitive event. Perhaps she thought he was her personal cuddle toy. Perhaps the hugs of Peaches, Cheryl, Cassie and others were a prank. Perhaps they didn't understand the professional distance rule. He shunted those thoughts aside, preferring to think about his professional stature as a trainer.

Easter's warning—*borders and rules*—dampened his urge to invite physical contact.

A quick glance at his watch showed five minutes past the girls' ten o'clock curfew when Sorelle Ebanetti crossed his mind. Why be nervous about her upcoming visit? Like the lyrics of an unforgettable song, she still lodged in the deepest recesses of his heart.

Long ago she promised him fame. With the passing of two decades, that promise had faded. In its place, anguish followed infidelity. Even now, the pain of their breakup resurfaced during a fleeting moment of sentimental reflection.

Yet a tantalizing spark of hope remained. He wondered if she recalled with fondness the good times they shared. And the intense love. Twenty years had passed. Yes, that might make a difference in how she felt about reconciling with him. But how would the once-famous model react upon learning his acting gig included almost two dozen female entertainers?

Solar lights illuminated the east wall of the house. He rounded the building while fishing an extra backdoor key—Easter's idea—from his cargo pants. In semi-darkness below the veranda, he paused and listened to an owl hooting in the distance before ascending the outside stairs to the first level.

With the girls asleep upstairs, his presence in the mansion den should go undetected.

After brushing past tropical foliage in the atrium, he keyed the kitchen door. The faint aroma of spices greeted him as he slipped through the kitchen and past the dining area, then into the den where the soft glow of a lamp reflected off a leather recliner. An embroidered coverlet draped over the recliner, its folds cascading in haphazard fashion. A floral perfume lingered on its fabric. He reached to turn off the lamp but a notepad on the lamp table caught his eye.

Curious, he read a handwritten note: *I'm here for you, coach. Need to talk? Your Scribe.*

How did Cheryl know he would sleep tonight in the mansion? From his shirt pocket he plucked the fortune cookie placed there from Ellie's. Opening it, he read its message: *Romance will come into your life in a very unusual way.*

"How unusual?" he mumbled. Would it be more unusual than two years ago when he befriended a nurse named Naomi who cherished his friendship? He wondered what she would think about his new job at Sanctuary Beach.

But now, amid a rush of hormones, he envisioned Cheryl descending the stairs to join him in the den for whispered endearments, or skit collaborating—whichever came first.

Just as he dismissed the vision as unrealistic fantasizing, a more disturbing thought jarred him. Suppose Goodnowe gained control of the girls? Would Patrick's role as their comic be eliminated? Why couldn't he read the man's next move and muster a defense? In a flash of insight he realized his wishful thoughts were not the best strategy. He could not expect Sorelle to become an ally.

A call to her New York firm could at least confirm her arrival time.

He shed his deck shoes and switched off the lamp. The recliner allowed him to lie almost supine. He must formulate a plan to outwit Goat. With his eyes adjusting to the darkness, he detected the slight movement of a figure on the lower steps of the stairwell. His first guess was the note writer. He wanted to call out her name and suggest a late-night chat.

Without a sound, the figure drifted upstairs.

Still mindful of Goat's deceptive ploy, he fell into a restless sleep and a troubled dream of naïve young women auctioned to slavers by a Brazilian shyster. But dreams had no meaning. Or did they?

ON WEDNESDAY MORNING Easter replaced Cheryl with a different actress.

For the Nothing Less video shoot, Goat urged Larry Lemoyne and his sidekick to haul props into the mansion library and arrange the ten girls in provocative poses. Goat lauded see-through peignoirs as standard fare, along with their nude-colored bras and panties.

The modern illusion of nakedness completed the glam look set by the Nothing Less brand.

"Less is more," Goat chimed to Larry who followed the man's directions.

Patrick wanted to ask, *How much more of nothing does it take to be fashionable?*

Following the lingerie session, Patrick staged a promo shoot for syndication on the Funtasy Channel. But after three hours of performing skits, the girls' antics struck Patrick as amateurish.

"It could be better," he confided to Easter after calling for a recess.

"Didn't think I'd be doing a TV show instead of staging a live event on the road."

"Rubleau's editors can fix its flaws," she said.

"But we have just one shot at this. Rubleau is expecting a file tomorrow."

"I know but the girls did great," she said. "His editors will see its potential and want more."

"Okay, so all we can do is wait for the TV honchos' verdict, right?"

"Come with me, Patrick." Easter ushered him to the patio and embraced him before pulling free to swing her arms like a carefree child. "Rubleau will grade it no less than a nine," she said. "But we'll get better, maybe get more innovative later. Besides, viewers love imperfection."

"How about spicing it with pedigree testimonials?" he said. "Like ten-second vignettes."

"Yeah, in a series," she said. "And show viewers the difference between misfits and pedigrees. The doofus crowd of misfits will do anything for notoriety."

"It could backfire," he said. "You know, public sentiment is hard to predict. Do you know any famous pedigrees we could recruit?"

"Plenty of them, yes, and they don't have to be famous." She looked at the bay as if lost in a moment of reflection. "I can instinctively spot pedigrees a mile away. It's in their bearing and healthy glow, especially that sparkle in their eyes. It's in their symmetry of form but also in their intellect. That kind of insight is instinctual with me, like a gift."

He leaned toward her. "Why not show viewers something altogether different?"

On impulse she embraced him again. "Okay, so what do you have in mind, handsome?"

He held her around the waist, as if ready for a waltz. "Let's show the girls as thoughtful and yet naïve, like the ingénues they are. Reveal their personal quirks. Give viewers a bit of insight so they can relate to them."

She spun away but hesitated at arm's length. "Their antics should really engage viewers over a thirteen-week run." She twirled beneath his outstretched arm. "They'll be captivated and we can inspire people. Know what I'm saying? You can tell my heart is into this cause, can't you?"

He slowed the impromptu dance. "Goat staged the girls with a nudie look in his lingerie shoot. I mean, why typecast them as something less than wholesome?"

Easter adopted a burlesque pose. "Wholesome? What does that even mean? Nudie is in. Look at the fashion mags and the award shows. You've seen designer gowns at Hollywood's red carpet events, right? Well, they're all lingerie lookalikes."

"Yeah, but look who's wearing them—the rich and famous."

"That's us," she said. "Maybe sooner than you think."

He chuckled. "Projecting, are we?"

She poked his midsection. "Just you keep on doing skits like 'Hot to Trot.' Remember? There you were, planting a stick-on tattoo on Vanessa's posterior when she says, 'Stick it to me, baby.' That's the kind of unscripted banter we need. I'm counting on you to do your job, Casanova. Train to entertain. Uninhibited, no less."

He leaned in close to her. "But in our promo, not the lingerie shoot, we want viewers to think."

"Right, and the vignettes can do that. Thinking is good but emotion counts for something, too."

"I'm okay with gimmicks like stick-on tattoos on derrieres, but what Goat's doing with lingerie isn't in harmony with our cause."

"Patrick, why be so starchy about everything? Just innovate." She folded herself into his body and swayed to prompt a continuation of the dance. "Imagine hyping a total genetic makeover, like we caught a wave on our way to stardom with Mr. Goodnowe's help."

"I've seen hucksters aplenty, Easter, and he fits the imagery." He turned away, miffed over her trusting Goat. "Pardon me while I retire to the den and do my job. Got skits to write."

"Hey, come back here. I'm in the mood to dance."

So Easter's priorities were skewed. Perhaps Goat had spun her deeper into his web. Yet it wasn't the Brazilian she had embraced with unusual fondness while breaking her own distancing rule, was it?

ELEVEN

Tally Schermer, a twenty-something waif, edited her script aboard Goat's luxury yacht. Her latest script, as usual, involved erotic scenes, but it needed a plot, or the semblance of one. Plotting, she had to admit, was never her strong suit. Perhaps her muse needed a prompt.

She searched all the familiar places where Goat kept his stash. On impulse she checked the safe behind a painting in the stateroom. To her surprise, it was unlocked. A collection of mailing tubes inside it contained an artist's rendering of satyrs. A watercolor she pulled from one depicted a goat-like demon ogling a group of nude women bathing in a pool.

A recurring Grecian theme in the artistry were young women caught off guard by lechers.

Tally wasn't shocked by Goat's prurient taste in art. He often bragged of his art collection being extensive. She toyed with the idea of selling some of the treasures—two small wood carvings and a few photos—to a museum, but only if she tired of her confinement aboard the yacht. In such moments, she wondered where she might escape, but she knew of no one in polite society who would welcome a lost vagabond whose specialty was scripting x-rated movies.

She couldn't reconcile her psychological dependence with her repugnance of him.

Goat's new assignment for her was a "breakthrough" script—soft porn for a group of glamour girls. It would have minimal dialogue. Its racy story line would explore risqué antics and insinuations of sexual indulgence. She proudly titled it *Star Harem*. Star implied celebrity. And acting on camera in the nude was something she assumed most actresses did early in their career. Had she not done the same?

Surrounded by her favorite amenities aboard *LoveLord*—a nautical residence she shared with Goat—Tally wanted to believe she was living the good life. In lieu of marijuana, a margarita should make writing the final scene a cinch.

As she stuffed the paintings back into their tubes and eased them into the safe, dissimilar objects drew her attention. Curious, she released the strings on a binder with a swastika imprint on its cover. It contained a thick cache of printed material.

She perused the literature and decided propaganda was boring. Even the photos held no interest. Except one. There was Goat in his younger days standing next to a Brazilian flag on his left and a Nazi flag on his right. Youthful men, all white, had gathered to salute with arms outstretched as he addressed them from a podium. A deep frown creased his face. Knowing what that frown meant sent chills down her spine. She tensed in the wake of painful memories and closed the binder. A strong cocktail would steel her resolve to write and forget that his abuse of her was chronic.

A HEAT WAVE enveloped Sanctuary Beach, causing breezes to shy away from the mansion. Easter strolled across the patio tiles to the umbrella canopy where Goat Goodnowe relaxed in a wicker chair. His gaze centered on the bikini-clad Sweethearts as he appraised their poolside antics.

"Look at this." Easter dropped a printout on Goat's lap. "A VP at Rubleau Entertainment signed it. Good, but how long before our show starts on the Funtasy Channel?"

Goat read the label on his cigar band. "*Arturo Fuente*. You don't mind, do you?" He lit up, not waiting for her approval. "How long? It depends on when I invite Sebastian Rubleau for an excursion on *Love-Lord*. A barefoot cruise is long overdue for our club."

"As in what, a fishing club?" She settled into a chair and peered at the girls. Some played a game of dump-the-rider with Danny in the pool, each mounting a companion's shoulders.

"No, not fishing," Goat said. "On our cruise we admire our latest acquisitions. Together we own the most valuable collection of erotic art in the hemisphere."

"Interesting," she said in a powder-dry voice.

"You see, I have the discriminating taste of an aficionado," he said. "And I'm fluent in several languages, so I'm at home from Berlin to Budapest." A tight smile showed his small teeth. "Perhaps too much at home. The Monte Carlo and Macau gaming houses banned me."

"Let me guess. You cheat at cards."

"No, that's the easy way. But I did win too often. I have a photographic memory."

"Really? You counted cards?"

He took a drag on the stogie. "Yes. Anyhow, like I promised last week, I can swing this deal for you. Sebastian Rubleau co-owns Orgo Cinematic. We can pique his carnal interest. He lives for beauty and since your girls are all ravishingly beautiful, we—"

Easter crossed her arms. "One problem," she said. "The Sweethearts don't turn tricks."

Goat ignored butterflies that soared past him. "And that's the type I try to recruit. Modest women are more alluring, you see. And a nice variety is always appealing."

"Oh?"

"Certainly. The English poet, William Blake, once said, 'The naked woman's body is a portion of eternity too great for the eye of man.' You see, eroticism must reveal naiveté as much as symmetry. We'll need naturals who can project a certain...essence. My personal picks are the same girls we shot on Wednesday."

"All ten of us?"

"Of course. I have a script designed to immortalize Danny's prowess with women." He removed a tobacco sprig from his tongue. "Do you know Nigel Pregnor is writing a biography about Danny?"

"Yes, and a gossip columnist says it's not exactly flattering."

"Right," he said. "But we'll offset it."

"How? I mean, you already have the lingerie video."

"Yes. We'll expand it to make Danny immortal." Nicotine smoke drifted from his mouth. "We'll transition it into a movie. With good editing, we can outwit censors."

"It will take a stand-in, not just good editing, to do what you have in mind."

"Pardon?"

Avoiding the query, she said, "Slack mentioned you had an offer we couldn't refuse, but I had no idea it would include this...this new wrinkle. So I'll have to ask you this; just how graphic will this thing be? No nudity, I hope."

He tugged at his goatee. "Depends on how the ten of you react to Danny's overtures. Of course, first we need to shoot a test scene here at the house—today."

She sat up straight. "Why today?"

"Allow me to explain something to you, dear. To be a leader you must be decisive. You either lead, follow, or get the hell out of the way."

"Okay, but I'll have to discuss this with Danny."

He gave her a baleful look. "I'll need a volunteer with Danny for my demo. Slack says he'll forgive your debt if you greenlight this new lingerie version."

A flicker of dejection showed in her eyes. "I owe him bigtime."

"Um, yes, he said it's in the six-figure range, but it's a write-off if you help me. Guaranteed."

She sighed. "Ten bodies in the buff?"

Goat drew deep on his cigar. "Of course."

"Mr. Goodnowe, that's a big order. By the way, how else does Slack fit into this deal? I imagine he wants to seduce the movie's leading lady, namely me."

"Not quite. Vanessa is his turn-on these days."

Following a face-palm, she stood suddenly and beckoned to Danny who left the pool with tug-of-war winner Vanessa on his back and Larry's camera in tow.

Easter grinned as the pair drew closer. "Something new is in the works. It's a bit different."

"You'll love it," Goat said in sharp contrast with Easter's hesitancy. "This movie will be a real classic, forever remembered by moviegoers."

His gaze rested on Vanessa. "You two follow me and I'll explain upstairs—" he managed a grin "—in one of the bedrooms. It'll add meaning for Nothing Less."

Inside the mansion library, the screensaver on Patrick's laptop offered a compilation of images. Naomi Savoie dominated the screen in a nurse's uniform. Had it been ten weeks since he had called her? He finger-pecked a quick message: *I'm directing what we hope is a TV series for a troupe of glam girls.*

Wait. Should he mention genetic matching? No, it might suggest a stake in the outcome.

Deleting it, he backpedaled to a more generic creation: *A special guest will arrive today from New York. Sorelle Ebanetti, the former cover girl is....*

No, that might raise questions. Delete.

Frustrated, he closed the laptop. What had fond memories of Sorelle done to him?

Sorelle: modeling icon, public relations guru, sole owner of Zipit Talent Management. Who could have foreseen her as a worldwide talent mogul? A woman with her clout, if an ally, would be a powerful one. Would being with her this time be better than the first go-round?

He wished for a relationship free of deception. Would she blame him for their rift? Would she remember cotton candy at a county fair?

Above all, he must not show himself vulnerable to her.

TWELVE

Easter adjusted the tinted visor shading her forehead against the glare of afternoon sunlight and watched Patrick, along with Vanessa and Cheryl, act out a Roaring Twenties skit on the sandlot. Observing them from the shade of palms near the backstop, Sorelle Ebanetti applauded the Charleston dance as it ended their lively act.

"It's a zany interpretation," Sorelle said. "And I love those glorious flapper outfits."

Patrick's jargon and couture—period cap and bare torso under bib overalls—allowed him to play an umpire who could entertain any Jazz Age crowd. As he departed the sandlot, he hoped his face paint also concealed his identity from her. "Haven't titled the skit yet," he said with a nasal twang. "Vanessa likes to play the ditz role, but it takes some doing for me to react as her foil without cracking up. She's perfected the cross-eyed doofus look for camera close-ups."

Vanessa gave him a token kiss. "Stumpy says I'm a natural, but if our act leaves laugh lines on your face, it's his fault. He writes the scripts."

Standing nearby, Easter cast a wary eye at Sorelle. "These two jokesters are a hoot but without Stumpy as our buffoon, it wouldn't work. Don't you think so, Ms. Ebanetti?"

Sorelle nodded agreement. "By the way, how did this comedy act get its start?"

Patrick crossed his fingers, hoping her answer would sound believable. As owner-director of the Zipit Beauty Fest, Sorelle might still be chapped over losing Cheryl, her grand winner, to Easter's troupe of entertainers. He knew the girls in the Sweethearts of America Show must appear to be on loan but not stolen; just a diversion from pageant life.

"It was a fluke," Easter said. "The Paladins were raising hell, uh, money for, you know, a kiddie cause, so I recruited girls from everywhere. Some borrowed, actually. Of course, some came from your modeling schools. Amazing how the auditions went. We have only one charity benefit to do next month. Then we're done. Their DNA is superior, too."

"Really?" Sorelle's tone hinted at disbelief. "Yes, my pageant also requires such a status."

Patrick winced. Why mention DNA? Pedigree could be a sore spot.

"You're such a welcome *bon vivant*," Easter said. "I have to get back to rehearsals now."

"Certainly," Sorelle replied. "As they say, break a leg...or two."

Patrick imagined Easter's fingernails curling into claws. He wished his thoughts could somehow be projected to her. *Rise above it, girl. This mind game is yours to lose.*

To his relief, Vanessa jumped into the tense conversation. "Me twinkle-toes and me go with you, Easter. Stumpy must now entertain his *destink*, uh...distinguished guest."

He winked at the pair as they passed, a coded thank-you for not disclosing his identity.

It seemed Sorelle had not changed. The cover girl look had earned her a fortune long before she founded Zipit Talent. Would she ever own up to being from Patrick's hometown of Bon Amite, a haven for football fanatics, freshwater fishing, and chinquapin trees?

"Care for a time-out stroll?" he said with a bow to Sorelle and a nod to the beach, a mere two-hundred yards in the distance. A minute later he strolled with her along Bon View Boulevard toward a Peninsula Road crossing and onward to the beach.

"I wonder how many girls from my modeling franchise she stole," Sorelle said.

He hesitated before answering in his modified voice. "Not sure, but Cheryl Decairo is one of her best trophy catches, uh...recruits."

"Yes, she won my Zipit Beauty Fest. She's supposed to be its ambassador this year."

"Lordy, lordy," he said, his twang intact to mask his identity. He must hold out for the ideal time. Perhaps she still relished surprises. Though she stood an inch taller than him at five-ten, even more of a contrast was her status. While he had struggled to develop a unique standup comedy routine, Sorelle had wowed admirers by developing a talent management empire.

Side by side, they reached the boardwalk beside Ellie's Restaurant and followed it to the sugar-white beach where fiddler crabs scurried in the tideline.

"During auditions, Easter and I couldn't agree on the number of girls for our entertainment acts. We compromised on twenty one. Danny swears it's an omen."

"Oh, he's always been superstitious like that," she confided. "Everything's an omen."

He chuckled. "He reminds me of the couples who consult a fortuneteller at our county fair."

Sorelle inhaled the salty breeze. "Danny's seen the Houdini movie a dozen times. He wouldn't sign with the Marauders unless they agreed to keep his jersey number the same. Same number ten worn in high school and college."

"It's like an amulet or something, huh?"

"Yes. And you don't want to know the significance he assigns to numbers at game time. Not even Gabe understands all his many quirks."

"Gabe?"

"His agent. I'm his talent manager but Gabe's the agent. He's also a friend of mine." She studied Patrick more closely. "Have we met somewhere before? It's uncanny, but you remind me of someone from my past, and for the life of me I can't recall who."

"And I betcha you've met gobs o' people."

"By the way, Stumpy, when is Danny supposed to return? He doesn't answer my calls. Easter doesn't seem to know, either."

Patrick thumbed toward the mansion. "Anytime you see Gert, his bodyguard, standing by the bus, you'll find Danny with his flavor of the day. Massage therapy, he calls it."

"Ah, yes, massage therapy."

"Is that my stomach growling?" he said. "Or is Mount Vesuvius erupting?"

She smiled. "Regarding dinner, it's on me. Unless, of course, you had plans to dine with your own flavor of the day. Is there a Mrs. Stumpy or perhaps a steady girlfriend?"

"Nope. Steady is not my style."

"Sounds like me."

Patrick slowed his pace. "Do you really want to be seen with a hayseed humorist at suppertime?"

She gently slapped his shoulder. "I have a high regard for comedians. Easter admires you, so you must be a special talent."

"Yeah, she appreciates a bumpkin who flubs his pickup lines."

"Perhaps she sees you as a trophy find," she said.

"Trophy find? What would she do, mount him—" he paused "—on her wall?"

She considered him a moment, head to toe. "Sexy humor is your schtick, isn't it?"

"It fits today's audience," he said. "Comedy is reality to me. But what're you in real life? You know, like when you let your hair down and shed your, uh...cares."

She studied her nails. "Well, my urges run in four-year cycles." Her eyelashes fluttered. "You're wondering if I'm in year-four, right?"

"*Youuu,* Miss Ebanetti, are so right," he said, his theatrical voice mocking a popular gameshow host. "Shall we pull the curtain back and see what you've won?"

Pausing, she toyed with a Star of David pendant on a silver chain about her slender neck. "To be perfectly honest, I'm weary of having to choose between boredom and stress. I'd like to simplify my life and find a strong, sensitive, trustworthy man. I prefer one who'll lavish me with affection. But me being so high maintenance, I can be difficult."

"Hmmm, studies show older women prefer money over men."

"*Older* women?"

"Uh, I meant to say mature."

She grinned. "In my forty-eight years I've never apologized for liking money. And in spite of its mileage, this face has never been lifted."

"I believe you. Does my humor rankle your sensibilities?"

"Is that a trick question?"

"Not at all, trick questions require more thought."

"On my part or yours?"

He chuckled. "Hey, you're good, real good."

"Thank you, maestro. Has insult always been a staple in your comedic repertoire? I'm not baiting you. The question only requires candor. Ever been married?"

Showing four fingers, he grinned and resumed his stride.

"Four times?" she said. "I take it you like weddings."

"About much as a fire hydrant likes a dog. Wise men say necessity is the mother of matrimony."

"Wiser women say it's the mother of pearls—" she elbowed him "—but only if the husband's bank account is substantial."

He edged closer to the surf. "Only a mercenary mama would say that."

"Or a pragmatic one," she said. "Shall we meet for dinner about, oh...sevenish?"

"Sure. There's an Italian place about a mile away, on the bay. Pick me up at the mansion. I'll be wearing khaki cargos and a pullover with a blue sailfish on it. After dinner, we can take a walk on the beach. It'll give you another chance to unload on me." His fingers partially hid a smile. "And seeing as how loaded you are, that may take a while."

She laughed softly. "I read lots of comedy material in my business." She removed her sandals and walked barefoot. "We should get along famously once I find where you're most vulnerable."

In his elation over their bantering, it saddened him to think how much they had missed over the years of being apart. Would they be able to move past their old love-hate relationship?

The surf washed over her bare feet as she stopped to hold his gaze, as if daring him to divulge his real identity.

He ached to tell her. But, like a warning whisper, a gentle breeze off the gulf seemed to counsel against it—*not yet, not yet.*

Among the three landlines in the mansion, Easter Beaulieu heard the wall-mounted one in the kitchen first. Dr. Henry Ronofski's familiar no-nonsense voice on the line surprised her.

"Are you sitting down?" the geneticist said.

"No," she said. "Should I?"

"Yes." He paused. "Genetically speaking, we may have found the goose that lays the golden egg. Of course, this time it's not an egg, it's sperm."

"I'm not sure I follow you, Dr. Ronofski. Is gold a metaphor?"

"Miss Beaulieu, what if I told you someone you know has the youth gene?"

She grinned to think a serious scientist could be joking. "What? Like the Fountain of Youth? I'm sorry. That slipped out before I could—"

"Right," he said, quickly interrupting. "This discovery may well define my legacy as a scientist."

She allowed a moment to process the significance of his words. "Danny? It's not Danny, is it?"

"Nope," he said.

A sigh of relief escaped her lips. "I'm glad. I mean, don't get me wrong, he has the macho image for it. It's just that..." She shook her head. "Never mind. If I'm supposed to guess, you could give me a clue, but to be honest I don't know many guys who deserve to have a thing like a youth gene."

"I understand, but this guy might fit the requiem for the proverbial Seeder, the one found in the New Scrolls. If so, then our regenerative cause has a spiritual dimension. I'll give his name to you on a secure site, and it'll be your privilege to let Eugenia know. You should know, too, he may need special attention in order to bring him in line with our genetics mission. You know what I mean, don't you?"

"Um, I think so. I agree that nothing is more important than our pedigree mission."

THIRTEEN

Sorelle Ebanetti tapped the horn of her rented Audi. Leaving the vehicle idling, she stood beside it and waited for her dinner guest. Chewing the earpiece of her sunglasses, she wondered what possessed her to accept an invitation to have dinner with a man she barely knew.

Clearly, the comic was respected and trusted by the Sweethearts, yet she was wary of all standup comedians and their reputation for sexual hijinks. But some mysterious quality about this man drew her to him; almost as if she had known him in another life.

Shoulders squared, her guest descended the front steps of the mansion. His shirt displayed the imprint of a blue sailfish leaping in the foreground of a charter boat.

As he drew closer, Sorelle's eyes widened. "Patrick! Ohmygod, it's you."

He spread his arms wide for a hug. "You like trophies so here I am, fresh-caught."

She held him tight before taking his hand. "You fooled me, you rascal, but it's a thrill seeing you again. How are you? It's been *sooo looong*."

"I can't wait to reminisce," he said. "Almost gave myself away earlier. Had to disguise my voice. I'm surprised you didn't figure it out."

"I've never been able to figure you out, love, so why would today be any different?"

He let go of her hand, rounded the car, and settled into its passenger seat. The rush of adrenalin over their reunion was proving more than he had anticipated. "Let's roll!"

Sorelle drove past a marina and soon turned at a sign: *Papa Romero's Italian Restaurant.*

Patrick's euphoria lingered as the car crunched over layers of ground-up oyster shells. Sorelle parked the car in front of the building. Hand in hand, the pair soon stepped up to a portico.

"*The Sanctuary Sentinel* said these weathered boards were salvaged from Jean Lafitte's pirate ships," he said. "It sank in the Gulf of Mexico—circa 1805."

Large clay pots on both sides of the entryway overflowed with colorful vincas and petunias. "Really glorious, don't you think?" she said.

"Yeah, the rustic look is a nice contrast with the delicate flowers."

On the bay side of the peninsula, the droopy foliage of a large willow covered the tile roof of the building. Inside the porch, a thick cypress door with vintage iron handles welcomed them to a semi-dark hostess station where an old ship's lantern glowed dimly.

"How quaint," she said while admiring a large pilot's wheel in the lobby.

An eye-level plaque gave a brief history of pirates who braved the Caribbean and Gulf storms in their quest for gold. A young woman led them to a corner table, its centerpiece a singular candle and a small bouquet of cut roses. "How cozy," Sorelle said. "I love a corner nook with candlelight."

She smiled as Patrick held her chair out. Sitting, she smoothed the blond hairline at the base of her neck, though no loose strands were visible where it swept upward in ringlets. A tortoise shell comb held the arrangement in place at the top of her head. "You like it?"

He seated himself across from her. "Sure, it's comfy. I reckon it was built to endure some really rough storms."

"Endure storms? What are you talking about?"

"Oh, you meant your hair. Yes, of course, it's beautiful."

The server, a swarthy young man with dark mane, presented

menus listing a Today's Special. He asked their preference of drinks. "I'd like a chardonnay," Sorelle said.

Patrick gazed trancelike into her icicle-blue eyes. "We'll have a bottle of it."

She moved the floral arrangement aside, slid her hand across the table to join his, and toyed with his gold-and-onyx signet ring. "Some fragrances give me a headache," she said. "No coffee unless it's decaf. Caffeine keeps me up all night."

"Really? And I thought you were tough as Teflon."

"Now, Patrick, I'm no Wall Streeter." She tugged at the sleeves of her tailored dinner jacket, its frosty blue sheen accented with copper buttons. "Shhh, listen. Recognize that tune?" In the near-empty restaurant, her eyelids closed midway through the soft refrains of the instrumental, *Don't Cry For Me, Argentina*, by concert pianist Pandolfi.

He squeezed her hand. "Is it still that meaningful?"

"Yes, of course. It was our song. But I'm just now getting over the shock of a hillbilly jokester who transforms himself into my old boyfriend."

"It was worth it," he said.

"What do you mean?"

"You know, seeing the surprise in your eyes, then your heart beating against my chest...."

She let go a deep sigh and fingered the topmost button of her silk blouse. "I wanted to cry and at the same time laugh. And how did you feel holding me?"

"Enthralled," he said. "You're more beautiful now than you ever were."

The young server placed stemmed glassware between them and poured from the bottle of wine. Their quick study of the menu resulted in both ordering the same dish. The candle flickered as the server spun and hurried away with their shrimp puttanesca order.

Releasing Sorelle's hand, Patrick lifted his glass for a toast. "Here's to us." With his mind on her instead of the drink, the first sip of wine dripped down his chin. Disguising his blunder, he held the glass in front of his mouth while unfolding the dinner napkin with his left hand. The loosely-rolled silverware slid from the napkin and fell clanking onto his lap. His startled reaction resulted in more wine spilling to dampen the white linen tablecloth.

His face colored. "Pardon me for dumping a load of scrap iron but my truck had a hiccup. Looks like it's spill-the-wine time. Shall I reconstruct the scene of the wine for the waiter?"

"Aren't you the clever one?" She watched him soak up the spillage with his table napkin. "Um, such a spectacle you are, given the wine will spot your pants down there."

The server returned with extra table napkins and refilled his wine glass before departing.

Dreamy-eyed, Sorelle lifted the glass to eye-level and gazed at its contents. "I have to be careful with wine. It makes me giddy...and loose."

"Oh, waiter!" He summoned the young man. "Pour more, yeah, more for the loose lady."

She waved the server away as she laughed softly. "Love, you're such a fright. Are you trying to put the make on me this early in the evening?"

"Yes, you're both appetizer and entrée. So says the big bad wolf who risks being charged with a felony for consuming Miss Ready Riding Hood." He cringed at the line's silliness.

She finished her drink and tapped the glass with her fingernails to approve a refill. "Just feel the moment and hollow..." she vibrated her lips, "and *follow* your heart."

"Cool. Do that again."

"Do what again?"

He imitated her lip vibrations. "That's the most sensuous thing I've seen any woman do."

"Are you spacey, Patrick, after only one glass of wine?"

"Must be the music."

"Pandolfi's, or the music in your heart?"

He warmed to the idea of heartfelt music and the rhapsody of the moment. "Ah, so you hear it, too. Is it the melody or the rhythm you like?"

"Both." Smiling, she waited for the refill before licking her lips and holding her glass aloft. "A cheer to us and our glorious reunion."

He clinked his glass against hers. "Here's to a woman who once thought spring practice was something done with a checkbook. How are you feeling? Tipsy?"

"Glorious, just glorious, thanks to the wine. And the music. How about you, love?"

"Just happy to be with Miss Glorious." The comic urge for absurdity overcame him. "Only to discover she's Little Miss Fortune, but I'm just thankful she's not Miss Guided."

"Patrick!" Her tone hinted at a threat. "Such *impulsions!* Are you quite finished?"

He imitated a cartoon duck's nasal tone. "*Quite!*"

She thanked the server who placed a dish of steaming pasta topped with a rich tomato sauce with capers, black olives, garlic and small shrimp, its aroma tantalizing. "More of this wine and I might start dancing on this table, naked."

"Ah, so many guilty pleasures," he said while directing the server's attention to Sorelle's glass. "Pour more, please, more-more-more. And follow up with a cup of robust coffee with caffeine."

"Must I remind you that coffee keeps me awake at night?"

"Yeah, but what I have in mind will keep us both awake—*all* night."

"Patrick Murph, am I going to have to shoot you?"

"Okay, but be gentle. Never been shot by a woman before. It'll be my first."

"Hah! It'll be your last if my aim is good."

"Yeah, like I'm worried. Woozy as you are, all you can do is aim. If you're lucky you'll hit only one of the two of me."

"Here's how it's gonna be," she said in a deadpan voice, ignoring the server who topped off her glass. Nonchalant, she opened her handbag, took out a .40-caliber Beretta with a gold trigger and placed it on the table. "First, we'll enjoy another round of the fruity-tooty froufrou, and then..."

The young man tilted the bottle to refill Patrick's glass as Sorelle continued her oratory. "...we go to Sanctuary Inn and if by morning you've disappointed me—bam!—I begin target practice till you give me an orgasm worth remembering." The server missed Patrick's glass by two inches.

Alone on the patio, Cheryl Decairo put the team log aside and opened her diary to narrate her private thoughts as long shadows slinked into dusk before nightfall.

Our comedy skits are improving day by day and the girls are excited about being entertainers. Yesterday, after our noon break, Freckles dared Patrick to show us the dance routine he used in his Pony Xpress act. In the mansion den he demonstrated a racy striptease. Amid cheers and catcalls, he refused a lap dance and ran lickety-split out the door. I'm told he set a record in the 40-yard dash at Bayou Tech. I believe it now. OMG, that Freckles! She changed the Weightloss Clinic sign to read Weightless Clinic. Only she has the audacity to do such a thing. Seems like that girl's dream is to have one of her pranks go viral.

Groundskeeper Buzz Cassidy spotted the fire while clipping a hedgerow.

Flames gutted the lower half of a tall condo lying one mile east of Ellie's. Sirens blared in the distance. Traffic stalled for miles on Peninsula Road. Investigators would later determine the fire had begun in a trash barrel near a barbeque pit. They blamed a discarded cellphone with its lithium-ion battery. Sparks and burning bits of trash breezed to piles of dry limbs ready for pickup near the condo.

Aided by a stiffer breeze, a small blaze soon became a giant bonfire that engulfed the cedar siding in mere minutes.

Trudy Mickelstein, a television reporter in Mobile, Alabama, made the scoop. She beat the competition by thirty minutes. Near the station's satellite truck, she talked with Spencer Lovejoy, leader of the Black Caucus of America and owner of a burned-out condo unit.

The big man's rantings would be good for Breaking News at Five. "No, ain't no such thing as a coincidence," he said. "Somebody got it in for me."

The activist directed his anger at what he described as a "cult of racists" he had traced to a plush mansion on Peninsula Road. He claimed they used eugenics to purge America of its "so-called inferior peoples." His inflammatory words further divided those in fear of genocide.

Hollywood celebrities arrived the following day to sign autographs and sell photos and treasured memorabilia to aid victims of the fire. A co-star in movies with Dan the Man DiNago arrived to auction off designer gowns worn at the Academy Awards television spectacle. A rock band showed up at The Hangout—musical heartbeat of the Alabama coast—to entertain during the fundraiser. As usual, U.S. Senator Boyd Blockton arrived to share media time with the glitterati.

After local fire departments doused remnants of the blaze, the Sweethearts resumed rehearsing their show in hopes of appearing on the Funtasy Channel while Larry Lemoyne kept his camera trained on them.

Rubleau Entertainment needed only a few more episodes.

Across Bon View at the Sanctuary Research Institute, newshounds from entertainment networks occupied student dorms —empty during July. They focused on celebrities, not displaced condo renters. Next day the Sweethearts' jog on the beach caught the attention of cable TV sleuths. The *Uptake* show, better at gotcha TV, led the field. Reporters with supermarket tabloids like the *Analyzer* followed up the reveal with human interest stories they could embellish and sensationalize.

A headline in the *Analyzer* targeted Danny DiNago: "Super Jock Hides Harem."

Not having to wait until the tabloid's release on the following Wednesday, the television media showed the attractive Sweethearts evading cameramen who skulked the mansion grounds.

In a moment of frustration, Freckles raised her T-shirt and flashed the paparazzi. A few million voyeurs shared it on social media. As a consequence, the host of *Uptake* dubbed the antebellum mansion a "hedonistic hideaway," adding that weeks earlier the area was stormed by "glamour freaks resembling a horde—" he emphasized *horde* "—of militant Amazons."

A pundit on television referred to the Sweethearts as "curvy cuties who promote eugenics, the pseudoscience made famous by Hitler."

Patrick grew irate at the newscasters and their soundbites. He could relate to the Sweethearts' dilemma. Following his lead, they had learned slapstick humor, yet this media ruckus misrepresented their pedigree cause.

The girls' angry parents called with concerns about their daughters' public image.

Easter tired of the pressure. "My sense of humor has flat-lined," she said while sitting alongside Patrick in a glider loveseat on the veranda. "What I need is one of those eureka moments."

"I'll conjure up something," Patrick said. "Why not brainstorm at the Bon Mot Diner? It's near a secluded fishing village off the beaten path."

Within seconds Easter tapped out messages on her smartphone and invited both Danny DiNago and Goat Goodnowe to a confab at the diner on Bon Secour Bay.

To offset Goat's unwelcome presence, Patrick insisted Sorelle Ebanetti attend as well.

"You're inviting Sorelle?" Easter said. "I had hopes for miracles, not misery."

"Miracles are in short supply," he said. "We'll have to innovate this time. By the way, why is Goat tagging along?"

"Good happens, Patrick."

"Nothing good can come from him. Why do you go along with his deals anyway?"

"Simple. Mr. Goodnowe is our intro to the Funtasy Channel."

"We're smart enough to know shortcuts don't work," he said. "Working his deal doesn't make sense. What am I missing here?"

"Wrong question, wrong time, Patrick."

Rather than force the issue, he tried to quell his anxiety as she stood to leave. Was he out of line for asking? He thought not. He lingered a moment on the veranda to watch as a large fiberglass vessel curled from the bay and slowed to dock at the Sanctuary Research Institute boathouse at the end of the pier. At the same time he couldn't help but wonder what devious scheme Goat, the Brazilian huckster, would introduce at the Bon Mot Diner.

FOURTEEN

After Easter accepted Goat's offer to drive the group to the diner, Patrick realized his anxiety was born of fear, distrust and uncertainty. Something about Goodnowe struck him as uncanny. Did the man have undisclosed paranormal gifts? Every shyster known to him exhibited shameless audacity, uninhibited bluster, and supreme self-confidence. The boldest told lies—big lies—without blinking.

Goat seemed never to bat an eye.

As an added precaution, the group left the house through its atrium and eased down back steps under cover of darkness. Goat's black Lincoln Navigator awaited them in the breezy garage. Given the vehicles tinted windows, Patrick hoped reporters would not associate it with the Sweethearts.

The journey eastward along Peninsula Road connected with the six-lane parkway where it then allowed a left turn on narrow State Road 10.

Patrick pointed to a sign on the back of a large utility truck. He read the words aloud. "*Caution: Frequent Steps*. It should read stops, not steps. Typical of Freckles' hacking handiwork."

"I'd have to question her judgment," Sorelle said.

Patrick tilted his Scottish tam-o'-shanter higher on his forehead. "It's a compulsion."

Sorelle's tone revealed mild concern. "Don't remind me."

Upon arriving at the Bon Mot Diner with its well-lighted windows contrasting with centuries-old live oaks, Patrick held its front door open. "I have kinfolk who work at an oyster processing place next door," he said before hailing a server. "We'll take the back booth, Charlene."

She waved. "Fresh coffee's brewing just for you, Patrick. Make yourself at home."

Red vinyl seats and checkered oil cloths engendered a nostalgic mood while on the facing wall a fisherman's net with clinging seashells appeared alongside the fiberglass replica of a trophy fish from the gulf—a blue marlin.

While sashaying along the aisle, Easter poked Patrick's ribcage. "Isn't this the diner that forbids you from working here again?" she said.

"Not sure what I did could be called work," he said.

Easter snuggled next to Danny in the booth while the icon's talent manager, Sorelle, squeezed in on the aisle side facing Patrick and Goat. Charlene took their drink orders and promptly left.

Sorelle winked at Patrick. "This is one of your old haunts, eh?"

"Yeah, my family keeps Bon Mot in business. At fourteen, I worked for my uncle, a shrimper just down the street. The next summer I landed a deckhand job on a charter boat. Met Hollywood stars on occasion."

The server delivered their drink orders and hurried back to the kitchen as Easter blew her drink straw wrapper at Patrick. "Some guys do it all," she said with a wink. "You filled in for the short-order cook here and burnt the bacon, set the kitchen on fire, and knocked up the pretty waitress—and all in the same day. That has to be some kind of record."

"She was on her lunch break," he said.

"Oh yes, a quickie, wasn't it?"

"I wouldn't put it quite that way," he said. "Anyhow, we had dated in high school when she was a cheerleader. I was a junior at Bayou Tech and home for Spring Break and the staff was short of help."

Easter grinned. "And you sort of filled in as baby maker, eh?"

"Hey, I married her, didn't I?"

Sorelle matter-of-factly chimed in. "You just hit a sore spot, girl."

"Sorry," Easter said, her gaze on Patrick. "Did I hit a nerve, Casanova?"

"Yes, you did," Sorelle retorted. "Mine."

"I forget you two are an item again," Easter said. "Oh, well...."

Sorelle addressed the group. "We have to give the media a positive, okay? And for godsake, why did Freckles flash reporters? Any Zipit student of mine wouldn't do that."

Danny shrugged. "The dailies might go for a positive slant, but not tabloids like the *Analyzer*." He cast a sidelong glance at Sorelle. "I told one guy yesterday his paper stunk."

Easter sighed. "Danny, what you said was, and I quote, 'All you *Analyzer* tabloid jerkoffs see life through your assholes.' So count on being branded a salty-mouthed jock because that'll go viral."

"Pro athletes deserve a life, too," Danny said. "Didn't they say I'm with whores?"

"No, *hordes* was the word," Sorelle said. "Scandals drive TV ratings up." She stirred her café latte. "But you have millions of fans following you, thanks to your mystique."

Patrick grinned. "Yeah, Danny reeks of mystique."

Sorelle's eyes shot icicle daggers. "Quote me verbatim, please."

Still directing the gabfest, Easter clapped her hands. "So what can we give the media?"

"With all his Super Bowl wins, we can tell them Danny was born of an immaculate conception," Patrick said. He mimicked the sound of a distant explosion. "Or why not hype him as the great Houdini reincarnated? Nobody escaped more traps than he did."

"Houdini?" Danny said. "Houdini faked his death because celebrity pressure got to him. And that tam thing on your head looks like a hot water bottle run over by a herd of Humvees."

Easter gave Patrick a rebuking look. "Houdini's legacy is sacrosanct. And another subject you must avoid is palimony."

"Sorry," Patrick said. "We comedians forget to take our game face off sometimes."

Goat rapped the table with his knuckles. "We do have one ace in the hole. Dr. Ronofski needs our help promoting selective breeding. It's the answer to emblot but it needs the right spin."

"Breeding?" Easter said. "We say mating. I meant matching. And what does our situation have to do with emblot?"

Goat sniffed. "I have a plan, a brilliant one. Eugenics will soon wear a new face. Guaranteed."

"Brilliant?" Patrick said. "Guess we'll have to take your word for it. And that eugenics word is another no-no. Regenerative matching is the correct term."

Easter shifted in her seat. Her outfit included tight capri pants and a mesh pullover from Bayou Tech. "After the tabloids finish with us, my actresses may need to *save* face, not wear a new face."

Goat braced his hands on the table. "To redirect people's attention to the human pedigree cause, we have to use drama."

A cup of hot coffee at his lips, Patrick hesitated to sip before speaking. "Define drama."

Goat ignored the request. "For people to believe in the gene matching cause, we need sensational slogans to indoctrinate them. But first things first. We know emblot is due to a stealth virus in the genes. It's a mutation on the x chromosome. About one in ten Blacks are carriers."

Patrick resisted the impulse to interrupt.

"Here's the best part about mutations," Goat said. "They're often lethal but also unpredictable. We can embellish emblot by showing the worst of it on TV. Fear causes people to panic but I'd like to reiterate; eugenics under our control can set them free if it's reimagined as genetic matching."

Patrick wanted to tell Goat that emblot needed no embellishment to inspire fear of Blacks and the panic-like prejudice against them.

Goat gazed into the eyes of the trio facing him. "Slogans can rally the rich without alarming the unfit. Like a dog whistle, code words are detectable by only the few. Like Jews; they know imbeciles in a society can lead to financial ruin. They put eugenics down here but —" his eyes narrowed "—in Israel they require genetic mating. In fact, they claim it's in the interests of national security. And Ta Sachs was reduced by ninety-five percent among Ashkenazi Jews due to genetic screening. That's eugenics."

"As goes Israel, so goes America," Sorelle said. "The Jews are God's chosen."

He pinged a spoon against the rim of his empty cup. "Case in point: They like to equate it with state-run purges, though twenty-nine countries—America topmost among them—taught eugenics, all without genocide. I mean, blaming Germany is as senseless as stigmatizing the Volkswagen as some nefarious invention."

Goat finished his coffee and fished a cigar from a shirt pocket. "Why blame good breeding for the Nazi's bad behavior? Bad politics and jingoism, not bad science, halted eugenics. But the general public's overreaction did the most damage."

The Brazilian's cigar lay on the table, unlit, as he continued. "Hitler weaponized eugenics when he infused it with the fever of nationalism." He held up a finger. "Horace, an ancient Roman poet, said, 'If we cannot state precisely what the problem is, we cannot solve it.' I suggest we can, and should, be willing to solve it."

"So..." Patrick began with a sigh of exasperation. "Other than your rants, what's the problem with our situation?"

A customer ambled to a jukebox in the corner and inserted a handful of quarters. Within seconds the Eagles belted out *Lyin' Eyes*.

Goat reared back like a man whose patience had well-defined limits. "We're the problem. While the unfit die from hereditary crap, pedigrees produce healthy offspring. So, why not reward them? Give bonuses so they'll make more babies."

Patrick's brow creased with curiosity. "What bonuses?"

"Bigger tax breaks," Goat retorted. "Five kids merit more breaks than two, three, on and on."

In the wake of Goat's presentation, a feeling of smallness rose within Patrick. He could interject comedy but it seemed out of place at the moment. "Goat, you think people are a commodity, right?"

"Yes," he said. "The idea is to make gene matching more palatable and trendy."

"And my girls can help with it through entertainment," Easter said.

Goat leaned forward. "On TV we'll show degeneration as unspeakably macabre."

"Degeneration is the norm," Patrick said. "Are you trying to sneak past the gatekeepers?"

Goat's hands stiffened. "It's about time someone did. If not us, then who?"

It seemed to Patrick the man's strategy failed to include people of color in his plan. Experience told him shysters set their victims up with a mix of truth and fables before prompting them to take quick action. At that crucial point, Goat would move in for the takeover. Easter needed to know that. Had she been blinded by her own bias? Otherwise, why side with Goat?

Charlene meandered past the group's table and smiled at Patrick but Goat's voice drew him back into the confab. "Our strategy is simple," Goat said. "We place the girls in the middle of a social reform. We all know Doc Ronofski's new study declares humans are an endangered species. To save it, we have to attack complacency. Since people are numb to retrogrades, we'll shake them up by showing pedigrees in strong contrast with the worst in society."

"Sounds risky," Sorelle said.

"Not so much." Goat said. "First, we need to find a Camelot-type figure, someone who's able to convince people that pedigree science is compatible with romantic love."

Easter rested her head on Danny's shoulder. "How do we accomplish that?"

Patrick's interest in conversation waned as his gaze lingered on Sorelle. He recalled the previous night when her dreamy eyes glazed and she spoke of primal desire. Could she sense that his love gears had no reverse and all conduits ran in one direction, all toward her? On the diner's jukebox, Carol King crooned the oldie, *So Far Away*.

Goat laid his hands on the table, fingers splayed. "Your telegenic Sweethearts are only part of the answer. The number ten symbolizes completeness, but think of another aspect of our cause." His voice low and secretive, he added, "Not a metric but a mystical one."

Easter shook the loose ice in her glass. "Mystical?"

"Yes," he said. "Freedom from fear of heritable diseases is not the only goal. Give people more positive inspiration. At issue is a grand genutopia versus a decaying dystopia. The mystique of pedigrees appeals because people need to believe in their own special destiny. We can link the Pedigree Nation, a new creation, to a superstar leader whose power to procreate is like no other on earth."

Patrick grinned. "Here we go with Dan the Man's Houdini act expanding as a super stud. Goat, you're having visions of grandeur."

Now more forceful in tone, Goat said, "We'll enhance that belief. Is it by chance that we, all of us, have converged at Sanctuary Beach? I think not."

Sorelle clapped her hands slowly, an insincere tribute to Goat's oratory.

The Brazilian wagged his head. "We must find a high-profile spokesman that we can instruct on how to finesse an earth-shaking opportunity, and on a grand scale."

Convinced that the man's scheme was like a deck of cards scored in a conniving dealer's favor at a blackjack table, Patrick wondered if Goodnowe saw himself elevated to spokesman—God forbid —for the movement.

Goat squinted hard. "We have to choose a PR front man, a genetic messiah."

"How you think, Mr. Goodnowe." Easter nudged Danny's bicep. "Do we need a savior type who can act as a front?"

Danny nodded absently, his eyes like those of a man who preferred his solutions be drawn by a coach in his Marauder's football playbook.

As if savoring an idea, Goat licked his lips. "Believe it or not, Danny could very well be the man of the hour. He has Ronofski's blessing to sire the privileged. Bear with me, okay? Let's suppose for a moment Jesus Christ had a wife. Yes, married to a woman. What would his children be like? They'd all be true to the original, their DNA far beyond ordinary. Right?" Not waiting for her reply, he continued. "Imagine Danny as a man among men, one who could affect the human gene pool with such positivity that his descendants are flawless."

"What?" Easter said. "Danny will sire children?"

"Yes, of course," Goat said. "Imagine his children endowed with celestial qualities." He gazed into mid-space. "It's coming to me. Yes, I see it."

Easter leaned in. "See what?"

Goat steepled his fingers as if to posit a revelation. "I see it clearly. People seek answers to flaws they inherit. Think about the cosmetic aspect of good breeding. After all, isn't vanity a cult industry? People spare no expense to be attractive."

Patrick blinked, amazed at Goat's persistence in suggesting a more audacious commercial angle.

"Danny is short for Daniel," Goat said, "and that's a Hebrew name. Don't forget, such names in biblical days had meaning, and especially messiah."

Easter's grin sat lopsided for a moment. "DiNago? An Italian messiah?"

"But suppose his ancestry is Jewish?" Goat said. "Danny, tell us your middle name."

His voice barely audible, Danny said, "Immanuel."

"Immanuel? Are you kidding me? Man, this is truly amazing." He looked at Sorelle and Easter. "Does anyone here know the importance of that name? Do we see its significance?"

"Jewish, maybe?" Easter said.

"It means God is with us," Sorelle said. "Immanuel is the Hebrew title-name for the Messiah, its perfect equivalent."

Goat spoke softly. "Immanuel. This is profound. You, Danny, could pass for a messiah."

Repulsed by the conman's assertion, Patrick's frustrations grew. "Listen, Goat, his given name is Immanuel. It's not some divine attribute. You just admitted he was adopted."

"Yes, adopted," Goat said. "But suppose he has no father."

"Get real, man," Patrick said. "You browbeat the Sweethearts into signing a release. Well, sir, intimidation won't work on me. I know what you're doing. You'd have us believe the bookies in Vegas were taking bets on Jesus all along for another Super Bowl win. Yet they never leaked that clue to high rollers. Danny's not some divine spook. He's a great quarterback, true, but he's one of us. Okay?"

Easter stared at Goat. "Yes, isn't your suggestions a bit sacrilegious?"

"I challenge you all," Goat said. "If we can determine his ancestry is Jewish, then what we have is something like a bona fide revelation right here in our presence."

Easter nudged Danny. "Are you a revelation, babe?"

Danny shrugged. "Whatever."

Patrick reacted as if he'd walked face-first into a spider's web. "Dammit. There's no Jewish link between Danny and some ridiculous prophecy. It's absurd."

Goat pounded the table. "I'll prove he's a supernatural genetic messiah. His acts can be shown as miraculous and easy to hype."

"Nothing doing," Sorelle said. "Danny's my client and I have the final say as to any embellished information about him."

"But—" Goat stared at her. "Imagine eugenics regaining the legitimacy it once had in this great nation. The world needs—" he wheezed "—a genetic savior."

Patrick shook his head. "Better not tell Doc Ronofski about a genetic messiah."

"Why not?" Easter said.

"Well, what if he starts hooking science up with religion? Critics already swear he's crazy."

"Crazy?" Goat said. "The Consortium for American Values endorsed *Pedigree Promise*, the best of his books. They know you don't fix stupid, you prevent it. Are we in agreement about my strategy?"

"Not unless we like kidding ourselves about your messiah fantasy," Patrick said.

"I much prefer fantasy," Easter said as she jangled the charms on her bracelet. "It's a lot more fun. Good happens. Don't you agree, Patrick?"

He stalled, trying to muster an answer. "Who, me? What would I know about fantasy?"

"My foot has a cramp in it." She nodded at him. "Would you mind?"

Patrick sensed a mischievous ploy as her toes poked his leg and a sly gleam crept into her eyes. He glanced at Sorelle before accepting Easter's bare foot.

"I decorated your bedroom last night," Easter said. "One good turn deserves another."

"Where?" he asked. "In the instep?"

Her jaw bulged with an ice cube. "That's a good place to start," she mumbled.

"Could we all meet tomorrow and discuss a saner strategy?" Patrick said.

"Tomorrow?" Easter said. "We just got here. Besides, I'm enjoying your foot massage."

The confab lasted another ten minutes before Sorelle paid the tab and left a tip for Charlene. "Ready to go?" she said. "I have calls to make."

Easter affected a lusty voice. "Ahhh, yes. Patrick's footsie expertise is second to none. He's a keeper, yes, definitely a keeper."

After departing the diner, Patrick pondered Goodnowe's audacious tactic.

A sense of impending calamity churned in his gut as the mental image of dominoes, all falling in a row, preempted what should have formed a rainbow of hope.

FIFTEEN

oon after breakfast Patrick donned chino walking shorts and
settled into the mansion gazebo to edit scripts. From the
corner of his eye, he detected movement from the mansion.

"We have to talk," Easter said as she approached and beckoned
him toward his van. She soon entered on its passenger side.

He slid into the driver's seat and placed a bottle of coconut water
into a drink holder. "Hope this little talk inspires a new skit. I'm
running behind and—"

"Just go." She placed a Gucci matelassé bag between them and
stabbed the FM radio button. "Drive by Sanctuary Plaza," she said
over the modern jazz. "Find a place to park...for privacy."

She buckled up before he wheeled the van away and turned east
on Peninsula Road. Absent the burned condominiums that once
obscured a view of the beach, colorful cottages stood strong amid
sand dunes.

She turned the volume down on the radio. "It's obvious Sorelle is
your lover. It's also obvious she knows exactly what she's doing,
Patrick. Pity you can't see it."

"Yeah? Like what?"

"She's still peeved because I persuaded Danny to join our gene-
matching program. Last night at the diner, the way you acted...." She
slapped the dashboard. "Sorelle's doing her best to divide us."

"Divide you and me? Hey, you were the one getting a foot massage."

"Be honest," she said. "Have you always had a thing for older women?"

"Huh? Just how old do you think she is?"

Easter angled her head to stare at him. "She's ten years your senior."

"So?"

"So is it her fame you're infatuated with?"

He chuckled. "If you must know, I was in a high school play when she met me backstage, said I was a talent. Or maybe a project. Her age was not on my mind. Turns out she had this thing for me."

"Thing, eh? I suggest you rise above the *thing*. You fit our pedigree program better than any man on the International Genetic Registry. You have the youth gene."

"What youth gene?"

"It's something you inherited," she said.

He chuckled. "Is that why I don't look my age?"

"Oh yes, your thirty-eight years do belie your youthful look, but little did I know till now that a mouth swab confirmed you have the special gene. At the time it appeared too unbelievable even to Dr. Ronofski. But I have to ask you something. Are you using us as a pit stop on your way to fame? It's us girls who deserve you, not Sorelle."

"What do you mean by deserve?"

"Patrick, to the Sweethearts you're more than a mentor, you're a babe magnet."

"Hey, I'm a coach. Period." He slaked his thirst from the coconut drink. "What you're hearing is frivolous pillow talk. Nothing to it. But what's with the flattery?"

She slapped his knee. "Why do you prefer Sorelle over us? You know we're good enough for TV without Sorelle interfering."

"But Sorelle has showbiz contacts," he said. "You—we—need *her*, not Goat."

Easter let go a cynical laugh. "Don't think I'm gonna allow that hussy to take credit for our hard work. She's a has-been. Sorry, Patrick, but I call it like I see it."

"What're you driving at?"

"Isn't it obvious?"

"No, but I know about the keepsake video," he said. "You can't deny some of the Sweethearts are being manipulated into a smut movie. Smut rhymes with slut. Is that mere coincidence? Think how the public will view them if it goes viral."

"Patrick Murph, do you really think I'd allow such a thing to happen?"

He waggled his leveled hand. "Hey, mistakes happen."

"But it's not a commercial flick, just something to make Danny appear more macho."

"Macho? Seems to me that's been overdone. Besides, Goat may sell the video to some sleazy syndicate. Think of the shame."

Her grip fastened on his knee. "That won't happen. I'll monitor it, start to finish."

"Monitor, huh? What you're doing is risking all that we've worked for, maybe even jeopardizing the pedigree program. That's not the Easter I know."

"Patrick, it's soft erotica, not even x-rated."

"Fine, but why must Dan the Man have to prove his macho credentials?"

"Well, a muckraker is writing a biography that questions Danny's virility."

"Okay, so somebody does a hatchet job on him," he said. "I'm sure Danny's seen worse in his pro career as an athlete."

"But Patrick, an erotic keepsake could put those bad virility rumors to rest. Whatever Danny endorses, people buy. He's a brand. His macho image has more than a little cachet. His status in retail sales is the alpha and omega."

He rolled his shoulders. "To me it's a sex tape. We recruited novices, not porn queens."

"Porn." Her voice deflated with a sigh. "What is it with you? My girls are not your daughters."

Patrick cringed. The debate had strayed into forbidden territory. "Then tell me this and I'm done. Is Goat using Danny's superstitions to exploit him and the girls?"

"Patrick, I can assure you they're not being exploited."

"I'm not so sure," he said.

She directed him to take a left turn and then a right on Main Street. Past the stop sign, Sanctuary Plaza harbored small shops fronted in cypress and sandstone. Engraved wooden signs, unique to each business, served as a play on words: Good Scents enticed shoppers to buy herbs. Gopher Broke Antiques teased a nostalgic impulse. Van Go Travel beckoned sightseers to rent an economical van. Pickle Derby Deli, its décor built around a dancing gourmet pickle, offered sandwiches in an old-fashioned ice cream parlor complete with a soda fountain.

Patrick soon reconnected with Peninsula Road. "Not to pry but why would a biographer think Danny is a phony if women everywhere idolize him?"

"Can you keep a secret? I really shouldn't be telling you this, but—"

"What? Like you think I'd stoop to leaking it to a tabloid?"

"No, but just between us, Dan the Man's mystique is based on illusion."

"Illusion? Hey, he's a football superstar, not Houdini."

"Yeah, right. Funny how celebrities can't survive without all the publicity fixers. You see, Nigel Pregnor interviewed women who had dated Danny, in particular students at Bayou Tech. Some claim he impregnated them."

"Interesting. Are you afraid the Sweethearts will make that claim, too?"

"No, Patrick."

"How long have you two been together? Two years, right? Long enough to know Dan the Man's bedside manner."

Her sigh faded into resignation. "If you must know, Danny is self-centered. Empathy? No way. Romance? No deal. He's been the romantic lead in several B-movies but behind closed doors he never sets the stage for Act One."

"I get it," he said. "He thinks foreplay is a number on a coach's dry-erase board."

"Yes. Sex to him is a bullet train that derails short of its station. And don't get me started on his performance anxiety. He's a psychosomatic mess."

Her disenchantment with him, he thought, was understandable. "So he fizzles out. Yet the aura of fame draws women to him."

A heavy sigh preceded her words. "Dr. Ronofski said he's a paradox. All juice. No seed."

"Whoa! He also said Danny's the one chosen to sire the privileged. Said it on the *Hotz*, too."

"Yes, but why ruin everything?"

"Everything?"

"Everything, yes. Unless we can come up with a plan B, the world can't be rejuvenated through pedigrees fast enough. If we fail to understand genetic implosion, we could be looking at Armageddon." She poked his arm. "You see how obvious it is, don't you?"

"You lost me at obvious."

"You know what, Patrick? I think you enjoy playing dumb."

"I'm sorry. So you want to speed up the mating process. Do you have a plan for that?"

"You better believe I do. We learn as we go and share what we know."

"This I gotta hear," he said.

SIXTEEN

Easter was not known for exaggeration but Patrick doubted Dan the Man's disinterest in the opposite sex. The idea of a macho sports star lacking sperm befuddled him.

She slipped her sandals off and propped her feet on the dashboard. "Months before those girls at Tech claimed they were carrying Danny's child, Sorelle ordered him fixed with a vasectomy. You know, for legal reasons. It's on his medical records but they're sequestered."

"Let me guess," he said. "Sorelle feared a palimony suit."

"Yes, but since she's the business manager of DiNago Diversified, she paid off every preggie claim. They're not supposed to talk about the settlement, but some girls have. I suppose Sorelle could've sued them on his behalf but who needs that kind of publicity?"

"A vasectomy is reversible, but if he's really biologically seedless and also useless in bed, the Sweethearts know it. Right?"

"Maybe, but they have unrequited needs. You know we're class-A pedigrees. Hispanics, Blacks, Asians, not just Caucasians. Better babies mean a better future. It's the essence of our program."

"Your words, my ears, but you made boyfriends off limits for the Sweethearts."

"True," she said. "We need a worthy man who can meet our genetic criteria." She squeezed his thigh. "And I'd prefer a man who's also, shall we say, easy to manage."

"Just hang a sign—*Apply Within*—and they'll come running, pedigree males no less."

She curled one leg beneath her. "Funny, ha-ha, but only you have the youth gene."

He gave her an eye-roll. "Yeah, right."

"No kidding. Dr. Ronofski speculates you may be one in a billion, so why dilly-dally with the likes of Sorelle when you have us Sweethearts needing you?"

He watched a truck loaded with propane cylinders move into an open slot ahead of him. Its large bumper decal read, *Don't Like My Driving? Call 800-CRY-BABY.*

"Well?" she said. "I'm waiting."

"Okay, I'm thinking. You do realize my thing with Sorelle is a love affair, not espionage, don't you? She makes me feel like I'm eighteen again."

"Patrick, get real. Unless you're an archaeologist, you don't fall in love with an old ruin."

"Uh-huh, good one, but the thing is she doesn't share your vision of a pedigree world. Tell me, if this pedigree promise to change society is so workable—and it's a big if—how do you prove to skeptics like her and that bald jabberwocky on *The Hotz* that it's the acceptable thing to do?"

Easter pushed her sunglasses up to her forehead. "Convincing Wynn Traynor and Sorelle will take time, but regenerative matching is urgent. In fact, it's a divine mandate."

"But you're talking about a hands-on approach. No, it's too off the charts, too far out in left field. No offense, but is good breeding an ethnic thing with you?"

She sighed. "I feel deeply for my people, and I appreciate diversity, but people are matched in many cultures for reasons far less noble than a pedigree priority."

Patrick's gaze rested on a parasailer high above the gulf. Brilliant colors in the sails contrasted with a dark cloudbank in the distance. The park soon came into view, a shady oasis facing Lake Shelby. On the gulf side of Beach Road, a sugar-white beach and turquoise water invited sunbathers.

The idea of intimacy with Easter stirred a yearning within him. Was she still off-limits?

"Don't shoot me for thinking but do biracial offspring inherit emblot?"

"Patrick, we don't mate with anyone who's die-cast to inherit horrible diseases."

"Just saying. And just wondering how to prevent things like that."

"With your help, perhaps we could use genetic matching to fight racism, too," she said.

"Well, I'm definitely anti-racist."

"I like that about you. But we have to ask why people of color seem to be targeted, like we have more defects. True, newborns of Irish descent have a greater chance of having spina bifida, and cystic fibrosis is common to northern Europeans. Still, forty percent more blacks have asthma than whites and fifty percent more die of prostate cancer. The H.I.V. rate for Blacks is eight times that of whites. There's a fourfold greater risk of sarcoidosis, an autoimmune disease. Our odds are greater of being infertile and we're twice as likely to get multiple myeloma and three times more likely to get fibroids. Why us?"

"And why now?" he said.

She slapped the dashboard. "It's the timing, yes! That's so insight-ful. I see it clearly now. It's a wake-up call the Almighty. That's it! He really does care about upgrading our genes. Patrick, you are an angel."

"Angels have wings. They fly. I don't."

"But they also deliver weighty messages, like you just did."

"Define weighty."

"Like urgent. Why now, you ask? Think how God must want us to see the urgency of genetic matching. See how my thoughts take flight? You inspire me. We can lift the idea of healthy genes to a higher plateau. Like Mr. Goodnowe said, we're set apart to share this saving knowledge."

"Forget Goat. He has two faces and one of them he's not showing you."

"Oh yeah? And what is Sorelle not showing *you*? That woman has snakes in her head. If you don't believe she's the most beautiful woman in the world, just ask her."

Patrick eased the van into the far left lane. "I'm aware of her vanity, but it's not fatal."

"Don't bet on it."

"You're being judgmental."

"Maybe so, but since when does a Christian wear the Star of David on a chain? God talks to her. So do married men. Both tell her what she wants to hear. That's bizarre."

He grinned. "Sounds like you have her all figured out."

Easter dialed the radio to a romantic tune before sliding closer. "You with Sorelle is such a waste, really." Her voice melodic, she added, "You know she'll never appreciate you like I do." Her fingers plied the thigh muscles above his knee and slid closer to a more erogenous, private zone.

He cradled her with his free arm while steering into the park entrance. Without stopping to drop money into a wooden honor box, he drove to a secluded spot beneath a bay tree at the lake and jammed the emergency brake in place. With the motor idling, he kissed her mouth and the contours of her neck, oblivious to a thunderhead closing in from the gulf, and caring less that Sorelle Ebanetti was capable of bringing her own kind of storm.

Amid the exchange of caressing and kissing, Easter hooked her fingers into the waistband of his athletic shorts, pulled them down, and gawked. "Ohmygod! Homo erectus. That is *sooo* flattering." She nodded toward the back of the van. "What are we waiting for?" She quickly leveled the back seats for more space. "C'mon, get with it, Romeo. Now!"

He crawled to the rear of the van and peeled off her jeans and halter top, her body so alluring he could only stare in awe. An ethereal light surrounding her head glowed briefly before it vanished. At a later time or another place he might have stopped to ponder the phenomenon. But not now.

"Do I look better than Sorelle?" she asked. "You know I do. Go ahead, say it."

"You're magnificent," he said while removing his shorts and

briefs. "No woman ever looked so good." He gathered her shapely body in his warm embrace.

"Tell me I have your heart," she said while kissing his face.

He grinned. "Yes, and anything else you want, baby."

"Promise?"

"Better still, I'll prove it."

Lying with her on a soft blanket, his foreplay included oral treats that soon led to gyrating full intercourse in sync with her escalating moans of desire. He marveled at each of her throaty syllables, sensuous purring and frenzied whimpers. Each vocalization invited him to follow the urgency of her advancing need.

Rhythm and momentum merged like the gulf's strong, incessant tide and her voice purled with the ardor of a mountain stream's turbulent cataracts. With her soul laid bare, he absorbed its essence and made her secrets his own. As the ascending force of their mutual ardor concluded, her eyes glazed amid the urgent tremors of an orgasm.

The visage compelled him to remain strong, ready to revive lovemaking.

"Incredible," she said while languishing beneath him in the steamy aftermath. "I never dreamed it could be this good, this consuming, the way you want me as much as I want you."

Breathing hard, he kissed her repeatedly. "Know what, baby, you're irresistible. I think I'm in love. The intensity of your passion, it's like something metaphysical, as if we've risen above the earthly realm to a superior state of being, like pure once-in-a-lifetime ecstasy. One woman I knew said I have a fear of intimacy, but with you the only fear I have is being away from you too long."

"Promise?"

"Count on it. I want you to be in my life, always and forever, no matter what."

She smiled. "Baby, that's the sweetest thing any man has ever said to me. And you need not worry about me being too possessive. I just want to know that I come first in your life."

"You got it, sweetheart," he said.

"First. Always first. That's not asking too much, is it?"

"I'm all yours," he said, relishing the aroma of her body.

"Patrick."

"Yeah?"

"Have you ever wanted a soul mate?"

"Of course, and now I've found her."

"Are you sure?"

"Uh-huh. And I can see us making this love connection every day. Lots of memorable times in each other's arms."

"Keep talking, darling," she said, her body writhing. "Take me again, yes, now. Now!"

Only dimly aware of the pelting rain on the roof of his van, he smiled as a crooner on the radio sang of young love. A powerful urge welled inside him. Still he held himself in check and pondered the forces that drove him to this moment. *The youth gene? Divine mandate?* Why was his arousal so mind-bending in its intensity? No woman had ever made him feel so needed, so wanted.

In that moment, an epiphany struck him like a velvet fist.

He envisioned Easter's breasts lactating and suckling a tiny infant. Imagining her as the mother of his child held him captive and carried him to a climactic moment inside her. In perfect harmony, her own climax erupted, her body tremulous and her voice blending in rapturous enjoyment of the moment.

He could not deny a sense of destiny between them.

Moments later, Easter studied his eyes. She seemed to intuit his thoughts. "You're a really deep thinker," she said. "Maybe I can talk with you about something way deeper than you've ever dared think about before. Since Dr. Ronofski says heritable diseases have reached critical mass, my idea is not only curative, it's transformative."

"Your words, my ears."

"Are you sure you'd like to hear it?"

"Anything to please you, babe. If it's as good as the vision I just had, count me in."

"Okay, you asked for it."

SEVENTEEN

His desire not fully sated, Patrick lay beside Easter and listened as pelting rain accompanied her chatter.

"I feel like I've already been transformed into a brand new life," she said. "Being the angel you are, you've inspired a grand idea...again."

He chuckled. "Like a contortionist maneuver?"

"No, not that. Seriously, there's more to our romantic interlude than meets the eye."

"More? My eyes have already met more than I expected, short notice and all."

"Honey, it's like a window has opened to something super grand," she said.

"I didn't think it was half bad myself. What did you have in mind? An overhead mirror? Rose petals? Jacuzzi?"

"No, darling, I'm talking about a revitalized future for us girls. You're a natural to, shall we say, rescue the Sweethearts."

"Rescue? Does this have anything to do with a lingerie video becoming an erotic keepsake?"

"Not really. In its anniversary edition, *SportScene* mentioned your exceptional stamina, so I'm seeing everything in a different light. It's like a revelation. Your lovemaking skills could fit nicely into our overall mission."

He watched her wiggle into bikini panties. "Babe, we already know our mission."

"Not totally," she said. "The article in the magazine said you're known as a marathoner, so that makes you, Patrick Murph, our pedigree movement's ideal paramour."

"What? Like skits on TV will include sexual innuendo?"

She fastened her bra. "Actually, you'll be Dan the Man's stand-in."

"Stand-in? Like I'll parody him on TV or something?"

"No, not parody him. Do you value solidarity among our girls?"

"You bet. And I treasure the rapport I've developed with them, too."

She lifted a hairbrush from her handbag. "So, just as I'm Danny's personal assistant, you'll do much the same for me, only more."

"More? More of what?"

"Like I said, we need a proxy and—" she poked him "—you're it. Of course, Danny is the star. It's his high-profile image we'll have to keep in the spotlight."

He shifted to a squatting position. "Okay, so Danny gets star billing. Are we talking about me portraying him behind the scenes?"

"Well, since you're the only man I trust to keep the Sweethearts, um...pumped, I have to agree. Strange, but before I fully realized the extended meaning, I've initiated you into a major role. Today is like a rehearsal for full-blown service."

Perplexed, he stared at her. "Would you like to clarify that word service?"

"Reproductive service, of course."

He laughed. "Yeah, right, like the girls would agree to that."

"Look, sweetie, you alone have the youth gene and we all know you're an overachiever. You're naturally qualified as the Sweethearts' pedigree propagator."

He jerked about to mimic the unsteady equilibrium of a drunk. "Whoa! This is crazy. You expect me to prop, uh...propagate?" He gasped. "Like in real-life fertilization?"

Easter nodded her head vigorously. "Yes, and with all the usual intimacies of a paramour."

"Whoa! What planet am I on? This one is wobbling out of its orbit. So now I'm a service stud?"

"Okay, mega-stud service if you insist."

"I'm not insisting."

"I have good reason for sharing you with them, darling. They need regular sessions with you. Your lovemaking will keep them rejuvenated and youthful. They deserve—"

"Hey, hold on a minute. I've done some foolish things in my time but bedding multiples wasn't one of them. Was it something in my résumé? Look, I'm a comedian. Period. I'm not some wild stallion trying to mount a mixed medley of mares."

"But you qualify. Besides, it has a noble purpose. It's regenerative. Why knock it?"

"Knock it? For starters, they wouldn't do it. Plus, when would I find time for you?"

She ruffled his hair. "Naturally, I come first, always, but I'm willing to make sacrifices."

"Sacrifices?"

"Yes, you know, for our program. So why can't *you*?" The light of amusement twinkled in her eyes. "Do I detect a fear of intimacy or is there some secret relating to, shall we say, your manhood?"

He huffed a retort. "I'll thank you to know I fear no intimacy."

"Okay, then what's the real issue?"

"What we're talking about is sport, not intimacy."

"But you're capable."

"Well, yeah, but—"

"Darling, this is your chance to be a real hero like Danny. Only better. More genuine. The girls have always admired you but now they'll, um...*love* you."

He found his briefs. "No, it's too...I don't know...outrageous."

"C'mon, honeybunch, my sharing you with the girls isn't easy for me, but it's for every one of them. If you won't do it for me, then think of the greater good. Imagine yourself as an actor with access to the best roles."

"Yeah, rhymes with holes, doesn't it?"

Easter lolled her head and sighed. "Look, we have to keep the girls happy. Just think one woman at a time. First one, then another." She fanned her face. "My girls are in the prime of their youth. C'mon, they need you. You'll keep them from straying. Besides, sex will bolster their immune system."

"You were planning this all along, right?" He pulled his shorts on. "Speaking of Vanessa, she's Danny's fav. He'd kill me if I even laid a hand on her."

She brushed her hair with long strokes. "No, our program comes first with him, too. No need to play favorites, either. Treat all the Sweethearts as equals."

"So—" he cocked his head and looked askance at her "—where's the punch line?"

"No gags, baby, just strict rotation. I'll give you a list each day."

"Each day? How many? Two?"

Nonchalant, she plucked a stray hair from the fabric of her bra. "Four."

He shook his head. "Four? Are you kidding? No way."

"Don't underestimate your ability," she said. "And don't be surprised if the most telegenic are in your starting lineup. Peaches. Cassie. Anastasia. All are starved for affection."

"What about Freckles?"

"Yes, of course. Sorry, I keep forgetting you two are close."

"Will the girls be on the pill?"

"No."

"Why not?"

"Well, the Scrolls predict—actually require—propagation. It's our destiny."

"Whoa! There's that word again. It's destiny to do this and destiny to do that. Do the Scrolls endorse a fertility rite, like in ancient times when young virgins were deflowered in pagan temples?"

"No, but it does include a spiritual component. You see, the Scrolls are linked to the pedigree cause, but we'll consider those details later."

"Oh, yes, details, details, details. Do the Sweethearts know about me and Sorelle?"

"Yes, but we all know you're attracted to her only because she has Hollywood connections."

He gave her a cockeyed look. "Suppose I reject this harebrained idea?"

"You won't get off that easy," she said, mockingly stern. "I've indoctrinated the girls about selective mating." She grinned. "Because it fortifies the immune system, it adds years to a woman's lifespan, maybe eons."

"And what does it add to a man's?"

"You'll die happy."

"And early, too, no doubt," he said.

She laughed. "I'll hype the proxy idea tonight when the girls study a new instructional video. It's titled *Treasure the Pleasure*. It's about technique, positioning, things like that."

"Did this bright idea occur to you because you were feeling threatened? You know, by Sorelle's fondness for me."

She adjusted her bra. "You're psychoanalyzing me. But that's okay. Sex activates serotonin, the love hormone, which in turn conditions us to accept your genetic asset. But I only speak as it's revealed to me, and I've been told pedigree reproduction is a divine mandate."

"Uh-huh. Have you considered the law of diminishing returns?"

She wagged her lecture finger again. "Think metaphysics. My spirit tells me the conduit of your mind and body, your psyche, will remain open."

"Open to what?"

"To divine energy, to epigenetic expression, to putting more super in your natural."

"What, like I'll be plugged up to some out-of-this-world energy source?"

"Right. You'll see when the time comes. By the way, when will you give Sorelle the boot?"

"I can't do that."

"Oh? Didn't you just tell me I was first in your life?"

"That I did, passionate moment that it was, but she has plans for me—career plans."

She cupped her chin. "On second thought, she may get suspicious of my intent to shape Danny's future for good. Okay, don't dump her just yet, but I'd better not catch you slighting any of my girls. By the way, you'll need to do seven, but staggered. Two per day, maybe three, and so on."

Stupefied, he shrugged and crawled into the driver's seat, thinking he could derail her absurd idea later. He glanced at the gauges within the dashboard. "We're almost out of gas."

"Speak for yourself, Casanova. How about I meet you on the bus tonight after curfew?" She smiled as she touched his groin. "From the looks of things, you're good for an encore."

Eighteen

A twelve-hour drive took Goat Goodnowe to central Florida and the headquarters for America's most popular supermarket tabloid. Its five-story building sat in the middle of twenty manicured acres where sprinklers jittered over the lush green lawn and a giant American flag hung limp atop a tall aluminum pole near the entrance.

On the glass door of the building, *Analyzer* appeared in gold lettering. Two uniformed guards greeted Goat in the foyer. On the top floor a receptionist announced his arrival into an earbud.

"Ms. Netll, your four o'clock is here." The receptionist nodded toward a nearby office.

The name *Jasmine Netll, Senior Editor*, faced him at eye level on her door. He fingered his bolo tie before entering her office.

"Come on," Jasmine said in a husky voice as she rounded her desk to greet him.

"Raul Goodnowe," he said without offering a handshake.

Jasmine lumbered back to her cluttered desk and squeezed her bulk into a worn leather chair, its armrests smothered by her forearms.

"If you got the goods on DiNago, lay it on me. I got deadlines to meet."

Goat held a tan attaché case beneath his right arm. "As Mr. DiNago's senior advisor, I have some shocking news about him," he said after seating himself.

Jasmine lowered her bifocals to peer at him. "Uh-huh. Let's hear it."

Crossing his legs, Goat showed the high gloss on his Mauri leathers. "Do you know the original meaning of the name Immanuel?"

"Maybe, maybe not. I know Miami is full of them."

"It literally means God is with us."

"We get all kinds," she said.

"It's Dan the Man DiNago's middle name."

"Anything else?" Her eyes glazed as she studied a flat desk calendar marked with coffee stains.

"Immanuel has returned to Planet Earth as a genetic messiah," Goat said, his tone hushed as he fished a lozenge from his pocket while shifting the attaché case onto his lap. "But he's different from what people expect of a pious messiah."

She perused the pages of his synopsis received days earlier. "Got an address for him?"

"Sanctuary Beach." He coughed into his fist. "Alabama."

"Really? He lands in Alabama? Is he lost?"

"No, he got beamed. You see, his DNA will produce a flawless offspring who'll restore Eden."

"You jacking me, man?"

"Not at all. My synopsis indicates the Sahara will bloom and the Kalahari spring up with lots of vegetation. That prophecy is due in our lifetime. In a nutshell, Ms. Netll, he's here to keep a promise, a longstanding one—perfect health. Guaranteed. But life isn't easy for him. Much like two millennia ago, he's still disowned by religious leaders. They especially despise a messiah who challenges monogamy. That new polygamy wrinkle can't be revealed until the second half of my series."

She flipped the pages. "Who the hell would buy into a Romeo messiah?"

Goat inserted the lozenge into his mouth. "For one thing, he's into genetic matching. That's why he services a healthy harem. And, true to his mission, the sperm he shares is free of inherited flaws, pure and undiluted."

"Okay." She placed the synopsis face-down and leaned back.

"Why a harem?"

"Why *not* a harem?" he said. "Messiah's vision has as much to do with aesthetics as it does with faith. He's very discriminating in his selection of beautiful women."

She rolled her eyes. "What?"

The lozenge changed sides and clacked against his teeth. "True, he's not exactly what the clergy expect, same as his first go-round. He shares his superior genes with his female disciples first, his harem if you please. In turn, they indoctrinate others. The result is pedigree babies."

She frowned. "Care to run that by me again?"

"It's basic biology," he said. "Match the right mates, eliminate heritable diseases and—bingo!—the DNA of Blacks no longer carry the emblot mutation."

"And he don't have in mind a master race?"

He squirmed in his chair. "I get what you're saying, but the pedigree cause has no ethnic bias. In fact, our genetic messiah embraces diversity."

"Still, my people feel put down by any hint of a supremacist agenda," she said.

"I understand, Ms. Netll, but emblot is a worse put-down. Suppose I told you Spencer Lovejoy has endorsed this program? Faith-based entitlements will help Blacks breed up to beat emblot. Twenty-thousand dollars each. No lie. At my clinic, bundles of cash from grants are there for the taking."

"Well, now that *is* a positive." She tapped the synopsis. "Any photos?"

Goat opened his briefcase and offered a manila envelope. "All color, five-by-sevens."

She slid the prints from the envelope with her beefcake hands. "Lovely women," she said.

"No airbrush and no photoshop. And you'll note the two mixed race beauties are among the most telegenic," he said. "All these lovelies signed my modeling agreement, too. These, in fact, will also star in a lingerie video, a keepsake for Immanuel."

"What else you got?"

"Something much more sensational, but first we need to agree on a price." He leaned back in the chair. "And I want them featured two weeks in a row."

Her gaze lingered on him. "I'll run this by legal. I don't know 'bout a breeder Christ."

"Why not? Look, *The Analyzer* is an influencer. This story is certain to cause an uproar but look at its impact on your readership stats. The numbers will run off the page in accounting. Sanctimonious firebrands see polygamy as a sacrilege, but we both know change has its price."

She grimaced. "But we're talking about a carnal Christ who sleeps around."

"No, he's much too circumspect for that. He's absolutely loyal to each of his beautiful wives."

She smirked. "So how does having a harem square with Christianity?"

"It may surprise you to know, Ms. Netll, that ancient Israel embraced polygamy. You see, it's through his wives that he blesses humanity in a spiritual way, too."

"Spiritual? This story is getting deep."

"Believe me, Ms. Netll, his generosity will resonate with modern females. One in six couples today are infertile. Worse, most male prospects are diseased."

Jasmine entwined her fingers on the desktop. "Yeah, but would you read an article titled 'Harem of Christ'?"

"I would if it said 'Miracle Harem'. That's your hook."

"Uh-huh, but where's the miracle in all this?"

Goat slapped his briefcase. "In his sperm, of course. It's perfect. So is his offspring. Once your readers understand his seed is a national resource, they'll buy that idea in a heartbeat. Make America Well Again—MAWA. It's the ideal catchphrase."

"Hmmm, how appealing is a wealthy messiah, though?"

"Ms. Netll, we both know evangelicals love prosperity, so it's as much about status as wealth. Ask any megachurch leader. But this messiah makes no plea for money. Ever. Plus—get this—when he sires perfect kids and they do the same, what do we have? A bankable treasure. It grows generation after generation, exponentially."

"Bankable, eh? Sound like you prophesying, Mr. Goodnowe."

He slapped his palms together. "It's like Immanuel returning on a white horse. His cleansing of humanity is done through gene-matching, like he propagates a pure bloodline. Who wouldn't love such sanctified purity?"

"White stud on a white steed sounds a bit too clever."

"Not if it's hyped by Reverend L.T. Moreau."

"The televangelist? How does he fit into this spectacle?"

Goat lowered his voice to a secretive level. "He's the forerunner. Like John the Baptist. And no doubt you remember the charges they lodged against Moreau."

"Uh-huh."

"But millions of the faithful now realize he was framed. But now he's been vindicated."

"Well, his new TV show is better than before," she said.

"And with a messiah on board, L.T's comeback is even more miraculous."

Jasmine smiled. "L.T.'s rallies were always sold out. I'll give him that."

"And lest we forget, he appeals to people of all colors. The man hasn't lost his touch."

"Well, okay, but just how many wives does Immanuel have?"

Goat stared into space, as if calculating the total. "Almost two-dozen—at last count."

She chuckled. "Busy man. Do we have the exclusive on this story?"

Goat showed double fingers. "Two weeks. After that, it's up for grabs."

"Long enough." She punched a button on her desk phone. "Sally, get Darnell and Nancy in here. And tell them to bring a contract." She faced Goat again. "We may pull out all the stops for this one. I believe you mentioned having something else to show me?"

Goat tapped the attaché case on his lap. "I have photocopies of a papyrus testament, in English. Very few people have seen it. It's really ancient."

"How ancient?"

"Almost two millennia." He released the snaps and opened the case. "Its cryptic language leaves no doubt *the* Danny qualifies as *the* Immanuel."

Jasmine took the copies and examined them. "Have the originals been authenticated?"

"Absolutely."

"Where are they?"

"The originals? A broker has them, a Parisian who deals in artifacts."

She grinned. "They could have a powerful ripple effect among believers."

He winked. "Any prophecy is open to interpretation."

"And embellishment," she said as she motioned to the editors. "Darnelle, kill this week's feature on ol' Sasquatch. We got something better."

The pair moved past Goat, one a short male with shaved head, the other a wiry young female with a bushel of frizzy pink hair and rose-tinted glasses.

The bald one spoke with casual insouciance. "What's up, Jaz?"

Jasmine grinned. "A genetic messiah. Hold the harem part for the second installment, then see what you can do with these shots of his women. And give the guy a darker beard. Traditional look. I think a halo would work, too, plus some phallic jewelry."

Goat thumbed his chest. "Open his shirt down to here and add more chest hair to contrast with his gold bling. Refer to Alabama beaches as a magnet for spring breakers. One more thing, but I prefer to negotiate in private."

Jasmine flashed a smile that showed gold-plated incisors. "We invented checkbook journalism."

"Oh, and be sure to send the final layout, text and photos, to a guy named Reggie." Goat offered her a small card. "His office is in New York City. He'll be expecting it."

"Is he your agent?"

"You might say that. He reviews everything I write. You know, for accuracy."

She raised her chin and smiled. "Yes, we do want it to be accurate, don't we?"

Goat gave her a thumbs-up. "And kick-ass entertaining."

NINETEEN

An hour before daylight, Patrick donned a pair of cargo shorts and left Easter asleep on the bus. Entering the mansion through its back door, he eased into the silent kitchen and brewed coffee. Soon after filling his mug, he took it to the den and turned on a lamp beside his favorite recliner. A slick magazine titled *Genomics World* lay open on the end table.

Curious, he thumbed through it and read a highlighted section: *Being genetically controlled, the lifespan of a species is not written in stone but adapts according to its circumstances.*

An experiment explained how a scientist created strains of flies with a longevity doubling that of the original population. *Doubling?* He pondered the idea as he sipped coffee and resumed reading. The author, a behavioral biologist, asserted cells could support lifetimes or even centuries of life because no fixed limits were assigned to the species lifespan. *No fixed limits?*

The scientist's conclusion stunned him: *Aging, therefore, is genetically malleable.*

He clung to the author's words, as if seeing the possibilities of an existence not shared by most mortals. He set the periodical aside and pondered longevity. Could malleable mean that regenerative matching—Dr. Ronofski's selective mating plan—was the prerequisite for a longer lifespan?

Would a test group of pedigree women validate his youth gene's potential? Even if he agreed to the proxy role, how would he find time for it? And it might also weaken his objection to Goat's erotic video, a spinoff of the telegenic ten's lingerie shoot.

Given Easter's need for power and control, her motives for justifying a pedigree proxy were transparent. He tried to imagine the betterment of society. But the Sweethearts were entertainers and motherhood might sideline their acting career.

How important was fame to them?

He wondered if the girls were informed by *Genomics World* that sex geared to procreation would allow their immune system to protect them against heritable diseases.

Easter's mandate intrigued him. First one, then another. How difficult could it be?

Assuming the girls had no clue about Danny's debility, they would still intuit that he was not a Don Juan phenomenon. Unlike him, Patrick realized women needed to be showered with affection, tenderly cared for, and genuinely loved.

He considered equally compelling thoughts. Easter was effusive in her praise of his performance last night. His status with her had improved. Could he leverage it into a means to defeat Goat's strategy? If his rapport with the girls continued to grow, perhaps he could sway them and Easter into rejecting the keepsake. But it would have to be done soon.

Caught up in the challenge, he almost forgot about the effect his new role might have on Sorelle. An itch irritated the underside of his wrist, one he knew sprang from anxiety. He must quell his troubled thoughts. A distraction may work. Penning a few comedy lines usually helped, yet nothing about a face-off with Sorelle inspired comedy at the moment.

Why allow her to interfere with his new status? He would have to play this new hand day by day and see what would develop.

PATRICK'S APPREHENSION persisted throughout the day, though none of the Sweethearts hinted they knew about his being offered the real-life role of paramour. As skit practices in the mansion gave way to deep shadows on the patio, his thoughts turned to the Swashbuckler and the anglers who gathered at sundown.

Instead he found Sorelle at a corner table preoccupied with texting.

"Busy day?" he said before taking a seat at her table.

Sorelle sat with her shapely legs extending into the aisle, ankles overlapping as she sipped a pink cocktail. "I sent a message earlier to my office before my secretary left for the day," she said.

His fingernails clacked a rhythm on the table top. "Don't let me interrupt your work."

"You're not. I just approved a hefty advance for a mid-budget movie. And I checked the stats on my perfume line before answering Gabe Casper's query."

"Agent Gabe, huh? My own agent says I'm not on track for another shot at the *Hotz*. Perhaps my showbiz profile needs upgrading."

"She's right. I say we time it to coincide with a movie role I'm working up for you."

"Really?" he said. "For me? Rehearsals for a charity game are chipping away at my time, so even if Wynn's show called, I might not have time to prepare."

She patted his hand. "Just wing it."

He rolled his shoulders. "I like doing that but success is all about preparation. Like it's difficult to rehearse skits when Easter keeps taking some of the most talented away in the middle or practice."

Sorelle tucked her phone away in a handbag. "She's incompetent. Why tolerate her? I would be willing to bet she has something going on that she's not telling you."

He laughed nervously. "Whatever it is, she'll tell me when she's ready."

"Not unless it's to her benefit."

"Maybe I expect too much too soon," he said.

Her fingers toyed with a Star of David pendant at her cleavage. "We all do."

Though Sorelle's ability to strategize his career as an entertainer could be helpful, it occurred to him that betraying Easter was not in his DNA.

He wanted to steer Sorelle away from a discussion about Easter. "I'm excited about the charity game," he said. "It's our debut wingding."

"Debut for what?"

"Oops, there I go again, fantasizing," he said. "No, it's only one game for charity. It'll be fun if we can pull it off."

"Such a waste of time," she said.

He offered a tentative smile. "You never know about these things. Suppose I take this glamour team on the road? I know it's risky but—"

"Forget road shows," she said. "Too much overhead."

Jacki the bartender took his order for a beer. "I'll find investors," he said to Sorelle. "Once they see the Sweethearts perform, their money will have to be hauled in by a Brinks truck."

Her laughter exploded. "You'd have a better chance of growing orchids in their belly buttons than raising venture capital for *that* bunch. Sweethearts! Hah! What kind of name is that? It's too trite. Besides, they're unknowns. No one bets on entertainers with no track record."

"Newbies are easier to coach, though," he said, miffed at her snarky attack. "I know an Atlanta socialite who'd spring for our financing."

Her icy stare scrutinized him and her voice chilled. "You know her that well?"

"Well enough to know she bets on the jockey, not the horse."

"Y'know what? I'm thinking of catching the redeye for New York early tomorrow."

"What? I've waited this long for a reunion and off you go again?"

"But waiting is the point, love. You didn't. And now a fling with some rich woman in Atlanta. Ha! I don't need a reckless gamer who thinks he can transform a bunch of wannabe stars into actresses. Easter said the charity game is temporary. She lied, didn't she? Debut, indeed."

"For the record," he said, "I go away to college and you get steamed and run around with a rich married man who has six kids. Clay was more than another payday, wasn't he?"

She gave him a smoldering look. "That is *sooo* not true."

"Why deny it? Everybody knew the rich auto dealer was a playboy."

"I never betrayed your love, Patrick, and that's the gospel truth."

"Truth? Your best friend Maggie swore to it."

"Oh, sure, jealous Maggie fed your suspicions."

"So did Clay."

Her voice hardened. "No, Patrick. Guys who do it don't talk. Those who wish they *had* done it do the blabbing." Her tone grew forlorn. "Now do you see what you did to yourself, and to me? You and I had a love so rare.... You know, to love is something, but to love and be loved is everything. I was so proud of you for going away to college. I waited. You didn't."

"But lots of people were talking about you betraying me. It hurt like hell."

"I'm glad you were hurt. Any man who'd believe cheap gossip deserves to be hurt."

"Gossip? My folks don't—"

"Yes they do. I was a consultant for Clay's string of dealerships. We flirted some but he was my client. My *client*! How could I know people were spreading lies? Sure, they envied my beauty and fame, but why would your parents believe all the slanderous gossip?" With hands cupping her face, her voice broke amid its tremors. "Why-why-why?"

"This is incredible," he said, shaking his head as swells of regret overtook him.

Sniffing, she wiped her eyes. "Admit it, Patrick, you judged me instead of defending me."

"But my parents said you had a baby long before you even met me."

Her eyes glinted in anger. "Not true. And I'm not that kind of woman. You should feel honored to know me. I also heard the rumors about our neighbor, Mr. Green. He respected Mom. She was not a harlot. No, but evil gossipers labeled her as one. I was devastated."

He swallowed hard. "I was so certain it was true."

She reached and squeezed his hand. "And now...you...know. I wonder what your mother thinks of me now after I built a talent empire in only ten years."

In a moment of reflection, he said, "She once said you'd have your heart's desire someday."

A stubborn resolve rose in Sorelle's voice. "And now I have. I learned a long time ago how to take care of myself, so money works for me, not the other way around."

A tinge of guilt pricked his conscience. Why talk of her betrayal long ago when his own tryst with Easter was so recent? Mired in self-reproach, the idea of being a pedigree propagator now seemed absurd. And whoever heard of a youth gene? Ronofski could be mistaken.

Sorelle finished her drink. "Do you guys have a contract with a production company?"

Her resilience, shown by the quick change to a business tone, intrigued him. "Easter has a letter of intent for a TV show."

"Patrick, all that's good for is to keep you from shopping your act to other producers."

"Yeah? Easter says the ratings have to be evaluated before they'll sign us on."

"Who's the producer?"

"Some guy named Rubleau."

She smirked. "Sebastian Rubleau. I know him well. He's a big leaguer, all right, but if the results are iffy on the first run, he'll cancel. And no explanation. If I made a proposal to him, though, he would accept it. You guys need a hard-nosed negotiator on your side."

"We're shooting for a thirteen-week run," he said.

"You have to get it right or it won't last a month." Her voice stiffened. "Easter doesn't know how to play hardball, yet she's trying—pretending—to manage the Sweethearts' career."

She took a lecturer's breath. "*I* have connections. *I* have clout. *I'm* also in daily contact with the top talent agencies in L.A. and New York. Who can Easter call? No one. But even I hesitate to promote your entertainers. Beauty can carry them only so far. You know acting, they only know reacting."

"Whoa! They know more than they let on, and I can tweak the scripts and—"

"Not listening, are you, love? The standup routine on your website: 'Make some noise, all you *claptomaniacs!*' And the one when you play a burglar stuck in a revolving door. When a cop shows up, your hip-hop slang erupts in the best impromptu I've ever heard."

"I kill it, don't I?"

"Absolutely. That pause and that look always slays me. You know how to set the audience up with that trademark look of disbelief."

"As good as Dan the Man?"

He detected a subtle smirk in her voice. "Patrick, his draw is due to the spillover from football fame, not acting skill. You, on the other hand, can make a script sing. Talent? Yes. Are you bankable? We'll see. Get your priorities straight. The Sweethearts are dead weight. They'll drag you down. With me, you'll be a star within five years. In fact, I have an opening."

An opening? As always, he was skeptical of her praise. "How do you know Rubleau?"

She leaned and kissed him. "I know all the producers. Want more than a kiss? Be my roommate tonight after dinner at Romero's. I promise to leave my Beretta at home this time."

He glanced at his watch. "I'm overdue a phone call to my daughter. I'll meet you there at eight."

Despite Sorelle's effusive praise, an uneasy feeling nagged him. Should he believe she wanted to sign him as her newest client? Managing talent was her life, but....

A call to his mother in Bon Amite might confirm his doubts about Sorelle, or put them to rest. Meanwhile, would Easter understand his quest for fame overrode the stirrings of amorous desire aboard the tour bus tonight? What had Easter said? *Don't dump Sorelle just yet.*

Was it possible that Sorelle's promise of movie fame was compatible with the pedigree priority Easter had so recently talked about? The idea seemed too far-fetched at the moment.

Which woman will better benefit my acting career? That's the question.

TWENTY

A stiff wind attended by rain blew in from the bay the following morning. The Sweethearts pranced in circles on the makeshift softball diamond. With their tank tops thoroughly soaked, they performed a scripted dance while hamming off-script for Larry Lemoyne's video camera.

Easter blew her whistle and ordered them to take cover in the gymnasium. "If we're about busty exhibitionism, then gear up and let 'er rip," she said as an aside to the girls. "Let's try some impromptu stuff. Show me spontaneity."

Larry's voice reverberated moments later off the cavernous walls of the gym. "Take one!" He aimed his camera at a petite gymnast who followed the chalk-marked bases. As she turned cartwheels, spontaneous applause and cheers from teammates accompanied her performance.

Next, the girls perfected Patrick's dance medley to depict a variety of sports.

Most impressive to Patrick was Vanessa's backspin, followed by a double axel leap. Her act, if enhanced later by computer-generated graphics, would feature a colorful double helix. The molecule's image could be superimposed on her freeze-framed midair jump. Its symbolism, designed to boost the concept of regenerative matching, could also be used in a television commercial promoting the idea of a Pedigree Nation. With West Coast editing, technical wizardry could make even simple acts spectacular.

Recalling Sorelle's critique—disparaging the girls as dead weight —angered him still. Drag him down? She had no idea of the Sweethearts talent. Nor their pizazz.

"Even the Globe Trotters will envy us," Easter shouted. "Good happens!"

As Patrick climbed the bleachers to oversee the new skits, Freckles came to bat shouldering a python prop. The catcher pretended to faint at first sight of the lifelike reptile's open-mouthed writhing.

The skits segued into Cassie acting a granny in a flower-print dress, wire-rimmed spectacles, and blue wig up in a bun. With tongue showing in a determined curl, she swung at a whiffle ball but missed the pitch while struggling to regain her balance on the polished floor.

Anchoring first and second bases, Sandy and Mandy moved in closer to lead the infield players with their chants of "easy out."

Vanessa bounded up the bleachers to sit beside her comedy coach. "These new slapstick skits are really funny," she confided. "Are you nervous about playing the Paladins in our debut gig?"

"Nervous?" Patrick said. "No, hon, I'm too busy following my instincts like a bee following its nose to nectar."

"Nose to nectar!" she said. "Is that a metaphor hinting at what you do with women?"

He grinned and pointed to the gym floor where Cassie stiffened at home plate while Anastasia lobbed the ball to her. Missing the first and second pitches, she wobbled momentarily but shouldered the bat and tucked the front of her granny dress between her legs. She pointed to an imaginary centerfield fence and loudly predicted, like the legendary Babe Ruth, where her home-run hit would go. Stepping into the last pitch, she popped it beyond the outfielder's reach before loping along the base lines, her arms wide like a gangly goose trying to chase an invader from its nest. On her arrival at home plate, her teammates happy-screamed like fans celebrating a clutch play in the World Series.

In harmony with the safe-at-home script, she led her teammates' cheer-song:

"She's a glamour freak on a winning streak
With a softball glove and lookin' keen
Struttin' her stuff for the TV screen
She's fast, she's lean, a scoring machine
Runs two bases, steals a third, and
Flies on home like a hummingbird."

In the spirit of a pep rally, Easter cupped her mouth and began a rah-rah session with the team. "You've no idea, girls, how famous we'll be this time next year. We'll give 'em the most, coast to coast, and come Saturday we'll all be—ta-daaa!—at Paladin Park in Florida."

Pumping her fists skyward, she continued. "A famous producer will watch us perform there. He loved our sample video. Sooo...are we happy yet?"

The girls cheered as she added, "And we'll grace the cover of *Sport-Scene* magazine."

Vanessa slapped Patrick's knee. "Lordymercy, coach, why didn't you tell me about all this juicy new stuff? When you don't remember, you forget, don't you?"

He smiled while anchoring a coffee mug on his knee. "Jot that one down, partner."

"Can you imagine us on the cover of a famous sports mag?" she said.

"Uh-huh," he replied. "Next thing you know, y'all might be cast in a movie."

"And just this afternoon," Easter shouted, "Danny was offered the starring role in a new motion picture. You girls—yes, *youuu*—will appear in it as mates of a famous buccaneer."

Vanessa did a double-take. "How did you know we'd be in a movie? Got a supernatural clue?"

He chuckled at her naïveté. "Nah, but I do foresee things."

"Like, in the future, you mean?"

"Well, the future being the only thing foreseeable, I reckon you'd be right."

She bumped her forehead with the heel of her hand. "Walked myself into that one, didn't I?" She pressed a finger to her temple.

"Incoming! Wait for it. An idea is parachuting to my brain. If you're big into foresight, tell me what I'm thinking right this minute."

"Well—" he tapped his forehead "—my crystal ball shows you're thinking about us giving you the lead role in Danny's new movie."

"Yep, like gung-ho-ho-ho." She elbowed him, suddenly serious. "Are your balls really crystal?"

Momentarily forgetting the coffee mug on his knee, he laughed too hard as some of the hot liquid spilled onto his sandaled feet. "Damn!"

"Oops! Did I do that?"

"No, it's my fault. Your humor caught me off guard."

Her voice changed to a seductive purr. "Remember how you were rapping when we first met and you said hormones beckon egg and sperm to pair? I reckon your hormones do beckon a lot, don't they? Easter said you're a sack master."

"Easter said that? Hon, I was just having fun with a rap song I made up."

"Uh-huh, like I believe you're not a real Casanova? Easter also said we gotta act more sensuous, so I'm thinking you'd like a massage aboard the Hooter Commuter tonight."

"Anybody hungry?" Easter crooked a commanding finger his way. "Lunch time. Now!"

He escorted Vanessa to the floor of the gym where she spoke more softly to him. "Think about it before your thinker gets all thunked up."

In an instant he knew Easter had informed them of his new surrogate role, but in the next instant he doubted it was how a coach should bond with players. Being hired to help them reach a level of fame they could not achieve on their own was understandable. And he didn't want to achieve fame for himself alone. The thought moved him to think of ways he could fine-tune the synchronicity between them. But something more personal had happened. He recognized the secondary prompt in their mutual quest was his growing admiration for each of them. Too, they had a larger goal to achieve.

Did achieving a genutopia mean the kind of synchronistic relationship Easter suggested?

TWENTY-ONE

Patrick imagined the sky spreading like pizza dough to welcome the heat as the girls left the gymnasium and crossed Bon View. On the flagstone walkway leading to the front of the house, moisture glistened on the concrete, steamed by the summer shower, a daily occurrence in August.

Easter waved her arms and directed them to follow her. "Let's go, girls! It's a pleasant stroll to the Pickle Derby Deli."

Not surprised that Vanessa's wiggle-walk in gym shorts yards ahead of him was intended to be a distraction, he faked a head count of the Sweethearts. "Pickle Derby Deli? Who's into pickles?"

"Me," Vanessa said. "But me not preggie."

"Oh yeah?" Cheryl said. "When was the last time you had a period?"

Walking backward, Vanessa made a show of counting the fingers on one hand. "Five days."

Cheryl moaned. "Oh...my...god. Vanessa ran out of fingers. What are we to do?"

With her dimpled showstopper smile, Peaches joined in teasing the troupe's make-believe ditz. "She can count to twenty but first she'll have to remove her shoes."

Dancing like a frustrated child, Vanessa flipped her long ponytail over her shoulder. "Why don't we grease Freckles' cabaret pole before her skit about a movie stuntwoman?"

"Yeah, now there's a skit with a slick twist," Patrick said. "On second thought...."

He ambled alongside Cheryl who followed the contour of the mansion driveway. "Write down all the impromptu stuff," he said. "Let's tap into any rich vein of ideas. Not to digress but level with me, girl. What've you heard about Goat's keepsake video? I know it's an extension of the lingerie thing but please tell me they're not doing hardcore."

Cheryl grinned. "Can I trust you on this one?"

"Yeah, I'm zipped tighter 'n a gobbler at a turkey shoot."

"Freckles said *Star Harem* is simulated, as in pretend. Goat must realize it's a sinker, though." She smiled. "You could be in it and pretend you're Danny's proxy, like in real life."

"Oh, so you know about the surrogate idea?"

"Harem star you are. Freckles can put in a good word for you, and you can put in, um...the rest."

He laughed over her oblique reference to *Put It In*, *Put It In*, a popular song charting strong on all radio stations. "Cheryl, tell me this: Who's in the running for best actress in it?"

"Ha! Like it takes acting, which is another reason I rejected it from the get-go. Sheesh! First, you tell *me* something. You do know Vanessa is Dan the Man's fav, don't you?"

"Yeah. What about it?"

"Well, you know an interloper would not be welcome in his machismo world."

Patrick slowed as his gaze focused on the gulf waters where distant anglers were surf-casting in the shallows. "Easter has my back with that but the proxy thing is not a done deal. Not by a long shot."

"Really? Okay, but what's up with Easter and Sorelle?"

"It's a standoff, like a clash of ambitions," he said. "You might say their stars are not aligned but they share the same orbit."

"Is Easter hoping Sorelle will sign off on Danny's career change?"

"Chances are, that won't happen."

"Sorelle manages Danny's finances, so is she holding back support from us to spite Easter?"

"You think?"

"One of us has to."

"Okay, I think Easter has to first convince Danny to free up funding. But to do that, he'll have to overrule Sorelle."

"Know what I think?" she said while cracking her knuckles. "Danny has to decide if his loyalty to Easter is stronger than his ties to Sorelle. Am I right?"

"Yeah, but it's about status, too." He wiped his brow on his sleeve as he stopped in the shade of a palm. "You see, Danny's like an institution. Thousands in his network look to him for their livelihood but in the meantime Easter is trying to raise his status in a different way."

"Oh, c'mon, Patrick, he doesn't need Easter for that." She lifted her visor. "I'm betting Sorelle will find a way to discredit her."

He studied the girls—Vanessa and Peaches—strutting but straggling behind Easter. "My guess is Easter's banking on TV syndication to solidify her position. And intuition tells me Danny does admire a visionary like Easter who sees genetic matching is the future, but his emotional ties to Sorelle are strong. God help us if she finds out he's into a skin flick. It has scandal written all over it."

Cheryl slapped her palms together. "So Danny feels the future is in Easter, right?"

"True, but only because he fears stagnation. You know, with his fans. But Easter convinced him pedigree matching will broaden his appeal by tapping into a wider audience. And it'll be done without reliance on American football. So yeah, I see conflicts ahead with Sorelle, and fairly soon."

"So which one loses?"

"Cheryl, hear me out on this, okay? Sorelle knows something you don't." He ignored a patina of sweat on his neck. "I've known players who're more at home in a locker room than in a love nest. For athletes like Danny it's about camaraderie and the challenge of the game. He's addicted to the rush. For some it's like the experience itself influences genes and alters a player's motivations."

"So where did you go right and Danny go wrong? You know, with women."

"Well, my feelings for a woman like you, for example, would never be at odds with my work because I see you as something precious." He closed his eyes momentarily while waves along the shoreline seemed to beckon him. "To me, every expression of love is its own reward. Love can touch a man's heart in profound ways, and nothing in this world exists more exquisite than that."

Head bowed, she walked beside him. "Wow, I could fall in love with your eloquence."

He nudged her. "I'm glad you feel that way, hon."

She smiled. "Just so you know, in her former life Vanessa was a cannibal, so if ever you do her, don't say *eat me* out loud."

"Jot that one down, too. To tell the truth, after a serious chat with Sorelle, I have misgivings over the proxy deal. She's a master at guilt trips."

"Easter said you're exclusive to us. Does Sorelle know that?"

"No, not yet. If she could, she'd try to ruin both Easter and the pedigree program."

"You *do* know a lot about her, don't you, Proxy Man?"

"I called Mom and got an earful about Sorelle. Seems one of her lovers took a photo of her with Clay, an auto dealer. Caught them in the act. Clay's goons fried his grits, so to speak. But Sorelle has a lie-and-deny mentality about such things."

"So how does it feel bedding a weirdo like Sorelle?"

He grinned. "It feels like the distance between us can't be measured in inches, but miles."

"Maybe you're trying to juggle Jello and pig iron at the same time," she said. "Can't be done."

"Yeah, I know. Mom says sociopaths wear many hats and one doesn't fit. She's also right about Sorelle's narcissistic tendencies."

"Sorelle unexpectedly turns into a vamp, right?"

"Yeah. Not to digress again, but this proxy thing smacks of polygamy. I mean, given that fifty-percent of marriages end in divorce, we all know about serial monogamy being the same thing as having plural wives, essentially, with kids everywhere, but how are the Sweethearts supposed to deal with it?"

"Hey, the Sweethearts come from a long line of pedigrees," she said.

"I know, but—"

"Patrick, we females are pragmatic, so we naturally adjust and opt for polygamy when there's a serious shortage of quality males."

"Wait. No joking, okay? You're justifying polygamy with environmental and social backing?"

"Yes, Patrick, but I'm copacetic with monogamy, too."

"Really?"

"Yes. It's just that many of us come from polygamous families. In fact, I have lots of half-sisters and brothers."

"And you'd agree to a plural arrangement?"

"Sure. Generosity and regenerative matching go hand-in-hand. That's been drilled into me since childhood." She smiled. "You do know that in a polygamous society, testosterone doesn't become a big issue. In fact, controlling it might be the best way to prevent wars."

"Ever been told how clever you are?" he said.

"Hey, Patrick!" Vanessa called from twenty yards ahead. "Look at this."

He watched as she and Peaches did a shimmy-shake with breasts bared. They recited a cheer-song with the act. "More bounce to the ounce, more tease to the knees." Too amused to finish, Vanessa giggled. "Lordymercy, ought to see the look on your face. Fun-neee!"

"I'm not believing this," he said. "You girls got me again."

Cheryl's expression changed as her sneaky grin broke into madcap laughter. "Wait, it doesn't have enough shock. But we're working on something and it'll be a lot more dramatic."

"You'd better be kidding," he said.

Cheryl cocked her head to one side as if appraising his physique. "Yeah, girls, I'd say he's ready. Do the gag right and he'll never see it coming."

"C'mon, enough teasing," he said. "Let's catch up with the lunch crowd."

A Jaguar driven by Danny DiNago sped past and stopped beside the bus. Danny entered without looking back. As though responding to a secret signal, Vanessa ran to join him.

Patrick's resentment of the superjock's celebrity status flared. A halfhearted attempt to reassure himself that Dan the Man was only a poster boy for pedigree mating—an impotent demigod and nothing more—failed to excuse the famous jock's audacity.

The Sweethearts' fondness should be reserved for himself, their coach, not Danny.

Excess hype over Dan the Man's gridiron heroics kept his status sky-high. And a fat-cat financial portfolio added even more to his social value. Symbolizing the epitome of robust health at a time when half of American males were either impotent, sterile, or carried venereal diseases helped to bolster the icon's brand.

Patrick remained hopeful that his appearances each week on the Funtasy Channel would improve his backseat status. And soon.

TWENTY-TWO

C heryl Decairo slipped away from her companions to the privacy of her bedroom. She listened to the girls' playful antics in the pool on the patio and smiled, glad they were preoccupied with a game of water volleyball.

True to her daily routine, she recorded her most recent thoughts.

Am I a misfit here? My refusal to appear in the keepsake video makes me feel like an outlier. Patrick dislikes it too. Some guy from a tabloid keeps tailing us, but only reporter Trudy Mickelstein has an exclusive on interviews with us. Tonight I want to conjure up skits for our weekly TV show. We girls have a big surprise for Patrick on the tour bus. We learned about one of his ancestors who was the best comedian of his day. His great-grandfather was a vaudeville actor. Is it any wonder Patrick excels as a humorist? It's in his bloodline.

ABOARD THE IDLING Silver Eagle bus, parked in a copse of oaks and palms, Goat Goodnowe placed his camcorder on the front seat and faced Danny DiNago. "We need to do another take of that last scene with you and Vanessa," he said.

Danny's hand rested on the hydraulic door opener. "Okay, so I'm a buccaneer," he said. "But the macho thing is a stereotype. It's not me."

"But the *Star Harem* script has you vying to become king, so both your heroism and hedonism are legendary. And your adversary is scheming to steal Vanessa."

"Who plays the thief?"

"Slack Creel. He acts as your evil half-brother, the one who envies your birthright."

"Slack?"

"Sure. He tries to ruin your bid for the throne."

Danny frowned as he stepped away from the bus. "Too predictable."

Goat lifted a lighter and a cigar from his shirt pocket before departing the bus. "By the way, why were you never injured playing pro football?"

"Pure luck." Danny stepped aside to let Vanessa exit the bus and walk to the mansion.

Goat shook the lighter. "Name a quarterback who's never had any injuries." Seconds passed. "I'm waiting."

Danny shrugged. "I think it's my lucky number ten."

"Maybe you've beaten the odds for another reason, champ. You have guardian angels all around you. Who's your birth mother? I have a good reason for asking."

"No idea," he said. "I was adopted."

"You might be surprised to know your true origin. Do you know what an incarnation is?"

"Some new twist on reincarnation, I suppose."

Goat sauntered alongside him until reaching the rear of the mansion. "Let's go up and sit in the atrium. I doubt you're prepared for what I know about your genealogy."

"What about it?"

"You don't have one." Goat searched his pockets for another lighter. "You might be surprised to know you have no family tree, man. You're about to turn the world on its ear, young man."

CONTOURED WINDOWS in the executive dining room of Samuel Crown's penthouse offered a view of the New York City financial district. The maître d' escorted Crown, a frail man with a permanent frown, to a table in a semi-private area.

Reggie Torgenthal levered himself quickly from a chair at the table and stood in deference to his friend's arrival. As the CFO of National Guaranty Trust, the British expat was recognized as second in command of the Central Order.

"How's it going with our supergenes project, Sam? Bloody well, I trust."

Crown slid gently into the armchair and nodded at a server for his daily Manhattan. "You should know our clinic is thriving on the Alabama coast," he said. "Goodnowe is moving DiNago into his new role as a genetic messiah."

Relaxing in his chair, Reggie grinned. "Indeed. I would imagine it'll take more than hype on L.T. Moreau's toady hoedown on TV to give him credibility. But I'm concerned more about Dr. Ronofski. Is he helping?"

"Yes, he's booked solid with lectures. He raves on about a meltdown of the gene pool. Since we stopped access to biotech solutions, research funds have dried up. Senator Blockton blames the fallout on activists who protest the cost of genetic engineering."

Reggie nodded approval. "Not too shabby, Sam. We'll be in position to purchase biotech stock for pennies on the dollar. But I don't trust the Senator. He skips AA meetings. It's time to replace him."

Crown squinted. "You have someone in mind?"

"Yes." A moment passed. "In fact, she and I are having lunch tomorrow at The Emporium."

"Is she the only one you're considering? Teddy doesn't approve of women in power."

The Brit smoothed his mustache. "That attitude is despicable, Sam. By the way, do we have any opposition on the breeding front?"

Crown tugged at the loose skin around his large Adam's apple before savoring the mix of Canadian Mist and dark coffee. "Easter Beaulieu's comedy recruit, a Casanova, had objections to our facilitator's leverage with DiNago."

"Oh? The man has spunk, eh?"

"Yes, Murph wanted to protect the glam girls' image but, thanks to Miss Beaulieu, he'll soon be a very busy man. The girls will need us to bail them out of the prickly situation. Meantime, this comedy guy has a valuable asset we can exploit."

"So I hear," Reggie said. "And rest assured my spy will keep an eye on Miss Beaulieu and Goat Goodnowe."

The Imperial Master frowned. "Who are you using to surveil them?"

The Brit grinned. "Someone they would never suspect. He knows who comes and goes at the local pub, and he'll report Murph's movements, too."

"Shouldn't that informant be a confidant to Murph?"

"Great idea, Sam. I'll have a chat with him." Reggie nodded at a passing stockbroker before he turned his attention back to the chairman. "Does Miss Beaulieu know you collected data from thirty-thousand pedigree families in northern Europe?"

Samuel Crown shifted in his chair. "No. We haven't tested her to the full yet. The Caucasians we recruit shouldn't be a shock, though she naturally has empathy for her own race."

"Okay, but what about Lovejoy and his Black Caucus group?"

Crown's expression changed to a stony facade. "Emblot is decimating those malcontents. God's curse remains upon them."

Reggie cringed at the radical interpretation of holy writ. "Is withholding hi-tech cures the only way to deal with them? It contradicts the ideals of the Order's social stance."

"That policy is outdated, Reggie. Anyhow, no one questions our good works."

Reggie proffered a wry grin. "And the Paladins' leadership is kept apprised of that?"

"Yes. Also, Teddy keeps them busy. He lines up charity drives and—"

"Teddy? You put Teddy in charge of public relations? Are you serious?"

"Of course, and I agree with his strategy. Blacks simply reproduce too fast."

"Sam, diversity is in line with our enlightened policy for the

Paladins. Besides, with Beaulieu's genetic porgram, we can include more biracial people like her to power our PR goals."

"Nonsense!" Crown's mouth scrunched in a tight line. "A young buck down in Knoxville had thirty kids by eleven women. All on welfare. I trust you're no traitor to our values. Ours is a righteous cause and you know it."

"Of course," the Brit said, his hands bracing on the armchair. "But our charter encourages the reproduction of the best across all ethnic lines, not just—"

"No! Far too many are flawed," Crown said, a blaze of anger in his gray eyes. "Too many."

"Bloody hell, Sam, we have to look at the whole panorama, not just people of privilege."

Crown's hand shook as he lifted the coffee and sipped it. "Takes forever," he said. "University liberals have long failed to honor our Aryan heritage."

Restless, the Brit squared his broad shoulders. "Be that as it may, the Central Order needs to be more inclusive. And please advise Teddy not to call them darkies. Must I remind you he wants to fill your shoes as chairman? He tells every bloke who'll listen. It's an affront to all of us. Especially to me."

Crown's gaze fixed on neutral space. "Teddy presents only a small behavioral problem."

"Small? He's become a threat to our unity."

"But his mood swings are being medicated. Lynda sees to that."

"Lynda? Sam, your wife is deceased, and Teddy's erratic condition has grown worse. But I'm your friend. Believe me, your son's issues have to be resolved, and soon."

"I assure you, Teddy can do the job."

"Really? Some in the Order are demanding action. He's upstaging me at our meetings. Even his charm is a thin disguise for his devious ploys. We'll not honor him as our leader. Not now, not ever. Our goals are in line with a timetable. Every day is crucial to our success. We both know Teddy's methods have no resemblance to our plan for better offspring."

"But he's undergoing psychoanalysis."

Reggie slammed his fist on the dining table. "I don't care what's wrong with him, genes or drugs or some schizoid mania. He's not to be trusted with privileged information."

"I'll take care of it," the old man said.

"I hope you do, my friend, because if this becomes an issue with the committee—and we know it will—Teddy will be processed out." He spread his arms wide. "No offense, but you're ninety-seven and fading. And your memory these days—"

"I'm in no mood for a lecture," Crown said. "It's time to take my meds."

Reggie stood. "And I have calls to make. Sorry to be so abrupt, my friend."

He glanced out the windows as light pooled in heavy clouds above skyscrapers of the New York skyline. "I hope you'll think seriously about me becoming Imperial Master. You know I'm qualified."

He braced against the table and squeezed Crown's hand. "I'm your ally, Sam, and I need your backing. I'll see you tomorrow on the fairway, my friend."

Samuel Crown lifted his hand in a begrudging farewell. The palsied hand trembled as he hefted a coffee cup and spilled hot liquid on the white linen tablecloth.

He grabbed his chest. "Lynda?" Turning his body slightly, his eyes searched the room. "Lynda! Why do you never come when I call you?" He gripped the cup tighter. "Answer me!"

SORELLE RETRIEVED a cup of her favorite tea—PG tips—as it steeped on the countertop before gliding her bare feet over deep pile carpet and settling in a sofa chair to read her messages.

The door burst open and Patrick entered her Sanctuary Inn suite. In gym shorts and a sleeveless pullover, his tight abs glistened with sweat from the morning beach run.

"Ah, the fitness fanatic arrives," she said.

"Hey, don't knock it." He flung the *Sanctuary Sentinel* onto a table by the window where Sorelle sat. "Fitness might help us get revved up for romance."

"In your dreams," she said.

Within fifteen minutes he had showered and made a cup of java from fresh-ground beans. He poured the hot coffee into his ceramic trophy mug, an award from his stint as a rodeo clown.

"This news report is absurd," Sorelle said. "Says here the *Analyzer* claims Danny was sent from heaven. Who makes up this garbage?"

"I'd say Goat Goodnowe," he answered. "Remember at the diner he insisted Danny could fit the profile of a messiah."

"Yes, but what's this about ancient scrolls telling how he will lead the way to enlightenment?"

He chuckled. "And sire offspring who'll inherit what's left of this earth."

"I can read, thank you."

Amused by her curt reply, he strolled to her side and massaged her neck. "Read on, then. It gets better. Among messiah's subjects are beautiful women, the details saved for a second installment—same tabloid but with glam photos."

"I suppose they all believe in eugenics."

"That word is prejudicial. They prefer to call it regenerative matching."

Tossing the newspaper aside, she said, "It's voodoo science, Patrick."

"I have doubts too but, after all, animals are crossbred to retain certain traits. My dad's treeing Walker hound's bloodline boasts winners going back four generations. He makes five-hundred-grand per year off one dog's sperm."

"Yuk."

"No yuk about it. If breeders only bred first-rate animals, problems like hip dysplasia could be completely eliminated."

"Enough, Patrick. Peddle your heresies somewhere else."

Retreating to the bedroom, he donned clean sweats before returning to her side. "I was told by Easter that believers consider the New Scrolls a godsend, and without good breeding, uh, matching, we humans will continue to suffer and self-destruct."

She stood and took a few steps before collapsing on the sofa. "I'm getting a migraine."

"But I just got here."

"Silence, please. This tabloid trash has to be dealt with before it slips into the mainstream."

He coaxed his feet into a pair of canvas Skechers. "Wish I could stay but I can't be late for our rehearsals." Hurrying past the kitchenette to the half-bath, he set his Timex on the vanity and applied sunscreen to his face and arms. The mirror seemed to brighten as he thought about Vanessa and her companion Sweethearts' progress in learning synchronized dance routines.

Sorelle called to him, her voice loud. "Patrick, tell me about Easter's video project."

"What's to tell? She wants me to rewrite some of the skits." He rolled his shoulders on approach to her, as though expecting a sparring partner. "The girls are talented but new to showbiz. Take Vanessa. Her fluid moves are a thing of beauty. That girl can flat-out dance."

Her imploring gaze lingered on his face. "You should be running the show."

He strolled to the window and peered out at the courtyard where cobblestones lay dappled by the shade of ornamental trees. Was Sorelle manipulating him, hoping to control the team vicariously?

He forced a grin. "How do you determine the sex of a cell?"

"I beg your pardon?"

"Easy," he said. "You pull its genes down. Vanessa came up with that new line. I'm giving the girls creative license and a shot at spontaneous comebacks."

"Okay, so a one-liner falls out of Vanessa's puckery lips once in a blue moon. But I say you're the one who should direct the shoot. Do you take orders or give them?"

He shrugged as he faced her. "A toe in the water is best right now."

"Timid, are we?" she said.

"We have that charity gig next week. I'll tell you more about the Paladins tonight at dinner."

Sorelle waved him off. "No, maybe tomorrow night. Gabe and I are pushing for a bigger contract with the Marauders. It'll be a glorious turning point for Danny. And for me."

"Do you happen to know anything about Danny's linage, like if he's Jewish?"

"Let's not go there, Patrick."

As he sauntered to the door and waited, Sorelle palmed her phone and joined him with a quick peck on the lips. A gleam of mischief appeared in her eyes. "I have to make some calls on behalf of DiNago Diversified's business. See you later."

He couldn't dismiss the uneasy feeling that her affections had drifted in a direction having little to do with romance. Halfway down the stairwell, he retraced his steps, mildly alarmed to learn his watch was missing. The door to her suite opened with little effort. With the carpet muffling his footsteps, his entry went unnoticed.

Sorelle stood at the far end of the sofa while pressing numbers on her cellphone. Her hair curled about her face, obscuring her peripheral vision. "Hi, Gabe!... Yes, I'm fine. And you?"

Patrick found his watch and decided to leave quietly so as not to disturb Sorelle's negotiations.

"That's so sweet of you, love," she said into the phone. "I'm all yours tonight and tomorrow... Destin? Yes, I love the beach." Short pause. "Three days?" She laughed seductively. "Admit it, Gabe, you can't get enough of me. But, if you insist...."

Patrick stopped, instantly alarmed as she continued the phone conversation.

"Don't you ever get any at home?" she said. "No, I didn't imply that I'd deny you." She giggled. "How irrepressible you are with your animal appetites."

"Poor bastard," Patrick said before he could stop himself.

Sorelle spun about to face him, a startled look in her eyes as her mouth hung open a moment. "What're you *doing* here?" Again on the phone, her voice little more than a mutter, she said, "Gotta go, someone's here, can't talk now." She swiped a finger across the phone screen too hard and it slipped from her hand and fell to the carpeted floor.

"Same ol' Sorelle," he said, shaking his head as he stalked from the room and slammed the door behind him.

TWENTY-THREE

Near the end of Gulf State Park off Beach Road, tourists found easy access to Lake Shelby but today's afternoon heat drove most indoors. After introducing Danny DiNago to Reverend L.T. Moreau in the parking lot, Goat followed the pair to the lake and lingered in the shade of a willow tree to watch the televangelist work his theocratic magic.

Moreau gazed up at a large cypress, its crown home to an osprey. "This is a historic moment," the preacher said. "What better place for God to bless a perfect match?"

Danny sent a translucent pebble skipping over the surface of the water. "Perfect match? Who, me and Easter?"

Moreau loosened his shirt collar. "Yes, it's predestined. A layman's untrained eye may see this lake in the natural like any other body of water, but to me it's the mighty Jordan. The Most High has led us here today to rejuvenate you and your mission."

Goat nodded assent as Danny looked his way.

The star athlete wrinkled his brow. "What kind of gig are you talking about?"

Moreau whistled as he gazed at the airborne osprey, its wingspan shorter than a bald eagle's. Distant lightning stenciled a dark smudge of clouds banking against the sky. "Is it true your name is Immanuel?" he asked.

"Yeah, but like I told Mr. Goodnowe, I didn't drop out of the sky like some alien."

Leaning, Moreau plucked a grass stem. "You do believe in God, don't you?"

"Sort of, yeah."

The preacher rocked back on his heels. "Sort of?"

Danny tossed another pebble, watching it skim the lake's surface. "All that *thus sayeth the lord* lingo makes no sense to me. Who talks like that anyway? It sucketh."

Moreau offered a pious smile. "Good. That means you don't have any convoluted ideas about the Almighty. You being an incarnation, you got no need to dwell on secular things."

Danny glanced at Goat. "Yeah, Goat says I don't have a birth mother."

L.T. Moreau clasped his hands behind him, his skyward gaze seeming to contemplate a lofty idea. "Ever heard of Melchizedek?"

"Mel who? Don't tell me a lawyer's in on this, too."

Moreau let slip a protracted sigh. "Melchizedek came along during the time of Genesis. The Bible says he had no beginning on this earth. Question is, did he get born up in heaven and then drop down to this earth? So you see, you're not the first to come down from heaven."

As Danny rolled his eyes, L.T. said, "The fact is, ain't no record of Melchizedek's birth in Holy Scripture. We can't trace his genealogy because he has no earthly history. You got no record of a flesh-and-blood father, either. We can make of that what we will, but I have the gift of interpretation and I'm telling you that *style* is what it's about."

"Style?"

"Yeah, man, style. It's no surprise our new-age messiah comes riding mightily on a snow-white stallion, not no farm donkey. Did Easter show you the New Scrolls?"

"Yeah, but it's all Greek to me."

Moreau chuckled. "It's mostly Hebrew with some Aramaic throwed in. Our translator did a right good job converting it to English."

Danny squatted to sort through the pebbles at his feet. "Preacher, I don't have a religious bone in my body."

"There again, the prophecy fits you." Moreau hitched up his pants. "The Scrolls ain't clogged up with platitudes. No thou and thee stuff, either. I'm about to enlighten you and show how it all fits." He moved from the tree toward Danny. "The prophecy tells how over time you'll find yourself empowered, filled to the goozle with power and wisdom."

"Yeah? Like I'll turn water into wine? Best I can do is turn wine into piss."

"Oh, what a charmer," L.T. said as he glanced at Goat. "He's got the aura, too." With his arms upraised, Moreau studied Danny's face. "It'd be a privilege to witness your anointing on this day as the genetic messiah."

Danny slung another pebble across the water. "If I'm so messiah-ized, how come young women are drawn to me like bees to a puddle of Pepsi?"

Moreau's arms fell to his side. "The Scrolls say you'll be anointed for polygamy. You no doubt remember Jonah, don't you?"

"Yeah, Jonah Ashford in L.A., but what's a movie director got to do with this?"

"No, just Jonah...in the Bible. He rebelled against God's mission, so he got swallowed up by a big ol' whale."

"Why? He didn't believe, either?"

"Believe? You betcha he did. But he was a stubborn man. For three long days and three long nights he wallowed around till the whale got as sick of him as God did. Then he got puked out."

The next pebble plopped and sank. "We don't have any whales around here, do we?"

"I'm just saying, my lord, after you're baptized, the message of the Scrolls will become as clear to you as these waters we're looking at."

L.T. sniffed as a breeze riffled the lake's surface. "You know, the river that feeds this here lake they used to call the Tallaquanock. In the Seminole tongue, it meant 'river that heals.' The early white settlers humored the natives living hereabouts and scoffed at their ignorance. But then along comes this old Franciscan monk. He blessed that very same water and pronounced it a cure-all. From then on, the local natives gained respect and lost their label as savages."

Danny cocked his arm to pitch again but lowered it. "People label me a superstitious nut but I get these vibes. When I see some good developing, I stick with its positive patterns."

"Same exact message right there in the Scrolls," Moreau said. "Tell you what, the Tallaquanock wasn't all that valuable till somebody respectable came along to approve it. Funny how an endorsement adds greater value. It behooves us to copy that divine pattern of goodness."

The preacher smiled, hands patting his paunch. "Yep, like Houdini once said, 'The more things change the more they stay the same.' Can I get an amen on that?"

"I think your point is a lot clearer now," Danny said. "Status gives an endorsement its value."

The preacher's voice boomed. "Oh yes, your IQ has done caught up with your spirituality."

Only ten yards distant, Goat aimed the camcorder for a profile of Danny's face.

Sweat stains expanded at the armpits of Moreau's white shirt as he removed his red bow tie and opened his collar. Waving his arms outward like a wand, his voice rose. "You see all this here water? Now, by itself water don't cure *nooobody*. It's got to carry the right *nuuu-trients* to help the body heal itself. Same with you. When you start the miracle process rolling, it'll keep on blessing all manner of people for generations to come. It's in the Scrolls."

"Got it," Danny said. "Like water, it evaporates but returns as rain. On and on, it never ends."

Moreau laid his hand on Danny's shoulder. "And when our Black brethren get *freeed* up from ailments their ancestors saddled them with, they'll believe in Easter's pedigree program."

Danny peered into the taller man's eyes. "Only thing is, this religious slant irks me."

The preacher wagged his head. "What you gotta do is *deeetox* and absorb the truth."

"Detox, eh?"

"By all means. Spence Lovejoy says Blacks are up for a rebellion if we don't kowtow to them. But they see you as a sports demigod. Only now, with you adding messiah to your credentials, they'll listen and buy our pedigree pitch."

"You mean, like I can actually stop race baiters in their tracks?"

"True, my lord. With what-all's going on, you can guide humanity to a place free of *hereditarian* malignancies."

"Houdini would be proud, wouldn't he?" Danny said.

L.T. smiled. "He certainly would. So what's to stop you from getting baptized?"

Danny spat in the sand. "Did you run this by Easter?"

"Ohmygod-yes," the preacher said, his arms tremulous with energy. "What a believer she is!" He gestured toward the lake. "It's time, my lord, it's *tiiime!*"

Following the preacher's lead, Danny shucked his deck shoes and waded into the lake.

Moreau followed until they stood waist-deep in the water. Goat's camera captured the moment from a distance. In mere seconds the submersion was over, the water flattening Dan the Man's dark hair against his head and shoulders as he rose from beneath the lake's surface.

L.T. Moreau raised his eyes upward, his voice thunderous. "What are the heavens showing you, my lord?"

Danny's gaze fixed on a moving object returning to the towering cypress. "A bird."

"Hallelujah!" Moreau shouted.

The osprey had sailed down to the water but, startled by the preacher's exclamation, curled its wings into a stalling pattern. On an edited video the bird would hover above Danny's head, its body bathed in brilliant light, its timing symbolizing a moment of divine approval.

The charismatic preacher would remind his television audience that the Scrolls never said a dove should appear this time around. An osprey would fit the new messiah criteria even better.

ALONG WITH THE SWEETHEARTS, Easter welcomed Patrick to her class after breakfast. "I know some will be surprised at what we're learning today," she said. "Dr. Ronofski's new book says a mysterious agent, an elixir in our chromosomes, rejuvenates cells for an indefinitely long life. Right, Cheryl?"

Cheryl smiled. "Yes, you see, during a woman's procreation cycle this mystery prompter kills all genes damaging her body, which enables us to live a long, long time."

"*Then* what?" Freckles said. "We stop procreating and die?"

"Use it or lose it," Vanessa interjected.

"In his book," Easter said. "Dr. Ronofski says sex is the catalyst that puts in motion an internal prompter. It signals the body to produce offspring."

She fixed a knowing look on Patrick. "To remain youthful, we have to put a healthy sex regimen in place. That allows Mother Nature to activate our prompter." She poked him. "You get my drift, don't you, Casanova?"

He gave her a thumbs-up but a disturbing image intercepted his focus. The idea of Sorelle with Gabe Casper wracked his mind after overhearing her on the phone with him. *Already she's been with that sports agent four days in Destin. Four days. Outrageous!*

"Hello! Earth to Patrick. Are you with us?"

Her question jolted him back from the distraction. "Yes, still on board, sir...uh, ma'am."

"Good," she said. "After class, we'll continue rehearsals, but you'll also give the girls massage therapy—four per day."

He looked askance at her. "But what about writing comedy sketches? That takes time."

"Yes, I know. But focus first on the girls' physical therapy."

After the class was dismissed, renewing a discussion with Cheryl about the Maubilla skit held a strong appeal to him. "I've been thinking about expanding the skit about DeSoto," he said.

Cheryl smiled. "Great. I'd love to hear it."

"Yeah, it impressed me because it recalls the historical account of Tuscaloosa, legendary chief of the Maubillians, and his disastrous conflict with the famous explorer."

Cheryl cocked her head as if trying to remember. "Yes, Hernando DeSoto. He killed thousands of the natives and burned their village, like maybe he was mad over not finding any gold."

"Right, but in that same village of Maubilla, he found something more valuable. Yep, stumbled right over a greater treasure than gold without even recognizing what it was."

"I don't understand."

"Well, DeSoto should've been evaluating the Maubilla maidens instead. They were intelligent and healthy and had perfect symmetry of form—like our Sweethearts."

"Okay, so he could have improved Spanish genes with a mix of native Americans?"

"Exactly," he said. "The villagers' genomes were a fount of holistic genes."

"Um, so DeSoto must have been a dullard not to discern the obvious."

"Yeah, like a typical mercenary. His perspective failed him. Greed for gold blinded him to the New World's most valuable treasure. If he had only known what the natives had to offer, he could've struck real gold by mating with them and in that way mined their regenerative assets."

On the veranda she sat beside him in the glider. "Let's think about giving the skit new meaning," she said. "Suppose DeSoto missed that golden opportunity due to his obsession with fame."

"Fame?"

"Yes, Patrick, fame. Almost fifty years earlier, Columbus made a name for himself. DeSoto had to best him, so he decides to cash in bigtime. The incomparable beauty of the maidens distracted him but even that was not enough to overcome his quest for fame. If you had been in his shoes, would you have made the same mistake?"

"Of course not," he said. "With all the knowledge we have today about genetic matching, I'd have been shortsighted not to appreciate such an obvious treasure." He did a double-take. "Wait, was that a trick question? Yeah, and I walked right into it."

She smiled. "Never saw it coming, did you?"

"I've been blinded by my desire for fame and lost my perspective," he said. "Is that it?"

"Yes, so far you've failed to see us as the real treasure," she said. "Fame is secondary to making pedigree babies."

He grinned. "And the other option is...?"

Unsmiling, she said, "Making a couple of dozen babies. If you can't see that, then you're just as shortsighted as DeSoto was."

Boxed in by her logic, the need to review his value system took control. "C'mon, let's go join the girls at poolside. We can collaborate on that skit later."

But an hour later, diminutive Dodie Appling also hinted at making babies. A break at sundown found him chatting with Freckles but she made no mention of his proxy obligation.

Having realized by midweek that the daily massages were meant to be a conduit to sex with the Sweethearts, he confided to alpha leader Easter that acting as a paramour with the ingénues was outside his deal with her. "I may need to rework my contract," he said. "Why the obsession with babies?"

Easter spread her arms wide. "Patrick, reproduction is the key to our survival. You know how it works. Babies are the future of our cause. Why do you not appreciate that?"

"I do. I mean I really admire the girls, but the responsibility of a large family blows my mind."

"Large family? Patrick, we're building a whole new world. Class-A pedigrees are in line with a sacred command, yet you're thinking it's a burden on you?"

Stunned, he offered no reply.

A secondary thought bothered him as well. His love for Sorelle still lingered. Yet he had to admit being enthralled with the girls. They needed him. But was sex really that essential to their well-being? Why were the Scrolls concerned with babies? True, propagating a pedigree offspring made biological sense. It prevented heritable diseases, but no mandate from the New Scrolls was needed to do that. Like Sorelle, he doubted their authenticity.

Could he ever cut his ties with Sorelle?

Perhaps she had a place in his life. He tried to imagine his fondness for the Sweethearts replacing what he had long felt for her. But fondness was not love. And how could a self-respecting man love—truly love—more than one woman?

During the next three-day stretch, he realized the Sweethearts were an idea factory for comedy scripts. He marveled at their creativity. After their creations yielded the quality he had worried about losing, he was inspired to write antics with more urgency.

SITTING ALONE, Cheryl gazed out the window of the tour bus. She watched wispy clouds and imagined them tailgating like motor homes at a playoff game. The fantasy helped to abate her anxieties over the glamour troupe's debut game. But her private thoughts must now be penned. She side-glanced Patrick across the aisle and hand-covered her words.

> *Our Saturday debut game is 90 minutes away and all the girls are eager to play. Yikes! Patrick has me rhyming again. The girls compete for his look of approval. Easter directed us girls to watch a second video today behind closed doors. It involved a lover's verbal techniques.*

She paused to consider the power of suggestion.

> *I'm reluctant to express my feelings to Patrick. I fantasize about him. I'm Eve and he's Adam—pre-fig leaf days. So glad my parents support genetic matching, just as their ancestors did before them. Mom says love means we always improve our genetic composition. The pedigree cause is our gift to humanity. I hope Patrick appreciates that. By the way he looks at me, I think he desires more than friendship.*

Gertrude the guard steered the Silver Eagle along Scenic Route 98. Its destination, Fort Walton Beach, would host the Sweethearts' debut. Danny DiNago sat near his security guard while Patrick sat across the aisle from Cheryl. He guessed the muse might be helping her siphon ideas for comedy skits from the wellsprings of her fertile mind.

Such deep immersion in thought was not unusual for a writer of comedy lines. Her long-range look signaled she might be inspired to create a surprising twist in her script, perhaps some unforeseen turn of events.

A similar look had been worn by a thirteen-year-old with an odd light of mischief in his eyes years earlier. He seldom spoke up for himself when older kids called him Stubby or Shorty. And at fourteen when leggy girls in stuffed bras called him Half-Pint. Or at fifteen when a gymnastics teacher upgraded him to His Studness after seducing him in her upstairs apartment.

His mystique had grown at Bon Amite High. An elusive runner, he racked up nine touchdowns in four games. A rival coach's pull-quote in the newspaper said, *To stop him you first have to catch him, and that's the other problem.*

But the coach's mistress had her own designs on Patrick to complete her personal playbook. An unexpected visit by the coach put the kibosh on that tryst. Caught in the middle of an act, Patrick had far less wardrobe than alibi at the time.

During his senior year, winning felt like losing. Until he joined the drama club.

His teacher said his acting skills helped fill the school auditorium. His classmates dubbed him Wiseass, though Wise Man was his role in a Christmas play where he carried a star on a stick. The audience howled as he portrayed a bored klutz and lifted a donkey's tail onstage, imitated a fart, and pretended to faint. After that night, he began to imagine life as a standup comedian.

Modeling icon Sorelle Ebanetti fed that imagined life during his senior year and assured him of fame as an actor under her tutelage. Finally, someone not only believed in him, but loved him. Their practice sessions took time away from his family's heritage lessons. So rather than learn about Murph traditions, he preferred lessons in acting and lovemaking with Sorelle.

For a decade he had strived to become famous on his own. Until he met Easter on the set of *The Hotz Show*.

Five months he traveled and helped her recruit young women laden with talent, each endowed with pizazz and crowned with the kind of beauty he could only describe as luxurious.

Destiny, it seemed, had far-reaching plans for him—plans involving genetics. But how could he have foreseen those plans would also involve an offer to mate with twenty-one women? He wondered if his parents, and especially his great-grandmother, could forgive him. She had labeled him a prodigal and forced him to forfeit his land. But why must she think of him as anything less than a humorist?

And why did being an heir to farmland mean more to members of the Murph Land Collective than his pursuit of fame and fortune?

No doubt Eugenia would question his relationship with the Sweethearts. The Murphs, with all their agronomic wisdom, would also be shocked to learn female colleagues were open to not only coital contact with him, but impregnation as well.

He cringed to contemplate his family's reaction to his newest list of prodigal sins. How could he face his closest kin without feeling shame?

Twenty-Four

Reminders of Patrick's prodigal label seemed to follow him like a shadow, yet he imagined fame as a comedian would offset the stigma.

He recalled the rocky start that had thrown him off course in high school.

In his hometown of Bon Amite, a famous model with icicle-blue eyes had promised to mold him into a megastar. Sorelle had the Hollywood contacts needed for success. With his days honeyed in hope, he staked his future on her.

In his senior year he had scholarship offers from a few football programs, but Bayou Tech was always in contention for end-of-year championship bowl games. And Tech was known for its theater department as well. With Sorelle's tacit approval, he had enrolled there. He assumed she was willing to rendezvous with him on weekends. After all, they were in love.

But she, too, had an insatiable desire for the spotlight.

Clay Mason paid her top dollar to be the TV face of his deep-south auto dealerships. Rumors of Clay's infidelity with Sorelle persisted. In hometown Bon Amite, the rumor became a scandal.

As the years rolled by after his breakup with her, Patrick thought finding Sorelle's equal would be easy. Four marriages proved him wrong. His romantic life had become habitual rebounding when he married in succession a waitress, a stripper, a secretary, and a chef. But now, like a fantasy come true two decades later, Sorelle was back. He had never felt such elation and, at the same time, confusion.

Once again she ignited his suspicions of infidelity.

Another thought confused him. His yearning for female companionship had been a constant in his life. But he wanted more. He wanted love. Abiding love. Passionate love. Would his affection for Easter reach the level of intensity he had once felt for Sorelle?

His reverie was interrupted as the bus pulled into Paladin Park at Fort Walton Beach.

"Girls, y'all look like centerfolds," Easter said. "Keep in mind the Entertainment Hall of Fame awaits us. Your debut here today is the first step in that direction."

Leaving the bus, the Sweethearts closed ranks and pranced toward the fieldhouse as spectators filled the stands. An overflow crowd lined the barricades of the ball park. The blaring of trumpets and the squeal of party whistles greeted the girls as they began swagger-dancing while lobbing air kisses.

Patrick took the lead, bowed to the crowd of spectators, and pretended to stumble in his unlaced brogans. Quickly regaining his balance, he pranced forward but, following an acrobatic flip, he pitched onto the turf, as if his equilibrium had lost its battle with gravity.

Vanessa feigned alarm at the pratfall and summoned Anastasia and Cassie to assist her in helping Patrick to his feet. As the trio dusted him off, their efforts soon resembled a flogging. He broke free but soon introduced a dance that prompted the girls to join him in a choreographed series of jazzy moves as each showed their ability to synchronize with the fast-paced rhythm.

Heads topped with a fez, the Paladins welcomed the act in a thunderous roar of cheering. Across the field near the opposing team's dugout, host members displayed a large banner with a crusader shield at its center—purple on an aquamarine oval.

The girls' dance exhibition ended with them again sending kisses to the cheering crowd.

As Patrick returned to the busy sidelines, a bearded man approached. "Appears to me y'got more'n you can say grace over." With a handshake he introduced himself as the head fez, chief of the

Fraternal Order of Paladins. With other fezzes gawking at the girls, the chief went slack-jawed as Vanessa passed nearby, her iridescent gold bodysuit a perfect fit. Her teammates followed in her train as the afternoon sun gilded each uniform in resplendent points of light. A gold sheen shifted along their shapely contours like the colors in a soap bubble.

Easter's smile exuded charm as she took command. "Glam it up, girls, and round the bases with your shoulders back and chest out. More bounce to the ounce, tease to please."

Patrick kneeled on the grass to inventory the contents in his comedy bag: makeup, bicycle horn, cap pistol, cowbell, wand, straw hat, red bandana—all items used in his slapstick acts.

A motionless shadow clued him that someone large hovered nearby. A sidelong glance revealed Danny DiNago standing with arms folded, his gaze on the field of play.

"Our gals look like goddesses, don't they?" Danny said.

"Yep, they do, but where's Larry Lemoyne, our videographer? And why didn't he drive us here instead of Gertrude?"

"Larry? Oh, he's riding over from the airport with Goat and Sebastian." Doubt seemed to cloud Dan the Man's tone. "They have my keepsake video. Guess we got our signals crossed."

Still on his knees, Patrick tried to tamp down a sickening feeling in his gut. It seemed to him a crucial moment, the missing video a betrayal by the Brazilian conman.

"I suppose you're real proud of what's on the video, huh?" he said.

"Don't know yet. I haven't seen it."

"Where do you suppose Goat is now? Rio? Morocco? Jakarta? Istanbul?"

"Hey, man, all I know is Goat needed Sebastian to critique the thing."

Patrick's voice grated in agitation. "Don't depend on Goat giving it back to you. Sebastian will market it to a porn syndicate."

"Goat says it's not porn, man. Guaranteed. Besides, it's nothing we'd sell."

"But *they* will." Patrick's anger welled up as he imagined Easter's ten most photogenic girls exposed on the internet in sheer lingerie, perhaps topless. "How will the Sweethearts react when the syndicate starts circulating your skin flick?"

"Ha! I've got an army of lawyers, Shorty."

Patrick shook his head. "You actually think hucksters fear lawyers?"

Danny thrust a finger at the entry gate. "See? There he is with an attaché case. And the guy with him is Sebastian. And Larry Lemoyne is tagging along. Eat crow, man."

Still riled, Patrick rose quickly to his feet. "But the video could still get away from you."

"No way."

"Yes, way. You're being played."

"You're the one being played. Easter's keeping you on the hook. Who made the first move—you or her? It was her, right? Yeah, I thought so."

Patrick swallowed hard. "She told you?"

"Of course. We have no secrets 'tween us. But I ain't pissed, okay? I have a higher mission now and no concern for things of the flesh. I got the calling, man. It's on video. Got an eagle coming down to show divine approval. I'll soon be appearing on Gospel Galaxy."

"What the hell are you talking about?"

"I'm taking charge of things here on earth, man."

"What things?"

"Everything, thanks to Reverend Moreau. He's like John the Baptist, forerunner of me."

Patrick's mind reeled in disbelief. "You're kidding."

Danny turned his face skyward. "The Reverend has the gift of interpretation."

Patrick spun about. "Of all people, they pick on you to pull off a hoax like that. You're risking everything. And for what?"

Danny cast a pitying look at him. "I admit I was plenty skeptical myself. But just so you know, from this day forward you'll refer to me as Immanuel. I have many things to teach and it's all from the sacred New Scrolls and—"

"Oh, c'mon, Danny, L.T.'s been using religion as a front to scam people for two dozen years, or maybe longer."

"No, God has quickened me to lead his flock."

"Quickened? Damn. You sound like L.T."

"Yeah, quickened, and not just here in America. I got dominion over the planet. But I gotta set Sorelle straight. She has no discernment about things beyond worshipping mammon."

"Mammon?"

"Yeah, you know, money. It all fits, you see. God sent Reverend L.T. to help us save the world. You'll see proof when we shake all nations and watch their treasures come pouring in. Pedigrees will fill God's house with glory. Don't believe me? Read the *Analyzer* this week."

"*Analyzer*? Look, Danny, I don't doubt your—"

"Immanuel, remember? It's my new title-name."

"Okay, okay, but look, I...I understand insight may be a bit supernatural but that charlatan L.T. Moreau has a long history of using people and—"

"Play ball!" The head fez's voice boomed over a megaphone as the Paladins clamored to get a closer look at the visiting Sweethearts. "The S-A-S got to strut their stuff but we have a surprise for all y'all. Our Buxom Beauts Shenanigan Team will outdo them. Big Mama and her Bigity Broads in their prissy pants are about to parade their stuff."

Danny dusted off his hands. "It's a moment made for the media, so go for it, comedy man. And may you be richly blessed today, y'hear?"

In his oversized brogans, Patrick high-stepped onto the field of play. "And now I've gotta be the funny man? What a freakin' farce this is turning out to be!"

IN NEW YORK CITY's financial district, Teddy Crown eased past the reception area of his father's high-rise office. Voices inside the chairman's office piqued his curiosity. Through the door, slightly ajar, he overheard Krista, his father's secretary, raising her voice.

"But what else could I do?" she said. "I tried but Reggie must not find me attractive."

"Nonsense!" Samuel Crown tapped a ballpoint on his teakwood desk, the rhythm signaling his impatience. "Take your time, gain his confidence. Reggie has everyone thinking he's in charge of the pedigree program; even convinced our facilitator on the Alabama coast."

"Why would he do that?"

"I don't know, but I thought you could find out."

Teddy opened the door wide. "*I* know, but I'm damned sure not saying till I know who's on the level around here."

Krista whirled to face him. "Teddy, you...you're supposed to be in Washington."

"Changed my mind. I have to keep an eye on you two."

"Paranoid again, are we, Teddy?" she said.

"You would know, Krista." He shook a binder in his father's face. "This report reeks of fraud. It's high time we exposed Reggie and his scheme to rule the Order. The man has no respect for me as your successor."

"Successor? That would be a presumptive leap, Son."

Teddy shook the binder again. "I think not, Dad. Who else has the savvy to fill your shoes? Did I not warn you about Reggie a year ago? He bet big on that overweight boxer in Vegas and the guy won, against all odds."

"Teddy, I'm aware he fixes a fight now and then. He has scams of his own but—"

"You're getting soft, Dad. Let's rub Reggie out. I can get the job done inside a week."

The elder Crown lowered his gaze and shook his head. "Excuse us, Krista."

Krista sniffed, executed a smooth pirouette, and left the room.

"Why confide in sleazy Krista?" the younger Crown said. "She leaks info to Sorelle. She can't be trusted. Presumptive leap, you say? Look at Reggie. He cutthroat a deal with Goodnowe."

Samuel Crown's voice grew weak. "Sebastian is on top of that situation."

"Sebastian Rubleau? He's another one we can't trust. He pals around with Reggie at the race tracks. Reggie is building alliances to force you out."

"Reggie and I go way back, Son. As usual, your concerns are misplaced."

"Don't patronize me, dammit. Sorelle is a demented liar. And

Zipit Talent would never be what it is today without Reggie's money. She's no friend. Use her like she uses you."

"I have. Sorelle doesn't appreciate class-A pedigrees, but she will."

"Yeah? Did you know her new lover is the comedian? Yeah, Sorelle was sent by Reggie to hook up with the Murph guy. He's an interloper trying to replace my hero. That's against nature."

"Teddy, the comedian is there to sub for Danny."

"Sub? How?"

"We're betting on him to bed the Sweethearts."

"You can't be serious. Why? What makes Murph so frickin' special?"

"He'll make an ideal proxy, Son. And he'll keep ratings high on TV with the new show. We're also distracting him with the girls so he'll keep out of our facilitator's way."

Teddy paced the room. "That doesn't compute worth a damn, Dad. Since when does a stupid-ass comedian rob a man like Danny of his rightful harem?"

Samuel Crown's voice grew weaker. "Son, Murph's genetic profile is exceptionally rare. We're depending on him to round out Dr. Ronofski's perfect progeny program."

"Don't tell me he's extraterrestrial."

"No, of course not. Dr. Ronofski believes he could be one in a billion, though."

"How can that be?"

"If you must know, Miss Beaulieu says a special gene makes him super useful as a breeder."

Teddy began shadowboxing, throwing punches at an imagined foe. "No! You don't get it, Dad. How many Super Bowls has Murph won? None! No way America's hero can be replaced. I can take that useless comedian out."

Samuel Crown sighed. "We'll discuss this later, Son. I have a dinner date."

"With who, Krista the slut?"

The elderly Crown pushed a button on the landline, rose slowly from his chair, and welcomed Krista back into the room. She rushed to his side, her look fixed sternly on his young namesake. The younger Crown stalked from the room.

"I overheard the slut insult," Krista said, her voice low. "I understand your affection for Teddy, but why is he obsessed with Danny? Are you sure Teddy is a copy of you?"

"Clones are not identical, Krista. He seems to be cursed, perhaps even doomed."

"Doomed? What do you mean?"

"No one is allowed to break the vow of unity." His breathing wheezy, he gasped for air while he searched a desk drawer. "My meds, where did I put them?"

"Here, hon, sit down," Krista said. "I'll pour some water for you."

Hands trembling, he accepted the glass. "I wanted a son, but now I have to ask if he's a son in the truest sense. Something is missing, some imbalance that makes him act, well...bizarre."

She searched the drawer and found the pills. "Teddy has no compassion, Sam."

He nodded. "And no real trust in me. I have to face it. Teddy can't be *me* made over."

She offered a chair. "A clone is a genetic twin, isn't it?"

"Who really knows about these things, Krista?"

"But isn't cloning horses how that Argentine polo player kept winning?"

He leaned against her, refusing to sit. "Yes, Adolpho... What's his name?"

"I don't know," she said. "Here, take your pills."

He downed the meds with a sip of water. "The comedian is on Teddy's hit list. But warning the guy would show our hand. Find an indirect way to inform him."

"Yes, I'll make the call to Sorelle."

"No, call Buzz, but tell him to be discreet."

TWENTY-FIVE

Sluggish waves rolled ashore at Sanctuary Beach and a soft breeze stirred a lofty copse of trees along Peninsula Road. Pelicans hunted for baitfish. By midmorning the blazing sun conspired with the high humidity to push the heat index to one-hundred-ten degrees, threatening dehydration. Crabs augered deeper into the sand.

Later in the afternoon on the patio, an umbrella canopy provided shade where Easter summoned Patrick to drink iced tea and relax in wicker chairs.

"This is for your edification," Easter said as she read from her iPad.

He listened while watching the Sweethearts in the pool play dump-the-rider.

Easter stressed a key word as she read to him. "'The more *equal* a society, the more heritability factors into excellence.'" She blanked her tablet. "Got the message? Your destiny is clear. You'll be our conduit between Heaven and Earth to help equalize society while there's still hope."

"Conduit? First, I'm a script-writing comedian, then a coach for twenty-one actresses. How do I convince my agent that my resumé should include conduit? Agents book entertainers, not flakes."

"You're no flake for believing—" Her mouth remained open while the ringtone on her cellphone interrupted her words. She motioned Patrick to follow her inside the mansion. "Hi Mr. Creel," she said into the phone while entering the parlor. "Yes, you'll be in our movie but you can't do that to her."

Patrick wanted to ask what the rich golfer had in mind.

"I'm not letting that happen," she said after a pause. "Take care not to violate my ethics, okay? See you tomorrow on the set." Sighing, she ended the call. "He doesn't love me."

"Who? Slack Creel?"

"No. Sorry, hon, but my thoughts jumped track. I'm thinking Immanuel caters to Vanessa and her every whim. When I told him about my love for you, he shrugged it off."

"Uh, one question," he said. "Why did you tell him about us?"

"Why *not* tell him? I wanted to test his reaction to the proxy idea." She raked back her hair, fully revealing her photogenic face with its light olive complexion. "Let's sit out on the veranda."

On the back lot, the tangy aroma of bay waters stole past tall pines and scraggly sand oaks. Far out on the bay a dark cloud, its underbelly ash-gray with sheets of rain, bulled toward the shoreline. On the south side of the peninsula, another bank of clouds, jagged with lightning, brought a corkscrew wind and the faint odor of rain.

He closed the double French doors and sat beside Easter on the glider love seat. "What's up? Is Slack being difficult about Danny's little movie?"

Easter sighed. "That man will never change. The film has one scene with him and Vanessa. You won't believe what he suggested. He's too hormonal." She flashed a disarming smile. "So tell me, hon, are any of my actresses madly in love with you yet?"

He pushed against the floor to keep the glider moving. "I'm getting to know them all better and I'm bonding with them."

"Bonding?" she said. "How about the populate mandate? Have you forgotten? I want you to put them in orbit. You know, like you do me. Well, not exactly like me. I'm way too theatrical."

"Uh-huh, but hey, with you I'm enthralled by it all."

She nodded at a mockingbird's pursuit of a flying bug landing on the far end of the porch railing. "Speaking of theatrics, Doc Ronofski sent a batch of videos. They show couples and their children, all exemplifying genetic misfits." She folded her legs into a lotus position. "To have humanity's devolving gene pool do a one-eighty turnabout, he says we have to create more urgency. We can do that easily, he said, by dramatizing the horror of dysgenic misfits."

"That could backfire on us," Patrick said. "Besides, we're about comedy, not horror."

"Darling, people witness the horror of its reality every day," she said. "They accept it as normal, some even saying it's God's will. That myth has to go. We'll hype the difference on TV."

He rested an arm over her shoulder. "Speaking of horrible reality, a monster hurricane is brewing out in the gulf."

"I know. It's not far from us, and it's the opportunity we've been waiting for. Immanuel wants to demo his first miracle."

"Miracle?"

"Yes, and just like that—" she snapped her fingers "—it'll boost his credentials."

"Huh? Just how does this boosting thing work?"

"Immanuel will command the storm to cease and desist. And standing at the end of the state pier at Gulf Shores—ta-dah!—we will be there for all the world to see."

"We? Who is *we*?"

"Danny and me. Imagine the networks competing for coverage of that event. Can't you just see millions glued to their TV sets, all breathless with anticipation? It'll go viral for sure. The media will eat...it...up!"

"So will morticians. They thrive on absentee IQs."

"Patrick, have you no faith?"

"Not when miracles have to be staged."

"But this is made for the media. It's high time Danny, uh—Immanuel—validated himself like the powerful messiah he is."

"But he could drown, credentials and all."

"So you think just because he can't swim, he'll panic? That's all the more reason to do it. You know faith without works is dead."

"Uh-huh, and faith without a backup plan is deader, and in the water. Even the beach mouse has a plan B. It digs an extra tunnel with an exit hatch below the top of its sand dune. State authorities will force you and your last-chance messiah to evacuate. It's a hurricane, remember. They suck—literally."

"No, darling. Immanuel will prevail. C'mon, let's go back inside."

He stood to follow her. "I'll need to know y'all's next of kin."

"Why?"

"In case a wave slaps y'all sideways from Sunday."

"But everything's in his favor," she said. "Besides, I'll be there with him."

"Not if I can help it."

"I hear you, yes, but don't worry. Our success is assured. In fact, it's foretold in the New Scrolls. They predict no harm will befall us, no matter what."

He tugged her forearm as she opened the French doors. "Look, Easter, I realize you can pull rank on me anytime. This glamour show is not my baby, it's yours, but you and this showbiz troupe are a big part of *my* life now, not to mention my future as an entertainer."

"Don't worry, darling. I know CPR."

I'm serious," he said. "I should have a say in what happens to you. I love you."

"That's so sweet of you," she said. "And it's really heartwarming to know you care."

"Care? Yes, I care. This is about life. Isn't life about good choices? Like choosing the best mate? Don't get me wrong, but there has to be a better way to dramatize Immanuel's, uh, whatever. Daredevil grandstanding like that is not the way to do it. It's just too risky."

She poked him playfully. "Just earn your proxy status and do right by the Sweethearts. Focus on the journey, not the destination, and remember to make eye contact while you're at it."

"Hey, you're the one who said don't fall in love."

"Not you. *Them.* It's okay for them to fall in love. Love builds unity. Please make each of the girls feel super special. That part of your role is preordained, too."

"Preordained? How would you know that?"

"Patrick, it's in the Scrolls. Seven different girls will become pregnant every six months."

"Which ones?"

"I don't know yet but when they start to show, they'll glow, so look for a nimbus about their heads. We know seeing is believing and believe me, you're sure to see it."

He studied her eyes. "Are you one of the seven? You know, to get seeded."

"No, not initially, but don't let my matriarch status stop you from romancing me."

NEAR MIDNIGHT CHERYL remained awake inside her mansion bedroom and reminisced over the prospect of being a star. Moments later in the den she settled into the lounge chair and jotted down her thoughts.

What buffoonery! The Paladins spoofed us in garish drag at their park. Redneck Boutique with gaudy Mardi Gras beads, pink wigs, reptile belts, tight Spandex pants, sequined mini-skirts, tattoos and bare feet with painted toenails. Patrick and I stayed behind on the tour bus at the mansion later, alone after the game. I asked why he confides in me more than the other Sweethearts. "Because you inspire confidence," he said. "Like the sun warms the soil to germinate seed, I write better because you inspire me to grow in my role as a comedy entertainer. I'd love to know that I inspire you, too."

She pondered the words before continuing.

I melt under the spell of his eloquence. He's a divine provision for us, but I hope he'll see us past the storm Buzz Cassidy said is destined to arrive here tomorrow. I'm scared. I've seen all the devastation on TV that hurricanes can bring to coastal towns. It's horrendous!

THE FOLLOWING DAY AT NOON, as customers gradually left the Bon Mot Diner, Patrick took a seat in its back section where the *Sanctuary Sentinel* lay askew on an oilcloth-covered table. Outside the eatery, a busy crew of carpenters hammered sheets of plywood over its windows.

A server approached him in a green uniform. Her elbows jutted outward. He recognized the folds of skin on her neck and her low-set ears as evidence of a genetic disease that affected the thyroid gland. She stood only four feet tall.

"Does Charlene still work here?" he asked.

"She's off today," the young woman said.

He grinned. "I know her from school. I wanted to talk with her about regenerative matching."

"What's that?"

"It's when you match the best human genes, male and female, to produce better babies." In an instant, he regretted his insensitivity.

She placed a glass of water on the table. "Better pray 'bout that one. What if their better kids turn out icky freaky?"

"Huh?"

"You know, like them punk babies in 'pocalypse movies. Mutant kids act paranoid crazy."

He wanted to reassure her but decided instead to order seafood gumbo. As she strode away, he studied the newspaper. Its bold headline read, *Emblot Victims Enraged.* The article revealed a scientist had refused bids on his technology for an emblot cure. The researcher, found dead in his garage, had no history of depression. *What the hell?*

The report mentioned stocks had fallen at gene editing companies. He wondered who might gain by denying cures for diseases that included Black males. A deep sadness enveloped him. Could the world have a worse disease to plague humans?

Hurricane preparations outside the diner triggered thoughts of his daughter in Sarasota. On his cellphone, Angelina's recorded voice reminded him the Ringling School of Art was first in America to award a doctorate to a woman. His daughter's salutation, "Life is short, art is long," brought with it pride in knowing his only child was thriving.

He left a message: "Storm's a-coming, I'm a-going. May you outlive art, Ange. I love you."

He tried to call Eugenia in Bon Amite and congratulate the centenarian on her birthday. Knowing she'd ignore it, he left no message. It vexed him to recall she had fated his prodigal status by setting him adrift without the customary blessing.

A call to Naomi Savoie, a friend in Georgia, ranked high on his list. He hung up before activating her voicemail. What could account for his restless behavior? Anxiety over a coming storm? He decided not to call his agent, opting instead to write new comedy scripts.

He ordered another bowl of hot gumbo as an idea slid from his subconscious. In the side pocket of his cargo pants he found an envelope. With a pen he wrote: *Nurse, I'm hot... Sorry, sir, but hot is not on our list of diseases... Well, what I mean is, I have a hot temp... Fine, call the fire department... But I'm not on fire... Okay, then take my lighter....*

The timing of inspiration was not his to question. Besides, what did a whimsical muse know of time constraints? For a comedy writer, ten minutes might become two hours.

He wrote almost as fast as the barrage of ideas filled his mind. After using all the space on the envelope, he scribbled on the newspaper. His notes found open spaces around shoe ads, across scenic tours, and on white wedding gowns. He wedged ideas next to astrology charts and green energy news. As phrases bombarded his brain, he jotted around editorials before also finding space near auto ads, real estate listings, employment ads, and finally, obituaries.

He growled as a phone call jolted him back to reality.

The voice belonged to Cheryl. "Where are you? The girls are nervous."

"Nervous about what?"

"The storm. It's gaining strength and drawing closer by the minute."

"Okay, but where's Easter?"

"Gone with Immanuel and still babbling about some miracle and telling us to stay put here."

"Stay put? No! Okay, I'm on my way there."

He tucked the newspaper under his arm, paid his tab for the gumbo, and left with dire thoughts of Easter risking her life. He tried calling her as he drove southbound on Highway 59. As each call failed to connect, he worried that the glamour troupe's fate hinged on Easter staying alive.

Frustrated, he spoke into the unresponsive phone. "Where's Danny? Why's he trying to prove a point about power? Damn him! My career depends on you, Easter. This is ridiculous!"

He continued calling her while trying to imagine the fallout from a dead new age messiah. The bad news itself might stymie the regenerative cause. Speeding faster, he breathed a silent prayer. Or was it a eulogy? Writing epitaphs, he reminded himself, was not in his job description. Nor did he want to be a pallbearer. *Please, not another hijacking.*

NEWS OF EASTER'S absence struck Patrick hard on his arrival at the mansion. As a stress reliever, he nailed plywood over glass windows alongside Buzz Cassidy and his crew.

During a break, Vanessa drew Patrick aside. "How could you forget about us?"

"Okay, I'm flawed," he said. "But what's a doughnut without a hole?"

"Uhm, yeast?" she said.

Taking her hand, he invited her to help find a storm update on his smartphone. Meteorologists gave the coordinates of the hurricane as fifty miles southeast of Biloxi, Mississippi. Updates speculated that it would hit the Alabama coast by six p.m. at ninety miles per hour.

Others predicted it would increase to one hundred twenty shortly before slamming Mobile Bay.

With his shoulder-length hair and neatly-trimmed beard, Danny appeared on streaming devices as the man whose power would neutralize the coming tempest. News of his predicament filled social media more than highway congestion and escape routes.

Shock-jock pundits dominated the airwaves with sensational exaggerations.

None were more dominant than Luther T. Moreau who had prerecorded himself with Danny for the event. "The Almighty," L.T. announced, "will soon prove his son's majesty. Immanuel stands at the end of the Gulf State Park pier. We await his validation."

A camera strapped to pilings on the pier streamed images to viewers who followed the drama in real time. A half-hour later, stronger gusts whipped sand and salt-laden spray across the yard at Sanctuary Beach.

Steering a golf cart, Buzz approached the mansion driveway.

"Don't waste no more time here," he called. "We'll get it head-on. Seventy-foot waves gonna wash house and all slap off this peninsula and dump it in Mobile Bay."

Patrick left the porch and joined him in the yard. "Dan the Man will stop it...maybe."

"Yeah, but go-go DiNago better do it in a hurry," Buzz said. "You got worries even without a storm, though. A nutty New Yorker's got you in his crosshairs. Y'all better be leaving the peninsula now or forget saving life and limb."

Patrick squinted his eyes against the wind as an empty trash can tumbled across the lawn. "I'm hoping Easter shows up but I understand we're taking a big risk every minute we stay here."

Arriving with the brim of her visor cap low, Cheryl studied Patrick's eyes. "Will we be safe on the bus, honey?"

"Yeah, we'll be fine. What storm can harm God's sweet angels? Count on me to keep y'all safe."

She pointed at huge waves along the shoreline. "Be glad sea oats are stopping erosion of the sand dunes," she said. "And we can thank beach mice for spreading the oat seeds." After a hug, she hurried into the house to join her companions.

Buzz's wide-eyed gaze followed her. "Man-oh-man, them gorgeous gals..." He slapped himself in mock discipline. "Danny's a big deal on TV, way bigger than the hurricane. He gets enough without pulling stunts like that."

"Enough? Enough of what?"

Buzz's eyes narrowed. "Publicity, man. What did you think I meant? Poontang?"

"Not hardly. What are the talking heads on TV saying about him?"

Buzz scratched the stubble on his chin. "Reverend Moreau says stopping the storm might run up the flag on the super jock's creds, but Bishop O'Brien comes on TV and says any dying Danny's gonna do just shows him to be a souped-up imitation."

"The Bishop said that?"

"Yep. Said Lloyds o' London got an escape clause on their insurance contract, something called a Martyr Exception. And no exceptions for radical activists, either."

"Cross your fingers, Buzz. Immanuel may go one better than Houdini and slip away without a scratch." He braced against a sudden blast of wind. "You mentioned some nut has me in his crosshairs. Seriously, is he a hit man?"

"Phone!" Cheryl beckoned to Patrick from the mansion doorway. "Emergency!"

Patrick ran up the steps. On the landline, Easter's voice crackled and broke in the airwaves.

"What's up?" he said.

"I'm with Danny at Gulf State Park. Stay put at the mansion with the...."

"Hey, your cellphone is breaking up. You can't weather the storm out there. Leave now!"

"I'll be okay...has to be done...no better time...."

"No! Too chancy. With you and Danny gone, no team, no solidarity, no nothing."

"Listen, baby, I love you but Sorelle's fat-cat attorneys are trying to—" her words came out garbled once again "—injunction against Immanuel."

"Don't do this, Easter. We need you. *I* need you. I love you."

"We'll make it...alive so do like...told you...." The phone died and cut her message short.

He hung up the phone to face Cheryl. "Let's help the Sweethearts load the bus," he said. "This storm is too close and Easter won't listen. I'm defying her order and leaving this death trap."

As the Sweethearts boarded the bus, Vanessa flipped a coin and called heads for a seat alongside Patrick. Tails won. Lips pouty, she took a seat across the aisle, stuck out her tongue at Cheryl, and drew a bottle of sherry from a bulging handbag.

"Time for party central to get cranked up," she said while holding the bottle high. "You do the honors, Patrick, but it's not champagne so don't expect much to happen."

With Larry Lemoyne driving, the girls gathered in the lounge area at the rear of the bus. They pushed the partition aside to reveal a wide-screen television, a wet bar, and a sofa bed.

Most of them stood watching updates of the storm's erratic

progress as television anchors and on-site reporters talked about the famous football player.

On the lighted pier, remote-controlled cameras zeroed in on Danny who stood alone. The wind whipped his white robe, unfurling it like a flag. Saltwater spray blew horizontally in hard gusts and bathed him in its gauzy haze. Newscasters gave viewers a continuous update.

Patrick's thoughts turned to Easter. Was she at the state pier? Had she found shelter in the area?

Immanuel's silhouette turned from gray to black on television as he clung to the side railing with waves crashing harder against the pier. Short of a miracle, the demigod would be swept into the roiling gulf waters. The girls sobbed as camera lights on the state pier dimmed. A few prayed aloud.

Patrick's fleeting thoughts of managing the entertainers alone without Easter struck him now as a real possibility. The Sweethearts' future now rested on the shoulders of Patrick Murph—comedy coach, trainer, conduit, failure.

Failure? No! He could not abide the thought of failing them.

TWENTY-SIX

As the hurricane positioned itself to blast the shoreline, Patrick hesitated to tell the Sweethearts that Dan the Man, being human, faced the possibility of drowning in vain to prove his messiah credentials.

Larry steered the bus along Peninsula Road as torrents of rain pummeled it. Eighteen miles east of the mansion, he turned and drove north on Highway 59, passing barricades that blocked all southbound vehicles. Short of I-10 he faced bumper-to-bumper traffic. Inching forward, the bus came to a standstill thirty miles inland at a small town known for its strawberry festival.

Patrick hurried to the front of the bus to better assess the potential danger. Only one block ahead, police officers in yellow raingear stood at an intersection while sheets of rain blurred flashing lightbars on their patrol cars.

Two men, their ponchos swirling like spastic dancers, pushed a stalled vehicle into the parking lot of a farmer's co-op. Torn from the building, a long section of tin roofing skidded along the pavement and lifted to crash into an RV outfitted with a satellite dish twenty yards ahead of the girls' bus.

Like a vicious reaper, the wind scythed through the town as a black cloud dipped low and turned pine needles into arrows. Limbs ripped from a tree clubbed the sheet-metal siding of the co-op, the noise like clanging cymbals. The yellow awnings of a convenience store tilted and rose precariously. Pieces of tile torn from a roof became projectiles. As if released from grenade launchers, the tiles rocketed across the road and shattered windows between the metal bars of a pawn shop across the street. Alarms added to the chaos in a stand-alone café next door.

During the melee, Patrick shouted for the girls to fasten their seatbelts. An eerie calm followed. It allowed a peek at the aftermath of nature's assault. All road traffic remained in halt mode. The store awning, suggesting a prehistoric creature with giant wings, lay sprawled and twisted across the highway.

"Close call," Larry said as he crouched near Patrick.

"Yeah, a tornado dipped down," Patrick said. "I'm more worried about Easter now than ever."

"Me, too," Larry said. "Talk about dodging the paparazzi, this storm did the trick."

The girls, some visibly shaken, unbuckled and huddled near Patrick. From the door of the bus a rapping sound surprised them. The WMOP news vehicle, a sturdy RV, had survived the tornado's assault.

Larry opened the door before Patrick could object.

A diminutive, dark-haired woman with sharp features set in a long face confronted them. Her perky demeanor familiar to viewers along the coast, Trudy Mickelstein introduced herself as WMOP's TV reporter. She and her cameraman, in their rubber boots and rain ponchos, hurried aboard. She easily maneuvered past Larry toward the girls, her microphone pointing in search of fresh news.

"Roads are congested in all directions," Trudy announced. "This storm is packing enough wind to rip your wisdom teeth out. How do you voyagers feel about riding in a top-heavy bus with disaster so clearly imminent?"

"*Immiment?*" Vanessa said as she emerged from the group. Facing the camera, she displayed a bottle of sherry as if to toast the reporter. "It's okay, we've got a good luck charm trapped in here with us. Lordymercy, y'all! Behold Pat McGroin." Her voice, mimicking the soprano pitch of an opera star, rose an octave above middle-C. "Bring on the *immimeeeeeent!*"

Patrick pulled her away from the journalist's ambush. "Sorry, but wine sets her tongue free of its hitching post."

"What brand are we drinking?" Trudy said.

"*Aphrodiiisiac!*" Vanessa blurted, eyes wide as poker chips and arms raised like a preening bird. "If this egg flips funny-side up, the yolk will be on us. Cluckety-cluck-*cluuuck!*"

Semi-apologetic, he said, "She's our team prankster. Pay her no mind or she'll show her behind."

"How's your comedy show doing?" Trudy asked, her mike moving in search of a wry comment. "After Danny DiNago's stunt today, your ratings should go through the roof."

Vanessa drank from the bottle. "Wanna hear a naughty one?"

"Told ya," Patrick said as Trudy nodded. "It's show-her-behind time."

Vanessa hopped onto Patrick's back. "This clown's stage name is Stumpy. Know why? 'Cause he has to stand on a stump to mount his mares. *Heee-hawww!*"

The pot-bellied cameraman began shaking in uncontrollable mirth. Trudy looked askance at him, her brow squiggling up as she shook her head, though a grin soon spread into a smile and smoothed the cleft in her pointy chin.

Amazed that Vanessa's antics seemed to relieve tensions, Patrick scrunched into a seat to avoid the WMOP newscaster. Vanessa's ploys were enough, he thought, to amuse the slim reporter and her portly cameraman.

Trudy's live report aired with the Sweethearts laughing in the background. "Of all the hotspots I've covered today," she said, "what could be hotter than girls celebrating till they reunite with Dan the Man—a.k.a. Immanuel. Is he Houdini reincarnated? That escape artist's road to fame ended in tragedy. But let's hope Danny Boy beats the odds. Not likely, though, unless you believe in miracles."

Soon after Trudy and her cameraman left the bus, the girls' upbeat spirit returned to gloom. It left Patrick wishing he could offset Trudy's assumption about the likelihood of tragedy.

An hour passed before reporters announced the storm had begun wobbling toward Florida where it became a tropical disturbance. Meteorologists expressed puzzlement. Some asked why the storm had suddenly lost its punch. Others speculated that an unseasonable cold front may have blunted it.

Another hour crawled by before a follow-up report by the Coast Guard assured Danny's fans that he and Easter were found alive. Drenched but robed, Danny said, "Upon my command the winds calmed and the waters stilled. I saw angels hovering within the torrents around me."

Patrick breathed a sigh of relief as the bus resounded with the girls' cheers.

A few Sweethearts adjusted recliner seats and relaxed to music on headphones. Patrick instructed Larry to drive to a nearby parking lot before he eased to the rear of the bus to join some who lay resting.

The girls, formless in the dark beyond the partition, stirred as he spoke. "I'm proud of y'all," he said. "You never lost hope and that's remarkable. Enjoy your sleep, girls, and sweet dreams."

Yet sleep eluded him on the bus. What were the odds of a severe storm suddenly waning so fast? Could a cold front move hurricanes in a different direction—in August? It defied reason. But, other than levitating, what might boost supernova Immanuel's confidence higher? Would he now be seen as more than a genetic savior? Even if skeptics scoffed at his miracle claim, none could deny the outcome. But what about next time? He might be credited for a bona fide one today, yet his next stunt—like that of Houdini—could be his last.

Patrick's thoughts lingered on his predicament. *Why am I into this wellborn business? How long will my youth gene obligate me to the pedigree program? Suppose gene matching is not a panacea? Will my agent backlist me on the comedy circuit?*

THE FOLLOWING morning at 11:00, Patrick picked his way past debris cluttering Peninsula Road in hopes of a cold brew at the Swash-buckler Pub.

Jacki gazed at him a moment, then at Buzz before offering each a draft beer in a frosted mug. "You'ens look like something left over from the saltwater breakers," she said. "I guess these are on the house. But I'm surprised Danny's hotdoggin' on the pier didn't get his butt killed. Reports say him 'n Easter done run off to Pensacola to join preacher Moreau at his TV studio. Then she'll fly to Tampa for a movie shoot at the Shamrock. Erratic weather makes you wonder about climate change."

"Bishop O'Brien is dumpin' on him," Buzz said. "Says he's a heretic. What'll Danny do next?"

Patrick raised a hand to interrupt Buzz's chatter. "Sorelle?" Through the breezy archway opening to the Sanctuary Inn lobby, her figure—along with her familiar runway strut—caught his attention.

Buzz's fingers curled to imitate binoculars. "She's double-timing to her room with a package."

Jacki winked at Patrick. "Where's *she* been all this time?"

"Away on business," he said. "I'm curious to find out where."

"Does she still want to kick Easter's keister?"

"It's a standoff, Jacki," Patrick said while finishing his beer. Seconds later he took the stairs and knocked on Sorelle's door with his rat-a-tat-tat rhythm. He entered in response to her voice. "Been safe from the storm?" he asked as she turned away. She stepped barefooted to the kitchenette, placed a cup in the microwave, and set its timer, all done without comment.

Without looking his way, she moved a package from a chair to her bed. "Your glamour troupe is broke, yet all you can muster is a question. How about a thank-you?"

"For what?"

"For finding out things you could never find on your own. It's called research. But first, you owe me an apology."

"Me? Owe you?" His hand gestured like that of an overly excited stage director. "What I heard was Gabe having to do *without it* at home and you're there for him."

Grinning, she removed a cup from the microwave, opened a box of decaf packets and eased one into the hot water. "So you heard friendly banter between colleagues. So what? I was busy negotiating a lucrative deal." She glanced at her Rolex First Lady, its diamonds glistening. "But next I need to grab a bite to eat, get my hair done, do some shopping, and relax with a mudpack."

"Busy girl, you," he said, imitating the Creole idiom used in his standup routines.

She frowned. "Busy? Yeah, I've been busy charming a man who owes me."

Chuckling, he said, "And did you collect without disrobing?"

She spun about to face him. "Stop it, Patrick. Hear me out. I know an information broker who can help us. When I realized the storm was headed to Florida, I took a private jet to New York. With me you could have a Hollywood future, but only if you get your head on straight."

He dropped into a sofa chair by the window. "Uh-huh, I can't wait to hear this one."

"Scoff away but Gabe helped me dig up things on Rubleau Entertainment." She stirred creamer into her coffee. "Here's the deal. To my dismay Sebastian is producing a slew of porno movies through a subsidiary. His partner is none other than Goat Goodnowe."

"Tell me something I *don't* know," he said. "I know they own Orgo Cinematic—together."

"But Goat scams investors and makes deposits in Antigua and Brazil and Panama."

He rose and stood at the window to gaze at the cobblestone courtyard below. "Yeah, some are wired to deceive," he said. "Like it's assimilated by their bodies without first going through egg or sperm, otherwise known as an epigenetic mark."

"Not that again." She moved to the loveseat. "Despite what Dr. Ronofski says, our DNA is part hobgoblin. We're victimized by carcinogens in the air and water, not just heredity."

"You'll get no argument from me," he said. "DNA can be altered by pollutants to cause birth defects, abnormal sperm, and infertility. Records show that's why we humans are at the lowest fertility level ever. To have better babies, what we need is, oh I don't know, better breeders?"

"Patrick, all our people were flawed. You can't redo your ancestry."

"True, but we have to start somewhere and I'm one of those who've never been sick. Neither have the Sweethearts. Diseases can be prevented with good gene matching."

"Interesting. But tell me what's in the gene matching deal for L.T. Moreau."

"L.T. stands for Light Touch," he said. "At least to me it does. Moreau claims to have the sort of wisdom that allows him to interpret the Bible plus a book he's calling the New Scrolls."

She aimed the television remote. "What a charlatan. Pardon me but would you care to watch one of my clients? He has the lead in a made-for-TV movie."

Patrick made a face. "Why not tell me what happened in Destin?"

Unblinking, she gazed at him. "If it matters, Gabe's fiancée was there in Destin with us the entire time. Edith doesn't mind that Gabe kids around with me. In fact, Gabe and I were busy discussing ways to finagle a better deal from Tookie Ward."

"Tookie? Owner of the Marauder's franchise?"

She shook a finger at him. "Patrick, this conversation never took place if you betray me. I have a tentative deal for a billion glorious dollars, including perks, all for Danny's football re-up."

"A billion? No jock has ever been offered a billion bucks."

She slapped the armrest. "Five-year package. It includes stock in thirty casinos, plus a biggie in Dubai and one in Hong Kong, not to mention other treasures that will remain undisclosed."

"Who's paying for all this, Tookie Ward's company?"

"Companies, love—plural. Believe me, this is historic, a splendid moment that'll shake the world of professional sports like nothing ever has."

Patrick grinned. "Does he know Danny's true identity?"

"Is that supposed to be funny?"

"Maybe. Is Weather God of the Year funny? If he can stop a hurricane, he just might be worth a coin or two held by the Federal Reserve."

"The storm slowing down was a coincidence," she said. "But it bothers me. I mean, suppose his next so-called miracle fails? It could be deadly."

"Exactly my thoughts. But how many people do we know who follow psychics?"

"Are you saying his miracles don't necessarily have to be real?"

"Well, look at Nostradamus. His predictions failed over a hundred times. Pro wrestlers earn big bucks faking it and they don't even have a punch line."

"Drum roll for the punster," she said in light-hearted mockery.

"Do you realize how much real history is whitewashed to hide injustices and outright atrocities?"

"I know, but my client is the world's hottest hunk and I can't bear the idea of him making a fool of himself. He must sign the new contract and keep playing football, then win a fifth Super Bowl. With so much on the line, it's scary to think Easter forbids him to play. Who does she think she is?"

He looked longingly at her, unable to deny the attraction that drew him to her. "When your neck is exposed, it brings back erotic memories. I gave you hickeys back then, remember? I always liked your hair pinned up in a stylish sweep, like cotton candy."

She lay back on the sofa. "Cotton candy? Oh yes, at the county fair. And it wasn't so long ago. I still can't resist your smile and those big baby blues. And the way you look at me. Some feelings never change, do they?"

Patrick knew his heart had accepted her back even as his better judgment counseled against it. Once again her charm swayed him, yet the miasma of doubt lingered. Was he nurturing a love destined to fail?

What was the saying? *Fools rush in....*

TWENTY-SEVEN

After the storm, Raul "Goat" Goodnowe moored his yacht at Sanctuary Marina. He and his Hollywood guest, Sebastian Rubleau, watched dailies of *Star Harem* in the yacht stateroom.

Goat muted the television. "An absurdity happened yesterday," he said. "We shot the *Star Harem* movie in the Bon Secour Wildlife Refuge. It's a scene made for Vanessa, but Slack Creel is the antagonist and he decides on too much realism with her. Creel is in character with his swagger and bragging about how much better he is at acting than fucktard DiNago."

"What? He called Dan the Man a fucktard? What a put-down."

"Yeah, Slack was drinking single malt whiskey. Vanessa freaked out when he pinned her down, but Danny steps in and slings him aside like a sack of potatoes. If a scene needed real drama, that was it. Slack takes a swing at Danny, still mocking him, but then he bolts away. Danny gives chase and throws a rolling body block, knee level, from behind on Slack."

"That's illegal," Sebastian said. "Referees eject players from the game if they do that."

Goat's gaze turned dreamy. "Yes, yes, yes, it can turn a man's spine into a noodle."

"Is Slack hurt bad?"

Goat sipped his tea. "You might say it'll be a while before he can putt a golf ball past his own shadow." He licked his lips. "It was such a thrill to watch."

Sebastian shrugged. "Yeah, well, shit happens. How many clients are you ripping at the clinic?"

"Fifty per day on average. The *Analyzer* will run the second installment of my story tomorrow. It'll feature ten of the girls, along with excerpts from the Scrolls."

"Okay, but what about the clinic? It is a gold mine, isn't it?"

"Megabucks every week, man. Invoices paid by government vouchers."

Sebastian squinted. "How much actual profit are we talking about?"

Goat hesitated as he nursed his tea. "A hundred grand per customer but we're supposed to issue a voucher of eighteen grand to each impregnated woman. Pregnancies have to be verified and then coded soon after their next monthly visit before payments begin."

"Ahhh, verified. That's the catch, right?"

"Right. Since they're never pregnant, we don't pay. It keeps them running in circles."

"Do they really think it's the so-called messiah's sperm they're receiving?"

"Yeah, like holy seed. We'll soon have billions in our offshore account."

"Good, but how does Senator Blockton prevent regulators from interfering?"

"Easy. Given all the cutbacks in regulatory funding, their lean team of investigators looks like Gandhi on a hunger strike."

"But what if some reporter gets wise to the scheme? Leaks happen, you know."

"No problem," Goat said. "Our media pundits will keep the public confused."

"But what if a gung-ho reporter follows the money?"

Goat drained his teacup and set it on the table beside a wood-carved satyr. "Here's the genius of it all. If Senator Blockton gets indicted, he'll have to take the fall for fraud."

Sebastian's gaze returned to the television screen. "Blockton has lost the edge. Drinks too much. But in a crunch he'll point to you as the mastermind. What then?"

Unfazed, Goat lifted the teapot and poured another cupful. "I have him on video molesting his wife's underage niece. She's thirteen."

"Very good, but what if the girl rats Blockton out?"

"No worries there either," Goat said.

"Why?"

"Her family knows she'll need more than a face-lift to be recognized if she talks. I don't play games. I once blew up a yacht in international waters to fake my own death."

"What about Danny's part in this flimflam?"

"He's no stud, if that's what you mean."

"No, what I mean is—" he leaned forward "—how do you pay him for using his name?"

"I'll deal with that when the time comes." Goat took Sebastian's glass and stopped at the wet bar for a refill. "He's not stupid but like most professionals, he's only smart in one area."

Sebastian sipped the rum and grinned. "Fucktard indeed. Ahhh, yes, feel the rush. By the way, when will the blushers be coming aboard for our barefoot cruise?"

"They're not."

A menacing frown swamped Sebastian's face. "Why not?"

Goat turned away. "They're busy cutting a DVD for the Gospel Galaxy show."

Sebastian tugged at his Fu Manchu. "No shit. Don't tell me I'll be flying back to L.A. without getting some glamour nookie. What kind of host are you?"

Goat sipped his tea. "A rich one if everything falls into place."

"Hell, I could've stayed in L.A. if I'd known about the no-show babes."

"Yeah, well, enjoy the clips. I'm off to bed."

"Do you miss being normal after the Jennorez incident?" Sebastian said. "You do know she lives in L.A., don't you?"

"Don't ever bring that up again," Goat said, his jaw muscles flexing.

"Sorry. Did I hit a nerve, partner?"

"I'm not done with that slut," Goat said. "Think I'll send her a gift—a special one."

Sebastian placed his half-empty glass beside the satyr. "Why gift a porn star?"

"She has to be reminded of my power," Goat said.

"See you in the morning, man."

Goat retrieved the glass and wiped a droplet off the statue's head with his finger. "Balsa wood. Stained, not varnished. Take your damn glass to the bar and find a napkin."

Sebastian stood, strolled to the bar, and placed his glass next to a Venus flytrap plant, its maw open, ready to ingest an insect. "Anybody ever question why you're so eccentric, Goat?" Under his breath, he mumbled, "Asshole."

PATRICK AND SORELLE dined on crab cakes at the Pickle Derby Deli before moving next door for ice cream at The Skoop. Small round tables and wrought-iron chairs with red vinyl seats, a checkered floor, and hanging Tiffany lamps reminded him of an old-fashioned ice cream parlor.

As he basked in sunlight refracted by stained glass windows and chatted with his famous guest, Sorelle finished her ice cream, examined her nails, and stood to go. "Ready?'

He smiled. "Not quite. Reminisce with me. Do you remember our first date? Eugenia, bless her matriarchal heart, refused to recognize your—"

"Not now, love." She shouldered her tote bag. "History will be made this afternoon."

"Oh? Something to do with Danny?"

"You said it." She walked to the door, leaving him to stay or follow.

He followed at a brisk pace alongside her until reaching Sanctuary Inn, a quarter-mile from the quaint shop. Sorelle took the stairs up to the third-floor suite. Once inside, she channel-surfed until an inset read, "Breaking News."

She turned up the volume. "Look, there they are, the two of them."

Patrick brewed a pot of coffee, full-strength Columbian bean. A sly grin crimped his face. Dare he perk Sorelle up? Today she had been far from perky, even rejecting his capricious overtures. Torture, he realized, was not limited to pain. His withdrawals, caused by her refusals of pleasure, was a special kind of pain.

"Who's the baby-faced guy standing to the left of Tookie?" he asked.

"Gabe," she said. "Believe it or not, I made him what he is today. Look, live on Sports Central. Everything becomes official today. Look at Tookie Ward, so dapper in his blazer. Shhh, listen."

"How I love thee," Patrick said. "Let me count the ways, but first let me count to ten."

"What?"

"Nothing. Just thinking out loud about a comedy skit."

Tookie Ward, the silver-haired owner of the champion Marauders, braced for his appearance on television with a sports reporter holding a mike next to him. "Our franchise is only in its ninth season, but we've done okay with Dan the Man," Tookie said.

"Done *okay*?" the reporter said in loud but friendly banter. "Just okay?"

His eyes belying over seven decades of robust health, Tookie grinned. "Well, after we evaluated his stats, I can tell you this. He's the most exceptional player I've ever known. And that's why today is special." Turning, he faced Gabe and said, "I know this might send shockwaves through all the world of sports, but today—" he grinned "—I'm offering *the* Danny a billion dollar re-up." He held up a finger. "With perks. Provided he keeps playing for the winningest team in pro football, our Marauders."

The reporter's jaw dropped. "Is that a billion with a *B*, sir?"

Sorelle danced in celebration of the historic moment. "Yes-yes-yes! The phone will start ringing any minute now. Know what this means, love?" She pointed to the package. "Sunday night I picked up these samples in New York. I can now go international with my cosmetics line."

The idea of a billion-dollar re-up struck Patrick as absurd. How could Danny or any other sports figure be awarded such a ridiculous amount? Yet the hype following Tookie's announcement meant ten times more money for Dan the Man in endorsements and appearances. It also meant money in Sorelle's bank account. But her human ATM must first sign the re-up deal.

What would be the crossover effect on the pedigree movement? Since Danny's value was rising sky-high as a sports star, the value of his genes would rise as well. And matchmaking pedigrees would mean the program's perceived value would also rise.

Did Tookie Ward's offer portend a larger scheme, one that would capitalize on Danny's image as a holy man? And how would it affect Patrick's role in the pedigree cause? No one had to know his role completed the deal.

"I didn't know you had a cosmetics line," he said.

"Yes, but at this very moment, Trudy Mickelstein is setting up to surprise Danny with more good news." Her arms opened wide as if to embrace the universe. "What a glorious day this is." She spun and faced the show again. "I have to call Gabe, then go to the spa next door. It has a facial advertised. This may take me a while. Did you make my coffee, love? Decaf only. Now run along and find something to do till I need you. Go downstairs. I have to take these calls, okay? I can't be distracted during this special time."

"I have to disappear just like that, huh?"

"Patrick, do as I say. Go-go-go!"

He pocketed the extra door key and set a cup of caffeine-rich coffee beside her.

Sorelle answered the call on its second ring. "Listen, Trudy, are you looking for Danny at the Shamrock?... Great! What I need is a memorable quote for a Highlight of the Year Award."

Shamrock? Easter was scheduled to be there with Danny for Goat's movie shoot that involved Vanessa. Patrick hesitated to leave as he watched Sorelle drink from the cup.

The phone rang again. "Hi there, Gabe! Can you believe we negotiated a cool billion? What a tandem we are. Who else could work Tookie for a record-breaking deal? So flatter me all you want, you handsome devil. You and me, mostly me, just made sports history."

Patrick closed the door behind him, chafed by Sorelle's indifference to him. He doubted the business tycoon had flown to New York for cosmetic samples. A delivery via drone to Sanctuary Inn was more likely.

Even as he fought to reject it, a sense of loss torpedoed his self-confidence.

But an equally strong emotion loomed—fear of an uncertain future. Goat Goodnowe remained an ever-present threat. And no doubt Dan the Man's newly-enhanced fame would have a positive effect on sales at the conman's clinic.

He must also shake the feeling that a force beyond his control was pulling him into the bull's-eye of a more troubling situation, one that portended great personal danger. How could Buzz know for sure that some rogue New Yorker would take aim at a humorist in coastal Alabama?

Crosshairs. The word itself suggested danger.

TWENTY-EIGHT

A parlor clock gonged nine o'clock as Patrick surfed television channels in the den. He slowed to watch wall-to-wall fundraisers, one for autistic children in need of special attention. Again, no focus on prevention.

Easter's name showed on the lighted screen of his phone. "Did you watch the news tonight?" she asked without saying hello.

"No. How'd it go at the Shamrock? Are you on your way home?"

"No, but I'll see you early tomorrow. I have an early flight. By the way, how's Sorelle handling Immanuel's rejection of the Marauder's big offer?"

"Don't know. Danny turned it down for sure, huh?"

"Yes, and as you'd expect, he's getting wall-to-wall coverage on TV."

"Okay, but are we prepared for Sorelle going berserk when she finds out? Somebody served her coffee with a fair amount of caffeine, so I'm not looking forward to chatting with her."

"Shame on you," she said. "But it doesn't matter. Rerouting his football career is in line with destiny and she can't stop it." A moment passed before her voice adopted a sultry contralto. "Patrick?"

"I'm here," he said.

"I know you may not want to hear this, but I'm in love with you."

"You are? I mean, yeah, I miss you, too."

"Patrick?"

"Uh-huh? I'm still here."

"I'm serious. I really, really love you."

He grinned. "What're you drinking, a Margarita?"

"Darling, I love your devil-may-care smile, your blue-blue eyes, your tight buns, your shyness, your dance moves, even that habit you have of rolling your shoulders, like something doesn't fit. It's all etched into my heart. This love surpasses genetic compatibility. Know what I'm talking about?"

"I get it. You're rehearsing your lines for *Lovestruck*."

"Love what?"

"*Lovestruck* is the new name for our new movie. My idea."

She chuckled. "Listen, I have plans to up your status as a proxy. But first, answer me this. Do you ever want to be loved? Like your next heartbeat depends on it? Like your heart spills over with it? Like the view of a sunset is all it takes to make you yearn for your lover's embrace?"

"Yeah, but I focus on something else, like sailing in the regatta with a pina colada."

"No fooling," she said. "Admit it, you're as hopelessly in love with me as I am with you. You're into me and you feel it deeply. My vulnerable side draws you to me."

Vulnerable? If she only knew. Even now his heart seemed to recognize that. Intimacy felt more meaningful with Easter than with any other woman. Some he had known to be adequate lovers, but she touched him with a far deeper tenderness and a profound caring.

"Bright girl you are," he said. "Not that I'll pretend to be less than human, but I can't see losing control, and that's what giving my heart to somebody means."

"So you think love is an illusion?"

"Actually, no. Love has that unforgettable face and seductive voice, a certain lolling of the head, and eyes so brown they melt this man's heart."

"Hmmm, so you do love me in the same special way I love you. Don't you, baby?"

"Does thinking about you day and night count? And how about the way my heart beats faster when I see you? Or the excitement I feel when we kiss? Or how your soft moans of ecstasy cause my entire body to quiver with desire. I'm so into you, I never want out."

"Are those your real thoughts? And don't say it unless you mean it."

"Genes don't lie and neither do I," he said. "You know what else? I always wanted to be with a lover without having to pretend she was somebody else. Believe me, that's you, Easter. Seriously."

"Love is real, baby," she said. "I need to ask you; do you ever imagine me being pregnant?"

He chuckled. "Matter of fact, I have. Strange as it may sound, it's a real turn-on."

"Really? You never told me. Do you realize the fruit of the womb is like arrows? That divine message also says, 'Blessed is the man whose quiver is full of them; they will not be put to shame when they contend with their adversaries.' Nice thought, eh?"

"So that's why Eugenia wanted to keep us kids close to her on the farm."

"A lot of kids is something to think about, darling. They vouch for our legacy of love, generosity and so much more. I really do love you. Goodnight."

"I love you more—nite-nite."

After their chat, it occurred to him that flawless genes were only part of the equation in the huge health game. Love suggested uplifting vibes. Whatever else love proved to be, no one could deny it was the main ingredient in happiness with its strong emotional appeal to the heart.

On television the time-lapse video of a charter boat showed it lingering over the horizon, dark against the sun's orb, its blazing rays painting the underbelly of a cloudbank orange and russet. As he marveled at the splendor of the vivid hues, Easter's words lingered in his mind, cooing dovelike and confirming the certainty of their future together.

But could he support seven mothers and their newborns with his limited resources? He didn't want to believe the New Scrolls were bogus but their interpretation rested with Moreau, a preacher with a dubious past.

And Easter had compromised ten of the most telegenic Sweethearts. Plus, she trusted a crook who promised to help fund her showbiz plans with a tradeoff deal that smacked of porn. Why had she waited until now to admit her love for him?

To Patrick, love had always been an absolute verity. Of course, it had strings attached, making it difficult to sort out the complexity of a lover's motives.

Though he tried to throttle his excitement, he couldn't shake the idea of Easter being his lover full-time. True, he could find a measure of fame without her. But with her, the regeneration cause made fame more meaningful. Not sharing his youth gene seemed irresponsible, yet maintaining a harem for procreation seemed unimaginable, not to mention unaffordable. And not to mention patently unlawful. And immoral.

Why did life's choices have to be so complicated?

<hr />

A HALF HOUR before the ten o-clock curfew, Patrick left Cheryl Decairo revising scripts in the mansion den before driving to what she called the Drink 'n Think, the Swashbuckler Pub. While he navigated Peninsula Road, his thoughts reverted to Wynn Traynor and how months ago he allowed guests to hijack his hopes of a comedy break-through.

Had it not been for that fluke, he might be a household name today, a star with his own televised comedy show. Yet being in Easter's employ was a welcome relief from performing on the road alone.

Soon after he arrived at the pub, he nodded at Jacki who slid a beer-filled mug toward him. On each television set—one at each end of the bar—a cable news show featured a segment on emblot. Russ, the *Uptake* anchor, confided that since emblot had become pandemic, a noted scientist who supposedly had a cure for the hereditary disease committed suicide.

The chyron below the news anchor's face read: *Suspicious death of scientist under investigation.*

As the newscast continued, Russ compared the epidermal mani-festations of emblot to scenes from a horror movie. The image of a victim's horrid face appeared onscreen, along with an inset—*No*

Special Effects. The news show cut to Spencer Lovejoy on Capitol Hill.

"The supergenes option is not off the table," Lovejoy said. "Genetic matching got to power up Black folk to take control of our *own* destiny, heal our own. We wise to gene engineering. I tell 'em to shove it, not love it. Ain't no frickin' reason for doing things outside nature's way."

With his curiosity growing, Patrick moved closer to the television. Still talking, Lovejoy stood beside Senator Boyd Blockton on the Capitol steps. Like a bobble-head, the Senator nodded agreement.

How had he convinced the Black activist to reverse his position? Kickbacks? Other than money, what else might have prompted Lovejoy to approve genetic matching?

"I'll have a Zany Zulu," the man next to him said above the televised voice. "PDQ!"

The mixologist, Jacki, wore a headset and continued to chat with someone. She ignored the PDQ —*Pretty Damn Quick*—demand for a drink.

Trudy Mickelstein's face appeared above the Breaking News caption on *Uptake*. Her debut on a national channel seemed natural. "On another front, Russ," she said, "the NFL brass refuse to comment, but it's that conspiracy of silence that adds to *the* Danny's unique mystique."

Unique mystique. Patrick grinned at Trudy's use of a rhyming phrase.

Removing the jacket of his pin-striped suit, the stranger sitting nearby at the bar spoke with an air of cynicism. "Whazit take to get a drink in this frickin' place?"

Irritated by the man's interruption, Patrick rapped his knuckles on the bar and waved to Jacki, his thumb indicating the new patron. A frown came with her effort to serve the man as Patrick resumed his study of Trudy's reportage.

Trudy appeared on the street outside the New York City news studio. "Speaking of sideshows," she said, "may I have a word with you, Reverend Moreau?"

Lingering beside Trudy, Luther T. Moreau towered over her, his suitcoat unbuttoned to show a gold cross anchoring a solid blue tie to his starched white shirt. With his slicked-back hair boxed on the neck, his ears protruded out like those of an elephant spooked by African poachers.

"I'm no sideshow, Miss *Steinmickle*. I *am* the show."

"And my viewers have ringside seats," she shot back.

L.T. grinned. "The faithful will recall how I prophesied a comeback for my global ministry. I'm here to tell 'em it's real." He looked at the reporter as if she were one of his minions. "I'm so glad to be back and so glad you asked, Little Miss Trudy."

"I didn't ask," she said. "But tell us what's happening with America's most famous athlete. We know his tectonic plates are causing an upheaval, but why groom Dan the Man to be a theocrat? Is he that desperate for fame?"

A glint of mischief shone in the big man's eyes. "Pooh-pooh him all you want but let me tell you that God chooses the lowly things to confound the mighty." Moreau wrung his big hands, dry-lathering them. "Fact number one—we've found ancient scrolls and they're the real thing." He placed his hand on her shoulder. "Fact two—they verify him as the one-and-only Immanuel. Fact three—he's got the power to deliver the goods, whether y'all admit it or not."

"Excuse me, sir, but—"

"Immanuel calmed the raging waters of a hurricane," he said. "How're y'all gonna deny that?"

Trudy shook her head. "But why do you say DiNago, a pro football star, is a messiah?"

He fanned his arm skyward in a wide arc. "Our man prevented a disaster to show his power over *temporal* things. Blows your mind, don't it? If y'all don't believe his teachings, then believe his works. He's no weenie."

Trudy suppressed an emerging smile. "Tell us about his not signing with the team, the franchise deal with the Marauders. Who's responsible for his change of heart?"

Moreau's eyes widened. "God, of course. But why toy with a billion bucks? The New Scrolls say the treasures of the land—all of 'em—belong to the Greater Solomon, our own Immanuel."

Trudy's mouth hung open momentarily. "*All* treasures?"

The preacher drew himself up to his full height. "For those out there in the know, that prophecy begins now. Messiah must ride on his white *steeed* to *victoreee*!"

Trudy winked at the camera. "Is DiNago seeking treatment for his messiah complex?"

Her question went unanswered as the big man turned and lumbered toward a limousine.

She brushed the spot on her shoulder where his hand had rested. "This is Trudy Mickelstein and I'm reporting from *Uptake* in New York City. Back to you, Russ."

As Patrick considered the exchange between Trudy and the preacher, he realized L.T. Moreau's oblique reference to treasure had a meaning beyond materialism. The public knew Danny as a sports hero, a veritable sports institution, but now it seemed Moreau intended to capitalize on his image as a bigger-than-life mystical force from another dimension.

TWENTY-NINE

The Swashbuckler Pub stirred with excitement, enough to keep the barkeep busy. A fun-filled mixture of anglers, kayakers, and recreational boaters played pool, corn hole, or darts—the normal weeknight crowd. All wore casual attire, except one.

In his tailored suit and high-gloss shoes, the dandy stood out like a barber's pole from a bygone era. His voice rang with authority as he demanded another Zany Zulu on ice. "Moreau's off target if you ask me," he blurted without offering Patrick a handshake. "You're Pat McGroin, aren't you?"

Patrick faced the young man. "Maybe. Who are you?"

"Just call me Teddy."

Uptake resumed its newscast. "In Alabama's port city," the anchor said, "Our WMOP-TV sports reporter Randy Palwick has Tookie Ward cornered in the real estate mogul's office. As owner of the Marauders franchise, he's well-known to football fans everywhere."

Sitting at his desk, Tookie appeared at ease with the reporter in his headquarters overlooking the waterfront on Mobile Bay.

"Our viewers keep asking the same question," Palwick said, his words in closed caption. "Why offer a billion dollars to a pro football player? Is Dan the Man that special, Mr. Ward?"

Well into his golden years, Tookie straightened his slightly-stooped posture. "Just do the math, Randy, and you tell me if Dan the

Man isn't worth it. Not only does he win football games, he exhibits certain intangibles that make him a rare asset." His eyes twinkled. "To leadership born, as they say. No one inspires a team like Danny does. Care to know why?"

The young reporter grinned. "Why, Mr. Ward?"

The old man framed his mouth with one hand, as if to amplify his words. "Because he gets in a zone. I knew a fisherman who was the first to win a million dollars in a bass tournament. He demanded more of himself every time he fished." Relaxing his hand, he added, "Competition can do that for you."

"You mean, like he's one hundred percent focused?"

"Yes, it's a phenomenal thing, Randy. Competition can force you into a zone of super awareness, a state of mind you won't get any other way."

"Okay, but what about the claim that he's a secular messiah, a genetic phenom?" Palwick asked.

For a moment the old man's expression remained placid, but then his lips curled into a smile. "Is that what reporters call hard news these days? It may explain a lot but that stuff really holds no interest for me. Never has."

Zone of super awareness. Patrick clung to the idea as the reporter wrapped up the interview and signaled a redirect to the news anchor. During the interim, he tossed a comment to Teddy, the stranger. "Seems to me Tookie likes to toy with reporters."

"Except in business," Teddy replied. "But the beauty of it is, he belongs to us."

Patrick's focus shifted from the television to the suit, detecting in his voice a recklessness all too common among braggarts. "Tell me more."

"We're behind the big offer," the dandy said. "We back Tookie's commercial properties, too, and we operate from our own island." He sniffed in a condescending manner during an awkward pause. "NGT is transnational."

"NGT?"

"National Guaranty Trust. No billionaire can have holdings like Tookie has without a banker floating them. Share the risk; it's our creed." Without moving his head, Teddy's gaze shifted back and forth between the dart players and Patrick. "We're into private equity funding and we take great pride in finding upstart businesses with lots of potential."

"You do? I mean, are you an executive at NGT?"

"I'm the acquisitions czar," he said. "In fact, I'm checking out a tip on some glamour girls who show promise as entertainers on TV. Do you know anyone with the Sweethearts, other than you?"

"How do you know I'm with them?"

The suit studied his drink and raised the stir stick to eye level, examining it. "I have my sources."

"Uh-huh. How do you guys make money dealing direct? Seems you'd be a mite better off talking with producers like Rubleau Entertainment."

Teddy stirred his Zany Zulu. "A smart czar goes to the source. We have in mind a joint venture. On TV the girls dazzle audiences. They also tie into something grander that'll make our IPO numbers zoom out of sight. It's a project Dr. Ronofski refers to as Perfect Progeny."

"So now we're actually talking about super jock DiNago, aren't we?"

Eyes blinking rapidly, the banker took a small sip of his drink and dabbed his lips with a napkin.

"Yes. Wall Street investors understand certain genetic links are an asset. The girls are clean energy to us. They have a good shelf life, and a perpetually long one with our backing."

"Who controls the supply?"

His eyes shifted to the dart players again. "A conglomerate. But remember—" his tone became secretive "—not everyone qualifies. Geneticists won't admit it but roughly twelve percent of people just don't get sick. They have superior genetic assets. We're positioned to assist in vetting them."

"Like some type of quality control?"

"Certainly." Teddy's black tie bunched on his neck like a goiter. "The power is in the pedigree. Qualifying gets pricey. We can't devalue Danny's sperm by selling to inferior mates, like Goodnowe is doing. The human race is too close to becoming extinct. That's why we operate on a grander scale, aided of course by our Paladin charity."

Patrick chuckled. "Yeah, the Paladins spoofed the Sweethearts' in our debut game a while back."

Unsmiling, Teddy glared at Jacki who served him another drink. "We intend to reject retrograde misfits and keep the best for Ronofski's breeding program."

Patrick hunched his shoulders, aware the man had no clue about Danny's lack of sperm. "Who else might be excluded?"

"The feebleminded in particular."

Patrick wanted to laugh at the young czar's reference to the antiquated word. "Ah, yes, all those feebleminded ones. How about other nettlesome people, like maybe those with slightly subpar genes?"

"Are you being sarcastic?"

"No, I'm simply amused by your audacity."

Teddy cleared his throat, his gaze traveling again. "As everyone knows, the wellborn must be favored. Or else, what's the point? Some mulattoes are admissible, but not Blacks per se. To manage any undesirables, we can engineer diseases such as emblot from our secret labs."

Patrick squirmed on his stool. "Engineer a disease, huh?"

"Yes. Our corporate hospitals can alter the DNA of certain human embryos. Medics introduce toxic generational diseases that can be covertly passed among them."

"How does that improve the gene pool?"

"It doesn't."

Patrick cringed. "So in your view, science is best used in creating a privileged social class. At the same time, you're justifying genocide."

"Genocide." Teddy squinted, as if the word challenged his comprehension. "How uncanny of you, Mr. McGroin. How easily you discern that the net result is all we're concerned with. But why not? Long term, it's in the world's best interests, and ours, to do exactly that."

Patrick shook his head. "Genetics without heart, devoid of humanitarian concerns. Right?"

Teddy fingered a mole at the corner of his mouth. "You must understand eugenics is the Holy Grail to us. It's been stigmatized but we will bring it back." He readjusted the bulky knot in his necktie. "Once this world is free of retrograde humans, our selection of pedigrees will grow exponentially."

Patrick marveled at his attitude toward an elitist caste system that kept the poor in servitude. He decided to listen and expose the czar's game plan to Easter.

"Kluuge backs the pedigree project, too," Teddy said. "That's why it recruits girls from Russia, Germany, Scandinavia, and England—classy breeding stock. Our philanthropy work with the Paladins is a perfect cover. Shall I tell you more? I also have an indoctrination video, but I should warn you, we do play dirty."

"Why not? I'm a sponge for information. Call me Pat, won't you?"

"Formalities are not my bag, either. To you I'm Teddy, but in the world of finance I'm addressed as Mr. Theodore Crown."

"Any relation to the Crown who financed Saul Buckalew in a condo scam hereabouts?"

"How did you know who financed him?"

"You just told me. Small world, isn't it, Teddy?"

THIRTY

Below the mansion's second-story veranda, the leaves of a silver maple shimmered like beads on a belly-dancer's hips. A kingfisher on its lowest limb studied an inlet of the bay for minnows before diving to snag one.

Patrick held Easter in a full-body hug on the veranda. "Glad to see you, sweetheart."

"Are you still in love, baby?" she asked in a plaintive voice.

"My love is boundless, sweetheart. And yours?"

"Infinite, yes." She kissed him. "You won't believe all the drama at the Shamrock."

"Why? What happened?"

"A lot. Trudy Mickelstein shows up and surprises Immanuel with news of the billion-dollar offer from Tookie. She comes charging into the penthouse with a camera crew, uninvited. Vanessa is midway into a scene, but Trudy spooks her and she flees in a panic out o' there— boobs bare."

"She barely made it out, huh?" he said.

"Hah-hah. Goat will probably scrap the keepsake project after that hullabaloo. And that's all I want to say about that. Do you know who gave Trudy orders to crash our keepsake shoot?"

He shrugged. "All I know is Sorelle wanted a quote from Danny for publicity purposes."

"She got a quote alright," Easter said as she released him and propped against the railing. "So how're you doing with the girls?"

"A reporter kept pestering us so we practiced our skits in the parlor. On a different front, I'm trying to keep track of Sorelle's schemes. Really I am, but my time is limited."

"So it is. By the way, which of the Sweethearts demands you the most?"

"Pick a name."

"Binged, didn't you?"

He sighed. "Actually, I'm still thinking about the proxy proposal. I mean, I'm in love with you, not them. Copulation would seem awkward, like I'd be cheating."

"What? Listen, it's your duty. Haven't you noticed a surge of energy you didn't have before? I told you the New Scrolls require a surrogate seeder. You fit the prophecy."

He shrugged. "I'd call it projecting, not prophecy."

"You have to honor the generosity law."

"What about the law of the paparazzi? I don't want my face in the *Analyzer*."

She tugged on his arm. "Come with me, I'm hungry." He followed her downstairs to the dining area where a queue of Sweethearts visited Wattanabe's buffet. The aroma of stir-fry vegetables—red bell peppers with shrimp, cheese broccoli and brown rice on the side—attested to his skill as a chef.

Easter soon led him from the kitchen to the atrium with two plates of food, one for each of them. Beyond the orchids, bromeliads and ferns, a portico opened to Stu Watanabe's backyard herb garden. Swallowtail butterflies flitted between nectar-laden blooms.

Easter sat near him and stirred a small mound of steaming rice into her vegetables. "I'll deal with the *Analyzer*," she said. "Did you know the Sweethearts—all of them—were groomed as pedigrees since their teenage years?"

He watched the kingfisher leave its perch and dive into the inlet, returning with a sunfish. "Yeah, after Cheryl mentioned her folk's pedigree culture, I assumed that about them."

Along the bay's shoreline, bass boats rocked gently in the wake of a passing skiff. Anglers with jackets covered in sponsor's decals cast lures toward downed trees, limestone riprap and reefs of bridge rubble where larger fish staged.

She tasted her food before continuing. "Have you ever been to Lookout Mountain?"

"Yeah, Chattanooga, to be exact."

"Well, deep inside a cave there, fish survive with no light. None. But suppose they were exposed to a bright light? Would the illumination help them to see? No. It's the same with bias. The darkness of materialism adds to the geneticists' blindness. When truth seekers challenge them, their hackles go up."

"Okay, but you sometimes refer to a mystic element in our makeup."

"Yeah. Let me explain. Do you realize our life experiences form epigenetic tags that are passed down from one generation to another?"

"Well, I've read articles in *Genomics World*, so I know quite a bit."

She waved her fork in midair. "Why are some folks optimistic and others not so much? Thing is, our behavior activates chemical switches to regulate gene expression and transmit information onto our offspring's DNA. That info is transmitted without passing through egg or sperm. In fact, it can modify our genetic makeup—our genome—cell by cell."

"Amazing," he said. "But weird."

"Weird but true." She dipped into the stir-fry and ate with gusto before continuing her lecture. "It's really esoteric," she said. "Empathy and generosity are among those transmittable traits. When I say you and the girls are assets, I'm talking about things like that. Each time you delve into the Scrolls, you'll begin to understand why we have to improve ourselves in order to be game changers."

"Game changers, huh? Not to digress but how long can you keep raiding Danny's discretionary fund? Seems to me our goals require big bucks. Any contingency plans?"

"No, but a miracle would be nice right about now."

"Doesn't Goat make payments to you?"

"Let's not get into that, okay?"

"Why not?"

"Life is about timing, Patrick. But I'll tell you this. Somebody should look into Sorelle's history. Seems to me she has an insatiable need for male companionship."

"Lots of men, huh?"

Easter fanned her neck with a napkin. "A friend of mine says she likes them to be younger and quasi-religious. Her former employer, so she says, was a drunk. She stole his client list and created her own talent company. Now that she's lost control of her best client, I expect her to go gunning for me."

He finished eating then posed another thought. "Speaking of timing, though, if you don't mind, I need more time to rehearse with the girls for our show on the Funtasy Channel."

Smiling, she poked his arm as she stood to go. "Along with your love sessions with them?"

He looked away. "Give it a rest, okay?"

"Okay, but did you know we have a wedding coming up soon for the girls? It's a prophetic part of the New Scrolls, so think aura like never before. You know, like a corona."

She secured her ponytail with a scrunchie. "The girls we selected had an effervescent glow about them. You'd hardly notice if you're looking for some spectacular aurora borealis. It's more of a nimbus, transitory and fleeting. By the way, you're Immanuel's best man."

"A wedding ceremony strikes me as too obvious, like you're flaunting Danny's masculinity."

"Patrick, imagine the pageantry in a celestial wedding." She took his empty plate and placed it on top of hers. "Have you not read the Scrolls in your spare time?"

"*What* spare time?"

"Okay, but remember, Immanuel gets credit for seeding them. Of course, the Reverend has to consecrate your seed, not Immanuel's. One blessing does it. No daily rituals."

"Arg! I'll be working with actresses who waddle around in maternity outfits."

"No-no, like I said, you'll impregnate seven every six months. Only seven."

"Seven is one-third of my crew."

"Sorry, but fourteen others are capable of doing the show. Oh, and since seeding involves sex, you'll need a boost."

He thumbed his chest. "No, thanks. My libido is naturally turbo-charged."

"Fine, but an aphrodisiac drink will help you establish the new norm."

He lowered his head as he turned to go. "I'll go find Sorelle and give you updates."

"Now? I just got home. We need to test the new norm. When does your obsession with Sorelle end? Never mind, I'll deal with that later. Right now, though, I need a massage." She held the plates to one side to kiss him. "Let's go upstairs."

He stalled, wanting to clarify other mysteries she had hinted about in the Scrolls.

"C'mon, baby," she said. "Know what I'd like? I want you to brush my hair. Mom used to do that. She said long hair is a woman's glory."

"Sounds like a new foreplay wrinkle," he said while following her to the kitchen where he placed empty plates in a dishwasher.

Soon alone with her in his bedroom, he closed the blinds so the softer light created a semblance of romantic ambience. He made a show of sniffing the scent of her body, the allure sensual.

"Like my body wash?" she said. "Mom takes pride in creating new scents from plant extracts." Fishing a hairbrush from her purse, she lay it on the bed. "She likes to combine the best flowers, the ones with the most appealing aroma."

Retrieving the brush, he kneeled behind her on the bed, removed the scrunchie, and brushed her hair with long, purposeful strokes. "Sounds like hybridizing," he said.

"Mom used to say we're not perfect in the arbitrary sense of never making mistakes, but we are perfect for our purpose. Good stock begets good stock. Still, the potential is there for an endless variety within that stock, so Mother Nature allows us to reinvent ourselves."

"Is that why our lovemaking gets better and better?"

Moaning pleasantly, she lolled her head back. "Are you saying I bring out the best in you, or you the best in me?"

"I'll go a step further and tell you a secret," he said.

"Uhm, I'd love to hear all your secrets."

"Well, then, did you know I'd never gone extra innings, so to speak, till you came into my life?"

"Not even with one of your former wives?"

"Nope."

"Why me? What's different?"

"Everything."

"Oh, c'mon, tell me one thing I do that turns you on so much that you go overtime."

"Well, with you I feel like we accomplish something significant." He brushed the underside of her hair. "And it's a feeling that stays with me long after we make love. It's like seeing a rare diamond take on a brighter luster. You exude an extraordinary brightness sometimes, like the bloom of youth, and your beauty seems more magnificent."

"Dad used to say Mom was like a full-flavored peach picked fresh off the tree."

"I like the analogy," he said. "I don't know how you do it but I feel like I'm being absorbed into you, like the essence of you and the essence of me merges into one organic whole."

"Ohmgod, the way you're brushing feels so good, baby. You have a sensitive touch, like not too hard, not too soft. I'm so turned on."

He crouched over her and fondled her breasts. "Found something new about you, didn't I? Yeah, must remember about brushing your hair before our lovemaking."

Unlike the hurried foreplay leading to penetration with Sorelle, he found Easter appreciative of his slower caressing. As always, he preceded the transition to intercourse with oral intimacy for a more intense arousal. Marveling at its profound effect on her, he explored different techniques while finessing her slowly to spasms of erotic delight. His gentle entry soon escalated to uninhibited gusto.

Unexpectedly, an aura, softly glowing, encircled her face and lingered a moment.

In those magical moments, they shared a passion more sensuous than any time before, the tender rhythm flowing freely between them, growing in intensity before peaking in orgasmic ecstasy. Deeply touched, he climaxed in perfect harmony with her orgasm. Her endearments, softly whispered and easily in sync with her moves, awakened in him a tenderness he had never known before.

Still infused with energy, his renewed desire drove him to continue pleasuring her. His follow-up performance surprised him with another climax. Restful but in awe of her vocal expressions of pleasure from the act, he wondered if this was the new norm she had mentioned. At a loss for words, it seemed to him a supernatural phenomenon.

Did it also mean he had achieved some kind of super-elevated status with her?

But a sudden rush of reality quashed hopes of a repeat performance. How could he support seven women and seven offspring? And seven babies would not be the finale. Mentally calculating the quota, he realized seven babies every six months and twenty-eight over a two-year span tallied forty-two kids in three years.

Which part of Easter's plan had drawn him to this moment; sex to revitalize or sex to regenerate?

Babies and more babies. Which part of impossible did he not understand?

To forget the impossibility, he imagined Easter confiding to him that Goodnowe was a conman. She might never do so but the thought grew in his mind as a probability. He must talk with videographer Larry Lemoyne. A deal with him would be a start in assisting her awakening to the reality he imagined.

Could he also convince the young man to spy on the clinic? It was a long shot fraught with risk but it was one he had to take.

THIRTY-ONE

Upstairs in her bedroom, Cheryl Decairo slipped into her silk pajamas, climbed into her bed, and rested against downy pillows. A ceiling fan circulated semi-cool air and slatted blinds at the sliding glass door allowed a view of the bay, its waters silvered by the moon.

The cadence of nature instilled in her a need to think in harmony with its rhythms.

> *Immanuel surprised us early today with twenty-one rings, each a diamond solitaire. Meanwhile, Patrick gleans info from genetic articles for use in our skits. We—us girls—will soon ambush him with a dramatic scene. We live for a Pernassus effect, that sacred place associated with drama, knowledge and song. On TV we grab the viewer's attention long enough to instill pedigree values in their mind. Patrick wanted spontaneity. Well, he'll have it—loads of it—because we're learning new skits clippety-clop fast. And Nature itself is on our side since pedigree living is in harmony with it.*

SORELLE EBANETTI STEERED her rental car into the circular drive of the mansion, lowered a window, and called to Patrick who paused midway up the front porch steps. "You deceived me, you quisling."

"Whoa! Time out." He descended the steps toward her. "Why do you think I deceived you?"

"You have to *ask*?" she said. "And Easter, too. She's still influencing my Danny." The caffeine-induced insomnia had a telling effect in Sorelle's eyes. "Who's behind this holy man nonsense? I know you must know, Patrick, so tell me."

He peered warily about before answering. "My guess would be L.T. Moreau."

She slapped the steering wheel. "Exactly. His so-called Hebrew scholar is a hack and the New Scrolls are a hoax."

"Okay, so he transcribed a vision direct from Macaroni."

Sorelle leveled her bloodshot eyes on him. "I'm warning you, Patrick, I've been up all night and I don't need your sarcasm."

"Fine," he said. "But you could fill in a few blanks for me, too. Goat Goodnowe is in on it and I'm also suspicious of a weird banker I met last night. Do you know a New Yorker named Teddy?"

Sorelle closed her eyes as her head fell back against the headrest. "My God! Teddy Crown hates me. What else can you tell me about their designs on Danny?"

He squinted in the bright sunlight. "I'll tell it to you straight, then. Conmen like Goat need a front. With super jock Immanuel as their draw, it's easier to con the mark."

"I need to talk with Danny," she said. "Do I make myself clear?"

"Okay, but if I were you, I'd seriously consider a compromise, maybe share control of him with Easter. You girls could find common ground and—"

"No thank you, mister smartass mediator."

He turned away. "You're the one asking for help, not me."

"Tell Danny I'm here."

"Tell him yourself."

"Patrick!"

"Okay, okay, I'll tell him, but that's all I'll do."

Perturbed, he continued walking. Minutes later, after notifying Immanuel in the mansion, Patrick watched their meeting from the front porch, then decided to creep down the steps and position himself in the shade of the garage. From there he could hear their conversation from a discreet distance.

Sorelle's voice zeroed in on the sports icon like a hypnotist. "I've been so terribly worried about you, Danny. You're like a son to me."

Danny spread his arms wide. "It's all in God's hands."

"Forgive my doting on you, love, but you have me to thank for your new billion-dollar contract." Sorelle started to open the car door but stopped short. Easter's fast pace down the mansion steps would soon put her in position to interfere. "Come with me, Danny. We need to talk, just you and me. Hurry."

Easter quickly approached the car. "Aha! You, Sorelle, are trespassing."

Sorelle's chin lifted imperiously. "*I* have a performance contract with Danny and you don't. *I've* performed and you haven't, so I'm on solid legal ground when I insist he's—"

"Phooey! I'm in charge. Immanuel is with me now and he's done with both you and football."

"Ha! Football is big bucks but you wouldn't know it if it bit you on your dilettante derriere."

Easter wagged her head. "Uh-huh, money rules your white ass and you'd do anything for it, and that stupid necklace makes you look stupider, like the hypocrite you are."

"Don't you dare chastise me, you loathsome poacher."

"Problem with you, Sorelle, you're two-faced. You stole your employer's business."

Sorelle's icy stare lingered on the younger woman. "I'll have you know I rescued—"

"No-no, you *stole* his clients like the thieving thief you are."

Measuring a half-inch between thumb and finger, Sorelle said, "I'm about this close to exposing your messiah scam and prosecuting you for criminal fraud."

Patrick moved a few yards closer, aware that the heated exchange could turn into a catfight, one he might have to referee without a whistle.

Easter shook a finger in Sorelle's face. "I'll sue you right back for defamation."

Sorelle sneered. "A thousand pardons, Miss Beaulieu, but you'd have to first *be* somebody."

Danny's hands waved for attention. "You girls, I have more important things to do than listen to you two bickering."

"This Jezebel's specialty is sleeping with her clients," Easter said. "A blood-sucking tick has as much class as she does."

Derisive laughter from Sorelle rose above the soft hum of the car. "You have no idea who you're dealing with, girl. I'll be back with a court order and—"

"No, you won't be *back*," Easter snapped. "What you'll be is *out*." She stepped back as the car crept forward. "Go see a shrink, y'hear?"

Easing away, Sorelle hurled a final insult at her adversary. "Pimp!"

"That does it." Easter reached for the door handle as she followed alongside the car. "How dare you show your slutty face around my man. Danny, get this deranged Jezebel off our property."

As Sorelle revved the engine, Patrick rushed in, pulled Easter away, and held her while Sorelle gunned the vehicle around the circular driveway and onto Peninsula Road.

Patrick shook his head. "You just alienated the missing linchpin in our quest for fame."

AFTER A BRIEF MEETING with Larry about planting a spy at the clinic, Patrick joined Easter in the den where she directed his attention to a Gospel Galaxy television program.

"Let's watch Reverend Moreau's show," she said. "But first, you have something new to tell me, don't you?"

He hesitated to answer, wondering if she had seen the *Analyzer* online. "Like what?"

Her breath feathered his neck as she leaned over the recliner. "Cheryl says you met a guy from National Guaranty Bank."

He side-glanced Cheryl who sat next to him. "Yeah, the guy looked out of place. His financial group buys into companies in need of a cash infusion."

"Hmmm, how much are they willing to invest?" Easter said.

"He didn't say, but we have to show global potential."

"Well, our genetic matching approach is not a commercial one," she said. "But our numbers on the Funtasy Channel are going up."

"Sorry, not enough," he said. "The pedigree base has to multiply like privet hedge on a fencerow. The bigger the numbers, the bigger the profits."

"And that means we'd have to speed up the reproduction of pedigrees, right?"

Patrick smiled. ""Exponentially. His word, not mine. Hundreds turn into thousands and then into millions. To them we're a commercial venture with banks in control—their banks. He gave me a video. It dramatizes mutations—some grotesque and others bordering on repulsive. Ever heard of Cockayne's syndrome?"

"Patrick, is this leading to a punch line?"

"No, I'm serious. With Cockayne's you may be nineteen but look ninety."

"Are you saying the aging process runs out of control?"

"Check. But in the banker's world, power brokers ignore emblot. And they're not above killing people who oppose their strategies. Does that, by any chance, disturb you?"

Cheryl leaned into their chat. "The video he gave you magnifies the worst diseases."

"That it does," he said. "I can see contrasting healthy specimens with defectives, but this video paints Blacks as a health threat, as if they're cursed. It's like declaring open season on them."

Easter arched her eyebrows. "Yes, but—"

"But what?" he said. "The video he gave me reeks of bias."

"Yes, Patrick, but showing a contrast helps advance our pedigree program."

He stared hard at her. "Even if it alienates people of color?"

"No, but we don't just prune invasive privet hedge, we uproot it," Easter said. "Our future as a species hangs in the balance. We humans —black, brown, yellow, white—are facing doomsday."

He shook his head. "Doomsday? Hmmm, sounds alarmist."

"But think about it, Patrick. Choosing a seriously flawed mate is inhumane."

"I'm sorry, Easter, but it sounds like you're taking a shallow view of the common good. I agree that little else matters if we humans can't have kids who survive, but we have to be inclusive. Being part Black, you should understand."

"Yes, but showing a contrast is like facing reality. It's not the negative you think it is. We can be inclusive yet favor certain individuals within each ethnic group."

"Okay, I'll see the banker again soon. I want to know more about their plans to engineer genetic diseases. That's scary. People who'd do that are weird, like they just tossed their last coin in the fountain and made the wrong wish."

"Okay, I'll look at the video. Do watch Moreau's show, okay? Cheryl, come join us girls in the library."

Gospel Galaxy, a program beamed by satellite from the Cathedral Center on Pensacola Beach, channeled Moreau's daily dogma.

Moments later, the refrains of a lively hymn ended on L.T.'s show and he stood behind a pulpit with Bible in hand.

The preacher's voice boomed. "I have many things to tell you but ye are not able to bear them at present. Those words of our Lord were spoken two-thousand years ago." He laid the Bible on the pulpit. "You see, people were not ready to partake of deeper truths back then. Some advancing had to be done. But the New Scrolls lays it all out plain for us today."

The choir chimed amen as he set the Bible aside and gripped the pulpit, his voice modulating for effect. "Oh yes, it...is...time, *passst* time for us to understand some godly mysteries."

Patrick wondered when the showman would get around to asking viewers for a donation.

L.T. gestured toward his production crew. "If anybody has doubts about God's divine purpose, we got a man here today who'll tell it to us straight. But first I want to show all y'all what happened last week at a big lake. See for yourselves, my friends."

On video, Danny's baptism at Lake Shelby took only a few seconds. Edited for special effect, it presented the osprey aglow as it plunged downward but made a quick upturn and climbed skyward. The dubbed-in music rose to a sentimentally majestic crescendo before studio cameras returned to Moreau.

Eyes wide, he said, "You got proof right there. We got the anointing of our messiah on video." A loud amen swelled in the cathedral. "This time our messiah will conquer death itself in a holy crusade."

Patrick winced. *Crusade?* Did L.T. understand crusade conjured up ancient conflicts between Muslim and Christian factions? A better word—campaign—would have sounded more palatable.

Easter returned to the den to watch the preacher. The telecast spotlighted throngs of people who stood with arms raised and eyes closed. All appeared to be in a catatonic state.

L.T.'s voice rose in volume. "Did y'all know Adam was not the first to foul up perfection?"

"Like, who else was available?" Patrick mumbled before Easter poked him.

L.T. continued. "Yep, it started with a supernova called Satan. So only from Jesus could we see the good stuff. Did we? No! Jesus begat no children. It wasn't God's time for it—till now. Yes, now!"

The preacher strode double-time across the carpeted platform, arms spread like an eagle's wings. "Today, our genetic messiah has a propagator mission with a spiritual dimension."

Patrick glanced at Easter who seemed to hang on Moreau's every word.

Moreau flowed into a fast-paced liturgy. "Y'all ever hear about the engineer who turned into a grease monkey? We use it or we what...lose it?" He eased back a few steps. "Adam figured he'd be living larger if he ignored his Maker's counsel. Mongrelized people today get all prideful thinking life's boundaries ain't made for them."

Mongrelized? Patrick did a double-take. The word had long been used by white racists.

Moreau shielded his eyes. "Adam, what's your helpmeet doing over by that tree? Talking to a snake? Snakes don't talk, man. Ain't you suspicious? The reptile said she could be like who? God? So listen, if the snake's right, why don't *he* have the unlimited power of God? Where has the snake's own independence got *him*? Duh!"

Moreau strutted. "Eve did what? Ate the snake? Oh, I see, she ate his message. Wrong choice, don't you think? I hear snakes are tasty." The audience guffawed. "Adam ain't about to let Eve get one up on him. No sireee! His wife says, 'Try it, you'll like it.' He don't question her. Double-duhhh!"

Head down, Moreau shuffled back to the podium, momentarily

silent as he wiped his brow with a handkerchief. "Adam was deceived. Still, because of him, we also inherit the bad with the good in us."

Easter stood close behind Patrick, her voice low. "He's getting to the good part."

Good part? Even if he conceded Moreau had charisma, he couldn't forget the man had swindled buyers in a condo scam, and later launched an outreach program to save runaway girls. But the girls had been forced to become breeders for an organ cartel. The recollection gnawed at Patrick's yearning for justice. Yet a jury refused the suggestion by prosecutors that Moreau had prior knowledge of the cartel's illegal practices. Smart lawyers, dumb jury?

Onstage, the televangelist stalled with eyes shut, as if an epiphany had mesmerized his mind. "So down at the fab shop they churn out a jillion gizmos, copy after copy, all identical. But what if they find a burr on their mold? They scrap it. If they use the flawed one, everything it makes won't do what it's supposed to do." L.T. grinned with eyes open. "Crankshafts won't crank, batteries won't bat, radiators won't raid, pistons won't, uhhh...excuse my boo-boo." The audience chortled. "God put a burr like that in Adam's genes." He paused. "Genes, g-e-n-e-s."

Laughter flowed again as he continued. "Do you folks—" he shook off a lingering smile "—do y'all see genetics as the answer today? Now where am I going with this? Hang on. Let's not lean on our own understanding. Remember the one about a believer who's on top of his house with flood waters all around? Yeah, a rescue boat comes along and he turns it down, saying he don't need it 'cause he's got faith. Again and again he turns down rescuers. He drowns. Up in Heaven he asks why he wasn't saved. The Lord says, 'Man, I sent every means on earth to save you but you refused them.' Friends, it's the same today. God sends a genetic plan and a genetic messiah. Don't tell me you ain't being rescued."

Easter propped against the recliner. "Give heed to his every word, hon."

Patrick rolled his eyes. "What? Give *heed*?"

Talking rapidly, the televangelist resembled a carnival barker. "You see, we may have faith, but in what? We reproduce but even our copies got burrs. What we're missing is a template without a flaw." Shaking a fist, he said, "But no more! The New Scrolls say our flaws are being removed one by one. We had to play the hand we're dealt but God done *interveeened*, done *reversssed* the curse of bad genes."

Moreau paused. "What I'm gonna do now is introduce y'all to the man God sent to renew us all." He turned to face a giant screen as it lowered behind him. "Behold the man!"

On video, the interior of a den featured a paradise-themed mural in the background. Appearing in a white robe with purple trim, Danny DiNago sat straight in a sofa chair.

L.T. addressed him. "Tell us, my lord, about your divine mission here."

Patrick wondered if the Sweethearts agreed with the elevation of a secular demigod like Danny DiNago to such a high plateau. And heaven forbid they discover themselves as sex objects in a tabloid. That reveal might put a double-whammy on their sensibilities.

Loud applause in the cathedral greeted Immanuel's onscreen presence. "So glad you consented to debut on my show," the preacher said. "So let me be the first to interview you, my lord."

Tanned and bearded, Immanuel seemed at home on the telecast as he spoke. "It's a privilege to share my thoughts and experiences with you, my brother. I've always felt destined for kingship, but it wasn't until I was baptized that I understood the spiritual dimension of it." He leaned forward in the tall chair. "Felt like I was in the midst of receiving a higher power to jump-start my mission."

L.T. Moreau's eyes grew intense. "When I baptized you, my lord, what else did you feel?"

"I felt wet. But then a big bird dives out of the blue. While I'm looking up, I see eternity. The air around me was supercharged, like in a magnetic field."

"Did you hear anything, maybe a voice?" Moreau asked.

"Yep, sure did. I recognized Easter Beaulieu's voice. I looked around but she wasn't there. But I could feel her there. You know, her presence. Being spiritually charged, I could hear her sweet voice. It encouraged me to be generous."

"Generous in what way, my lord?"

"Well, the Scrolls say a spirit of generosity will identify those who're blessed with good genes."

L.T. squinted at the camera. "Now, about Easter Beaulieu, enlighten us about her role."

Immanuel smiled. "The Scrolls say a prophetess will inspire hope in the pedigree plan. She must know I don't need a patent to be potent. So, along with her girls, we'll bring about the great awakening."

Patrick's thoughts lodged on Immanuel's impotence. Did the sports icon view his new role as a lark? He insinuated more than he explained so that believers must rely on code words and phrases.

The preacher nodded. "Some followers may doubt your need for more than one bride, my lord."

Immanuel leaned back in a relaxed pose. "Well, look at it this way. When a majority of men are diseased, the least we can do is produce pedigrees. Polygamy is nothing new. Montezuma had what—four-thousand concubines? One Chinese emperor had ten-thousand. King Solomon had only a thousand. The Scrolls mention me having a senior wife but she has an attendant. He's a courtier who takes care of secular matters. Whatever she tells him to do, he does. You might say he's my go-to guy, my proxy."

Jolted by the icon's words, Patrick straightened. "Huh?"

Easter leaned and wrapped her arms about Patrick's neck. "See, my darling, you're my one-and-only main man, my beloved courtier."

"First I'm a proxy, then a conduit, and now a courtier," he said. "I'm hung with all three."

Easter ruffled his hair. "Hung is right, and it'll bring us closer than you ever dreamed."

On the telecast, L.T.'s gestures became more emphatic. "Again, it's the fulfillment of a divine prophecy. But my lord, what about Easter's lovely entourage, the Sweethearts?"

Immanuel smiled. "This coming Saturday, they'll be wed to me. The wedding will be televised, so I'm doing things in a transparent way as their future husband."

L.T. indicated his television audience with a circular motion. "This was foretold in the sacred Scrolls, too, now in book form. Y'all can own a first edition fresh off the press."

As the video blanked, the live broadcast resumed. "Are y'all ready for a land of milk and honey? Immanuel's wedding will give us a taste of it. I promise no shock but you'll be surprised at what I have to say when I officiate it."

THIRTY-TWO

"Finally, it's over," Patrick said as the preacher concluded his presentation.

"Now I want to show you Immanuel's future wives," L.T. said.

In a flash Patrick imagined viewers seeing a contrast after viewing the *Analyzer.* Would they dismiss the tabloid's images as mere phantasmagoria?

Prerecorded, the video captured the Sweethearts strutting across the auditorium stage in glitzy white evening gowns. In the forefront, Easter introduced them.

Patrick marveled at the irony—strut-walking onstage in modest gowns but appearing nearly nude in a notorious tabloid. If Immanuel had enough chutzpah to foster a lie by posing as a harem keeper, did that suggest his proxy, his secular stand-in, might be an accomplice to fraud? Given Patrick's past run-ins with civil law, such an unsettling prospect was hard to flush from his list of worries.

———

DURING THE NIGHT Patrick dreamed about luminous wings lifting Easter up and suspending her in midair. Her ascendancy seemed related not so much to distance as to some mystical elevation. A beatific aura, accompanied by celestial music, framed her face. She looked at Patrick, her soft gaze lingering on him as he stared in awe at her beauty. Then, as suddenly as she appeared, she was gone.

In his bedroom, he turned to make sure she was sleeping peacefully beside him.

Though skeptical of miracles contrived for the occasion, Patrick shared her desire to help people. His lifelike dream beckoned him to identify with her quest. He tried to imagine himself, along with her, destined to lead a new world—a retooled humanity—in its pursuit of disease-free lives.

Was he the lifeline, the secret weapon for a genutopia of pedigrees mentioned in the New Scrolls?

How much of their success would depend on Patrick being her courtier? *Why me?* he wanted to ask. *I'm an entertainer, not a world changer. The solo fame I wanted is now a more distant goal.*

It occurred to him that King David, an ancient king, had been chosen while simply a shepherd boy without social standing. So status was apparently not the only measure of someone's potential.

A half hour before sunrise, Patrick insisted the girls run the beach to avoid the paparazzi. Soon after breakfast and a shower, Easter summoned them to meet with L.T. in the mansion library.

The girls filed into the room, their eyes wide with anticipation. The preacher stood facing them, his palms grinding together and clapping to gain attention.

"I don't like dropping by so early but this briefing can't wait," he said. "It's important to y'all's future—all of y'all."

Standing with the girls, Patrick stationed himself as their wingman. He cringed at the possibility of Moreau revealing the contents of the *Analyzer*.

Moreau continued. "Don't get shook by rumors. Some out there are saying Immanuel's intent is to monopolize all the best-looking women. Others say the feds will raid this mansion. They don't take kindly to polygamy but the Almighty will deal with our enemies in his own way and in his own time."

Cheryl raised her hand. "Will it affect our nuptials this Saturday at Gulf State Park? Should we move it to a secret location?"

"No," Easter said. "And don't forget wedding rehearsals tomorrow. Plus, before we leave this room, Cheryl will announce the seven of you who're predestined to become pregnant first." She swung her arms by her side like a restless child. "After the wedding reception, we'll take the bus to a seaside resort in the Florida Keys. It's the perfect place to dwell on spiritual things. And Patrick, while we're away, you'll stay here and create enough skits to last all season long."

"It's me against the world, huh?" he said.

She smiled. "In a little while I want you to entertain a few of the Sweethearts in the library. Why not start by reciting your new jingle to set the mood?"

"Sure." He grinned. "Aptitude and attitude went out to play, aptitude won the game but attitude the day. No small task for a courtier." He faked strumming a guitar. "Need *stray* in there somewhere."

Easter laughed. "Well done. But it's now time for Reverend Moreau to officially consecrate you for your proxy mission."

"Thanks, but I can *concentrate* on my own."

"Nice try," she said. "Please make an effort to conduct yourself as my loyal servant."

Servant? The word, as his great-grandfather Landon would say, stuck in his craw.

The televangelist stepped forward to face Patrick. "Bow your head." His breath redolent of mint, L.T. affected a solemn tone. "I hereby confer upon you the duty to fulfill divine promises found in the sacred Scrolls. As Immanuel's surrogate, you are knighted to service his lovely celestials. You'll honor their nuptial right to you by letting loose your juice to reproduce. Amen."

The preacher backed off as the Sweethearts applauded. He promptly departed the library. Easter closed the door behind him as Patrick smiled. "Let loose my juice to reproduce? How original."

"Listen up, everybody," Easter said. "Cheryl has important news to share with us."

Cheryl pulled her blond hair back in a ponytail before reading from a notebook. "So here we go. First on the list to be seeded is—" she glanced at Patrick "—Freckles Lambert."

"Ah, yes, the perfect prank," Freckles said. "Surely you can do better than that."

"No, I'm serious," Cheryl said. "Being a prankster doesn't exempt you. Second to conceive will be Anastasia Andrews, followed by Dodie Appling and Peaches McCollough. Take a bow, girls."

Cheers erupted as the young women bowed low from the waist. Cheryl's gaze rested on the only Australian among them, Cassie Wellington, whose braided blond hair hung to her waist. "As your loving family would say in the land Down Under, you'll soon be clucky."

Cassie whirled in place as the group applauded. "Fantastic," she said.

"Lastly—" Cheryl's gaze roamed "—we proudly announce the Canadian twins...."

Cheers drowned out the names of Sandy and Mandy Dupleiss as they rushed to hug Patrick.

Given time alone might be a welcome change to write skits, he thought. The girls would return after a week away and regroup. What might happen then? He tried to imagine their expectations and demands. Perhaps he had seen more anxious moments of anticipation, but he couldn't remember when.

WHILE WAITING for Easter to arrive with updated instructions, the seven Sweethearts milled about in the mansion library with Patrick and perused framed photos on the wall that illustrated Slack Creel's famous charity tournament. A few photos featured the Paladins alongside their female caddies.

For a fleeting moment he imagined the Paladins using the library for strategy sessions, but then his thoughts veered to Goat, wondering if he was the one who submitted the Sweethearts' photos to the *Analyzer*. Would a link in the tabloid steer the curious to the keepsake video on the internet?

Eyes closed, Anastasia cheered the photos. "Wooo! Do I detect something super sensual here?"

Patrick grinned. "Seems those guys like to spoof everything, as if life is one big game. What I'm feeling, though, is a deeper sense of responsibility and it concerns you girls."

Dodie winked. "I'm good so long as my kids inherit your genes," she said.

Easter entered the library and snapped her fingers loud. "Time now for you girls to channel your instinctual pedigree passions."

"Instinctual?" Anastasia said.

Easter waved to Cassie. "Please share a few truisms you found recently."

Cassie recited from memory. "Geneticists agree that the human female mates for good genes. It's instinctive. So the male who provides her offspring with his superior genes will be naturally attractive to her." She grinned. "So what does our paramour have to say about that?"

Patrick winked at her. "Take it from me, if chemistry and charisma are what we adore, then those must count for more in your final score."

The girls moved to sectional sofas as Cassie quoted verses from the Scrolls. Key words sounded familiar to him. *Paradise. Jubilee. Stewards. Swords into ploughshares.*

Cassie's tone lowered to set up a conclusion. "The Chapter also says, 'The teachable will inherit the earth's enormous bounty and repurpose it by seeking new treasures, the kind money can't buy.'"

Easter faced him squarely. "Did you know our ancestors practiced selective mating? It began in earnest about a hundred years ago. The idea is, when we help one of us, we're helping all of us. A spirit nation has an instinctual need for better, faster propagation."

"Spirit nation?" Patrick said.

Easter shook her hair back. "Yes, we're not confined by artificial boundaries. Also, the Scrolls mandate a multiplier effect among all ethnicities. Or words to that effect. It says colors, I think, but I'm paraphrasing."

"I get exponential growth and repurposing with a different value system," he said. "But really, who practices polygamy these days?"

Easter spread her arms wide, as if to embrace the group. "We all come from families who favor polygamy. Maybe yours do, too. Would that surprise anybody?"

"Yeah, me," he said as they laughed. "By the way, how do these pedigrees hook up?"

"Families rendezvous year after year," Anastasia said. "Some travel thousands of miles."

Patrick nodded. "So, as great-granddaddy Landon would say, they favor courtship."

Easter stood with feet spread wide. "Exactly. It gives parents a chance to size up future spouses on behalf of their offspring. And when the time is right, wedding bells ring. Enough questions for now. Time to toast the chosen."

Turning from the Sweethearts, she opened a fridge behind the wet bar. "This LoveLife drink is only one key to our success."

He examined the label on a spare bottle as Easter filled eight goblets with the golden liquid: *Love nectar concentrate...use sparingly.* She darkened the room with a dimmer and lit votive candles. Each cast a glow on sectional sofas in the room.

After giving him a parting hug, she spoke in a hushed tone. "Remember, as a paramour you must act instinctually. Do not disappoint." She hurried from the room and closed the door behind her.

"Hey, where you going?" he called after her.

From the popular *Lovers Only* CD, romantic lyrics from the stereo system filled the room. The love song spoke of touching the heart with the flame of desire, causing him to mull Easter's setup for a private send-off in the library. Even with goblets of liquid laced with an aphrodisiac, a menagerie struck him as absurd. But perhaps their innate modesty would move them to mirror his self-control.

"Ignore the potion," he said with a wave of his hand. "Love should be a meaningful time, not an assembly line, so Easter's clever endeavor to enhance romance is off the charts for me. Pardon my witty ditty, but we need to glow and go 'cause we have skits to rehearse for our TV show."

Peaches moved closer to him. "Okay, but just so you understand, I'd love to bear your child."

"But wait, we have things to discuss," he said. "Profound things."

Cassie's voice rang loud with enthusiasm. "Good. Let's talk about babies."

Anastasia joined the lyrics of the song. "We're made for love, baby, and love was made for us, for real. Just believe it and receive it and never say it's surreal, just know our love is true, baby."

Patrick looked from side to side, perplexed. Would Eugenia, his great-grandmother, approve of plural wives, especially mates who wanted dozens of children? Kids? Okay. Polygamy? No way.

As the song ended, Peaches led them in a cheer-song: "Dozens, dozens, dozens of babies!"

"Okay, okay," he said. "But I want to tell you a secret. Brace yourselves for a shock. What I have to say has to be said and who better than me to say it? After all, I lived it. Yes, I lived it."

The young women quieted and seated themselves, awaiting his revelation.

As Patrick gathered his thoughts, he decided full disclosure would build trust. It may also distract them from their obsession with making babies.

"Me. In high school. A spelling bee. I'm being asked to spell perpendicular. I'm bored. First, I pronounce the word. I get as far as *perpendick*. I say it twice, slowly, and yes the accent on the D-word is deliberate. Yes, sniggers all around. Yes, teacher scolds me. Yes, I don't give a flying fig." He paused. "But that was then. Anything for laughs."

He popped his fist rhythmically into the palm of his hand. "Humor has to mirror life. My life, by the way, was anything but humorous until I was invited here to train you girls. In fact, I was an unhappy comic. When Easter gave me the title of Casanova Comic, it fit, but not for the reason you might think. Now she's added courtier. It's more than a title and, like other titles, it's an obligation."

He grinned. "Courtier suits me fine. Fact is, it inspires me. Why? Because here with you I have found my true calling. Here I've found genuineness and love and meaning. Your future. My future. It's all inseparable. That's the good news, but I have even better news."

Peaches flashed a dimpled smile. "How much better? Like better babies, right?"

"Patience, please, I'm getting to that." He winked at her. "Let's assume all you girls are ready for motherhood. So, all you fertile Myrtles get pregnant, which is the fruit of love, but—" he waved a finger crosswise "—funny thing, I'm not into exhibitionist sex. I don't have a voyeur bone in my body."

"We can help you overcome your hang-ups," Dodie said.

"Hang-ups?" he said. "I'm not a prude, if that's what you're thinking. I do love you, all of you, and I believe through love we can become a part of something bigger than ourselves. We can—"

"Why be shy?" Freckles said. "We're not."

"I'm not shy," he said, unsure of which direction his extemporaneous speech was taking him. "I'm just saying we don't need a ménage. And aphrodisiacs may stimulate us, true, but it could also change the chemistry in our brain. If so, copulation would soon feel like a big letdown. Why not work *with* nature instead of trying to bend it with some exotic elixir?"

Dodie raised her hand. "We don't need an elixir, but we do need you, voyeur or not."

Mandy Dupleiss, her voice quivery, spoke. "The Scrolls endorse polygamy, so why don't we, you know, ditch our inhibitions?"

Cassie's voice rose more assertively. "Yes, ditch our inhibitions. Ditch 'em, baby, ditch 'em."

Befuddled, he searched their faces in the candle-lit room, wondering why his reasoning failed to reach them. They had flirted but never whipsawed him with manic enthusiasm.

He breathed deep and exhaled his frustration. "Why aren't we in sync? What's up, girls?"

"Why reject us?" Cassie said. "Like, we're not fat or ugly."

"It's not you," he said. "Listen to me. All my life I've been doing things off balance. Like, as a youngster, I used to dream of hitting the comedy jackpot. That didn't sit well with Dad. He wanted me to be a naturalist and do battle in the ecology wars."

He interlocked his fingers behind his back and shifted from one foot to another. "The other thing is, we Murphs rely on an elder picking someone for us to marry. By elder, I'm referring to Eugenia, my great-grandma. But the thing is, I broke away to freelance. I hated regimentation." He shook his head. "My rebel nature and lack of self-esteem had me crossways of the rules everywhere in those days. But when I met Easter, my life changed. I admire her leadership skills but I don't agree with her shortcuts. Like the keepsake thing she asked you to make for Goodnowe."

"I'm not proud of the keepsake, either," Anastasia said. "We got snookered."

He folded his arms. "Maybe now I want to be a good example, okay? I do cherish being your coach and your mentor and I care deeply for you—all of you."

"We care deeply for you, too," Cassie said. Her companions chimed agreement.

"Love revitalizes," Anastasia said. "We feel it and we look to you for bunches of it."

Still standing, he took Anastasia's hand and kissed it. "Glad y'all feel that way. A moment like this is what I call *thumos*." He smiled. "In ancient Greece, thumos meant a special time when all that is best within ourselves blends with all that is eternal for a perfect synchronicity. It's like a happy reunion between reason and desire."

"Wow, that's so eloquent and romantic," Anastasia said. "It gives me goosebumps. Woo-woo!"

On a roll, he continued. "To me, your upcoming pregnancies will be the highest of achievements among women with superior genes. Problem is, Immanuel takes all the credit for your progeny. Not that I want people obsessing over my youth gene, but Immanuel's claim to it is bogus."

Anastasia stood and hugged him. "Have faith, baby. It'll work itself out."

"But his image doesn't square with reality," he replied. "Why must we tolerate an illusion?"

Cassie curled her arm about his waist, competing with Anastasia as she snugged him closer. "So it's partway illusion," she said. "Get with the plan, man. Imagine it as real and it will be."

"Okay, but this wall-to-wall hootenanny Easter cooked up is—"

Cassie interrupted. "Okaaay! How about you helping us create an impromptu skit?"

"Skit?" he said. "What's the premise?"

She smiled. "Let's do a comical wardrobe malfunction while we're dancing with you."

Patrick pinched the bridge of his nose. "That's the kind of dance that blew up my act with the Pony Xpress. Women were screaming and rushing the stage and—"

"We know," Cassie said. "But we number only seven, not hundreds of out-of-control fans. I mean, what could possibly go wrong?"

"A lot," he said. "Next thing I knew, cops were raiding the club."

Anastasia chuckled. "Okay, but that's all the more reason to do this. We can recreate that event and purge it from your bad recollections. It's the least we can do for you."

"Yeah," Peaches said. "It's just us girls and you trust us, okay?"

He studied their faces. "This isn't a prank, is it?"

Anastasia pulled clear of his reach. "*Whaaat*? Are you implying we're more trouble than a pack of prickly porcupines at a nudist convention? C'mon, relax."

Dodie laughed. "Yeah, dance with us. You're the official courtier."

He shook his head. "How can a man say no to sweet girls like you?"

"That's the spirit," Freckles said.

He peered about at them. "Remember, no monkey biz."

Cassie hurried to the bar and poked a button. A song blasted from the stereo system, its lyrics matching the beat of a bump-and-grind favorite by Christina Aguilera.

In perfect rhythm, Anastasia's sinuous moves set the pace and drew her companions closer to corral him. The Texan exposed her bosom and the rest quickly followed her lead.

Inspired by the music, his excitement rose as they encircled him to demonstrate their shimmy-shake, their bodies swaying, twerking, and coaxing a wardrobe mishap.

Cassie and Dodie had pinned him on the sofa when the library door suddenly swooshed open.

Uniformed officers, their silhouettes backlit by the glow from the parlor lights, rushed forward. Whistles pierced the air. A voice shouted "Vice Squad! You're all under arrest." The girls shrieked as though a fallen sky had enveloped them.

Patrick sprang to his feet, arms raised. "Whoa now, don't get happy-trigger. We, we, we're just having a fiddle, uh...little fun. It's not what it likes, uh...looks like."

"You like looking?" the female officer said in a harsh tone, her pistol aimed at his groin. "Being tongue-tied is the first sign of guilt, sport. If you can't pronounce it, don't announce it. And I dare you to make me call for backup. I'm gonna report your ham-it-up-harem to the news media."

He waved his arms above his head. "But we, we—"

"No we-we about it. Just fess up to your crime. A proxy gets no passes here."

"Proxy?" he said as the Sweethearts burst into a paroxysm of laughter, palms slapping as they danced about the room in festive celebration.

"Not again," Patrick said while palm-slapping his forehead. "I should've known you girls were setting me up. Easter, where did you get those uniforms? Is Larry in on this?"

"Whoeee! We gotcha good this time!" Cheryl said as she removed her police hat.

Vanessa brandished a fake pistol. "We ought to reenact this raid for our TV show."

He shrugged. "Hah! I was just stringing y'all along. Didn't fool me one bit."

"Admit it, we gotcha good and you fell for it," Cheryl said.

Easter hooked a thumb into the wide leather belt of her uniform. "It took perfect timing but hey, good is still happening." She bowed like a matador. "We've gotta go now. Show's over." She turned and motioned for her mock squad to follow her into the parlor.

He stood motionless for a moment after Easter's exit. Slowly turning, he faced the Sweethearts and grinned as a comical notion teased his mind. "She gives me the heebie-jeebies," he said. "Call me a proxy, a paramour, or a Casanova but I'm dutiful to the beautiful and I don't stammer over glamour. I'll call the shots from this *flay dorward*, uh...this day forward."

Tight-lipped, the girls sniggered at his stuttering mistake.

He trigger-pointed at Cassie. "Join me an hour before lunchtime for a massage. Dodie, I'll take care of you at midafternoon. Freckles, you're mine around suppertime. Anastasia, we're on tonight. I'll do you twins first thing tomorrow. Peaches, you can go up to my room now. Yes, now!"

He assumed the stance of a drill Sargent to speak forcefully yet playfully. "No more *pwanks*. It throws my timing off and ices my *bwain*. Besides, we don't know what tomorrow will *bwing*."

"Why the big concern about tomorrow?" Cassie said while fastening her bra.

"Because my instincts tell me we'll be facing a big challenge, and soon," he said.

"Woo-woo," Anastasia said. "Sounds spooky."

Relaxing his stance, he held fast his playful mood. "Whatever it takes, *meself* will protect all *ye* damsels from all manner of assorted villains."

Cassie snort-laughed. "We expect *yeself* to not be so callous with *ye* phallus."

Like a jump ball when a basketball is tipped out of reach, it occurred to him that depending on intellect and experience to outwit the Sweethearts was more fantasy than solution. Another wonderment crossed his mind; giving the girls a massage could be risky. Suppose he decided to go a step further and satisfy their baby-making request? Would it improve his rapport with them, perhaps raise his status?

Or would sexual intimacy complicate their trusting relationship with him?

THIRTY-THREE

On the phone from the Sanctuary Inn lobby, Moreau sounded frantic. "The girls are bunched up in the *Analyzer* and they're all jaybird naked," he said.

Easter stopped on the stairwell of the mansion parlor and clutched her smartphone tighter. "Who would dare put us in that rag? Where's Mr. Goodnowe?"

"Well, I think after dark he'd most likely be on his boat," Moreau said.

"Find him! I need to know who betrayed me. And hurry! And call me right back. I have to know who's responsible for releasing our photos to that trashy tabloid."

Easter waited ten minutes for the preacher's next call while pacing the parlor floor. Her mood grew darker by the moment. She phoned Moreau. No answer. Jogging the distance in six minutes, she arrived at Sanctuary Inn and found a copy of the *Analyzer* in the Swashbuckler Pub.

From a barstool in the pub, she ordered a Scotch and soda. Her anger burned hotter after seeing her girls, including herself, in the tabloid. The montage of photos filled two pages. Two feature pages! The telegenic ten wore only thongs or sheer teddies, and in some photos their breasts were exposed.

The article embellished Danny DiNago's exploits as a genetic messiah but Christian leaders lambasted him, their harshest comments shown in prominent quotes.

One pull-quote in the text, a statement by Father O'Brien, stood out from the others: "No one can deny DiNago is pretending to be the storied Christ, but he's also used quite shamelessly by a notorious charlatan on Gospel Galaxy TV."

Easter suspected polygamy would offend the sensibilities of those who revered the teachings of Jesus but this pictorial flaunted plural wives. The *Analyzer* now scandalized her girls for grifting, not the respectable harem shown earlier on L.T. Moreau's television show. And the gaudy bling, never worn by Immanuel, further cheapened his all-American image.

"Another Scotch, Jacki," she said while studying the double-page narrative again.

"Better slow it down, girl," the barkeep said. "You're way past tipsy."

"But my girls have been shanghaied." She spread the tabloid layout on the countertop. "I'd like to know who gave our pictures to the *Analyzer*. It had to be Sorelle. Somewhere that snotty-nose Jezebel is gloating about it. But she'll pay, yes, and today by god is payday. I want to claw her evil eyes out and feed 'em to the crawdads." She downed her drink before slamming the empty glass on the countertop. "Another one, Jacki, and make it a double this time."

Easter had knocked back her fourth drink when Jacki turned away and straightened a wall plaque depicting a stylized shark, its mouth open wide as it chased high-stepping stick figures of human waders. The irreverent caption read, "Fishers of Men."

With her back turned after serving a fifth Scotch, the barkeep sent a text message to her closest friend, Buzz Cassidy. *Stump's main gal likkered up. Call him b4 she finds a victim.*

PATRICK WONDERED if the text message from Buzz was a ruse: *Come b4 u gal gets booted from pub.* The gadabout was known for his wacky sense of humor, so why take him seriously?

But he also knew Buzz could be semi-serious. As usual, time was a factor. The day had passed in a blur, starting with a few of the Sweethearts pranking him. He was not inclined to shut down his laptop.

An hour before the 10 o'clock curfew, he continued to ignore the message on his phone, instead putting the finishing touches on a skit he had written with Vanessa Wynley in mind.

Yeah, my boss asked me why I was ticketed. Well, duh, I didn't use my turn signal. You know, my blinker. When he asked why I didn't use it, I told him I'm saving my blinks.

Something about Buzz's message nagged at him. He donned a T-shirt, sweatpants and Skechers before tiptoeing downstairs and out the back door. If nothing else, he would quench his curiosity about Teddy, the audacious young banker whom he had met at the pub.

Ten minutes later he approached the bar and spoke to Easter as she teetered on a barstool.

Easter slapped the collage of photos with the flat of her hand on the countertop. "Shame, shame, shame! Our honor got all used up. Can't let 'em get away with this."

"Get away with what, sweetheart?" he said.

"It makes us look like huzzz...hussies. We won't lie this takin' down. Call me a lawyer. We got rights. We'll sue 'em ass off."

"Easter, you're drunk. Come, let's go sleep it off and deal with this tomorrow." He held her arms and struggled to lead her from the bar to the Sanctuary Inn lobby. She balked before reaching the entry doors and flagged Buzz Cassidy who happened to be sauntering into the lobby.

"Sorelle's a bitch," she said to Buzz. "And y'know what? I'd never okay a naughty video but for owing Slack big money."

Noting Buzz's puzzled look, Patrick urged Easter along until spotting Sorelle in the hotel lobby. As Sorelle rushed toward him, he shook his head in a not-now signal but she ignored the warning, her intent soon apparent—confronting Easter.

"Hey, you!" Sorelle shouted. "My office called about an exposé of Danny in the *Analyzer*. You won't stop till you've ruined my client's image, will you? What in God's name were you thinking, idiot-woman? Have you no scruples?"

"Slut!" Easter shot back. Eyes glazed, she jerked hard against Patrick's restraint and leaned into Sorelle's space. "You put our *pish-tures* in that rag."

"Oh, but you're the guilty one," Sorelle said. "And don't deny it. My best client is—" stopping her rant, she frowned "—you're drunk."

"Your fault," Easter said. "You got the gall to low-rate me? You be shame, you."

Patrick held Easter's arm after wedging himself between the two women. "Let's go. Here, this way to the parking lot. You can sleep it off in my—"

"I should've known," Sorelle said as she tugged on Patrick's arm. "I hold you responsible as her accomplice, Patrick. The nerve of you allowing Orgo to slime Danny on the net."

His grip loosened on Easter's arm. "That'd be Goat and nothing to do with me. I swear. Scout's honor."

Sorelle's voice echoed in the lobby. "Don't you ever deceive me again, Patrick Murph. You hear me? You've cheapened yourself just by associating with tramps like Easter." In a glass-breaking octave, she shouted, "She's a poacher!"

Easter skirted Patrick, lunged and stiff-armed Sorelle. Instantly recovering from the jolt, Sorelle charged her adversary and ripped her blouse, exposing her braless chest.

Bear-hugging Easter from behind, Patrick pinned her arms back and shuffled her away from the scene. Easter kicked but Sorelle strolled out of reach with her head held high.

"Everything's fine," Patrick said to pacify bystanders—Teddy Crown among them—as Easter wilted in his arms. "She, uh...she's just a bit tipsy."

"See you around," the young banker said while eyeing Sorelle. "What a piece of work."

Too preoccupied to answer, Patrick lifted Easter as if she were a drowsy child and carried her to his van. Buzz followed and opened the door on the passenger side. With a slight breeze stirring over the parking lot, Patrick placed her in a recliner seat and lowered the windows two inches. She slumped like a ragdoll as he closed and locked the door.

Buzz lingered nearby. "You gonna keep her tucked away till she sobers up?"

"Yeah, I want to corner a banking czar before he leaves."

"Is the banker buying?" Buzz said.

"Buying drinks? No, not that I know of. Why?"

"That ain't good. Who's courting who?"

"The Yank with the bank has lots to gain but so do I."

"You buy the drinks, bohunkus, and he'll have you pegged for a sucker."

"Hmmm, so you're thinking he's a con?"

"What can I say? He's a banker. All he's got is money, though. What you got's worth more'n what he's got, else he wouldn't be showing up this far from wink city."

"How do you know Teddy?"

"This here's *my* turf, Stump. Me and Jacki, we make it our *bidness* to know everybody. So see I'm subbing for the limo driver this week and I pick your guy up at the airport. He brags too much so I hear stuff. Cheryl, the smart blonde, she's in love with you. Know how I know? Jacki says she's an open book. But the besotted one here's hot for you, too. All the smart money's on a bigger catfight later but my chips are on this'n."

"If you only knew," Patrick said. Leaving Buzz to puzzle the answer, he reentered the pub, his eyes scanning like radar, but the banker was nowhere to be found. Why would the man dislike Sorelle? *What a piece of work*—the man's exact words. And Easter blurted about being indebted to Slack Creel, the golfer who had earlier forewarned him not to risk being her business partner.

Knowing the Sweethearts' future as entertainers hung in jeopardy, he must assert himself as their leader, take control and sort through the options on their behalf.

While strolling to his van, he imagined himself empowered for this new crisis. Just as he served as Dan the Man's proxy, he also had alpha ranking as Easter's courtier. Oh yeah, even if he refused to be their baby maker, he would honor his newfound status and man-up to rescue the Sweethearts.

THIRTY-FOUR

One mile from the Sweethearts' mansion, Goat Goodnowe stood alone on the wharf at Sanctuary Marina where a dozen boats docked alongside his yacht.

Minnows chased insects drawn by lights along the pier while speckled trout and flounder, hungry for baitfish, lurked below. Only ten yards away the bay waters roiled as a largemouth bass snatched an unwary bluegill.

Goat waited for a visitor he admired above all other marine life. With its row of fang-like teeth and compressed torpedo-shaped body, the barracuda instilled fear in its prey. The predator would often venture into the murky harbor where it attacked any glistening object. Goat affixed Tally Shermer's big earrings to the end of a fishing line and jigged it a few inches below the water's surface.

He repeated the jigging until the main attraction attacked. "Good boy," he said.

Goat's luminous watch revealed it was time for *Informed*, his favorite television program. He soon boarded his yacht and signaled for Tally to fetch a mix of rum—Kraken ninety-four proof—and cola. The embattled opinions of Dr. Henry Ronofski on *Informed* appealed to the Brazilian's taste for intimidating adversaries. As the show's host, Paula Bradley's journalism met Goat's combative criteria.

After introductions to the television audience, Bradley began the interview. "Let me start with a question, Dr. Ronofski. As a famous genetics wizard, why do you insist eugenics is not pseudoscience?"

The slender scientist's owlish eyes seemed to ponder the question. "Actually, pseudoscience is what ideologues are doing when they ignore dysgenics. Genetic mismatching is a huge health issue, yet many scientists today focus on individualized hi-tech treatments that favor the rich and have no regard for nature's solutions."

The woman's eyes, tinted with blue shadowing, lowered to refuse his gaze. "Really? You would dare blame scientists who rely on genetic engineering?"

"They're wedded to the medical system," he said. "Its solutions are too speculative."

Dagger-eyed, she stared at him. "But eugenics is experimental, too, isn't it?"

"Not really. I've often said the few have sabotaged the many, and now here we are at a point of no return. Too many have passed along flawed genes, so let's hurry along with holistic matching, shall we? Of course, it's another reason why I favor plural wives...for some."

The host pushed a loose strand of hair, stylishly streaked in gray, over her ear. "Most people see genetic matching as a cozy excuse for polygamy, which is illegal."

"I know, but if pedigrees were free to practice polygamy, they could reverse the human condition. The focus on genetic engineering doesn't help the masses. Besides, we know most people don't have genes worth sharing."

"Elite pedigrees, eh?" She lifted her chin, a tactic reserved for moments when a Q-and-A session called for condescension.

"Touché," Ronofski said. "How else can we offset genetic deterioration? Fact is, we're besieged by taxes to fund those with severe flaws. Meanwhile, our pedigrees are hard-pressed to procreate more offspring, and fast."

Bradley's eye-roll mocked the scientist's message. "And polygamy will solve that, you say?"

Ronofski shrugged. "Listen, we know the least intelligent are having the most children. We pity them, but pity fails us. We should solve the dysgenic problem before the misery quotient is unbearable. Imagine this; society lost five-to-eight IQ points over the last half of the twentieth century. And with so many states banning abortions, the number of misfits is off the charts."

Curled in a sofa chair aboard *LoveLord*, Tally threaded silver earrings into her earlobes before continuing to clip her toenails. "Bullshit!" she shouted at the television, "Ain't no such thing as misfits."

Goat glared at her. "Do that later, okay? And put away the damn nail polish, too."

Ronofski continued. "For example, look at the increase in illegitimacy, child abandonment, and high school dropouts. Those things lead to criminality, another heavy expense."

"But how do those things relate to your precious pedigree doctrine?" Bradley said.

"Isn't it obvious?" he said. "Look, pedigrees add value. Always have. But after one ideologue on the far right twisted eugenics to justify genocide, and hijacked the movement, radicals have condemned genetic matching. As a result, misfits today are incapable of discerning that the science is legit. So they reject our program. Look at the cost of that rejection. The worst diseases have doubled. If we fail to stop them now, they will plunge us into a cataclysm from which we cannot recover."

"By the way, eugenics led to a world war and the Holocaust, Dr. Ronofski."

Ronofski shook his head slowly in dejection. "If we're to follow that reasoning, then the science itself rather than its hijacking will be discredited for leading us into war."

"Oh, c'mon, that's ridiculous," she said.

"Ridiculous? Science used enemas to treat the Spanish Flu, and infant mortality hit forty percent. Since then, rational people realize ignorance was to blame. But hate inspired by nationalism brought us to an international war when Hitler nationalized, militarized, and delegitimized eugenics. But with our enlightened perspective today, we know science wasn't at fault. A dictator callously misused it. So we don't blame eugenics and we still buy Volkswagens with no regrets."

The host's smile more closely resembled a smirk. "Okay, but why say polygamy is the answer?"

"Because we favor pedigrees who happen to have the right balance of genetic assets."

"I don't know, Dr. Ronofski. It all sounds like a slippery slope to me."

"Oh, but dysgenics is the slippery slope, my dear. It's in free fall; has been for many generations. On the flip side, if those with top-tier genes were matched, we'd see an upswing in human rejuvenation, and at a dramatic speed."

The host snapped her fingers. "Just like that, eh? Only the fittest survive."

Ronofski's gaze lingered in mid-space. "To quote my book, 'Survival of the fittest is not the test; life is about reproduction of the best.' It's no surprise that better genes produce better babies."

The host squinted at her smartphone screen. "Here's one for you. 'Studies show married women among people of color have twice the odds of being infertile.' Twice! So, rather than neuter people like pets, you'd let infertility just run its course. Why? To eliminate reproductive competition, right?"

Goat tensed, sensing a trap. The book-smart scientist might fall for it. Would he tacitly endorse a form of passive genocide?

Ronofski frowned. "A better question is, are we so cruel as to bequeath to our offspring a legacy of killer diseases? Refusing to prevent those diseases is immoral and inhumane."

"Still, the modernist scholar equates eugenics with Nazism," the host said.

The scientist bristled. "If that's true, then modernist scholar is an oxymoron. The Nazis hijacked eugenics for a reason. As I've stated in my book, Communism never advocated genetic matching. Just the opposite. Yet Stalin's record of genocide is the worst in history. The point is, my dear, we need not use eugenics as a pretext for slaughtering millions. Misguided ideology will do."

"But that can't happen in a democratic America," Bradley said.

"Let's not be naïve, Ms. Bradley. Immigrant kids were locked in cages by a president's executive order and forty percent of Americans approved. Regarding Americans, do you realize one in six suffer from mental illness and four percent are sociopathic? But those studies aren't accurate—it's worse. So what happens if those with the most flaws reach critical mass? Sorry but a bad consequence oftentimes has an equally bad cause, and we're seeing it become worse with every generation."

Stiffening, the host said, "But according to your book, we humans have built-in inhibitors against diseases, except emblot, which sounds like a racist assumption."

"Not at all," he said. "And your racism claim only distracts from the real issue of degeneration. I have always felt sorry for those who have emblot. We know it's not exclusive to Blacks. More study is needed to understand the disease and its anomalies."

The host's eyebrows arched. "Let's cut to the chase, shall we? What can we do to help Blacks avoid emblot?"

The scientist sighed. "We'll show them how to help themselves. We obey our instincts. We humans, no matter our race, subconsciously endorse genetic matching by choosing a healthy mate. We want to be wise but nature is whimsical. Who knows which Blacks may benefit? But know this; good genes, regardless of ethnicity, have always been an envy asset among those who choose wisely."

"Envy asset?" she said, hands fluttering. "Sorry, but it sounds, well...terribly vain."

"But we're human, dear. You see, we already make choices based on good bloodlines. Resistance to disease among our pedigree people is not just natural immunity, it's innate. In fact, we intuitively seek a mate in much the same way that birds do."

"Seriously, Dr. Ronofski, we're not wild birds."

The old scientist's thick eyebrows hooded his eyes. "Correct. However, my DNA sampling of birds produced an interesting discovery. I found the partner of some monogamous birds was not the biological father. A scarcity of male birds led female birds to invite the company of males other than their regular partner."

"Okay, so some females are dingbats," she said. "No surprise there. But they are the exception, not the rule. Right?"

"Not so fast. These had extramarital affairs, if you will, and even shared their favorites with other females. But think, dear. We're seeing a scarcity of human males here in America, so females are—"

"Dr. Ronofski, no way are we ready to accept polygamy in America."

"Listen, dear, scarcity isn't the only reason. Plural wives are more often found in countries with heavy disease loads. Again, women prefer disease-free mates with good genes. Also, just as female birds seek a male who's a good provider and defends a territory with plenty of food or shelter, it's the man of means who's better at facilitating polygamy."

"Yuk," she said. "Now we're into rich guys with mistresses. How unromantic."

"It's not a new phenomenon, dear. Look at icons like Dan the Man DiNago. First, he represents genetically superior people at a time when many married couples are infertile. Second, he's rich. Third, he's disease-free. Naturally, women instinctively choose the superior mate."

Tally spat at the television. "Superior, my ass!"

Goat thrust a finger toward the television. "Dammit, Tally, shut up and listen."

Paula Bradley continued. "So why you? How is it that only you are able to recognize or identify the so-called youth gene in DNA? Has that finding been peer reviewed by other scientists?"

"My colleagues aren't interested in reviewing it."

"Why not?"

"Who knows? Their peers have long obsessed over equality. As to why me, well, why not me? Think about it. If anyone is sharp enough to find an unusual gene, fine. That's one thing. But an ability to recognize it for what it is, to understand it, and to see its regenerative value for human achievement, well, it's just too much for some to wrap their mind around. A mutation like that might bring radical changes to our society. Of course, change that robs them of riches from hi-tech is not acceptable."

"What if DiNago's seed is—I don't know—weak? Or his youth gene unreliable or even bogus?"

Ronofski glared at her. "Reproduction will always find a way. I happen to believe in a prophecy favoring pedigrees. It relates to divine intervention that favors believers who practice genetic matching."

"How quaint," Bradley said. "Will we have to eat kumquats or mate with aardvarks to avoid the pestilence of not being pedigreed?"

Tally laughed uproariously. "Kumquats! Aardvarks!"

"For the last time, Tally, shut your damn pie hole," Goat said.

Now irate, Ronofski said, "You said pestilence. How about Hunt-
ington's disease? You inherit it and lose muscle coordination. Then
around age thirty you develop psychiatric problems. Do we know why
the incidents of it are not calculated accurately? You bet we do. Americans refuse screening for it out of fear. Why? It's simple; genetic
discrimination from health insurers. That's why it's undercounted, so
in reality it's many times higher, which skews the entire calculus."

"What's your point?"

"Well, does it concern you that if the disease burden is light,
research funding can't be justified? Why are we not able to detect such
discrepancies? Could it be, collectively, our low IQ?"

After palming her face, she continued. "The leader of your cause,
Easter Beaulieu, is of African ancestry. Will your genotyping include
biracial mating to assist Mother Nature in her balancing act?"

"You would think so, wouldn't you? But to what end, may I ask?"

She sighed. "To prevent emblot, of course."

"Perhaps, but biracial mating is no panacea. Most of those
afflicted by the emblot mutation are beyond the reach of genetic engineering. Too expensive. So yes, hi-tech offers a false hope."

Tally frowned and jumped to her feet. "What? Did he just write
us off?"

"Luck of the draw," Goat said as he aimed the remote and raised
the volume.

Bradley's tone softened. "Yet our attitude must not be cavalier. As
you state in your book, it's condescending to say, 'There but for the
science of genetic matching go I.'"

Ronofski nodded. "Right, so why not be compassionate and help
achieve an equitable balance? And since our goal is to live in good
health, why not combine our best genetic assets? Give nature a shot at
the solution. Who knows? We might even live to be two hundred and
yet show no signs of aging."

Tally shouted at the television. "Dream on, you old fart! You
don't have a frickin' chance in hell of seeing another twenty, much less
two hundred. My people will outlive your skinny ass."

Goat lay the remote aside and stood, his gesture beckoning Tally
to follow him.

"Where're we going, Goat?"

Leading her across the deck, he indicated the precipice along the gunwale. "Stand here so your silver earrings are easier to see. Now, look down at the water."

"Why?" she asked as she leaned over the edge. "You lose something down there?"

"No, Tally, you did."

"Me? What did I lose?"

"Your mind," he said as he pushed her overboard. "Try out-swimming a barracuda, bitch."

THIRTY-FIVE

Stu Watanabe knew his employer seldom took advice from a subordinate, not even from a man who managed his properties with efficiency, or prepared meals on a par with any certified executive chef in America. And taught his protégés to emulate his culinary skills.

Wealth, not gratitude, was the endgame and golf the means to that end for Slack Creel.

On his drive to a hospital in Pensacola, Stu pondered why such men were so oblivious to their ancestry and the joys of life. For them, attaining one goal only created another, thus real satisfaction eluded them. The chef pondered his own forebears and their value to his present-day happiness. As tradition dictated, Stu's middle name—Makoto—meant *peace*.

Stu traced his ancestry to Emperor Saga of the Ninth Century. As the propagator of forty-nine children by thirty wives, Saga had been considered a demigod. It was customary for a royal family or clan to be accepted as the most dominant god—the *kami*—which defined their ancestry.

How, Stu wondered, could any man of either common or royal ancestry think of himself as self-made when his DNA was a composite of every tribe that had gone before him?

At the hospital Stu easily found his boss's room. He sat at Slack's bedside and spoke softly. "I hope you are well today, Mr. Creel."

Slack removed the oxygen mask from his face. "Hell, I'm anything but well. What's on your mind, Stu?"

"Mr. DiNago says he will settle with you for damages," Stu said. "His company made an offer on all your properties. The mansion, pub, restaurant, research center, and golf course."

Slack Creel closed his eyes. "They must know I'm behind on my property taxes."

"That is true, Mr. Creel."

"Sorelle was in here earlier. What are the glamour chicks doing, still dodging the paparazzi?"

Stu grinned. "They are busy with wedding plans."

Slack's eyes opened wide. "Wedding plans? Oh, that's right, they've got that big shindig at the park." He sighed. "Goat says the money should start pouring in from our internet venture, so maybe I won't be selling Ellie's and my other properties right away."

"Mr. Goodnowe has something on the net?"

"Yeah, Easter's glam girls, all ten of them, with lots of *exposure*."

Stu averted his gaze. "Does Mr. Goodnowe share any of the money he makes with the glamour girls' leader, Miss Beaulieu?"

"Hell-no! Sort of ironic, ain't it? Danny doesn't know I screwed his gals without laying a hand on 'em." He chuckled but winced in pain. "That's what I call poetic justice."

"Are you sure Mr. Raul Goodnowe will pay you a share of the money?"

Slack's brow wrinkled below his thinning hair, a matted comb-over. "Why wouldn't he?"

"Well, his boat could take him far away. And fast. And with your money. Has he paid you from his online sales?"

"Not yet, but he will."

"Does he use an offshore bank?"

"Stu, you read too much conspiracy crap."

"Sorry, Mr. Creel, but Mr. Goodnowe's history of good deeds is questionable."

"Nah, Goat's too smart to double-cross me. He'll shoot high-concept movies with Easter's glam gals. We've got leverage. She's in my debt big-time."

Stu frowned. "Her girls no longer pose for Mr. Goodnowe. Miss Beaulieu feels humiliated."

Creel groaned. "Hell, they wanted publicity, they got it up the wazoo, and in a tabloid. So much for gratitude, eh?"

"Sorry, they do not see it the same as you, Mr. Creel."

"Why not? Look at the stars in Tinsel Town who got their start with a skin flick."

Stu checked his watch. "It's time for me to go, Mr. Creel."

"Well, give my regards to Easter and remind her we have a deal. She'd better not think about crawfishing on me. I've half a mind to sue her anyway. Tell her I will if she tries double-crossing me." He sneered. "Humiliated, my ass!"

PATRICK SAT NEXT TO BUZZ, both attentive to Jacki who placed small paper napkins beneath their beer mugs.

"That jerk in the three-piece suit left you a message," she said. "Says he'll be conferring with a couple of executive partners, something about equity investing."

"No kidding?" Patrick said. "He must like hanging around you here at the Pub."

Jacki frowned. "Next time he talks nasty to me, Buzz is gonna bust his chops."

With fists cocked like a bare-knuckles fighter, Buzz straightened his wiry frame on the barstool. "Damn right I will."

"Can't blame you," Patrick said as he sipped his brew. "Sorelle knows Teddy. He hates her. But Sorelle's on the outs with me right now, too."

"Slack Creel wants to lease his mansion to the victims of burned-out condos," Buzz said.

Patrick's voice rose in alarm. "Hope he doesn't kick us out."

Buzz winked at Jacki. "Don't bet on it. It's listed. Slack either can't manage his money, or it flies out to Vegas where booze and broads soak up anything not nailed down at the gaming tables."

Jacki scowled. "You're the one brought that banker guy in here, Buzz."

"Yup! Got paid good, too," Buzz said. "I took him by that new clinic, the one selling Go-Go DiNago's joy juice. Mr. Goodnowe wouldn't see him and he got pissed. Me, I figure the suit had best cool down here at the pub. That man's jumpier than a trigger-happy coke-head at a Shot Show."

"Teddy doesn't scare me," Patrick said.

Buzz grinned. "Said he'd like to ram a 'lectric cattle prod up Sorelle's rectum."

Jacki winked. "He needs schooling in proper etiquette."

"That Sorelle, she knows stuff," Buzz said. "I betcha she could tell you some secrets, Stump. Knowledge is power, you know, and you don't wanna bet against an inside straight."

Patrick swigged his beer. "Yeah, but would she know anybody at the *Analyzer*?"

"Don't know but she was sucking up to Slack this morning. Danny-Do-Right did a number on him. Slack's bitter mad but Sorelle's laying the blame on Danny's bunny girl."

"Bunny girl? Oh yeah, Easter." Patrick drained his mug. "Sorelle threatened me, too. Says she'll sue me, as if I'm a co-conspirator."

"Aw, she don't mean it." Buzz scribed a number in midair with his finger. "Score one if you can make it up to her. She likes fresh seafood. Knows lots of things you need to know 'fore it's too late." He splatted the countertop with a glancing blow. "Take it or leave it."

Patrick slid a credit card toward Jacki. "An insider could be the ally I'm looking for. Think I'll invite Sorelle to a culinary treat. Can't hurt, I suppose."

To offset the scandal about Danny and the telegenic ten, Patrick needed a savvy contact with the *Analyzer*. Sorelle had said she knew beaucoup people. Would she know anyone at the tabloid? A story, a weird one, hopscotched through his mind. If he could spin it into something bizarre for the *Analyzer*, it might nullify scandalmonger Goodnowe's published story.

The story's content must challenge a reader's disbelief. The belief bar among readers of tabloids being near zero, how difficult could it be to con them with a fantastical story? As its originator, he must remain anonymous. How could he conceal his identity as the author? Sorelle may know someone who could help with that, too.

It was a longer shot than the one he'd planned with Larry to monitor Goat's clinic, but the extra counterpunch couldn't hurt, either.

THIRTY-SIX

Patrick waved to his brothers who returned to the Gulf State Park launch after they fished Lake Shelby. In the distance they held up a stringer showing their catch of speckled trout while Patrick gave them a thumbs-up and continued grilling flounder filets in the shade of a towering cypress.

Distracting him, Sorelle entered the area and found a parking space. Attired in a frilly blouse to match a pair of slim-cut white jeans, she reminded him of the same stylish couture that made her famous as a top glamour model two decades earlier.

On her approach, she made a show of sniffing the air. "Ahhh, grilled fish. And I just happen to be ravenously hungry."

With his midriff bare below a tank top, Patrick bowed to her from the waist. "Got a mighty fine day for a cookout, m'lady. Have a seat, relax and enjoy yourself."

"That I will, but why here?"

"Because we can talk in confidence away from crowded restaurants and—" he thumbed toward his brothers "—my nosy kinfolk."

She waved to the anglers as they loaded their boat on a trailer. "So what's the real purpose of our meeting?" She propped her sunglasses on her head and continued in a more blasé tone. "I imagine you have your reasons but remember, you owe me."

"Everybody owes you." Forking a sample of the grilled fish, he offered her a taste test. "A friend of mine says you might have some insider info I need. Hope it's not some malarkey about Easter."

"You're pretty tight with her, aren't you?"

"She's like roux in gumbo," he said. "All the other ingredients won't taste as good without the right base." With platters set near the hot grill, he scooped up fish fillets and added garlic bread, potato salad, and baked beans to the plates before walking alongside her to a picnic table. "I'm curious to know who has clout enough with the *Analyzer* to jeopardize my girls career as entertainers."

"Are you referring to their Funtasy TV deal or their keepsake video?"

He wrinkled his brow in disbelief. "How would you know about that?"

"I know everything, Patrick. A secret to me is like a yellow house. It announces itself. By the way, the Marauders lost an exhibition game last night. They need my Danny back on the team."

"I know, I know," he said. "Guess I'll work on a solution, but help me sort this out. Seems to me something sinister is lurking out there, manipulating us behind the scenes."

He sat across from her and waved to his brothers who left pulling their bass boat with an SUV.

Sorelle tossed breadcrumbs to approaching seagulls. "Who taught you to cook?"

A line from his standup days tracked his mind. "A chef who knew how to avoid salmonella and angry wives. One wife I tried to tame but she was way too wild. I tried everything; kept ER doctors on standby, a lawyer on retainer, and shamans on call. Plus an exorcist when things got really bad. She was sixteen." He grinned. "Her shoe size, of course."

"Ha-ha-funny." Sorelle kept a straight face as she ate. "I'm well acquainted with sinister. Try this on for size. Conglomerates control broadcast media. They test a matrix audience for reactions. Sanitized news is then released to manipulate the public discourse, so red alerts are nixed."

He nibbled the grilled garlic bread. In the distance, an osprey snagged a fish in the lake and flew to the top of a cypress. "But the *Analyzer* scandalized my Sweethearts. It may have ruined their image, along with their entertainment career. I'd like to know who's behind it."

She shot him a doleful stare. "You asked if something is working in secret to control us. How about a cabal of billionaires who think fair is just another word in Webster's somewhere between fable and fantasy? Do you know what globalism is?"

"Yeah, free trade." Taken aback by her smirk, he asked, "What? Too vague?"

"Yes, but that's how the wealthy want to keep it—vague."

"Why?"

She ate more fish before sampling the baked beans. "Best meal I've had since forever. Love the seasoning." Her gaze shifted to a faraway place. "To answer your question, consider this scenario. Let's say I'm in charge of a transnational corporation. So long as stocks are climbing, I really don't care if the environment goes into convulsions."

"Not me, I'd raise hell," he said. "This planet is the only one that's livable."

"Nice viewpoint, but I'm the CEO in this scenario. The board of directors can vote me out if I bypass the game plan. Gone would be my lifestyle—private jet, yacht, mansion, art collection. You'd have to know I'd reached my position of power by backstabbing my way up the ladder."

"Okay, but I happen to favor collaboration," he said. "You know, for the common good."

She grinned. "You're too idealistic, love. Follow me on this, okay? Have you ever noticed how all the news is choreographed like Orwellian double-speak?"

"Not really. Is that how corporate honchos deceive us?"

"Yes. Newscasts are about distracting us with fearmongering, celebrity scandals, and hate-filled rhetoric. Corporations that control commerce can deceive us because they own the airwaves. Financial firms own half of all daily newspapers. Money is power. In fact, if you heaped all the billionaires in one big pile, they'd represent the world's third largest economy. We're talking trillions of dollars."

"Seems to me they have tons of traction," he said. "How do they use that kind of leverage?"

"Well, let's suppose my corporate empire makes huge loans to your developing country. Now you can build roads, hydroelectric dams, seaports—the works. Can't pay off your loan? Not a problem. But your debt obligates you to me."

"Okay, but I can pay it back as long as I'm solvent. After all, I'm autonomous, right?"

"Yes, but I'm cunning. I leverage the debt. Your government cabinet is staffed by my corporate agents. I exploit your natural resources. Of course, I install a military base in your country to protect my investment there. Now I *own* you."

He squirmed on the bench. "Sounds ruthless, not to mention sinister."

"Exactly. But the enormity of its scale is even scarier."

He swallowed a morsel of food. "How so?"

"Well, for every dollar I take from you in gas, gold, or timber, less than three percent goes to the laborers you supply who slave long hours for peanuts. I ruin your environment, too. No more sustainable farming, so I've added to your country's poverty. Your people get sick. Many die."

"And why would I tolerate that?"

Because you, my handpicked dictator, enjoy obscene riches. You're now a *Richistani*."

"Wait. What if I decide to call your hand and nationalize my assets —gas, gold, timber?"

She pinned her hair up with a barrette. "You wouldn't dare."

"Why not?"

"Because with our media power, we'd brand you as a tyrant and overthrow your regime in a military coup. Or we would assassinate you. Omar Torrijos, a democratic president of Panama, went down in a plane crash. We knocked off Jaime Roldos in Ecuador and Allende in Chile. I could go on."

"So if I try, I die? That's surreal. But you're assuming corporate empires work the dark side."

"Patrick, we *are* the dark. When we're done sliming you, TV viewers will fear and hate you, but without knowing the backstory we've kept hidden."

"Seems to me a fair number of people would oppose you."

"Perhaps, but we can discredit them. After all, our reach is unlimited. Who has media power? Not you. We can either control or obliterate your group—your choice."

"Where I come from, that's not considered a choice," he said.

She wiped her mouth with a napkin. "Still resistant, eh? But you do have one ray of hope. Some corporate heads associated with the Central Order do favor gene matching, along with a trophy wife and a mistress of their choosing."

"What're you implying?"

"Well, your girls are vulnerable, aren't they?" She smiled, apparently relishing the idea as she motioned for him to follow her. "More fish, please."

He trekked to the grill alongside her. "But why did they trash my girls in a sleazy tabloid?"

"Admit it, love, your glamour troupe will need rescuing by...guess who? The Central Order. On the net and in tabloids these guys create a crisis only they can resolve. Need money? Good. They'll help you restore the girls' lost credibility. But of course you'll owe them bigtime."

He frowned. "Dare I ask what happens if I refuse their help?"

A deep sigh preceded her words. "Do you really want to go there? What is it with you and that defiant attitude? You'd be risking health, money, and friendships for an ungrateful world, a world that will end on a sour note anyway. You have to cooperate."

"No! It's a trap, always a trap," he said. "The fascist tyrants only care about me cooperating so they can manipulate my genetic assets. They want control for one reason; to grow their fortunes."

"Okay, Patrick, I agree. The Central Order honchos are all delusional but selective breeding for self-preservation, not fortunes, has been their obsession for eons. Because they can't patent your youth gene, they'll certainly try to exploit it. That has to mean controlling you."

"Ah, you know about the youth gene. Who are these jerks? Name one."

She lingered a moment before sitting at the picnic table. "A few you'd know. Goat Goodnowe plays a role but Easter is key. Throw in televangelist L.T. Moreau plus U.S. Senator Blockton and you have religion and politics. Both are allies in the cabal's ambitions."

He nodded. "How do they know about my youth gene?"

She whiffed as if weary of the Q&A. "Believe me, they know who's packing the goods after Dr. Ronofski approached them for a private equity investment. To his chagrin, they turned him down in favor of a method much more corrupt—enter Goat Goodnowe."

He studied the self-satisfied glint in her eyes. "How did you know about my youth gene?"

"Well, I had a clue but it's nice of you to finally confirm it."

A mix of anger and sadness flooded his senses. "Sorelle, I'm guessing you've known all along about the Central Order and how they operate, yet you chose to play their game, which is how to control me. So give me the big picture. You could have opposed their scheme. Why didn't you?"

She smiled. "I thought maybe I'd work my way into their good graces and learn what they know. With that knowledge I'd use their greed against them. Isn't greed the undoing of every tyrant?"

"Sounds a bit risky," he said.

"Yes, but then it dawned on me that I'll need partners like you to assist me. Besides, they can give you a deal that will mean never having to worry about money again. You'll be set for life."

Patrick gazed at the lake without seeing it. "Uh-huh, sounds like a sellout to me. So what's in it for you? You came south to restore a relationship with Danny, your demigod client. But it seems you found something equally valuable—the youth gene. And that little gem happens to be in my possession and you need to pry it loose. Is that how you beat the cabal? You would use me to beat them?"

"We don't beat them, love, we *work* them. They're not any smarter than us. I know a guy who's leveraging to become the next Imperial Master. Believe me, Reggie can help us reform the Order."

"Reform? Not likely. Why work with bad boys?"

She sighed. "For once, try being pragmatic. If billionaires are reduced to zero status, the entire economy collapses. Who'd replace them, some ruthless dictator who thinks democracy is a disease and then ransacks our country's resources? They would surely nationalize my talent empire. You see, while the Order may be bad boys, they're *our* bad boys. But don't worry, we'll have our share of influence."

"You mean money, don't you? We'd be allied with the big money."

"Yes, money is leverage," she said. "The glue holding everything together for them is a heady sense of entitlement. But what if shareholders insisted that corporations form a different kind of alliance, like maybe a re-chartered B-Corp, a benefit corporation? Its goals would extend far beyond supersizing shareholder profits. It'll respect social justice and good environmental outcomes."

"Okay, now you're the one who's being idealistic. You know their good deeds are a front."

"But Patrick, it's a triple-play. We would have principles geared to people, planet, and profit; all tied to high finance."

"I follow you but who'd want to live by those lofty principles in a world run by—you'll pardon my sense of justice—greedy capitalists who stockpile all the money?"

"We haven't worked that out yet, but—" she grinned "—remember I operate in the heart of the financial world. A few of the players believe ethical changes are necessary."

He shook his head. "Yeah, right. Corporate heads are all talk."

She tapped the table, her fingers doing a rhythmic arpeggio. "Maybe so, but my friend at the top considers pedigrees to be a rare bankable asset. Pedigree people could be a business model, like a social vehicle that reimagines world markets."

Patrick squirmed on the bench. "Like commercializing my DNA, huh?"

A strand of blond hair, loosed by a breeze, lay against her face. "Yes, you're marketable."

"Okay, so you profit bigtime, too."

She rolled her eyes. "Of course."

"But you know the Central Order won't respect my independence."

"Patrick, I have a plan for that, but first be my eyes and ears. Share everything you learn with me, and only me, especially about Easter. Do that and I'll help you reach stardom in Hollywood."

"I dunno. I need an in with the *Analyzer*. That rag clobbered us. I'd like to turn it around with a story of my own. It has to restore the Sweethearts' good name."

"And if I do that, you'll help me get Danny back, won't you?"

"Wait, Danny's past the deadline for a franchise re-up."

"Yes, and Tookie isn't easy to convince but he'll extend it for me."

"Don't cut Easter out of the deal," he said.

"What is it with you? Infatuation?" She vibrated her lips like a pony clearing its nostrils. "She's not your ticket to fame. Even her name is ridiculous, like she stole it from an Easter bunny. Besides, her failed attempt to become a talent agent speaks for itself."

"But her partner was Slack Creel, the lecher, and she wouldn't compromise. I insist she not be excluded, and that's that."

She grinned as if harboring a secret. "Okay, I'll have Nigel Pregnor collaborate with you on a story for the *Analyzer*. He has a good rapport with its senior editor."

"Hmmm. Nigel Pregnor. Isn't he the guy who's writing a tell-all book about Danny?"

"Yes, but he owes me. He wants writing credits for a docu-drama I'm doing about Danny."

"You don't miss a trick, do you?"

"Of course not."

"When you're hobnobbing with Reggie, do you pretend to be interested in genetic matching?"

"Of course," she said. "But remember, breeding for better stock like a eugenicist could lead to genocide."

He shook his head. "Genocide? That's a scare tactic, Sorelle. I don't get it. Why the hypocrisy?"

"What hypocrisy?"

"Well, here in America the Jews are against gene matching but Goat claims that in Israel they're copacetic with it. Why the double standard? I mean, if it's good enough for Jews, it should be okay for us Gentiles."

"Maybe so, but that's beyond my purview, Patrick."

"And what about your friend, the guy who wants to be the next Imperial Master? Has Reggie convinced you to believe in genetic matching?"

"Heavens no." She laughed. "But selling it is different."

"Really?"

"Yes. Its potential can't be denied for a global market."

"Ever bought a yellow house?"

"No way," she said. "You don't buy yellow, you have to be *sold* yellow."

"Would you sell one?"

"In a heartbeat."

"I thought so. Remind me not to buy anything from you."

THIRTY-SEVEN

Alone in his van, Patrick drove home while reflecting on his meeting with Sorelle.

Capitalism had no conscience. Its megarich CEOs had deceived the masses. They exploited loopholes, vacated regulations, and hijacked vulnerable projects as well as governments and business leaders to establish a self-appointed ruling class, a shadow government of plutocrats.

Generosity was not part of their value system. Rather than share their bounty, they monopolized markets. In doing so, they created income inequities that victimized the poor. How could Sorelle expect them to welcome a new way of doing business?

Greed seemed to be a chronic downside of epigenetics.

But perhaps Sorelle had found a chink in their collective armor. Would her friend, the financier, side with a world run by pedigrees? Was this power broker's values free of avarice?

Arriving home, he spotted Easter in the shade of the mansion garage. He admired the sheen on her chestnut-brown hair as she approached for an embrace. The hug, aided by the scent of shampooed hair, enhanced her appeal. Gentle kisses covered his face with reminders of her affection for him.

In response to his nuzzling her neck, an audible breath hitched in her throat. She stepped back to look into his eyes. "Feels good, baby, but where've you been?"

"Oh, just shopping for a halo," he said. "But I couldn't find one bright enough for you."

She lolled her head to one side, her eyes blinking away his attempt at humor. "Listen, you'll be giving the brides away on Saturday but you missed rehearsals today. And the twins were asking about you. Massage therapy, you know. They always feel slighted when—"

"Hey, hey, it's exactly two-fifteen on the dot," he said. "Lighten up, okay? That Yankee banker stood me up last night and things got a little complicated after that but I'll tell you about it later." He grinned. "Provided you lay off the Scotch."

"If you must know, funnyman, I have a low tolerance for alcohol, but don't try to distract from the issue." She poked his bare midriff. "The girls won't let you off the hook. Neither will I. Know what I'm saying? They're habited to your attention."

Her scent reminded him of fresh-cut roses. "On Saturday I'll go to the wedding outfitted like a hillbilly."

"Patrick, it's not a circus."

He grinned. "Are you sure?"

"Okay, what's bothering you now?"

"I really don't want to be photographed."

"Why? Ashamed to be seen with us?"

He knew this agonizing moment would come. "It's my past. You see, I was involved in a scam years ago. My face was plastered all over TV news. It still haunts me. So I'll need heavy makeup."

"It can't be that bad. What happened?"

He took a deep breath and slowly exhaled. "The company I worked for sold condo units on spec. The project went belly-up. I was a stockholder with no cash investment but, as it turned out, a whole lot of liability. They left me holding the bag, but not the money bag, and I had to face a judge. Alone. He smirked a lot during the hearing."

"I see. Tell me more."

"The builder was a wealthy contractor from Texas. His MO was build and bankrupt, but L.T. was the sales manager—my boss."

"The Reverend? Wasn't he an unwitting partner?"

"Unwitting? Hardly! He went to prison for fraud in another case a few years ago."

"I know, Patrick. Sloppy bookkeeping put him away. His CPA

embezzled a small fortune. I read the court documents. A prosecutor distorted the facts."

"Maybe so, but I don't trust L.T. I worked behind the scenes to help convict him back when he ran Castaways Outreach and funneled runaway girls—hundreds—to a phony rehab place in a little town called Dewberry. I think the legal term is human trafficking."

"But Patrick, prosecutors withheld evidence. They framed him."

"Framed him? No way. My daughter was lured into their rehab. She had a baby there."

"I'm sorry, darling. We can talk about it later." She ruffled his thick hair. "See? Who'd recognize you at the wedding without your tam? And dark retro sunglasses will add to the disguise."

"But the IRS might spot me."

"Wow! You do get around, don't you?"

He buried his hands in his pockets. "I took cash-only jobs so they couldn't garnish my wages and went incognito in comedy clubs as Pat McGroin. And now on TV."

She held him tight, kissing him repeatedly. "In the van. Now!"

"But the twins want a massage," he mumbled between kisses.

"They can wait. You're so bad with that boyish look and I'm *sooo* in the mood for you."

"What, no hangover today?"

"I prayed it away this morning. I embarrassed you at the pub yesterday, didn't I? It did sort of complicate things for you, I'm sure. Forgive me? C'mon, I wanna make it up to you."

THE FOLLOWING day Patrick dined with Easter at The Landing, a posh restaurant overlooking Perdido Pass where charter boats chugged through to the gulf.

The day had started out beehive-busy: beach run before sunup, followed by a shower, breakfast, a workout in the gym, time in a genetics class, and skit drills—all done before noon. After lunch, at one o'clock, directing skits took priority. At two-thirty he gave Anastasia a massage, followed by coaching the girls for another Funtasy video to be edited by Rubleau's company.

At five p.m. a half-hour with Cassie preceded a swim in the pool before the evening meal at six. A fourth Sweetheart, Peaches, completed the massage therapy rotation at seven.

He soon realized the quality of his scripts had suffered. Time had become a luxury. He could not abide imperfection on their weekly variety show on TV. Something had to give. The upcoming wedding held no promise of relief.

———

PATRICK JOINED Immanuel late Saturday morning in the gym adjacent to the college.

After a cursory greeting, the superstar took a break from lifting weights and wiped his bearded face with a towel. "I hear Easter's upset over the tabloid," he said.

"That would be your best assessment, huh?" Patrick said. "I think she's panicky about Sorelle wanting to get even with her for poaching. Can you imagine those two combining their talents, though? Why don't you have a talk with Sorelle? Easter is a valuable asset to you."

"And valuable to you, too. As a manipulator, she almost equals Sorelle."

Patrick grip-tested a couple of barbells. "I hadn't thought of Easter in quite that way."

"Yep. Those two should be equally yoked, pulling together, but Sorelle keeps score."

"I know. Cross her once, pay her twice. The wedding's at six. Have you seen the girls today?"

"No. It's bad luck to see a bride before the ceremony."

"Look, Danny—"

"It's Immanuel. Call me by my title-name."

"Fine, Manny, uh...Immanuel, but these girls want to look perfect. That's a daylong prep, so getting them to the Gulf State Park on time will take a miracle."

"You're the one who'd better get with the miracles."

Bemused, Patrick hesitated to reply. "I'm into pratfalls, not miracles."

"I'm talking about you actually being one, man."

"Me? A miracle? How?"

"Like in football, man, split the uprights. You need to do more for them than massaging."

Patrick double-blinked. "Okay, but in the meantime, what miracles will you be doing?"

His faraway gaze suggested deep thought. "I'll be memorizing the Scrolls down in the Keys so I can build up my flock's faith."

"Okay, but you just insinuated the girls want more than things like that."

Immanuel gave him a light jab. "Yeah, and the Scrolls say your energies are channeled best for it. You'll excuse me now while I go find Sorelle and straighten out her attitude."

Patrick spared him a glance. "Glad you thought of that all by yourself, boss."

"No boss to it. Humility becomes me. As for Sorelle, it won't be the first time I've had to smooth her ruffled feathers. She's like a mother to me."

Mother? Patrick considered the word as Immanuel departed. Someone, perhaps Immanuel, must end the rivalry between Easter and Sorelle.

His thoughts turned to his own dilemma. His debt to the IRS had to be settled. If federal marshals found him and served an injunction, how would it affect the Sweethearts' trust in him?

The thought weighed on his mind as he imagined the turmoil.

But now he must serve as Immanuel's best man. *Best* man? How ironic. A sports icon was to be wedded to twenty-one women in name only. And not one betrothed to Patrick.

How had his world become such an odd mix of fantasy and reality?

THIRTY-EIGHT

A motorcycle escort led the bus through Gulf State Park to a
spot where Lake Shelby offered a backdrop of live oaks
festooned with long strands of moss while a gentle breeze
contributed to the comfort enjoyed by nineteen-hundred wedding
guests.

Gertrude, the bodyguard, helped the brides disembark from the
bus in a flourish of beauty and pageantry while Larry Lemoyne and
his partner stood nearby and gazed at the gown collection they had
designed for each of the Sweethearts.

At the far end of a carpeted walkway, Larry's work crew had
woven white orchids and teacup roses into an arched trellis on the
platform behind the podium where L.T. Moreau waited to officiate
the nuptials. Also arching high above the walkway at its midway
point, an arbor of matching floral colors offered more evidence of
Larry's artistry as a decorator.

Moreau nodded toward a band behind the podium where a choir
belted out a medley of jazzy songs. Handlers on the ground guarded
accordion-release boxes. Each contained painted ladies, a species of
butterflies with three-inch wingspans. All would be a fluttering
surprise when released.

Soon after the brides swished free of the luxury coach, graffiti
artists assailed it.

Riding with Immanuel, Patrick sat in the rumble seat of a 1928

Model-A Ford, the position symbolic of his ceremonial status. The gold-plated car clackety-clacked as if to announce its driver, Patrick's great-grandfather, as the event's grand marshal. He wondered how Easter knew where to contact Landon Avery Murph, the slender centenarian.

The old man pointed at the graffiti on the tour bus: "Wet dreams on wheels," he said. "No biting below the belt." He stood beside the car and peered over Patrick's shoulder. "What a lolla-palooza this is. These modern flappers have a great sense of humor, don't they?"

Landon's appearance—no crepe skin, no turkey neck, and no sagging flesh—solicited admiring glances with his starched white shirt, gray slacks, red suspenders, and black Stetson hat.

"Nice getup, Grandpa," Patrick said as he jumped from the rumble seat. "Like vaudeville."

"Yep. Back in the good ol' days, Eugenia and I were stage actors. Should have seen us. We'd be adlibbing and before you know it people got to laughing so hard they plumb forgot to breathe. Had some big paydays in our heyday, too."

"For how long was Eugenia your comedy partner, Grandpa?"

"Long enough, son. She named this old Ford after the most famous sex symbol in Hollywood—Betty Boop. Boop had cleavage, a short skirt and a garter belt. The National Legion of Decency forced the movie studio to tone her down. Imagine doing that to an animated cartoon character. Speaking of sexy women, my favorite real-life lady friend was Margaret Sanger. She was our mentor."

"She fought for women's rights, didn't she?"

"Yes. She helped mostly poor women who begged for birth control, but wouldn't you know church leaders declared her first pamphlet obscene."

"Obscene? Why?"

"Because they thought birth control was like playing God. It was outside the norm. Most think of genetic matching in the same way today, yet they accept degeneration as normal. And why do they fault Margaret for associating with eugenicists back in the nineteen-thir-ties? What next? It's like blaming us for accepting hygienists as neighbors."

Patrick glanced at his watch. "Let's go, Grandpa. I'm the groom's best man today."

Landon stalled. "In the spring of twenty-nine, Eugenia gave birth to our first child. So I took on another comedy partner but danged if she didn't get pregnant, too. Before I retired, I'd taken on a dozen more partners."

"Wish I could hear more about 'em but—"

"Oh, you will. I'll be at the soiree."

"The what?"

"The reception, son. You know, the party. Hang in there with Easter and she'll fill you in. By the way, Eugenia never called you Runt, and that's a fact."

Leaving Landon with Immanuel, he smiled at his great-grandfather's ability to leave a listener wondering about his former comedy partners.

Patrick sidled to the perimeter of the area cordoned off by velvet ropes. Photographers aimed two-dozen cameras at the Sweethearts but only photogs from *Affinity*, a bridal magazine, milled about the restricted ceremonial area. Trudy Mickelstein ordered her cameraman to photograph the brides as they gathered at the head of the processional walkway.

According to plan, each bride was to glide along the trail of rose petals toward the altar. During their walk, a canopy with winged awnings on each side provided shade. At the altar they would face the preacher in a group ceremony.

Their satin gowns ranged in color from turquoise to coral, lilac to daffodil yellow. Each off-the-shoulder design, with cleavage as the focal point, featured bodices of embroidered lace, seed pearls, and iridescent crystals. The fabric, with its beaded accents and loops gathering at the waistline, arrested the eye. Small orange blossoms glammed each headdress.

Televangelist L.T. Moreau steadied himself on the lectern. A canary yellow tie with blue dots matched the handkerchief in the breast pocket of his navy blue suit. His cologne drifted on the breeze.

Danny DiNago, listed only as Immanuel in embossed lettering on the program, sported a pearl-white suit in contrast with his dark beard and mane. He stood erect and statuesque in front of the altar, waiting for the first bride to approach. Behind him, a slender mahogany box with a custom-made, inlaid mother-of-pearl bouquet design, lay open. Its interior, lined in red velvet, cushioned the diamond rings, each in its own slot. Easter had hinted that, all total, their appraised value "exceeded the annual income of plastic surgeons in LA."

Patrick positioned himself close to the groom. "What must you be thinking now, oh high one?" he asked, his voice low.

Immanuel matched the comic's tone. "I wonder if the prenups were recorded at the courthouse."

"Sorelle had your lawyers take care of that, no doubt."

"Who tipped off those guys to mark up my bus?" Immanuel said.

Patrick grinned. "A freckled female. It's a wedding tradition in the South. And just yesterday she hacked a letter in a church message board. It reads *God Resigns* instead of *God Reigns*."

"It figures. What's with the dark sunglasses, man?"

"My eyes are sensitive to photo flashes."

"Jesus!"

"Addressing yourself, my lord?"

Immanuel chuckled. "I forget who I am sometimes."

"Yeah, it's called identity crisis."

"Nah, just a brain fart. *SportScene* says you ran for four touchdowns in the Swamp."

"Nope, six. Two were called back for penalties."

"The writer also said you had out-of-this-world stamina, said you must be *on* something."

"Yeah, extract of green persimmon," Patrick said. "It has pucker power. It puckers the lips to keep the biorhythms in sync with other bodily BS incidentals. I'm kidding. Actually, my blood carries lots more oxygen than others."

"If you say so, pee-wee, but you'll need to do more than show the Sweethearts a good time in the sack, puckered or not."

"More? I gotta do *more*? Like what?"

"Like show them what our cause is all about, man. The Reverend consecrated you, so you gotta keep them faithful, not just, well...."

"Pucked?" Patrick grinned. "Okay, but the proxy idea wasn't mine, you know."

"Wasn't mine, either."

"Say, does my being indoctrinated, consecrated, and manipulated have anything to do with your seedless status?"

"Watch it, funny man, we don't bandy that about. Sperming is *your* game, not mine."

"But it's *you* the girls are going to the Keys with, not me."

Immanuel nudged him. "They'll be back soon enough. You're marked as my proxy, and that's an honor above all honors. But I rule them. Your job is to procreate on my behalf. Like you're a stuntman in a movie, there to make the star look good."

"Movie, huh? I'd title it *Spermaticus* and enter it in Cannes, Sundance, and a dozen others."

"Get over yourself, man. I'm the star—always."

"No, you're the whole damn Milky Way. Who needs the constellation with you around?"

With the tapping of a baton, the preacher's music ensemble was alerted to start the wedding march. Patrick strolled along the carpeted walkway to the arbor before escorting Easter down the aisle. A jazzy rendition of "Here Comes the Bride" charged the humid air. An electric guitar, flute, keyboard, saxophone, trumpet, drums, and violins assaulted the ears of spectators.

"You call this music?" Patrick mumbled as a flutist missed a few nuance notes.

Easter squeezed his arm. "It's New Age Jazz. Refreshingly different, don't you think?"

"Uh-huh, *real* fresh." As they drew close to Immanuel, Easter took the groom's hand but her side glances fell repeatedly on Patrick.

Stepping away, he joined the semi-circle of Sweethearts at the arbor close behind Easter and Immanuel. Peeling smoothly from the group, he stood near the ring boxes as the choir swayed, their voices humming softly like bumblebees caught in a gourd.

Patrick returned Easter's smile and wondered if guests noted her interest in him.

"Dearly beloved," Moreau said, "we gather here today to witness our messiah's marriage to his loving brides. This marriage is recorded in heaven as it is on earth." He gazed down at Immanuel and Easter. "This holy act goes beyond brides who'll help erase our birthsome flaws. It restores the type of innocence we find way back yonder in

Eden." His lofty gaze swept the audience. "Polygamy ain't for every-body but the Scrolls declare it's an option."

He pounded the podium. "We gotta stop all this winking at adultery and divorce. Polygamy is not the abomination. The real sin is bringing up kids in homes with no daddy."

Moreau's arms fanned toward the bridal group. "We gotta make polygamy legal for pedigree people. Irregardless of that, the women you see before you today are virtuous forerunners of a brand *neeew* age." He swayed in place as harmonious approval from the choir resounded over his voice. "I realize man's law forbids it but God's law can *overriiide* man's secular law."

The preacher paused for loud amens, then spoke as if infused with a metaphysical gift for homey eloquence. "God's people ate pork when it was God's due time. Well, now's the time for polygamy. The earth is being prepared for a genutopia."

Eyes glazed with tears, Easter bowed her head and glanced side-long at Patrick.

Goosebumps covered his arms. It seemed she exuded an ethereal charm not evident to him in days past. He wanted to put into words the adoration, the longing she stirred within him. It seemed no camera could do justice to the love reflected in her large brown eyes.

He ached to be the one accepting her wedding vows and giving his own to her. Dare he imagine her allied with a greedy megaopoly and subjected to the whims of a Central Order honcho?

L.T.'s nod was Patrick's cue to place a ring on the Sweethearts' fingers as the official courtier. To each he whispered *I love you* and embraced each one as they voiced the same sentiment to him. But, before giving Immanuel the ring for Easter, he held her in a long embrace. If only he could say aloud she belonged to him, heart and soul, not to some demigod. The pro baller had no right to her.

Instead, he suppressed the lump in his throat and backed away.

The televangelist's voice boomed as Immanuel slipped the ring on Easter's finger. "Behold the groom and his brides!"

His loud voice signaled the butterfly wranglers to open the boxes. Wings fluttering, hundreds soared in every direction. Spectators cheered and applauded. Patrick closed his eyes, knowing Easter shared the same longing to be together with him. Breaking suddenly into a reverie, the band played the Battle Hymn of the Republic. Like many things he considered oddball in the wedding, a patriotic song seemed not only out of place but disrespectful as well.

The strangeness of the event seemed to mock him as anger fought for the space love had filled. A tightness bunched in his shoulders. His jaw muscles flexed with annoyance. Why must he be ignored in such a prestigious gathering, as if he was dispensable? If not for him, how could Immanuel pose as their husband? Dan the Man had credentials in football, but what about the illusion he also created as a macho lover? All hype. No substance. Lame.

As Avery Murph would say, *It's not the whistle that pulls the train.*

Score one for a witty great-grandfather, his favorite ancestor, but he needed more. Much more. He needed validation.

THIRTY-NINE

Surprised later by the Murph clan's presence at the wedding reception, Patrick watched them mingle before he tugged on Cheryl's sleeve. "Let me introduce you to mama'nem," he said.

His mother, Savannah, along with his father Carson and grandfather Jeremiah, exuded a gracious and hospitable attitude common to the Murph tradition.

"I get it," Cheryl said. "Mama'nem means your mama and all the rest of them."

"Right," he said. Among his three younger brothers, two of them shook her hand. Oscar, the least talkative one, offered no cheerful salutation.

Patrick's mother apologized. "Oscar takes after his dad. Back in the day, Carson was so shy *I* had to propose to *him*. Right, dear?"

"Yeah," Carson said. "Those dazzling blue-eyes got to me. You knew I'd agree to anything you wanted, though."

Savannah smiled. "Oscar here won't even license his patents out."

"Patents?" Cheryl said. "Patrick, you never told me an inventor was in the family."

Patrick nudged Oscar. "You name it, this bro invented it."

Landon Murph entered the circle. "I'm Patrick's great-grandfather," he said. "I taught him how to do standup and juggle but he took it a step further and started juggling girlfriends."

Cheryl winked. "Ahhh, that's another thing he's never confessed to."

"But my wife Eugenia, she's the one," Landon said. "Whooeee! She could out-dance them all. Been preaching good genes for years on end, too."

"She seems to be missing at our reception," Cheryl said. "Is she well?"

Savannah rolled her eyes. "She's well alright but she's still miffed at Patrick."

Cheryl's arched eyebrows signaled concern. "But he's such an outstanding dancer and coach."

"We know," Savannah said. "But he's a free spirit, what she calls a will-o'-the wisp."

Landon spun around, his baritone voice echoing stage drama as he welcomed Patrick's seven sisters. "Hey there! How's my gorgeous girls?" They all hugged him. "I'm thinking y'all can't forget a toddler who rode the prized pig at the county fair." He laughed. "Yep, the judges gave Patrick a ribbon instead of the pig."

Arms open, he offered more embraces, this time to the approaching Sweethearts whose smiles reflected their eagerness. "Speaking of humor—" he chuckled "—Patrick used to draw an audience by imitating a donkey braying. He'd always end it by saying, 'A family that *brays* together stays together.' We all need a little levity, don't we?"

Cheryl unexpectedly kissed Patrick on the mouth. "It was fun meeting your kinfolk, darling." She waved farewell with fingers fluttering. "I'll wait up tonight for a bedtime story, okay?"

His mouth gaping, Landon sputtered, "Is she pranking you, son?"

MOMENTS LATER, Cheryl boarded the Silver Eagle to quickly jot down her thoughts.

Patrick swears I'm the ideal woman after I opted out of the telegenic ten lineup. When the butterflies took flight, my heart lifted, too. They represent a new beginning. Like today. I'm one of the wives who'll usher in a new era of health. Yesterday, Freckles altered another sign: leading edge is now leaking edge. My own kissing prank was noticeable today. Patrick was not his jovial self. Sadness was in his eyes. For some reason wedding festivities dampened his spirit but I'll keep cheering him up. I kissed him yesterday after my massage. I hope he obeys the Scrolls and proves his love is real.

IN THE BALLROOM of the Gulf State Park Lodge, Patrick sipped punch from a party cup and greeted the Sweethearts' family members. Among their parent's offspring, girls outnumbered boys. The exchange of contact information among the young singles amused him.

He knew family land would be parceled out to them as an inheritance on their wedding day, but only if they abided by communal rules. He wondered if some, like him, would spurn those rules.

As guests roamed the reception area, a photographer focused on the girls at the tiered wedding cake while the brides crowded Immanuel. Their outfits, an exhibition of décolletage, complemented the excitement over a traditional dance reserved for Immanuel. One by one they danced with him.

"Okay, ladies, it's time!" Easter shouted before bridal bouquets sailed in the direction of single females who had positioned themselves for the catch.

During the festivities, Patrick escaped to a lounge near the vacant infinity pool. A reporter's remarks on an elevated television demanded his attention. A politico said, "Were it not for DiNago's status as a sports celebrity, Alabama officials would not ignore polygamy laws."

Seconds later the previews of a docudrama enticed viewers to learn about genetic diseases. The host, a popular actress, faced television cameras. "Why are genetic disorders so distressingly common? Some genetic maladies such as Down syndrome has increased from one in eight-hundred to double that number. Here in Louisiana we asked an expectant mother with three youngsters, all with Down, why she persists in having more children with the same condition. Her answer? 'Because we love them.' Could it also be because social services makes it affordable? And why is a disease like emblot no longer confined to people of color in America's multiethnic society? Stay tuned for the perplexing results."

Shaking his head, Patrick moved through the crowded lobby, eavesdropping, but not expecting his great-grandfather to slow his forward progress. Landon placed his hand on Patrick's shoulder and stage-whispered. "Couldn't help but notice Cheryl kissed you, not to mention you hugged all the brides at the wedding. Is it the fashion these days to upstage the groom?"

"I had a point to make, gramps. Immanuel called me pee-wee."

The old man shook his head. "Listen, son, a man's height says nothing about his stature. These women admire you for who you are, and it seems that's considerably high. A word of advice, though. Don't rock Immanuel's boat or you'll have us all ducking for cover."

Patrick wanted to ask what he meant but Sorelle's voice startled him from behind. "Well, now, are we hiding an all-night drunk, or is this your way of selling celebrity sunglasses?"

Facing her, he affected a nasal tone. "Name's Pat McGroin, ma'am."

Sorelle winked at Landon. "And is that supposed to satisfy nosy reporters who want to know more about your unusual relationship to Danny's harem?"

To Patrick's relief, Larry Lemoyne tapped Sorelle on the shoulder. "Nigel Pregnor is here asking about you." Larry summoned a portly man in a tux to her side. "He insists you know each other."

"Adios," Landon said in deference to Nigel. "I'm gonna seek out the brides' whereabouts."

With Landon's departing, Sorelle welcomed Nigel with a hug. "So, how in the world are you and how's the biography coming along?"

"Much too slow," Nigel said as he watched Larry glide toward the punch bowls. "My publisher awarded a modest advance. How about you? Have you opened a vein lately?"

"You know me," she said. "Ghost is the way to go these days. I pay, they write."

Nigel wiggled his eyebrows. "Indeed, that's the easy way I suppose. But what brings so lovely a legend as you to a celebrity wedding? Is another miracle in the making, or is marrying a select pastiche of calendar babes enough for your client?"

"Oh *puh-leeeze*! Enough of this claptrap, Nigel. What's on that trenchant mind of yours?"

He grinned. "I'm just scouting for the usual mucky tripe. Sorry but I have to ask what's with the rumors of discontent between you and Miss Beaulieu?"

Sorelle assumed the aloofness of a priestess. "I'm here only because Danny insisted. Eugenics is an obsession with Easter. She's Danny's main mistress. Or malady, I should say. And she's ignoring the stigma of Margaret Sanger even after we had Sanger's name removed from Planned Parenthood."

Nigel clasped his double chin. "Ah, so she's the reason you're opposed to pedigrees."

"Not really. It's just that Easter and L.T. Moreau have fooled Danny into thinking he's a messiah of sorts." Voice low, she said, "Little do they know what I've learned about those Scrolls."

"Is Easter also behind the layout of all those prima donnas in the *Analyzer*?"

"And on the internet," she said.

Nigel frowned. "What could possibly be her motive?"

"Well, let's see. It seems she's indebted six figures to her former business partner who's vested in Orgo Cinematic, in turn owned by a Brazilian named Goodnowe. Both men are pawns of a kingpin, a porno producer in Hollywood who also owns a channel for TV comedy."

"Ohmygod, really? How scandalous. A name, please."

"Sorry, I can't betray a colleague." She winked. "But do your homework, Nigel, and whatever you write in your syndicated column, do make it as much *fun* as fantasy."

"Fun, eh?" Nigel grinned. "Meet me for drinks later. We'll talk book promoting, too."

"Yes, let's talk," she said with a beguiling smile.

As the writer ambled away, Patrick recalled Nigel being the one Sorelle wanted him to contact and collaborate with on the phone about a tabloid story; one that would offset Goat's own exposé.

"Smooth," Patrick said as he nudged Sorelle. "Real smooth, but why deceive Nigel? Does it even bother you? I mean, you know it wasn't Easter behind the layout in the *Analyzer*. Why not make peace with her?"

"Not happening." She turned away to greet reporters who knew her as a quotable source of entertainment info.

THE FOLLOWING MORNING, Patrick cornered Larry Lemoyne about a temp service that could surveil Goat.

Afterward, he hugged the newlyweds as they boarded the bus, then saluted Immanuel.

"Find a carwash," he shouted to Larry. "Removing graffiti won't be easy."

As the bus faded from view on Peninsula Road, he retreated to the solitude of the mansion. But finding no emotional comfort there, he drove to the Swashbuckler in hopes of locating Buzz. Instead he found Sorelle sipping coffee while poring over a document at her corner table.

"Whatcha up to today?" he said. "Saving the world or shaving points?"

She tucked the papers away in her satchel. "I made a concession on Danny's contract."

"Only one?"

"Yes, but I'm not backing off the billion. Everyone knows he's worth it. So here we are, six days past the September deadline. But tell me, did the wedding reception survive me?"

He pulled out a chair. "I'm surprised you showed up," he said. "I'm thinking Nigel took the hint about our fun-fantasy show. But will he really place my bizarre story in the *Analyzer*?"

"Yes. He owes me. Call him. Together you two can conjure up a fantastic scenario for that rag. Oh, I asked Vanessa if she was shocked that her photo was in that scandal sheet."

"You didn't," he said, eyes wide in surprise.

"Yes I did."

"How did she react?"

"Oh, typical of someone in denial. Imagine Easter trying to

explain that one away. By the way, a major studio in Hollywood wants me to put a package together. It means I'll have to find a scriptwriter, director, and actors for a movie project. I often collaborate on high-concept movies. What would you say if I cast you in it?"

"Okay by me. But I do have one request. I'd like the Sweethearts to be in it with me."

"Um, yes, it could use more glitz. Are we negotiating, just you and me?"

"Yeah, but Easter makes the final call. I don't bargain without her."

"Oh, come on, you're smarter than that. No one needs her—not the girls and certainly not you. Look at what she's done. Compromised my client. And she's sold her soul to the *Analyzer*. Ten girls! What's next, a porn release?"

"It wasn't Easter's idea. Goat masterminded it. So, about your movie. My girls are eager to—"

"The script is about high stakes fraud," she said, interrupting. "Goodnowe's character is exposed for funneling millions into his clinic. My surveillance proves it. The movie garners sympathy for Danny by centering on Easter as a seductress."

Patrick cringed. "Is this how you work the system? You would exploit Easter and her girls like Goat is doing?"

She removed her reading glasses to peer at him. "Consider what Easter is up against. You can't beat multinational power brokers."

"I know, I know, but like you said, we can *work* them."

"Exactly. I'll undermine Easter the same way she did me. Poaching someone else's talent is over the line, really reprehensible, and I want you involved in exposing her."

"Me? How?"

"The movie script calls for a court jester who doubles as a PI. Easter plays a talent poacher. In turn, Nigel reveals the real-life parallel."

He decided to play along. "Got it. What else?"

"Go into Easter's files and give me the phone numbers of each girl's parent."

"Why?"

"Listen, once they hear my take on events here in Sanctuary

Beach, they'll want to strangle her." Her icicle-blue eyes narrowed. "Talk about grief, when they turn up the heat, you'll see Easter wilt like month-old lettuce. I can depend on you, can't I?"

He grimaced. "Maybe you should have Gabe Casper do it."

Her teeth clamped momentarily onto her bottom lip. "Jealous, are we? He doesn't love me. You do. Now's your chance to prove your love beyond any doubt."

Patrick's mood darkened. "Have you always denied your addiction?"

"Addiction?"

"Yeah, addicts are great manipulators."

"I'm a pragmatist," she said.

"Addicts are known to flaunt their addiction in hopes of some brave soul rescuing them."

"Are you the—" her fingers marked an air quote "—*brave soul* in this fantasy?"

He leaned toward her. "You're so afraid that if you *are* found out, you might lose face with all your friends. Hey, give 'em credit, they already know."

"Don't be absurd."

"Twenty years ago you did the same thing, Sorelle."

"I have no recollection of—"

"Oh but you do and I'll prove it."

"You'll prove nothing. You hear me? Nothing."

"Listen, Sorelle. When I left for Tech, you became this other person, this panicky child whose father stayed boozed up. You cheated on me, then went into denial about it."

"*Puh-leeeze!* Spare me the pop psychology."

"That's why you had so many affairs," he said. "You wanted acceptance and love."

"You're pathetic. I never knew you were so jealous of my freedom, my beauty, even my fame."

"Look, Sorelle, I was only eighteen when you had me thinking I'd be a big star. You exploited my infatuation with you and you fed my obsessing with fame, so I left home too early. I missed out on the land collective's training. While other pedigree kids learned a practical purpose, I learned nothing. But those illusions you helped to create are over. It's time for me to move on."

"Don't kid yourself, Patrick. You can't stay away from me. Never have, never will."

He stood to go. "I already have."

"Addicts don't manage enterprises like DiNago Diversified," she said. "Your attempt to mimic a shrink is laughable. Look in the mirror. You're the addict, not me."

He walked away. No need to rebut her. All hope of a romantic reunion was over.

On his drive back to the mansion, he pondered his dilemma. How could he honor the sacred law of generosity mentioned in the Scrolls? Did they really foretell a proxy would seed pedigree women? He had no time to read them and verify, but prophesies were often vague and open to interpretation.

Was the movie role Sorelle offered now off the table? When would he learn to control his temper with her? How would he plant an outrageous story in the tabloid? A new sense of responsibility for the Sweethearts clung to him like barnacles on a ship. He had to somehow restore their good-girl image.

Even so, a sense of hopelessness attached itself to him. It would not let go.

FORTY

Deep in thought, Patrick drove his van a few miles from the mansion to Bon Secour National Wildlife Refuge and walked in search of solitude among tall timber. Blue jays sounded the alarm to alert forest dwellers of the stranger's presence in their habitat.

Why must he feel like a casualty in the wreckage of romance? Sorelle suspected a romantic link with Cheryl, yet it seemed only Easter could drive her to vindictive madness. What if she found out Easter had designated him as Immanuel's proxy, service provider to the gene matching cause?

I know everything, she had said at the park.

Easter had said Dr. Ronofski's book, *Pedigree Promise*, asserted polygamy was approved for the ancient Israelites, so why not in modern times? At the moment the need for a confidant overwhelmed him. That someone was only a phone call away.

He returned to the mansion and paced the floor from den to parlor, back and forth. He breathed deep to prepare himself. As he thumbed numbers on his smartphone, he pictured Naomi Savoie in her two-bedroom cottage at the end of a cul de sac, its tidy porch festooned with fragrant mint, basil, and other herbs she used to create culinary delights.

One year ago her Jeep, already a decade old, displayed the standard peach color on its Georgia license plate. And a decal had read, *Dewberry Hospital—Staff.*

"Do I know you?" Naomi said after his opening greeting on the phone.

He chuckled. "I get it. You're wondering why I haven't called you lately."

"Not really." Her voice had a chill in it. "After all, you're a professional joker."

"Well, you know comedy writing works best on the piranha principle. You reduce it to its bare bones. So what've you been doing in my absence?"

"Your absence? My-my, I hadn't noticed."

"I get it. You're miffed."

"We have to talk," she said in a sterner tone.

"Something wrong?"

"You have to ask? It's been weeks."

"I have a surprise for you, Miss Savoie."

"I have one for you too, Mr. Murph."

"Naomi, I know you're ticked off, rightfully, but could we meet in the middle? You know, in Tallahassee, 'bout noon tomorrow? It's a midway point and—"

"No, I'm having an estate sale."

"You're moving?"

"No, it's for Mom, just one of those things people do. You know, to make ends meet."

He sensed the dejection in her voice. "How's work going at the hospital?"

"I was fired."

"Fired? Why? What happened?"

"My conscience got in the way. It's a long story."

"Are you looking for work?"

"Actually, I have my severance pay and two weeks left on my vacation. I'm pampering myself while I consult an attorney. Last night Mom and I went to a symphony in Atlanta. I wore a new gown and her Mikimoto pearls. A doctor complimented me. Other guys noticed, too."

"Men don't just notice you, Naomi, they ogle."

"Mom tells me I should date."

"She did, did she? When can I see you again?"

"Well, Pat, it's not like you don't know where I live."

"Naomi, have you ever heard of the Sweethearts?"

"Can't say that I have. What are they, singing valentines?"

"Actually, they do comedy antics on the Funtasy TV Channel. Think actresses, hon. Ever heard of Danny DiNago?"

"Who hasn't? He's a super jock. Did a few movies, too."

"Right. I met him in New York awhile back. He and the Sweethearts are in the *Analyzer* tabloid and they're virtually nude. And then he marries them—all of them."

"Is he an exhibitionist?"

"No, but he thinks he's a mirror of Jesus Christ."

"Like...he walks on water or something?"

"Not yet, but he did a pretty good job of redirecting a hurricane here on the coast."

She whistled low. "So this imposter gets married in a nudist colony. Why?"

"No, hon, it was a big family thing right here at Gulf State Park. And guess who was there? Our favorite crook—Light Touch Moreau."

"*The* L.T., the preacher you wanted to kill?"

"Kill? I never said that. I had a score to settle, that's all. He did the honors at Danny's wedding. You should see the rings. The brides wore enough rocks to ransom Cuba."

"How many women did he marry? Two? Six? Eight?"

"Twenty-one."

A moment passed. "Let me get this straight. One man has twenty-one brides? Did the makers of Viagra need a new gimmick? Isn't polygamy illegal? What's this world coming to?"

"Hold that thought, Naomi. Do you know what regenerative mating is?"

"Is this a cow-and-bull joke?" she said.

"No-no, it's matching the healthiest people, like better breeding for better babies."

"Yeah, Pat, better grapes make better wine too but it doesn't excuse alcoholics. Where's all this nonsense leading, and where do *you* fit in?"

Fit in? He held his mirth in check. "I'm in the middle, sort of." He waited a moment. "Are you still there?"

"Yes. I had to sit down. Let's start from the beginning, shall we? Danny DiNago marries a bevy of women in a cult and you're in the middle of it. But knowing you, why am I surprised?"

"You'd have to be here to understand."

"I can't," she said. "I'm negotiating to get my supervisory job back, with full benefits. Besides, you don't want *me* there. I'd have the messiah committed to a mental ward. What, exactly, do you do there in the middle of all that craziness?"

"I'm their director."

"So they're dancers? Is this your latest fantasy, an entourage of flip-tail girls?"

"I'm coaching them to act in a comedy show, so they're all on a trial run with Funtasy TV. In our show, we're like the Globe Trotters, only we—"

"Play basketball while yodeling in the nude?"

"No, that nudie thing was a fluke. The filmmaker talked them into it. He's a conman."

She let go a belated sigh. "And you're in the middle."

"Yeah, but I could explain it better if we were face to face."

"As you would say, 'Your words, my ears.' Talk to me, Pat."

"Well, you see, I'm in the middle because I have to stop this jerk from shafting the Sweethearts. The girls are all gone now, though. They left me here with L.T. Moreau and the huckster and Sorelle Ebanetti. She's a talent manager and we're all 'bout to have a show-down before sundown, so to speak."

"Sorelle? Hmmm. How long has *she* been there?"

"Not long. We rub each other the wrong way but she's locked horns with Goat Goodnowe, the conman. But here's the deal. I have to figure out a game plan before the girls come back from Florida."

"They're coming back? Christamighty."

"Yeah, this weekend. In the meantime, I need more brain power, namely yours."

"Why me? They have a messiah."

"Well, for one thing, I'd like to restore their good-girl image. As for Danny, he's above the fray, way above. And speaking of genetic matching, it'll take a special sperminator to upgrade the gene pool. Believe me, this messiah is on a big-boy mission."

"Yeah, right. If he's a messiah, why not figure a way out of his own problems? Does he have to go through some kind of learning curve to do a miracle? Does he need a diagram?"

Patrick sighed. "No, he needs Houdini. One more thing, hon; the conman runs a genetic fertility clinic. Problem is, Danny's sterile. No sperm. So guess what? It sort of puts the fertility cause on pause. But that's why I need your expertise."

"I don't do fertility, Pat."

He laughed. "I know, but you were so clever at the rehab place. If not for you, I—"

"No, you masterminded that one."

"Okay, but drive down to Tallahassee tomorrow. We could make up for lost time."

"You can't recover time, Pat."

"Watch me," he said. "Time stands still when you're present."

"Sorry, you're on your own. But keep me in the loop. This is intriguing. Bye-bye."

"Naomi, are you seeing that—" the phone clicked off— "doctor?"

He ambled to the patio to view the bay where gulls, pelicans and a heron competed for bycatch tossed to them by marine biologists near the boathouse.

Patrick suspected greedy fortune seekers, like hungry birds, were scheming to exploit his youth gene. Fleeting thoughts of a better world crossed his mind, but the greed of mega-rich corporate CEOs quashed the imagery.

Could it be that he, a 38-year-old man, possessed the genetic key that would save the world? If that was true, what tactics could he use to keep his genetic assets from being hijacked by unscrupulous power brokers? But despite such concerns, his craving for fame persisted.

FORTY-ONE

The absence of familiar sounds in the empty mansion intensified Patrick's solitude.

Thinking of a hot breakfast at Ellie's, he strolled along Bon View Boulevard to the restaurant. A table near the floor-to-ceiling windows presented a consoling view of the empty beach.

Birdie Mae served fresh coffee before taking his order for fried eggs, grits and wheat toast. After offering a Sunday newspaper, she lingered to chat. "Since the girls left, Buzz says ain't much to see but fat tourists and sand. I'd say most need to cut back on their feed. Even the disabled ones in wheelchairs are decorated with ugly tattoos. How'd y'all's wedding go?"

"Birdie, you haven't lived till you've seen such spectacular beauty." He held the newspaper at eye level. "Look! We made front-page news in the *Sanctuary Sentinel*."

She squinted at the photo feature. "A beautiful bunch they are, and I know you must be missing them mightily. Word is, you're sweet on that Easter girl."

He peered closely at the newspaper text. "Uh-oh, says here the State AG's office could charge Danny-boy with bigamy *and* polygamy. Whoa! Says Immanuel could also be leading us to anarchy."

"Is anarchy a bad thing?"

"Compared to deeper tax cuts for the rich, it's not bad at all."

"You're an educated man, Patrick, I can tell."

"You just made my day, Birdie Mae."

"Aw, you're just saying that."

"No, I mean it. How many men have told you that lately?"

"Well, let me think. Reverend Moreau said I made his day, but that was yesterday. He's got a movie star girlfriend now."

"Yeah? Who might she be?"

"Tall woman with an accent. Wears too much makeup. Might be hiding her bitter years."

"Is that all she's hiding?" He chuckled. "She could be a doozy of a floozy."

"Well, even Jesus hobnobbed with republicans and sinners. Gotta mix with all kinds, you know."

He considered the unintended play on *publicans*, a colloquial word used for Jewish tax collectors in first-century Rome. As she trudged away, he marveled that the big draw at Ellie's was more than food and drinks.

So L.T. had a woman who tried to mask her age, did he? Interesting.

SORELLE WAITED until midmorning to call Sebastian Rubleau, the Hollywood movie mogul. Like so many on her list, he owed her a few favors.

She skipped a polite hello. "Sebastian, I'm sending a couple of treatments to you. They're based on traumatic events in the life of a super jock with a messiah complex."

"Great," he said. "Who do you have in mind for the lead?"

"Danny DiNago."

"Your top money maker has a messiah complex?"

"It's hot news, Sebastian. A eugenics cult shelters him, but by the time we get to the production stage, I'll have Danny deprogrammed."

"The Marauders lost again yesterday. When will he return?"

"Soon. I need your help in another way, too."

"Just say the word."

"Kill the deal with Orgo Cinematic."

"Orgo? What's that, some new contraceptive device?"

"Cute doesn't cut it, Sebastian. Goodnowe is your point man and he's conspiring to make Danny a party to fraud."

"Sorry, but I'd rather not alienate him. We've got—"

"Listen, Sebastian, your partner released a private video of my client on the net and Danny didn't sign a release, so I'll be suing Orgo. You don't want center stage when the feds link you with a man like Goat, do you? Neither of us want that, do we?"

Sebastian's voice hit a low note. "I'll take care of Goat's bungling."

"Not good enough. What you need to do is emasculate him."

"Emasculate? What an odd choice of words." He sighed. "I'll need a week."

"It's more urgent than that, Sebastian. Call me when you're ready for script talk." She killed the connection. Next on her list was the Central Order's CEO, Samuel Crown.

She knew who would answer the phone. As usual, Krista would keep the call a secret.

THE VOICES that once echoed in the mansion filled Patrick's memory as he recalled the girls' antics. He ached for their teasing banter, mock quarrels, shrieks of surprise, and pranks—all sounds that marked their domain. How easy it was to picture them in the den, the library, the patio, the parlor—and on some occasions for massage therapy, his bedroom.

He needed to feel their presence, not just flashbacks.

While sitting on the patio, he contemplated a chat with Angelina, but opted for a text message. His daughter responded with a photo of her recent watercolors. Three had won top awards in a regional contest in Florida. His text to her read, *Truly amazing art. Love you bunches! Dad.*

Next he called his mother and asked why Murphs had no history of divorce. She laughed. "In our clan, divorce is anathema and alimony is something that grows on trees in California."

"Cute," he said. "Does Eugenia still think of me as a prodigal?"

"Well, Patrick, since you didn't consult her about your plans or even return to claim the land as your birthright, can you blame her?"

"Hey, that was twenty years ago. I've learned a thing or two since then."

"She does keep tabs on you, though. I'm tending to my horses now. Call me later. I love you."

"Love you too, Mom. I wish you and great-grandpa had done the Charleston at the reception last weekend. Tell the folks there I love them. Eugenia, too."

Time dragged across the noon hour during lunch at the Pickle Derby Deli. The sound of patrons rang hollow to him. Buzz might be caddying and the pub would not open until late on a Monday. He considered calling Easter but decided hearing her voice would only heighten his loneliness.

Later that afternoon, he made a futile attempt to write a humor sketch at the Bon Secour Diner. And even later in the den as a sluggish sun clocked out from the dayshift. When a languid moon checked into its nocturnal duties, he yearned to hear Easter's throaty voice and feel her naked body in his arms.

At ten o'clock he returned home after ambling along Sanctuary Beach and opened his laptop. A review of the girls' profiles revealed photos showing various stages of growth—adolescent to adulthood. Other photos showed siblings—twenty to fifty of them. Siblings or cousins? Hard to tell.

He could almost hear the girls as they responded to Easter's good-night curfew call, each answering in a distinctive voice.

Cassie's voice had echoed a simple *g'night* while Dodie's resonated in a gleeful rap-song ditty. Anastasia's response trailed in a lengthy *nighty-night everyone*. A brief response spilled from Peaches who chimed *sweet dreams*. The twins reminded him of songbirds while Freckles' voice mimicked an opera singer, its high-pitched falsetto eliciting giggles.

Vanessa, with her charming mix of girlish enthusiasm and grownup seduction, would take aim at his status in a screechy voice. "A lovely one to all y'all, and to our *Casa-nooo-va*, I'm still *waitiiing*."

Each unique voice played like a recording in his head, a poignant reminder that he had become more attached to them than he realized. Each seemed like an extension of his dreams of fame.

His thoughts took a dark turn to Goat Goodnowe at the clinic.

With Larry Lemoyne driving the Sweethearts' bus to the Keys, his availability to feed Patrick reports through his informant at the clinic was also gone. A young intern at Goat's clinic had warmed to Larry's overtures and hired a receptionist from the Lemoyne Temp Agency. With the intern serving as an unwitting spy, Larry used both him and the receptionist to monitor Goat's daily routine.

Patrick decided his next move must be field-tested.

A QUIET BREAKFAST at the Bon Mot Diner allowed Patrick to reflect on the events leading up to his proxy dilemma. The girls' public relations snafu, along with sinister plans he imagined the Central Order had for his future, added to his vexation.

Which of the issues took priority? Resolving the conflict between Easter and Sorelle over control of Dan the Man's wealth had to be done, but generating interest in genetic matching topped his short list. After all, a genetic meltdown leading to an apocalypse—god forbid—seemed a possibility.

As degeneration became the norm, the evidence was too pervasive to ignore.

A mishmash of fundraiser infomercials rife with heart-tugging anecdotes had become a moment-to-moment reminder on television and social media of a dysgenic society. A visit to food or merchandise stores yielded live evidence of genetic maladies. Desensitized shoppers often averted their gaze. A slew of charitable promos for weekend disability contests like Genetic Disorder Olympics highlighted autism, sickle cell anemia, and Down syndrome as constant categories.

Everyone knew someone who suffered, yet few people wanted to admit that child abuse, a pet project of the Paladins, was linked to psychological toxins inherited from genes.

Despite the urgency of preventing genetic flaws, that long-range objective had a bridge to cross. Dan the Man must return to football. Patrick had suggested the rivals—Sorelle and Easter—cooperate, but both women were obstinate. So which was most important, Easter's pride or the standoff over control of Immanuel's fortune? If the pair refused Patrick's mediation efforts, a mighty rift would occur in Easter's program.

In that event, would the promise of a genutopian society fade into obscurity?

Perhaps, but he could talk with the two women separately. They should—no, they *must* —choose which was better for the greater good. In that moment he realized the Sweethearts' absence had led to an unexpected solution. Dysgenics was deemed a curse by Doc Ronofski. To prevent it required more than a genetic messiah. It demanded a savvy negotiator.

The psychological effect of his loneliness now seemed a small price to pay for this sudden eye-opening epiphany.

HAVING SURVIVED the humiliation of her forced fall from the shyster's yacht, Tally Schermer responded quickly to a secret invitation the following day.

Five minutes into their meeting she signed with Sorelle's talent management agency. "I have lots of connections, Tally, and Hollywood needs talent," Sorelle said while offering the young script writer a pen to sign her name. "That talent is you. But I'll need a favor."

"Yeah, sure," Tally said.

"Take records from the clinic tonight. You have a key to Goat's office, don't you?"

"Yeah, I'll do it for a hundred bucks," Tally answered. "Can you pay me now, in cash?"

A CALL RECEIVED on a smartphone in Atlanta was answered by a private investigator. "Yes, Mr. Goat, we are working on it day and night. My people say the woman is well-connected."

"Well, *my* people want dirt on both her and Murph, pronto," Goat said.

"No sweat. A guy at the Bon Amite Hospital is feeding it to me. You want it quick?"

"Yes, jot down the address. Send it by private courier. Why hasn't the surveillance guy called me this morning?"

"He reports at noon and again at seven, sir."

"No, not good. I need a faster update. Sorelle is cunning and I'm not about to be cornered by that bitch. My next move depends on timing. *Perfect* timing."

———

FROM A CORNER TABLE at Ellie's, Patrick typed new ideas on an iPad. He side-glanced gulls perched on a railing outside the windows, as if each awaited Labor Day tourists.

He fingered the growth of downy hair on his neck. A visit to a barber was long overdue.

Ten scripts later, he left Ellie's and strolled along the boulevard to the mansion. On its lowest step he paused as a skit idea slipped free of its enclave. He typed fast, eager to capture the scenario.

In the scene an attractive blonde in a coffee house spills a book from her handbag. Bystanders snicker as the young woman scoops it up and, thinking quickly, gives it to a clueless male behind her. "*An Idiots Guide to Sex*," she says, reading its cover title aloud. "It's for you, hon; happy anniversary."

Once converted into a skit, it could delight viewers of the Funtasy Channel.

Clever acting by Easter or Cheryl would enliven it. But both were gone. Too bad. Without them, the mansion seemed a humorless vacuum. Even Stu Wattanabe had lost interest in the mansion, focusing instead on managing Ellie's restaurant.

Life itself seemed to be stuck in neutral.

Who else was available? Once inside the mansion den, the obvious answer jolted him. He must call her. He took a deep breath, scratched his five-o'clock shadow, and tapped her number on his phone.

Naomi answered seconds later. "*You* again."

"Yeah, it's me, sitting in a rose garden, waiting for ideas to bloom." He chuckled. "Say, do you remember when we first met? You had me at *hey-wo*. How does that sound to jumpstart a new skit?"

"Pat, be serious. Whatever my verbal flaws, none resemble Elmer Fudd's hello."

"Yeah, I know it's corny but audiences like the silly stuff."

She groaned. "Anyway, what's happening with your pajama party? Still no PJs?"

"No, hon, Sorelle convinced Tookie Ward to offer L.T. a wad of cash if the preacher can swing Danny back to football. So far it's a no-go for DiNago. Meanwhile, Goat Goodnowe may be defrauding customers at the clinic. In fact, I'll be Sorelle's lookout tonight when Tally creeps the clinic. Tally's writer who lives on a yacht with the conman."

"You don't say. Why would Tally betray Goat?"

"She took a bribe from an interested party. And no, it wasn't me."

"I have to ask you something, Pat."

"Go ahead, take your best shot."

"Does Sorelle intimidate you?"

"No, not at all. The look-see tonight is risky but it has to be done. By the way, my confiding in you would make her nervous. You don't lie. That alone would intimidate her."

"You mean, the mighty Sorelle Ebanetti has an issue with the truth?"

"And how! The friction that woman creates could light up a city. She's been trying to turn me against Easter."

"Why, because the sunrise service in Alabama rises too early?"

"What? Sunrise service?"

"Yes. A sunrise service celebrates the resurrection. Easter. Sunrise. Get it?"

"Witty you. No, Easter is my boss' name. It's a takeoff on some ancient goddess. Anyhow, I'm thinking since pedigree matching is free, it's the way to fine-tune my mojo."

"Pedigree? Sounds elitist."

"Uh-huh," he said. "But it beats the alternative."

"What alternative?"

He chuckled. "Degeneration. Ask yourself, where are we humans right now? We're here, stuck on stupid. Think about being *there* and not here. It's all about *being* something different to get there, at least in a wellborn sense."

"Wellborn?" She made a grumbling sound. "Now there's one for the ages."

"But selective compatibility is the answer. Society must find its equipoise, its balance, and with better babies comes better thinking and better choices in all areas of our lives."

"So, you're really deep into this pedigree thing, aren't you?"

"Well, yeah. And we use comedy to reach people. It can open the mind to things that matter, and the gene matching program matters if we want to prevent heritable diseases."

"What will they think of next?" she said. "Keep me informed and stay out of trouble. I know how you are, Pat. You can't resist a good fight. Bye-bye."

FORTY-TWO

Like a veteran hunter scouting for trophy deer, Goat Goodnowe knew his quarry well. Stealth, refined by a lifetime of experience, led him to remain poised as he entered the yacht stateroom to watch Tally edit *Star Harem*.

He slid into the comfort of his recliner. "How long have we known each other, Tally? Six years? Seven? Only a unique person can last that long in our business. Too many pitfalls. Being psychic helps, of course, but I've always been tuned in to mystic powers."

Tally refused to look at her benefactor as she worked from a squatting position on the floor.

"I've never told you," he said, "but a shaman in Brazil took me into his confidence when I was twelve and performed the sacred rites. Some call it sorcery. It combines the spiritual forces of ancient Babylon with Christian tradition. The older boys in my village taunted me for having spiritual gifts."

She paused the video as Goat continued. "A voice, sometimes a vision, warned me about future events. I ignored them until the day my friend drowned. I should have warned him the footbridge was not safe to cross. But why should I be burdened with such responsibility? Of course, I rebelled at what I didn't understand, but the force—" he groaned "—would not let go."

Tally stiffened, her hands unmoving, overcome with a sense of foreboding.

"It wasn't guilt that drove me from the village," Goat said. "I had learned not to ignore intuition but it hardly describes such an awesome gift. Only one other time did I refuse to obey that sixth sense. Celeste had insisted we visit her parents in Rio de Janeiro. I stayed in a bungalow, she in the big house; a proper arrangement among her aristocratic kin."

Goat walked leisurely to the bar and poured hot tea. Returning, he placed the cup within reach of the lampstand. "A chaperone saw that we behaved, yet a week without her had driven me crazy. I was desperate to be with her and talk of bacchanalian excess. Little Nita, her younger sister, overheard our plans for a secret rendezvous."

Tally fidgeted, forcing herself to be attentive to his story.

He sighed. "Little Nita. She loved to flirt. Her features were refined, her eyes devilishly daring, her voice oozing with charm and confidence." He sipped from the teacup and cleared his throat. "She was delectable."

After a ten-second pause, he continued. "Previous to her arrival, I resisted the voice telling me to leave the hacienda. I opened a bottle of rum. One drink. Yes, just one. Then another. And another. The rear door squeaked open at ten, right on time. The perfume was Celeste's but the body was Nita's. Her visage was inebriating, like the rum."

His eyes closed momentarily. "A white rose adorned her dark hair and a peignoir, shimmering in the moonlight, caressed her body. My gaze lingered on her mischievous eyes. I took her into my arms, the feel of her supple body luscious to the touch. She confided Celeste would not be coming. Seems she had spiked her sister's drink. At first she giggled, pretending to resist. I knew by her smile she wanted it. She was mine, body and soul—all mine."

Tally's fingernails pressed hard into her bare knees. "Goat, you don't have to tell...."

"But I must. The anger, you see, must be reconciled with the love." His cup clinked hard against its saucer, his gaze distant. "I was not very gentle with her. No regard, actually, for her tender age. She became hysterical. Her frantic efforts to leave excited me even more. It was such a delight to see her like that, panicking in pain. I sometimes revisit the scene, on video, as the need arises. It's exhilarating."

With the tension constricting Tally's voice, her words sounded hoarse. "You recorded it?"

"Yes, the video camera sat on a tripod."

"That's creepy."

Goat shrugged. "To each his own."

"So—" Tally breathed shallow "—why'd you do it?"

"I don't know, but *not* knowing is the beauty of all mysteries, isn't it?" He held his head high. "I assured her the experience was good for her. After all, she came to me. *Me!* In my Satyr mask I tried to pose her for close-ups and...." His voice trailed into a mumbling reverie before its clarity returned.

"Celeste found us the next morning. She made a scene, screaming. Her brother came running to see what alarmed her so much. One look and he knew his little sister was now damaged goods. Wish I had captured the anger in his eyes on video."

The words faded into temporary silence, as if a casket of secrets lay buried in his subconscious. "The son of a bitch broke my jaw. Celeste drove the car toward the hospital but her father caught up to us, shouting obscenities. His sons dragged me to an abandoned shack. My mind went numb when the father brandished a box cutter."

Goat's voice turned plaintive. "Celeste saved me from being hanged. Her father swore death was too good for me. Instead, he put the blade to my neck and my gut, threatening me with death, but then he decided my scrotum was the best option."

A deep sigh preceded his next words. "The poet says when someone dies we feel diminished, but I must say we suffer things far more diminishing. Medics did what they could but weeks passed before I examined my lower regions. Shakespeare said violence begins with betrayal, quite often from a friend we've trusted. We humans are a treacherous species. It's the Judas gene. Wouldn't you agree, Tally?"

She nodded assent as Goat stood slowly and left the room. Her hands tremulous, she hurried to the bar and slugged down brandy straight from the bottle to steady her nerves and prepare for what she knew had to be done.

At the corner of Japonica and Main, two patrol cars loitered side by side as police officers on night duty exchanged pleasantries. Tally hid in the shadow of the clinic behind a large garbage bin. Her mouth dry, she licked her lips and wondered if they expected a break-in.

Still jittery as the cops motored out of sight, she hurried to open the back door to the clinic. She snapped her penlight on, jammed Goat's key into the lock, and winced as the hinges squeaked loud.

Once inside, she aimed the penlight along a hallway to the reception area and illuminated empty cardboard boxes in a closet. The odor of cigar smoke lingered in the room, a reminder of Goat and his excesses. Suddenly skittish, she hurried back down the hall to her boss' private office.

Her heart beat faster as she filled two boxes with documents and loaded them onto a dolly from the utility room. Needing a third box, she returned to the reception area. The tobacco odor grew pungent.

A faint clink, perhaps a lighter, alerted her to possible danger. On impulse she jumped for the front door and twisted its knob. It refused to budge. Flushed by panic, she tried to kick it open.

"Stupid, go out the back door," she muttered to calm the anxiety overcoming her. "Ain't no way I'm rolling this damn thing to her frickin' hotel."

Rushing to the receptionist's desk, she poked luminous digits on the phone. "Sorelle? Tally. Can you help me tote this stuff?"

"Help you do what?" Sorelle said. "Where are you?"

"At the clinic. I got some boxes full o' papers. They're too heavy and—"

"Boxes? I thought you knew to use a flash drive."

"What? No, I don't know the access code."

"Okay, let me think. I'm on the other line, so give me a minute and I'll see what I can do."

"Hurry up, it's spooky in here."

"Wait. Is the back door locked?"

"No, it's open." Tally placed the phone back on its cradle and moved slowly away from the desk. The fog and stench of a cigar filled her senses, engulfing her.

"Going somewhere, Tally?" the gruff voice said.

She screamed and fell back against the desk. A shadowy form

slowly rounded the desk and a thin flame sprang upward from a gold-embossed lighter, its eerie glow flickering over Goat's facial features.

Fear immobilized Tally's body.

Clink! The snuffed light preceded Goat's steely voice. "You'd betray your only friend?"

Her low whine became the soul of terror within Goat's enveloping cigar smoke. "Please oh-no please Goat don't kill me please-please-please!"

"Kill you?" he said, his voice feigning sympathy. "It's not your appointed time to die. Besides, you're no good to me dead."

FORTY-THREE

S orelle decided the daft girl would have to wait. Having put her call to Hollywood on hold, she switched back to finalize a prickly issue with Sebastian Rubleau.

"What do you mean, you don't know what's going on?" she said. "He's your partner, Sebastian. You promised to fire Goat."

"Sorelle, I agreed to do it, but wait a week or so."

"No, *days*. Now it's down to hours. You're in collusion with him. Surely you have better sense."

"It got past me, okay?"

"No, Sebastian, you're in a dogfight for profits. This puts you in hot water with the FBI. With their spyware monitors, they can link you directly to Orgo, then to Goat's scam at the clinic. Have you even called him yet?"

"I'll be in the area soon."

"Did it ever dawn on you to use a phone?"

"You don't handle Goat Goodnowe with a phone call. He has to see the fire in your eyes."

"Fire? I'll show you fire! Check the wall safe aboard Goat's yacht. You'll find training videos for white supremacists and Jew-bashing material. Celeste Jennorez and Slack Creel will testify to more. How's this for a sound bite? 'Hollywood director Rubleau promotes neo-Nazi cult.' You have one day, Sebastian, to kick him off our showbiz planet. Few people can afford to be on my bad side and you're not one of them. Got it?"

"Okay, I'll handle it."

"You'd better or I'll handle it in a way that it'll never have to be handled again. I'll side with the feds. Fact is, I'm picking up evidence tonight that could put Goat in federal detention."

IN THE SMALL retail area of Sanctuary Beach, Patrick drove his van across the intersection of Japonica and Main and parked outside a mini-mart to blend with other vehicles. Minutes passed before he spotted her.

Sorelle walked around the clinic to the back entrance, away from a streetlight on the front side facing Japonica Street. She may need help if Goat showed up without warning. Having planned each step with Sorelle earlier, Patrick hoped Tally's heist of office documents would go smoothly.

He crossed the street to the clinic and approached its rear door. A dim light illuminated empty parking spaces. A cell phone rang, the sound barely audible. Without warning, the door swung open and Goat appeared with a handgun.

Goat sneered. "Come join our little parley. You can tell me later how impressed you are with my preternatural knowledge of your arrival."

Patrick looked about for Goat's SUV. Like Sorelle, he left no evidence of his presence. She was trapped inside. He moved cautiously toward the open door. "I wouldn't buy stock in it," he quipped.

"Always ready with a *bon mot*, aren't you?" Goat said. "Burglary is a felony, so this meeting is deadly serious."

Patrick walked lead-footed through the doorway but stalled a moment in its threshold to listen for any unusual sounds before entering the man's office. Tally and Sorelle, seated and facing Goat's desk, looked up without greeting him. Tally whined.

Sorelle sat straight with arms crossed and glared at Goat as if he had ticketed a foreign diplomat. In a pullover and faded jeans, she appeared fashionable and poised.

Goat sat behind his desk and commanded Patrick to sit next to Sorelle. Atop the desk he placed a Beretta, its finish silver and its trigger golden—Sorelle's gun.

"Do you see the problems you've created for yourselves and this pseudo-comedian?" Goat said.

His tone prosecutorial, he continued. "My first thought was to sit back and watch you leave with the files in your possession. Law enforcement would arrest you for grand larceny and conspiracy. And since you'd be in possession of stolen goods, I would sue for damages in civil court."

With his gaze on a cigar burning in the ashtray, he ignored Sorelle's scoffing. "Instead, I chose a more prudent course. Let us look at what we have here, shall we? I've done a fair amount of sleuthing and found some very interesting things about you troublemakers."

Sorelle stomped her heel on the floor. "Out with it. I've no time for senseless prattle."

Brandishing her pistol, Goat lifted the cigar from its ashtray. "I'm advising you, Ebanetti, to hold your tongue until my presentation is complete."

He drew deeply on the cigar. "Patrick Roland Murph. My dossier indicates you've been divorced three times. Another wife died. As a comedian, success has eluded you. You also tried rodeo clowning."

The smoke drifted lazily from his nostrils. "Your stint as a dancer with the Pony Xpress was cut short. You pay no taxes." He lifted an eyebrow. "Interesting how you were implicated in a condo scam. A federal shakedown on a business you owned broke you. Couldn't pay those stiff fines, could you?"

Goat turned slightly to focus on Tally. "And *this* is the kind of two-bit loser you're siding with against me, your mentor?"

Patrick eyed Sorelle's handgun, wondering if it was loaded.

"Sorelle Myita Ebanetti," Goat said as he swiveled his chair slightly to face her. "It seems long before you met this failed salesman, third-rate comic, would-be rodeo clown, stripper, whatever—you had to help your retarded mother raise two sisters."

"Mom was uneducated, not retarded," she said.

"And...a man you called Uncle Nate was your mother's lover. His last name is Greenburg, not Green, which means your heritage is

Jewish. You intuit that fact, thus your link to the Messianic Hebrew Fellowship and the Star of David icon."

A tight smile creased his face. "You became a manipulator like Greenburg. At nineteen you slept with the owner of Bon Amite Auto, a married man who had six kids."

"I beg your pardon, I never—"

Goat interrupted. "Oh yes, he seduced vulnerable women and you were no exception."

She inched forward in the chair. "One more word and you'll pay dearly for—"

"Stop right there, you slut!" Goat lifted the pistol in a threatening gesture. "Earlier, at sixteen, you and a high school coach slept together. Later you targeted the town mayor but it was the DA who taught you how to be discreet."

She started to rise. "I'm not listening to this filth."

"Sit down and shut up." Goat clenched his teeth. "You made a lucky modeling connection. It led to your being hired by a New York talent agency." He laid the gun down. "However, you couldn't go to New York at the time since a handsome Italian in Bon Amite had impregnated you."

Looking sidelong at Patrick, she said, "Don't you dare believe a word of this...this...."

"Hospital records confirm it," Goat said. "You refused to look at your newborn son. A nurse left the infant in a barn later. She knew relatives would adopt him."

"Lies, lies, lies!" She shook her head. "Obscene lies!"

"Obscene but true," he said. "After a ten-year stretch in modeling, you returned to recapture your childhood. You seduced Patrick Murph but he went to Bayou Tech where girls fought for his attention. To spite him, you hooked up with Clay, the auto dealer." Goat lifted the Beretta as if to admire it. "You wish to have your gun back, but I have one more surprise for you." He grinned. "You see, by rejecting your bastard child decades ago, you face a far more serious predicament now concerning your son."

Patrick twitched in his chair, dreading the huckster's next revelation. If only he could spoil the man's theatrics, yet curiosity compelled him to listen.

Goat cleared his throat. "What I'm about to tell you has been verified in several ways. It can't be contested. You had a brief but well-publicized affair with a client, a talented young sports star."

"You're out-of-your-mind crazy, Goodnowe," she said.

Goat smirked. "Your dating him made headline news. If only you had known your client, Danny DiNago, was also closely related to you."

Sorelle's face twitched. "That's really far out, too bizarre for even the *Analyzer* to print."

Setting the gun aside, he slowly clapped his hands in mockery. "And that's exactly where it will appear, in the most widely read tabloid in America, unless...."

Patrick tried to make eye contact with her, his thoughts muddled. But a more scandalous thought crossed his mind, one from which he feared to draw an inference.

"How dare you!" Sorelle shouted. "You, sir, may as well join the Hemlock Society because life as you know it is over. Do you hear me? Over!"

Goat leaned forward, his voice soft. "Ms. Ebanetti, Dan the Man DiNago is your son."

Her hands gripped the armrests of the chair, voice emoting like someone in a winless deadlock. "Oh...my...god. That's the most insane thing I've ever heard. My lawyers will sue the hell out of you."

"Emerson DiNago?" Patrick blurted. He instantly saw Danny's resemblance in her.

As she ranted, Goat opened the center drawer of his desk, withdrew a dark folder, and opened it. "Court records say Randall E. DiNago swore in a petition filed at the county courthouse in Bon Amite that his son, Emerson, was the father of the infant Daniel Immanuel DiNago. I quote, 'The court allows full custody of the child be assigned to said petitioner.' Unquote."

Her face colored. "It's a lie. I'll take a DNA test. I'll not be humiliated by this."

Goat slid the folder back into the drawer. "What you *will* do, Ebanetti, is pay me ten million dollars to keep this report out of the mainstream media."

"That's extortion," she shouted.

"Yes it is," he said. "Wire the money to an account at the Caribbean American Bank in Antigua by noon tomorrow. I'll give you the routing info. But you'll have to take your chances with the tabloid scandal. After all, you're so good at PR. And they probably owe you a favor."

"What do you take me for? A fool?"

"Hardly," Goat said. "You know Danny is the victim in this scandal, and you the cause."

Tremulous with anger, Sorelle shook her fist at him. "You sorry bastard, you deserve hellfire!"

Goat stifled a faux yawn. "Incest is unforgivable. If you fail to do as you're told, your client will leave you in order to save face. Ironic, isn't it? Oedipus' good image, however, *will* be salvaged."

"What?" she said.

Goat tapped the tabletop with his knuckles. "And for that you can thank certain power brokers who see you as an obstacle to their goals. You know them well, and your arrogance in making demands of their Hollywood producer does not impress them."

He opened his arms wide in a casual stretch. "Oh, by the way, the money you wire will be paid to Crown Consultants."

Sorelle's face blanched as Patrick placed his hand firmly on hers, trying to offer solace, but she removed it. With the charge of incest, he realized she had taken an emotional hit. Goat might ruin her image with publicity. He wasn't sure Sorelle could find a way to overcome it.

How could she unknowingly bed her own son? What were the chances? Strange as it seemed, in spite of her betrayals, he felt badly for her.

FORTY-FOUR

After being released by their captor, Sorelle and Patrick departed the clinic and rounded the building to cross its frontage before speaking.

"I'm so sorry you had to go through that madness," he said.

Sorelle's eyes narrowed. "Leave me alone."

"But I was just as shocked as you by Goat's accusations. What kind of man would dig up dirt from your past? He has no scruples, even kept your gun. Was it loaded?"

Her pace quickened as she veered away to follow Japonica Street, putting more distance between them. "Forget it, Patrick."

Slowing his pace, he watched her hurry along the dark street toward Sanctuary Inn, then veered clear of her and trudged to the mini-mart.

From the veranda outside his bedroom a short time later he mulled the potential blowback of Sorelle's dilemma. How did she feel about Danny now after learning he was her son? He knew of no one who might sympathize with her.

Needing a new perspective from a savvy confidant, but with no bars on his smartphone, he sped downstairs to the den and called Naomi Savoie on the landline. She answered on the fourth ring.

"Crown!" he blurted. "Isn't there a business in New York called Crown Consultants?"

"Well, *hey-wohhh* to you, too," she said. "Yes, Crown Manhattan is a bank, and our hospital billing is handled by Crown Management. It's on the—wait for it—*innnernet!*"

He smiled at her chiding. "But I need your perspective."

"Well, then, here goes. In my lawsuit against my employer, my attorney says that both Crown Consultants and National Guaranty Trust are in a joint venture with other financial monopolies."

"Monopolies are no surprise," he said.

"True, but one report says they control a *uuuge* chunk of world trade. A Swiss bank, second largest in the world, is one of their confederates."

"Okay, so they have clout," he said. "Anything else?"

"Yeah, ten banks own eighty percent of America's assets. Want to hear more? *Hey-wohhh!*"

Patrick chuckled at her Fudd imitation. "A banker named Teddy bragged about Crown backing Ward's offer of a billion to sign Immanuel—Danny DiNago—in a re-up deal with the Marauders."

"Think he'll go for it?"

"I don't know, but Crown's corporate managers might coax Danny into leaving Sorelle's talent group. If that happens, they can wrest control of Dan the Man's brand. That would put the Sweethearts under their umbrella, too. And me. Along with my, uh...assets. My guess is they also want to put Easter on equal footing with Sorelle."

"Hmmm. Sounds like Easter's an up-and-comer. How old is she?"

"Twenty-six. Yeah, she may be easier to control than Sorelle. Hey! They'd play one against the other. Just now thought of that. Remember, too, that Goat Goodnowe is a master con."

"You seem out of sorts tonight, Pat. I sense your anxiety."

Was his stress that obvious? "Goodnowe might be crazy but he's no dummy. He's got Sorelle on the ropes and she has too much pride to go down without a fight. She needs leverage."

"Are you still in love with her?"

"Goodgodamighty! Where did that come from?"

"You need to say it out loud, Pat. Then you can get with it or get past it. To do less is unfair to both you and me. I'm no dimwit. Nothing burns hotter than an old flame. I knew it was a woman when you didn't call me for so long."

He grew weary of the pretense. "Life shouldn't be about hurting people."

"I'm not people, hon, I'm Naomi."

Sensing the ultimatum in her voice, he said, "This is confusing. A woman who'd sell to the highest bidder is disgusting."

"Is Sorelle the only one who does that?"

"What do you mean?"

"Well, look inside yourself. You obviously have a stake in saving her. Ask yourself why. When does it stop? Why be with someone toxic who makes bad memories?"

"What really disturbs me is her pattern of deceiving people."

"And where does that lead? To disappointment, right?"

"Yeah, she came from nothing and now nothing is denied her."

"Enough about her. Who else keeps you hanging around Sanctuary Beach?"

"I have a score to settle with L.T."

"Really?"

"Yeah, and I want to prove, at least to myself, that I can beat a losing streak."

"Losing streak? Pat, without your ingenuity, we couldn't have stopped that donor organ cartel and rescued your daughter. L.T. went to prison. Isn't that enough?"

"No."

"Talk to me, Pat. You're smart but you have a blind spot."

"Yeah? And what might that be?"

"An obsession with fame."

He sighed. "Years ago a redhead named Ginger worked in my sales office. We hit it off and got married. Eloped, actually. No time for a honeymoon. I'd been promoted to sales manager."

"Let me guess. You impressed her by breaking sales records."

"Uh-huh. My bonus included company stock. What could go wrong? The owners even made me a partner in Buckalew Developments. The deal was rock-solid. I'd learned Saul Buckalew was related to another empire builder, a guy named Samuel Crown."

"So that's why you were asking about Crown Consultants," she said.

"Partly, yeah. I can still see the empty sales offices. L.T. Moreau was a no-show. Days passed. I faced fraud charges. I walked around in a daze. Ginger's father asked if I was a retard, said it in front of guests, said they'd never had a criminal in the family. I suspect Ginger divorced me to save face."

"That's a shame. What happened to the money?"

"I've no idea."

"So you learned something about hucksters, didn't you?"

"Sure did. Got an education about how the legal system works, too. It's rigged."

"I won't ask what happened there, but—"

"By all means, ask. After my divorce, I started my own company. Talk about an obsession with fame, I made it bigtime, partly because I wanted to clear my name, but guess what? The rogue FTC busted me, and all because I'd used the words *realistic income* in my ads."

"So?"

"So they decided it was deceptive advertising. Never mind audited reports backed up my profit projections; didn't matter. I didn't see it coming but federal judges usually side with the prosecution."

"But you could've taken it to a higher court, couldn't you?"

"Nope. Too expensive. The nominal fee a lawyer charges becomes phenomenal in an appeals case. I cut my losses and moved on. My self-esteem shrank, along with my bank balance."

"I now understand why you prefer humor with a bite to it," she said.

"Yeah, but what I don't get is Sorelle hooking up with the Central Order. She's convinced herself that she can transform them. That's really messed up."

She yawned. "It's past my bedtime but listen, you have to stop saving Sorelle. Okay?"

"I promise she's off-limits. Socially, that is. I'll help Easter and the girls entertain on the Funtasy Channel. I trust them, but not Sorelle Ebanetti."

Naomi said goodnight, but it sounded like goodbye.

But he had no time for regrets, he told himself. His next call would be an urgent one to Nigel Pregnor, the biographer who would collaborate on a bizarre story for the *Analyzer*.

FORTY-FIVE

Assisting the clinic receptionist meant Tally Schermer was also obligated to prepare tea for her boss. With the hot liquid filled to the brim of an oversized mug, she took mincing steps to his office.

Tally rapped softly on Goat's office door before entering. Her hand trembled as she set the mug on his desk, causing the liquid to overflow and burn her fingers. Shrieking, she jerked her hand away but snagged the handle with a finger, causing hot tea to shoot up like a geyser and drench his paperwork. Gasping, Tally quickly gripped and steadied the mug, now almost empty.

Goat dropped the phone, scooted his chair back and leaped to his feet. Obscenities preceded his scowling reprimand.

"Sorry, boss," she pleaded. "My fault. I won't ever do it no more." On impulse she grabbed the *Analyzer* and dabbed the spilled liquid, oblivious to smearing newsprint photos on the desktop.

Goat retrieved the phone. "Hello, you still there, Senator? Damn!" In an instant he grabbed the ceramic mug and flung its remaining contents in Tally's face, then pitched the mug hard at her. As she fell back, it ricocheted off her forehead.

Arms upraised, Tally stumbled backward over a chair. She fell awkwardly, gripped her side, and tried to rise but slumped back on the floor. On the floor, Tally pleaded for an ambulance.

"What are you, a fucking retard?" he shouted before poking a recall button on the phone. A small recorder, plugged into a port on its backside, captured the politico's words.

"Senator?" he said. "Are you there? Good. Did they approve another grant?"

"Not yet," Blockton said. "But a coll, uh, colleague from Justice dropped by my office today. He says a whistle-blower's been badmouthing a certain pedigree project on the Alabama coast."

"What of it?" Goat said.

The Senator continued to slur his words. "It don't meet stab...'tablished criteria by the national 'cademy of shitfaced sciences. The board claims Perfect Progeny Clinic is bogus crap. And something 'bout funds misapplied. He says it'll be big news in the mee...media."

"That's good news, Senator. It may take a little drama for good breeding to be recognized."

"Yeah? Well, it gets worse. T'anks to you, gossip rags are showing pictures of messiah's curvy cuties. *Biiiiiigggg* feature."

"The more exposure the better," Goat said. "And social media is like a preview that'll set up my movie. It'll help in hyping DiNago's centerfold harem."

"No good, Goat. Your messiah is shameful to decency and reli'jon."

On the floor, Tally pleaded. "Please, Goat, I need an ambulance."

As an afterthought, he tossed a heavy-duty stapler at her but missed. Removing wet documents from his desk, he let the spilled tea drip onto the floor. "Typical politician, aren't you, Senator? It takes extremes to move people's sensibilities before they'll change."

"What kind 'o change?"

"Radical change, man. What other kind is there?"

"Listen, Father O'Brien says DiNago's mocking the church. Just so happens plegamy...polygamy's on his shit list. Don't forget O'Brien makes a big *contritution* to my 'lection."

"Then give him part of your take, your percent."

"No-no, what's mine's mine."

"Then do your job, Senator. By the way, you do recall the girl at your party, don't you? I have it on video. Did she bleed much? How old is she? Thirteen?"

"Shut up, Goat! When will you start *shending* my money? It's two months overdue."

Goat put flame to his cigar again. It failed to ignite. Cursing, he pitched a brass paperweight at Tally. The missile careened off the wall an inch from her head. He plopped the phone down and rounded the desk with fingers clenched in a fist. This time, close-up, he couldn't miss.

Tally screamed and drew her legs into a fetal position.

———

FOLLOWING a surprise call from Sorelle who shared her findings about Goat, Patrick watched a pair of brown pelicans synchronize their dives into the breakers of the shoreline surf.

He found a receptive area for a cellphone signal on the beach and called Naomi. "Good morning," he said. "Bet you can't guess what shyster Goat's done now."

"Rounded up more fallen angels for the tabloid?" Naomi said.

"Good guess," he said. "Brace yourself, hon. Sorelle said Goat swindled the feds out of ninety million in government grants, and I suspect he's still luring people into buying Immanuel's sperm. But guess what: it's fake. He has to be selling phony sperm after Danny wouldn't cooperate."

"That's *real* fraud," she said.

"You betcha. And she says Tally signed rights to *Star Harem* over to her and—"

"Slow down, Pat. What's a *Star Harem*?"

"It's a movie script, hon."

"Wait a sec. What kind of people would hire a shyster to steward grant money?"

"The same kind of people who want something more, like the elimination of emblot carriers, mostly Black males. And the best surprise of all, Sorelle knows their methods. Tally's on video telling about Goat's cult of white supremacists. And she got a signed admission from Slack Creel that he was tricked into backing *Star Harem*, the sexy movie. Her surveillance people also recorded a conversation between Goat and Senator Blockton. Some leverage, huh?"

"Is recording in secret legal?"

"I dunno." He sloshed his feet in the surf's edge while trekking along the shoreline. "Hon, I hate sharing bad news but Sorelle's at the hospital consoling Tally. Goat beat her up."

"What? He beat Tally? Are you serious? How bad?"

"Broken ribs. Concussion. Head trauma. Internal injuries could result in bleeding."

"Oh, to be a judge," Naomi said. "I'd give him the max."

"Me, too. A police report says a clinic intern found her beaten by unknown assailants."

"Unknown? Oh, I get it. The intern is Goat's alibi."

"Yeah, and others who work there back up the story. They say what Goat tells them to say. I wouldn't be surprised if they're all Aryan sympathizers."

"Sick cowards! A reporter needs to investigate it."

"No budget for that. This isn't Atlanta. Journalists here go after easy stories."

"You need a real pro, hon, so bring Atlanta to you."

"Yeah, Ada Golden might help us here at Sanctuary Beach."

"Right. She could do a job on Goodnowe like she did on those rogue surgeons at the Atlanta transplant center."

He backtracked toward Ellie's. "But this is minor compared to the organ cartel case."

"Don't be so sure, Pat. I'll bet Goat has lots of connections inside the Beltway."

"Yeah, and Easter is somehow involved."

"How do you know?"

"Because she owes Slack Creel lots of money, and she was real evasive when I asked about the profits at the clinic."

"Why?"

"Don't know."

"Then keep asking."

"Slack once advised me not to be her business partner. She owes him plenty and she may have caved in an exchange deal. How else does a sexy keepsake video make sense?"

"Okay, that could mean Easter's conscience is bothering her. How well do you know her?"

"Well enough. She's my boss. I need to help her see Goat for what he really is."

"Go for it, Pat, and be sure to call Ada Golden."

"Okay, but here's a thought." He reversed his trek and strolled along the boardwalk to connect with Bon View. "What are the odds of accidental inbreeding? Who keeps a record of heritable diseases at sperm banks, or the sperm donor's genealogy?"

"Pat, what's up with all this genealogy talk?"

"Sperm banks aren't regulated, Naomi."

"So?"

"So Ada could tie it in with an investigative report on Goat's clinic."

"But why the sudden interest in sperm banks? Are you a sperm contributor?"

"Hah-hah, funny. They couldn't pay me what I'm worth." He quashed the urge to joke about the proxy mandate. "Seriously, who tests the sperm donor's DNA for heritable flaws? Thousands who buy sperm can't trace the guy who fathered their children. Catch you later. Gotta go and call Ada."

He kissed the phone, emitting a loud smack, and within minutes drove his van along Peninsula Road until finding better reception for his phone. He left a text for Ada Golden: *Breaking med story hot enough to melt cold steel. Let's talk.*

FROM HIS OFFICE in Sanctuary Beach, Goat Goodnowe phoned his surveillance guys the following day and was told Ada Golden's TV crew was spotted at his clinic. "What? Why the hell would medical reporters be snooping around here? I want answers."

After instructing his crew, he signed off and glowered at Chad, the young intern. "Who tipped off an investigator about my clinic? A reporter like Ada Golden could blow my plans for us here."

"Investigator?" Chad said. "Is that what she was doing?"

"Dammit, don't tell me you forgot about the conspiracy."

"What about it?"

"Sorelle sent her Jew friends here to beat Tally senseless. Remember?"

"But the reporter is a Black woman."

He gripped the young man's shoulders and shook him. "I told you about the Jews of olden times. Being couriers gave them access to secrets between empires. They learned to network, make big money deals, and take unfair advantage of both sides." A spate of coughing stopped him momentarily. "Not one of them can be trusted. Now they've bribed a Black reporter to front for them."

Chad nodded. "Sorry, boss, guess I forgot."

"Forgot? Hell, man, when those Zionists see Immanuel advancing in power, you tell me how they'll respond." A few seconds passed. "I'm waiting."

"They'll, uhhh...they'll shame him, like at Golgotha. Then they'll kill him."

"Well said, Prince Chad. They're the most powerful lobby in Washington, better known as the great harlot, Babylon the Great. Have you visited Tally today?"

"No, sir, but security at ICU is tight."

"Find out who might be siding with her. And burn this clinic if we have to vacate it. Then we'll sail for Rio. Remember, we exercise dominion over all things entrusted to our care. We will prevail."

"Sure thing, Mr. Goodnowe," the intern said as he obliged his boss with continued chants. "We will prevail. We will prevail. We will prevail."

"Damn right," Goat said.

FORTY-SIX

Patrick's heart soared in anticipation of greeting the Sweethearts after spotting the Silver Eagle stopping beneath palm trees at the mansion.

The girls disembarked from the bus, ran across the yard, and bounded up the steps. But finding the house empty, they doubled back and joined him by the open-air garage. The tenor of their reunion clued him to their intent.

"Save a horse, ride a cowboy—yeee-haaa!" Easter yelled as she and her girls embraced him.

The sounds of jubilation echoed off the walls after the girls ushered him inside the house, their continued hugs delaying his progress from parlor to den. Easter soon proposed a toast by gathering an array of stemmed glasses and pouring merlot into them.

To Patrick the mansion's heartbeat was now restored by the Sweethearts' endearments.

"Good happens!" Easter said. "Let's draw straws to decide who'll pair with him in a sexy skit. The girl with the shortest straw auditions first with our new Twitchy Itchy dance."

"Twitchy Itchy?" he said. "This isn't another prank, is it?"

Easter poked him. "Ahhh, now there's a question that calls for reassurance. Folklore says some men can't deal with women who're overcome with twitchy-itis."

Vanessa mimicked a swooning young lass. "All this twitchy talk has me reeling with the feeling. Forget straws. I say we let him select one of us for a special massage. Me-me-me!"

With a chopping gesture, Easter interrupted. "Tell us, Casanova, whatcha been up to in our absence? Did you give Sorelle her walking papers? How hard did the door hit her derriere on her way out?"

"Yes and no," he said. "But first tell me about this new Twitchy Itchy dance."

Easter curled her forefinger, luring him. "We'll have to show you, but you need to participate."

"Define participate."

"It means we have the itch to match your twitch so treat the heat, babe, treat the heat."

He studied her eyes. "I need a minute to collect myself. It's been a week, you know."

"Seems more like a year to me, handsome," Easter said.

Soon after sharing their new dance by demonstrating it in the den, they welcomed a round of chatter. But cornering him later, Easter led him from the den to his bedroom where intimacies resulted in an hour of lovemaking. The week-long absence without the feel of her body against his revived a pentup yearning more intense than he thought possible. No woman in his past had expressed such longing in her caresses than Easter Beaulieu. Her every move seemed to find something in his psyche that revealed a level of sensitivity he never knew existed.

During an interlude, she propped up on a pillow and gazed into his eyes. "I think our love was meant to be, baby. You seem super-charged."

"You bring out the best in me," he said. "Never met a woman like you. The vibes are unreal."

She kissed him. "Tell me about your week alone here."

Gathering his thoughts, he decided to level with her about his calls to Naomi Savoie. "I told her about our mission and its troubles. Got some good advice, too."

Easter studied his eyes, as if to discern his motives. "And did you satisfy her curiosity?"

"I sure did. And she laid some words of wisdom on me."

"Is she a pagan?"

"Pagan? Now you sound like great-grandma Eugenia."

"Look, Patrick, you shouldn't share secrets outside of our group. Is she one of us?"

"No, but I trust her."

"Why? Does she share our hope of regenerating people?"

"Not really, but she's intelligent and cares enough to help."

"I doubt it."

"I'm not believing this," he said. "It's a big world out there, Easter."

"True, but we grow as wisdom directs us, remember?"

"Yeah, sounds like regimentation, the kind Eugenia believes in, but I'm autonomous."

She grinned. "Says the man who delays impregnating the chosen."

"By the way, I invited reporter Ada Golden to expose Goat's corruption at the clinic."

An exasperated sigh escaped her lips. "Okay, but you should've run it by me first. Being my courtier means you're a loyal team player."

He nuzzled her neck. "Sorry 'bout that. I reckon some ancestor passed along a rebel gene. Maybe I just need help settling down. You game?"

"Baby, I have something to tell you that's bigger than all of us. Can you keep a secret?"

He studied her soulful eyes. "Uh-oh, I know that look."

"You need to know about Reggie," she said. "We can either win with the Central Order or win without them, but it's best to include them. Let me tell you why and how. You listening?"

"Your words, my ears," he said.

On Monday the girls sorted through wedding photos to fill their albums, all spaced neatly on the library floor. The doorbell chimed twice. Easter finger-combed her hair and raced through the parlor to answer it before Stu Watanabe did.

"I'll get it!" she shouted. "Probably a package." At the door she faced a sheriff's deputy.

"Easter Beaulieu?" The officer placed a document in her hand. "You've been served."

Mouth agape, she watched as he retreated across the porch and down the long steps, not looking back. She closed the door, unfolded the document, and read it during her slow walk back to the library. Her voice rose in volume. "One-hundred-eighty-thousand dollars? Patrick! Look at this. Slack Creel is suing me for the debt I owe. Why? I mean, of all times, why now?"

"Honey, that's chump change to Immanuel," he said. "Lean on him. He'll spring for it."

Her eyes moistened. "I can't ask him to do that."

Patrick rolled his shoulders. "Goat's clinic draws a crowd. He owes you a lot, right? Must be like maybe a million by now. Know what I'd do? I'd hit him up for an advance."

"Yes, he owes me," she said. "I ought to strangle Sorelle. She's most likely behind this. Really, who else could be so diabolical?"

"Maybe so, but you need her."

She summoned him to follow. "Dream on. You ride shotgun. I'll drive."

"As you wish."

In the open-air garage, the personalized tag on Immanuel's Jaguar, *UNZIPIT*, brought a smile as Patrick thought about the irony. A messiah unzips? Not an image devout people would welcome.

Easter pressed the key fob and within seconds slid onto the seat to drive. Patrick cringed, amazed at how fast she backed out and gunned the car down the driveway.

Speeding along Peninsula Road, she took a hard left into Sanctuary Plaza. The Jag hugged the curb as she sliced onto Main Street, blew a stop sign, and shot straight to the clinic. Seconds later she braked hard and parked in a slot marked *Reserved for Staff*.

She led the way into the crowded lobby. "I don't need an appointment," she said to the wide-eyed receptionist. "My name's Easter Beaulieu and I'm here to see Mr. Goodnowe."

Patrick winked at the receptionist whose blond hair, streaked with flamingo pink, curled loosely about her oval face. She pointed to the hallway. "Second office on your right," she said. "And if anyone asks, I never saw either of you."

Patrick blew a kiss at her while pivoting to follow Easter. If his guess was right, the alpha female goddess of pedigrees would learn more about the huckster today—none of it good.

Chad, the young intern, stood at the end of the clinic hallway. He froze like a bird dog on point after spotting Easter and Patrick, then ducked into a side room.

Easter's quick steps brought her to Goat's office door. She opened it without a knock, her voice that of a field general. "How's business? The overflow of customers says you tapped into a goldmine."

Without turning from his computer, Goat gave her a quick glance. "I'm busy." Spotting Patrick with her, he did a double-take and swiveled his high-back chair to study the uninvited guests.

Patrick invited Easter to sit close by.

"I'll get to the point, Mr. Goodnowe," she said. "Mr. Creel is putting the squeeze on me for a debt I owe." She opened the document. "This is a court order. It gives me ten days to reply and I don't have it, not even a dime of it."

Goat propped his elbows on the behemoth desk. "What brought this on?"

"Mr. Creel holds a grudge, apparently," she said. "The money he's demanding is... Look, I can't count on DiNago Diversified to approve a loan to me."

"Why not?" Goat asked.

"They listen only to Sorelle," she said. "Plus, I would never presume on his generosity."

"Why not negotiate with Slack?" Goat said.

"Are you kidding? He and Sorelle are closer than Siamese twins."

"And that poses some sort of problem for you?"

"She controls the purse strings at Immanuel's company."

"Float a loan, then. Current bank rates are reasonable."

"Yeah, right, they require collateral." She fidgeted with the document. "Anyway, I need money to pay my girls, like an advance from the money you owe me. Six figures, please. And you must also cancel my debt to Mr. Creel."

Goat's expression remained impassive. "Debt? What debt?"

"Right, like you suddenly have amnesia? You promised Mr. Creel would cancel my debt to him if my girls performed in your video, the one you said would only be modeling lingerie."

"Can't help you," Goat said, still poker-faced.

Slack-jawed, she gasped. "What? Why not? You used us for more than lingerie videos."

"We have a performance contract, Miss Beaulieu, and its stipulations are clearly in my favor. As it turns out, Immanuel's acting skills in the erotic arts are nonexistent."

She shook her head. "But it's plain to see you're doing great here at the clinic."

The tapping of Goat's fingers on the desktop signaled a countdown. "I could speak with Slack on your behalf, I suppose," he said.

The fake sincerity in Goat's voice set Patrick on edge. "You know and we know you're not about to do that, Goodnowe," he said. "Slack is already sideways with you after you failed to repay the money back that he invested in your naughty video."

"What?" Easter said. "Slack is behind the keepsake?"

"A half-million dollars behind it," Patrick said. "Goat's not only double-crossed Slack but you as well. It's a thing among shysters, you see. The rush comes with the riches."

She glared at Goat. "So it wasn't Sorelle who ran our video on the net, was it?"

"Nope," Patrick said. "Goat masterminded that one."

"But I...I had the only copy," she said. "Nobody else was authorized to—"

Patrick interrupted as he patted her arm. "Goat apparently made duplicates. Yet all the money generated from internet sales goes to Orgo Cinematic. Right, Goat?"

Goat sneered. "The *Analyzer* probably hacked into it. Blame them."

"No, you betrayed me," she said.

"Don't discount the recognition you girls gained," Goat said. "You're lucky Rubleau didn't insist on a barefoot cruise first."

"More BS," Patrick said. "You deceived Easter and soiled the Sweethearts image as neophytes. Truth is, you won't pay Easter or Danny or Slack. Your intent was always to defraud them."

Goat pushed back a few inches from his desk. "Nothing personal, but I'm not a bank."

"Ah, yes, it's the ol' business decision copout," Patrick said as he looked askance at Easter. "Of course, the media will have to be informed about this rip-off."

Easter wagged a finger at Goat. "Your clinic is through. Finished. Done. Deader 'n dead."

Goat thrust a stiff forefinger back at her. "I'll sue your ass off, bitch."

"What a laugh," Patrick said. "You can't risk prosecutors knowing your rich clientele bought fake sperm."

Goat's eyebrows raised a notch. "Prove it, smartass."

"Okay, you asked for it. Immanuel had a vasectomy years ago. Imagine the lawsuits your—"

"Patrick!" Easter said.

Goat snorted a laugh, the sound menacing. "Interesting. Very interesting. And strange, too. So, we have a sports icon who shoots blanks, do we? Plus his acting is just as dismal. The macho image is an illusion after all, isn't it?"

"Forget Danny," Easter said. "Your clinic is defrauding the gullible."

"You have to realize life's not a beach, Miss Beaulieu," Goat said. "It's an undertow, and that's where you are now, whoring down and enjoying the ride."

"Whoring down?" Easter said.

Goat leaned forward, elbows on the desk. "A fortune awaits us if you convince your telegenic ten to compete in the Kluuge Ultra Nude Pageant. Easy money. I guarantee it. I'll set it up tomorrow."

Patrick stood, his teeth clenched and jaw muscles working. One step toward the door in a feigned departure served as his misdirection ploy to throw Goat off guard. He spun about with feet planted wide, his hands gripping the edge of the shyster's desk. One upward heave of the wooden monstrosity sent the humidor and other loose items cascading in an avalanche toward Goat.

Drawers slid open, spilling loose items in a clattering noise as Goat's eyes widened in surprise. He braced against the desk but, powerless to escape its oncoming descent, scrambled backward, twisting as he fell. The desk crushed the armrest of his chair and pinned him under its mountain of mahogany. Hoarse grunt-yells preceded his screams, all laced with shrill profanities and groans of agony as he struggled to free himself.

Patrick jerked the office door open for Easter but found Chad standing like an obstruction in the hallway. In one swift motion he slammed the young man against the far wall. His slim body bouncing with the recoil impact, Chad dropped a clipboard and stumbled toward the exit door. A trail of scattered papers marked his departure.

Patrick closed the short distance between himself and Easter in the hall, slowing only to pluck a rose from the vase on the receptionist's desk.

"Thanks for the insider info," he whispered to the festive-haired blonde.

Rose in hand, he ushered Easter outside. "Good happens when we give it a little nudge," he mumbled while walking alongside her.

FORTY-SEVEN

Outside the clinic, Easter slipped into the driver's seat. "I despise that man," she said. "You might've killed him, Patrick. I heard something crunch, like maybe a hipbone."

"Sorry, but it was payback time," he said as he eased in on the passenger side.

She looked away. "How do we counteract the *Analyzer* layout and his internet posting?"

"For starters, Ada Golden hopes to find some incriminating evidence, maybe enough to indict Goat for fraud."

"So why put me through this face-off with him?"

"Well, this one thing, Easter, you had to see for yourself. Goat was allowing you to think he was helping you outsmart Sorelle. But all the while he was swindling taxpayers under Danny's good name."

She revved the motor and drove toward the plaza. "Okay, what about government oversight?"

"That's another boondoggle," he said. "With understaffing and no whistle-blowers, that's a no-go. But now we have to restore the image of your pedigree program."

"How?"

"We'll start with Sorelle helping to book you on TV talk shows."

"No way I'm working with her."

He clutched the dashboard as she braked hard at the plaza stop sign. "Listen, if Sorelle agrees to back us, we can hold onto the team, the program, and *the* Danny. And I'll prepare you to go on the *Hotz*. It's high time we challenged viewers to think of pedigree reproduction in a whole new light."

Easter gently bumped her forehead on the steering wheel. "I don't need her."

"Don't be obtuse, sweetheart. Danny will lose advertising contracts if football is allowed to fade from his persona. Give him another year to win that fifth Super Bowl."

"But this is about life, not football."

"And it's also about promoting that life. Work my plan and the ripple effect will swell into a wave of popularity like never before. With her contacts, Sorelle can help us command the spotlight."

"But Danny is mine now. I can negotiate for him."

"Yeah, right, like you can borrow a dime from his company. He's being lionized by his fans now, but don't depend on it to last."

"Why not?"

"Fans are fickle," he said. "If he doesn't return to football, you'll see what I mean. No football, no Danny. And no Danny, no celebrity to vouch for your program. Without that, why a messiah? I don't think you want him sidelined. And with viewer ratings soaring on the *Hotz*, you'll do just fine."

He gently touched her arm as she steered the Jag toward home. "Easter, physical fitness is never doubted, right? Fine, but what about genetic fitness? Health pros know heritable diseases are killing us but they're hamstrung by the profit motive." He tapped her knee. "Besides, you can hype the relevance of genetic matching like nobody else, so you'll gain status."

"Status?"

"Yeah. So long as Danny is making money, Sorelle will share control of him with you. I know how she thinks. I dislike L.T. but he does put the right spin on our pedigree process. As for Goat, he'll fade away fast."

She guided the Jag along the highway before taking a right on Bon View. After parking in front of the house, she spoke softly. "It was best Mr. Goodnowe didn't pay me. All verbal. No paper trail."

"Good thinking," he said. "By the way, Sorelle is making a docudrama. It's about her top client, and the word is out that consultants don't come cheap. You game?"

"Consultant? Yes, I'd like that."

He grinned. "One thing bugs me, though, and I can't stop thinking about the contradiction."

"What?"

"Why didn't you tell Goat from the outset that Danny was sterile? You never let on during that first meeting that he was impotent, either. You negotiated as if Danny's sperm was liquid gold."

She grinned. "Dr. Ronofski agreed that I should play along and make Goat show himself as the fraudster he is. You see, I wanted to impress Reggie Torgenthal by using Sorelle's manipulator tactics. And I'd rely on you to come through for me."

"Me? How?"

"Well, you're not sterile. Can you imagine how relieved I was after you agreed to serve as the real proxy to Immanuel? But I had second thoughts about using your sperm for Goat's clinic. If the law were to find out, you'd be charged with conspiracy to commit fraud, along with me, and I...." With eyes lowered, she slowly shook her head. "I couldn't bring myself to do it."

"You had a crisis of conscience, didn't you?"

She nodded. "I didn't want to deceive or hurt you, the man I fell in love with."

Smiling, he leaned closer and cupped her chin. "I believe you."

"I do make a fuss over Danny, don't I?" she said. "But I do it for appearance's sake, baby. Call me shameless, but my seducing you in the park was a power play to beat Sorelle at her own game. But falling in love was not part of my plan."

"I understand," he said. "And if I hadn't been obsessing over Sorelle, maybe I could have figured a way to stop Goat long before now."

She kissed him. "I should've told you everything from the start. I didn't even tell you I've known about your youth gene all this time."

Pulling away, he peered at her suspiciously. "What do you mean by all this time?"

"Well, Dr. Ronofski looked at your ancestry. He hinted before we appeared on *The Hotz Show* that your genetic profile was superior to most. But little did he know how rare your DNA was."

"Who else knew?"

"In the beginning, just us. We wondered if radical corporate types might target you if they found out you're so unique. It made sense to use Immanuel as a diversion to throw them off."

"So they'd think he had the youth gene, right?"

"Yeah, but Dr. Ronofski let it slip to Mr. Crown of the Central Order, but the grand poo-bah said he wouldn't tell anybody except Reggie. Best I can figure, Mr. Crown's mistress eavesdropped and then tipped off Sorelle about a youth gene. Sorelle still wasn't sure who had it, yet she knew it couldn't be Danny. She flew down here to snoop around and find out. Apparently, her strategy was to control how the treasured gene would be used, but it was also her covert way of beating Mr. Crown for control of who had it. Now we know the truth about her ethics and commercial ambitions."

"I'm glad you outmaneuvered her," he said. "Can you do something like that with the Central Order kingpin?"

"I hope so. Like I told you yesterday, Reggie is idealistic. At last he's in the driver's seat. With his influence, he could have hurt us worse than a bizarre story in the *Analyzer*, but he didn't. I'd like to know why. I'll know after I meet with him in New York City. C'mon, let's go find a spot we know is secluded. We'll work on a script that'll work on the *Hotz*. Yes, have Sorelle book me on the show."

"Okay, but how do you feel now about us turning this whole thing around?"

An aura surrounded her smiling face. "Naturally, I'm happy to know you're a savvy peacemaker. And when I think of the hope your youth gene gives us, I'm overwhelmed; so much promise with each new generation paying it forward. But we're not done turning it around. You'll always be the catalyst."

He gazed into her eyes, realizing he was one with her, like a soul-merger, though it had been less than a year that he had known her.

She smiled. "So...when do I go on the *Hotz* and counter the scandal with our comeback story?"

"Friday," he said as he kissed her. It occurred to him that if testosterone was nature's trigger, he had become trigger-happy of late. Breaking the kiss, he said, "Drive to Sanctuary Inn."

"You're just full of surprises, aren't you?" she said, her tone sensuous.

Fingering the rose from the clinic, he offered it to her. "You're the real surprise," he said. "One look at you and it's easy to believe love is not a fantasy. Is that sentiment too mushy for you?"

She wheeled the Jag down the driveway and swung onto Peninsula Road. "Nothing's too mushy when we're in love."

FORTY-EIGHT

A makeup artist in the studio applied a light-diffusing foundation to reduce the glare on Easter's face, adding to the allure of her flawless complexion on the late-night talk show.

Wynn Traynor, host of *The Hotz Show*, introduced behavioral geneticist David Frankl. Many scholars, he said, regarded the esteemed professor to be the final word on human evolution.

Final word? Pondering the attribution from the den, Patrick studied the professor's demeanor. The man's short forehead and deep, self-important frown gave him the look of a raptor.

Wynn lay a copy of the *Analyzer* on his desk without announcing its relevance to the show's topic. "Welcome to the *Hotz*, folks," Wynn said. "Where to begin? I think we'll start with Dr. Frankl. Let's talk, sir, about biases. Are the New Scrolls truly prophetic or merely drivel authored by some deluded do-gooder? And what about people who say they never get sick?"

The professor smoothed his beard. "The Scrolls are aged artificially. But in spite of the hoax, a certain academic is using them to prop up his bias. Regarding the never-get-sick people, self-reports are notoriously unreliable. They deny or forget obvious symptoms."

The host grinned. "Seems to me people are easily hooked by hoaxes. Any idea why?"

"Simple," Frankl replied. "The gullible are drawn by the mystique of quasi-religious movements. They have a need to feel special. It's absurd for a so-called messiah to say he can change the gene pool among humans by mating with so-called pedigree women."

Wynn turned to his counterpoint guest, his gaze lingering a moment on her cleavage. "Welcome to the show, Miss Beaulieu. It would seem you've been duped by—"

"Not so fast!" Easter wagged a finger, calling attention to her telegenic face and its olive complexion enhanced by bronze undertones. "Genetic matching is not a fallacy. In fact, pedigree people in their procreative beneficence bring beneficial changes—measurable changes."

"Changes? How? By following Dan the Man as some kind of supergenes savior?"

"Genes matter," she said. "In the spirit of collectivism, regenerative matching is still the most effective way to upgrade the human gene pool, and Immanuel can get the job done."

"Oh, really? Do you believe he's perfect?"

"Have I ever said perfect? No. Perfection is an ongoing process. Our procreation is enhanced by candidates who come from imperfect people; not to say they don't have some perfect assets."

"So he gets the job done. Ha! How did this eugenics thing get so bizarre, so...so fanatical?"

"Fanaticism or zealotry?" she said. "Zealous describes us better. Also, eugenics is a misnomer. What you call eugenics we call genetic compatibility. Think about it. Do we stop giving medications because a quack doctor misdiagnosed someone's disease?" Her voice rose. "No, we ignore bugaboos as temporary setbacks. Sad to say, scientists favor genetic engineering only because it's so profitable. Does it benefit the upper class? Yes. Does it cure emblot? No. Why try to overcome nature? Work with it."

"Are you saying gene editing isn't legit?"

"No, but has it been successful as a cure-all? Again, no. True, it has made some in the medical field rich. Fine, but our solution is not only free, it's also effective." Easter slapped her knees. "Imagine the sticker shock when patients review the cost of their medical procedures. By the way, what recourse do patients have? None! Zilch! Zero!"

Wynn faced the professor. "Seems like zealots are easily exploited."

The old man cleared his throat. "Yes," he said. "First, a sense of urgency is present. It's often linked to some dire need. In this case, a cure for emblot. Also, a popular athlete is being used to sway the cult victim's mind."

Wynn Traynor's gaze drifted from the professor to Easter. "Don't shoot me for asking, but is Danny DiNago having visions similar to someone in a psychotic state of grandeur?"

"Oh, Wynn, is that the best you can do?" Easter said, her tone sardonic. "May I suggest you give your viewers credit for having a teensy-weensy bit of intellectual curiosity?"

"I concede," he said. "But I have to ask how Danny is holding up with his harem."

As Patrick pondered the show's setting, he realized Easter's charisma would captivate viewers.

With a twist of her head, Easter tossed her chestnut-brown hair back. "Good happens, Wynn."

"I'll bet it does. Please go on."

"Well, he's known for his, shall we say...stamina."

"Okay, I'll buy that." He gave her an expectant look. "Tell us more."

"Wynn, few people know his legacy goes back to ancient Israel."

In the den, Patrick smiled and raised a thumb to the Sweethearts around him. "Good move. She's taking command by framing the topic."

On television, Wynn tugged on his earlobe. "So how is history relevant to Danny's stamina?"

"Look, Wynn, we both know the Israelites in times past practiced polygamy, okay?"

"Yes, that much we can accept, but what's the relevance?"

She grinned. "Your real question is *why* the Israelites would do that."

"Let me guess," he said. "The chieftains needed backup singers in their Man Cave Rock Band."

Easter rolled her eyes. "Look, the health and wealth of patriarchs was a big deal. So nature's law of selection prevailed. You see, scientists can't deny that many of us have an innate resistance to disease and never get sick. In fact, nature favors females who procreate healthy offspring."

The host slapped the *Analyzer* lying on his desk. "Really? Why favor females?"

Easter swirled her hair. "Wynn, would you agree the hand that rocks the cradle rules the world?"

"Fine, but do you have regrets about how you've handled critics of your cause?"

"My only regret, Wynn, is allowing our entertainment troupe to be exploited by Mr. Goodnowe, a professional conman."

"Yes, but the *Analyzer* has a bizarre story this week about Goodnowe's strange collusion with an alien force," the host said. "Tell us more about that."

She lolled her head. "Mr. Goodnowe's motive all along, in addition to fraud, was to degrade our pedigree program by smearing our good name. And once he trashed our image, his corporate backers in New York City might exploit us with private equity funding in a takeover bid. Yes, it's about control."

His look quizzical, the host said, "Wait, what about the alien, the mystery baby in the *Analyzer*?"

"Actually, the article says the child was taken away by Mr. Goodnowe's agents. As for the other infant, Immanuel, nobody at the hospital knew where he came from."

Leaning toward her, Wynn said, "Be straight with me, okay? The tabloid lists Nigel Pregnor's byline. Sorelle Ebanetti, it says, was impregnated by extraterrestrial aliens. She gave birth in Bon Amite, a small town in Alabama. But—" he rolled his eyes "—Sorelle's alien child was stolen by the conman's agents and taken to places unknown. Can you tell us where?"

"The Middle East," she said.

"Why?"

Easter pointed at the *Analyzer* on his desk. "To join the anarchists. The alien child is trained in psychic warfare. His mission is to create chaos, confusion and division here in America. But he has no use for gobbledygook codes, algorithms, and cyber disruptions. In fact, mind control is his specialty."

Dr. Frankl crossed his legs and loudly cleared his throat. Wynn ignored him, instead raising his hands in mock supplication. "How does mind control work on an entire population?"

"Like a fascist, Wynn, he and his cohorts play on people's superstitions and fears. His lies are camouflaged to appear as the truth. It's no secret that anarchists can hijack the mind with a conspiracy theory. Radical ideas, if implanted endlessly, lead to paranoia. An example are gullible guys believing that the males in our pedigree movement are trying to corner the best-looking women and put 'em away in a harem, never to be seen again." Bouncing both hands off her thighs, she added, "Not true!"

"But—" Wynn tucked his chin. "—some geneticists claim your program is actually eugenics in disguise. Plus, it distracts from their curative gene editing efforts."

"Curative? Ha! Profiteers manipulate healthcare. These same neoliberals are idolatrous."

The host leaned back in his chair, his brow wrinkling. "Idolatrous?"

"Yes, idolatry is an attitude. They're infatuated with wealth and they worship rich power brokers."

"So you're anti-capitalist."

"No, but why not view human assets as real wealth? Look, our heritable traits are much more valuable than material wealth. We should view the beneficial genes as a resource and pass it on at no cost, like the creator of the polio vaccine did. Yes, pay it forward. That's how good happens."

Wynn folded his hands at chin level as he rocked back in his leather chair. "The world you wish for strikes me as a utopian dream."

"Absolutely," she said. "We're all gung-ho about physical fitness. Genetic fitness is even more important. So yes, a genutopia is certainly possible. But again, it's a collective effort."

His fist jutted upward. "Aha! So you'd create a perfect pedigree society. Good luck with that. You do realize the freeloading associated with communistic socialism failed in Russia, don't you?"

A coy grin preceded her reply. "You're being facetious, Wynn. Remember what Anatole France said. 'To accomplish great things, we must not only act but also dream, not only plan but also believe.'"

"So believing makes it so?"

"In a sense, yes. Believing makes it possible to actually do something. What you're about to see is millions joining our cause and creating a virtual nation *within* each country on this earth. And it's for the greater good—always."

In the mansion, Patrick joined the girls' applause. "Doing great, isn't she?" he said.

Easter looked into the eye of a studio camera. "Ten percent of people, maybe more, never get sick. Why not consider the common good and share that asset? No, it's not about race or privilege. It's about giving voice to your choice. My program encourages people to begin choosing without losing."

"Red alert," Wynn said. "Do you think high IQs are a commodity?"

"Save your red alerts for a real crisis," Easter said. "Think about it. Who doesn't want a sound mind? Smart people are better equipped to detect the deceptions of the rich and ferret out corrupt leaders who would exploit us. It's not some fantasy for the few. No, our way benefits all humanity."

Wynn bumped the heel of his hand against his forehead. "Let's get back to the *Analyzer*. Okay? The alien child, now a grownup psycho, rallies anarchists to oppose democracy, right?"

"Yes, he tries to control all commerce, too, Wynn. But our Pedigree Nation is wise to his every move. The first step in dealing with deception is to detect it, but we can intuit it well in advance."

The host eyed Dr. Frankl. "What about global anarchy in real life, professor?"

The old man's voice droned, "Some scholars think an ideological war is a real possibility, but it's nothing new. At its core is repression in the guise of liberation. Simply put, eugenics is a slippery slope that usually leads to social chaos, followed by polarization."

Patrick nudged Cheryl seated next to him in the library. "Hang on, girls, here it comes."

"Nonsense!" Easter said. "A slippery slope is no contest when compared to a genetic minefield that leaves people maimed or dead. So yes, let's talk about chaos and tell the mother of the child with spinal muscular atrophy, a disease that destroys nerve cells in the spine, about slippery slopes. Tell her about the astronomical expense of treating it and why a quarter-million Americans go bankrupt each year due to high medical bills."

She waved her hands. "Forgive me, Wynn, but I need to take a step back and clear up something in the story, the one in the *Analyzer*. Sorelle Ebanetti is the mother of the hybrid alien, not the mother of Immanuel. The child is taken to a place where he leads the great rebellion."

Wynn scratched his bald pate. "No?"

"No, our messiah was not born of a human," she said. "He appeared to us incarnate, straight out of heaven. Immanuel's appearance at the hospital in Bon Amite was supernatural. And when the alien baby in the crib next to him was stolen, a nurse feared baby Immanuel would be stolen, too, so naturally she removed him and found a trusted elderly couple who later adopted him."

"Okay, but who is this elderly couple?"

"We call them Grandpa and Grandma DiNago. Earlier at the hospital, nurses told Sorelle that her child—the alien—died during birth. You see, they were protecting themselves. Can't you imagine the panic over a stolen baby? Sorelle had been sedated. Anyway, the trauma of having lost her child caused her to block it from memory." Taking a deep breath, she continued. "But both thefts went unreported for obvious reasons. In some institutions it's called CYA— cover your ass."

The host spread his arms wide. "Wait. Did some soap opera writer botch that script? Is there a mother out there somewhere who'll claim Danny? Hold on, I've got it. Danny could provide us with his DNA profile."

"Wynn, he has no human origin, remember?" Easter said.

"Are you saying a screening of his DNA would fail to reveal his ancestry?"

"Right," she said. "It would prove nothing. An incarnation isn't easy to comprehend, is it? After all, it doesn't fit our limited frame of reference about humanity."

Stagehands laughed as Wynn's crossed eyes and pursed lips mimicked a fishbowl guppy.

Easter's voice exuded kindness. "The real marvel is how this genetic messiah changes people so they become more generous and loving. Imagine a world led by altruistic people like him."

Wynn quickly leafed through the *Analyzer*. "And that's due to his genes?"

"Yes, and the sacred Scrolls say he's to be the epitome of goodness."

"Okay, here we go again, the sacred versus the secular," he said, his gaze drifting skyward.

"Look, Wynn, if we hold dominion over the best genetic traits, all the other things the Creator has entrusted to our care will naturally follow. The process is orderly, not divisive, and it leads to peace and solidarity and the pure language of truth."

Wynn's head wobbled. "One last question about Danny," he said. "At the risk of sounding a bit crude...." He reacted in mock surprise to laughter from the audience. "Now cut that out. When was I ever crude? Danny has a harem of how many gorgeous young women?"

"Twenty-one," Easter said.

He wiggled his eyebrows. "I can imagine how he proposed—your egg, my sperm, spread 'em."

Easter eyed the cameras with a chiding, dour look, as if words escaped her.

Wynn offered only a grin. "But how did things go on his honeymoon? C'mon now, give us the lowdown."

"Lowdown? You mean other than admitting everything fit?" she said, as if unaware of the sexual innuendo that roused the guffawing studio audience.

"I would certainly hope so," Wynn said, his contorted grin provoking raucous laughter. "I mean, you know, super stud that he is... Really, though, was a week long enough?"

"Oh, but Wynn, it took less than an hour."

He gasped. "One hour and he's done with twenty-one brides?"

"Yes. How long should a wardrobe fitting take, anyhow? It had to match the luggage for our trip to the Keys."

"Oh, okay, I get it—*that* kind of fit. Oh yes! Everything fit. Indeed...it...did."

She shrugged with hands upturned on her lap. "What other kind is there?"

Wynn flung his hands outward in an exasperated gesture. "Please, just tell me about his brides, okay? Was he able to handle the conjugal aspect of his husbandly duties?"

"I refuse to answer on the grounds it might inseminate...uh, no, I mean incriminate, no, I mean intimidate me."

Wynn's hand slid over his face like a descending curtain. "Just stick a fork in me, folks," he said in his trademark sign-off. "I'm quite done here."

In the Sanctuary Beach mansion, the Sweethearts laughed and cheered and applauded.

Elated, Patrick hugged each of them. What more could he ask of their leader's timely presence on the most-watched show in America? Recalling his snafu on the same show months earlier, he knew this episode was a rare win. The girls now had a better chance at returning to a credible standing.

"Takes teamwork to make a dream work," he said as the Sweethearts danced in jubilation.

"I feel sorry for Easter," Cheryl said. "She had to make a ridiculous *Analyzer* story sound more credible than it is. Imagine how confused viewers are now."

"That's the idea," Patrick said. "Who's gonna believe Goat's earlier story in the same tabloid? Most will believe our version because it spoofs Goat's story and nullifies his threat to extort money from Sorelle. I'm thinking she owes me something."

FORTY-NINE

hortly before noon the following day, Cheryl Decairo helped
Larry Lemoyne search the tour bus for a wedding ring Vanessa
lost during the Sweethearts' trip to the Keys. During the
search, Larry found the ring near a stereo console. But he also discovered a dial missing on its stereo sound system. Curious, he dislodged a
miniature camera from the tight space.

Cheryl examined the object with him. "Is it a reset button?"

"No, it's a camera. Why would anyone hide a mini-camera on our
bus, unless...."

"Unless what?"

"Uh-oh!" he said. "Isn't this lounge area used for massages?"

"I wouldn't know," she said.

"Well, if a surveillance camera recorded someone's tryst here,
someone else could be a voyeur."

Cheryl glanced warily about. "Suppose more than one was
installed. Should we tell Easter? No, Patrick will know what to do."
She gasped. "Someone might be watching us now, remotely. Larry, I'll
have to report this."

"No," he said. "I'll do it. I want to see the look on Patrick's face."

Minutes later, Larry dared to interrupt Patrick's confab with
reporter Ada Golden in the den where, without explanation, he
slipped three tiny cameras into Patrick's hand.

"Ahhh, proof from the clinic?" Patrick asked. "Good. More help for federal investigators."

"Guess again, Casanova. I found these focused on the lounge area of the bus."

Patrick studied the videographer a moment before finding his voice. "Who'd have the gall to secretly record us?"

"Us?" Larry said, shrugging while only partially concealing a sly smile. "Beats me, but don't tell the Sweethearts."

Patrick wondered if his tryst with Easter was recorded. "Who'd be interested in watching candid videos of the girls? Oh yes, weeks ago Slack Creel mentioned spying on them."

"If there's more to this than meets the eye, Easter might know," Larry said.

Patrick tried to hide the tension in his voice. "Why Easter?"

Fingers interlocked, Larry stood on tiptoes like a ballet dancer. "Just because." He turned away while waving a limp-wristed farewell. "Got things to do, like explain to Vanessa that doing a split has nothing to do with a banana. She's such a hoot sometimes. Ciao, y'all."

"Yeah, see you later," Patrick said. "Let me know what you find out."

"About what? Splits?"

"You know what I mean, smartass—surveillance on our bus." He shook his head, chuckling at Larry who left the room with hands fluttering. "Who'd do such a thing?"

Ada's mouth twitched with a near-grin. "Not to pry, but is Danny on your list of suspects?"

He shrugged. "We have a more pressing issue, Ada—a conman. Why not call Senator Blockton and rattle his cage? Ask him about an underage girl. Sorelle's people surveilled a private conversation and she says Goat knows the senator raped the girl."

"Yeah, and suppose Goat is using that to renege on a kickback to the senator," Ada said. "As the grant-funding facilitator, Blockton would expect a hefty payment."

He nodded. "And Goat is probably thick with the Central Order. He could be their exit guy, the one who terminates the old Senator."

"Yes, so Senator Blockton might be feeling insecure," she said. "He could overreact."

"Right. We're on to something, Ada. If Blockton is due a payment and his pressuring Goat leads to bad repercussions, it'll be game over for the Senator and he knows it."

"Think, Patrick. We need to pry a tell-all from Blockton."

"Just tell the Senator that somebody is making noises about him on a rape video. As you said, he could panic. He might even side with prosecutors in a plea deal for immunity."

Ada's eyes, white in her ebony face, widened in surprise. "You know how a fraudster thinks."

"Yeah, sometimes."

"Is there something you're not telling me, Patrick?"

"Well, yeah. You see, I collaborated with Nigel Pregnor and he authored my bizarre story in the *Analyzer*. Later, I figured Goat would wonder who's manipulating who. Goat plays a major role in that fiction. He knows Nigel's friend is Sorelle and she in turn knows Central Order people, so—"

"Yes-yes!" Ada said. "They could be behind Goat's clinic rip-off of government grants."

"I'm fairly certain of it, Ada."

"Did I ever say you're a gentleman and a scholar? But wait, your story has aliens breeding with humans. You knew that's the kind of bizarre thing readers of the *Analyzer* love, and love to believe."

"Yeah, Nigel said scandals involving sex, money and celebrities are what editors count on. But actually, a hybrid offspring is plausible. In fact, their being fathered by aliens has a precedent."

"Says who?"

He juggled the tiny cameras. "I do. In those ancient days, they were called the Nephilim."

She chuckled. "People from Nephilodium? Beat you to the punch line, didn't I?"

"I'm serious, Ada. In the book of Genesis, rebel angels left Heaven and took attractive women as wives on our planet. The Nephilim were their progeny. Like I told Nigel on the phone, their progeny had superior strength, but those mighty men could only breed two deep."

Her brow furrowed with a look of consternation. "What? Too deep? You're joshing me."

"No, it's like you match a horse and a donkey to get a mule. Two is the end of the line."

"Okay, you're talking about two different species. I didn't see *too deep* as meaning exactly that."

"Not from the country, are you?" he said, smiling.

"No, but I've heard weirder lines in comedy clubs. Too deep? Damn!"

"My grandpa used to say two is the limit for hybrids down the genetic line."

"Ah-hah!"

"Ah-hah what?"

"As you say, Patrick, angels took on human form to mate with women, right?"

"Yeah."

"Well, isn't that an incarnation, like Immanuel claims to be? And wouldn't nature's law prevent his *first* generation from reproducing their own kind? His dynasty of hybrids would be a dead end with no future after two deep. He would therefore have no genetic legacy. Right?"

Stunned, he realized Ada was right. "Yeah, being hybrid, his offspring—if he had any—couldn't reproduce their own kind."

"Patrick, this means his potency is suspect. He's a fraud."

"I know, but you're missing a biggie, girl. That reveal validates the New Scrolls."

"How?"

"Well, they were right all along to mandate a proxy. You know, a surrogate on his behalf."

"Okay, but if an incarnated being has biological limits like that, then Immanuel is married to women who will never have grandchildren, at least not by him. Will you tell them that?"

"No, but I'll tell Easter." He understood now why a modern-day proxy in Immanuel's stead was necessary. "Immanuel is taught by L.T., so he must know divine law forbids spirit people from mating with humans. No wonder he's been reluctant to bed women. And no wonder the Scrolls predict a proxy propagator. And all this time I was dubious about all that."

"But Patrick, he's not the genetic messiah that Moreau brags about."

"Yes, but there's a couple of things you're overlooking," he said. "First, he doesn't need to be a propagator of pedigrees. He has a stand-in. Second, his image as a macho hero is all-important to their pedigree cause. So long as he's the great endorser of products, his fans will continue to buy stuff."

"I understand commerce, my friend, but Easter needs to set the record straight."

"But what about the youth gene?" he blurted. "If he doesn't have it, who does?"

"What youth gene?"

"Oh, that's right, you don't know about that. Well, according to Easter, the Scrolls say some guy has a divine mandate to share the youth gene with pedigree women."

"You mean like the genetic messiah who Immanuel is supposed to be but clearly isn't?"

"Yeah, but what if...somebody else, not Immanuel, uh...had it and became his, uh...surrogate? You know, by default. Or, says the Scrolls, by design."

"Okay, so the proxy guy has the youth gene. Sounds like quite a stretch for someone. Um, you wouldn't happen to know who he is, would you?"

Patrick marveled that the vibes between Ada and himself had always been vigorous. "Girl, you are too curious." Her reasoning had drawn the right conclusion but he feared it would expose himself as the foretold proxy. Perhaps he should change the subject. "By the way, in my article for the *Analyzer*, Goat shops this alien child to anti-Semitic terrorists who're rooted in the magical arts."

"Well, Patrick, we both know the Middle East is still volatile, so your story dovetails logically into Immanuel's arrival on Earth. It's almost like you were inspired to write it to embarrass Goat."

"Well, yeah, sort of." He motioned her to follow him to the kitchen. At the fridge he filled two glasses with ice before glancing back at her. "What'll you have?"

"Ginger ale." She opened a cabinet door. "But with a shot of Canadian Mist."

"Good choice," he said. "When Easter returns from New York this week, I'll see to it that she's there with Immanuel when he signs with the Marauders. And I want the Sweethearts to share in his new contract, too. My girls are extraordinary performers." With a half-smile, he poured the drinks. "The top banker in New York City invited Easter to meet with him in his office. I prepped her for it."

"Someone had the clout to arrange it, eh?"

"Yeah, Sorelle. She thinks he's the key to getting rid of Goodnowe."

Ada leaned on the bar. "Good, but my next phone call will be to Blockton. I want to spin this thing out of Goat's control and rattle the Senator with a bluff, like exposing him for raping the girl. Is it really on video? Do you happen to know her name?"

"No name, even if I knew it. She's only thirteen."

"Thirteen? Okay, that's all I need to know." She frowned and shook her head. "Are you evading my question about the guy with the youth gene?"

"Ada, you're not the type to spread rumors, are you? I mean, if you were me and you were not sure if the youth gene is myth or reality, or you doubted its potency...."

She grinned. "It's you, isn't it? You're the surrogate. That explains Easter's fondness for you and Sorelle's battling her for your loyalty."

"Didn't take a scholar to figure that one out, did it?" he said.

"Didn't take a gentleman, either," she said with a coy smile. "Gotcha."

"Yep, beat me to the punch line."

"My friend, it must be tough straddling the fence between Immanuel's fame and your lack of it. How are you dealing with that? I mean, you've got the family jewels, not him."

"Immanuel is handling it better than I would," he said. "Besides, it takes fame to sell the goods. My one shot at fame was hijacked months ago but looking back, seems it was for the best."

"How long will you keep it a secret?"

"I don't know, Ada. I really don't know."

FIFTY

Easter Beaulieu strolled into the Manhattan Tea Room, top floor of National Guaranty Trust on Fifth Avenue, and settled into a sofa chair. As Reggie Torgenthal's guest, she recalled the banker hinting on the phone about his commitment to her success.

She hoped this meeting would provide more than token support for her plans with the pedigree cause. Otherwise, why would he invite her to meet him in the bank's penthouse?

Looking dapper in his tweed jacket, the Brit stopped at the wine bar before offering his guest a glass of Dom Perignon. His thick mustache failed to conceal the repair to his cleft palate.

Knowing life dealt an uneven hand—always had—she tried not to stare.

After a sip, she nodded approval of the vintage wine while wondering if he admired her status as Immanuel's chief adviser. Did not ancient folklore suggest matriarchs were the force behind every royal throne? Emboldened by this knowledge, she resolved that no mortal would ever exploit her again, least of all Goat Goodnowe.

After kissing her hand, Reggie offered a toast. "I commend you on your television appearance, my dear. Such great stage presence. Such vocal appeal. Such poise. You exhibited more élan than any guest in recent memory."

She smiled. "Thank you, Mr. Torgenthal. I'm lost for words. Here

I am, actually talking with the most powerful financial guru in America."

"Ah, so it's not an act," he said as he sat across from her in a love seat. "I'm enthralled to see that you're as charming in person as you are on the telly."

"Professor Frankl didn't think so," she said before sipping the wine.

Reggie grinned. "In your hands, my dear, it was no contest."

"Well, okay, but was I too harsh? I was only trying to be emphatic."

"Indeed, your points resounded with clarity and wit."

She jangled the bracelet festooned with tiny charms on her wrist. "That's very kind of you and I appreciate the compliment but Dr. Frankl is an educated man. I felt inadequate. Hope it didn't show."

"Call me Reggie, won't you? The professor was boring but you...*you* mesmerized viewers. You brought to life some great phrases. But the slam dunk was when you compared the cobwebby old cliché about slippery slopes to a genetic minefield that leaves victims maimed or dead."

"I had a good coach," she said. "And I followed his script, more or less."

His eyes narrowed as if taken with a poignant thought. "The concept of exploiting human traits for their genetic value intrigues me. And you showed gene matching as one that inspires hope in a world starving for meaning amid all the current chaos and disinformation."

"I try to speak to the heart," she said.

Reggie nodded. "That's because you speak *from* the heart. But if I may, this one thing you could make clear to me."

"Okay, but you may need to ask twice." Laughing softly, she lolled her head to one side. "I'm nearly deaf from listening to the sound of my own importance."

His gaze flitted over her legs. "Just wondering what you meant by Immanuel's perfection being a work in progress. As you may know, his fans view him as needing no improvement."

"You mean, like I'm challenging his perfection?"

"Yes, something like that."

"Well, Immanuel is not infallible." She shook her head. "Sorry, but the Bible itself says Jesus, as the son of God, was *made* perfect by the things he suffered."

"The Bible says *that*?"

"Yes, in the book of Hebrews. And Confucius said, 'Better a diamond with a flaw than a pebble without.' Real perfection for humans is a process. People identify with that. It leads to immortality —" she grinned "—eventually."

"Eventually? Do you believe a deathless body is really attainable?"

"Yes, but with this caveat. It's conditional. The principle is that if we take care of our genome—our life as a living organism—it'll take care of us."

"I see. By the way, do you envision your matching program as a global endeavor?"

"You bet I do," she said. "You realize we're not doing it for bragging rights. Even among people of privilege, equity matters. They understand people of color need our help more than most."

"Yes, level the playing field, as they say." He raised his glass in a salute to her. "Most of my colleagues do not favor spreading our wealth to achieve equality. But I can see karma working in my favor, provided I'm generous."

She crossed her legs at the ankles. "I'm elated to know you feel that way. The Pedigree Nation is about sharing, and the residual effect benefits everybody." She smiled. "And you may call me Easter."

Reggie's eyes twinkled in amusement. "I'm not one to set off a donnybrook, but I must say your worldview is challenging, yet understandable and quite delightful."

"Just so you know, Reggie, I have power backing, even without an immediate funding source to see us through. I'm referring to divine help, of course."

He raised his eyebrows. "Of course. Immanuel did stop a hurricane, didn't he? And yesterday at the capitol building, lightning dispersed a crowd of anti-polygamy protesters. But I must ask if outing Goat Goodnowe was your call."

She lifted the glass of wine to her lips. "I confess, yes it was. He may be valuable to the Order, but he lied to me. In his absence I'm perfectly capable of filling the void." Smiling, she took a sip of wine. "We must think in terms of a genutopia, though."

"Right, but who wrote the bizarre story linking Goodnowe to the theft of a child?"

"You can credit Patrick Murph, my script writer, but Mr. Goodnowe forced our hand. Did you know he threatened to blackmail Sorelle by exposing her as Immanuel's mother?"

Reggie grinned. "Ahhh, checkmate. Murph is more cerebral than I thought. You, too."

She shifted positions in the chair. "Thanks, but I'm here because we need an influx of cash, but untainted, to promote my program worldwide. We also need our TV show to go global, and fast. It's in its third week now and ratings are inching upward. This is one great opportunity for a backer with deep pockets and good connections. Know what I'm saying?"

"Consider it done, my lady. I'm not without resources."

She raised her glass to him. "Regarding the terms of your assistance; we need a lifeline, not a life term. I'm well aware of the deception involved in private equity funding. You overload a company with debt, then sell your stock shares before it goes bankrupt. I'm glad Mr. Crown turned down Dr. Ronofski and his request for an investment. It forced us to find a better way."

"I like the way you think, young lady. We share the same vision. However, it takes a high degree of professionalism to manage a project of the magnitude you envision."

"Yes, I realize we've had to deal with a certain stigma. So in addition to funding, would you like to assist us with your management expertise?"

He smoothed his mustache. "That I can do. Don't worry about the eugenics stigma. Pendulums swing both ways and I have the means to see that it swings in favor of your group's best interests."

Easter finished her wine and set the empty glass on a coffee table. "Convincing skeptics, and that includes Patrick, was difficult," she said. "But now that he sees the big picture, I have no doubt about his commitment. He's rock-solid in favor of our pedigree movement."

Reggie nodded. "Good. A word of caution, though. You'll want to stay away from a colleague of mine. His name is Teddy. Teddy Crown. I'll be happy to airdrop a photo of him for future reference."

"Does he pose a threat?"

"Yes, he's a psychopath. The silly boy once suggested, quite impossibly, that we should patent DiNago's genes and retail them to the vanity market. If he offers monetary backing, reject it."

"Done. Like I said, we have divine backing, so...anything else?"

"Be patient with Sorelle Ebanetti. Rest assured I won't allow her to bugger our deal. You might want to think of her as a mentor."

"Well, to be honest, I've always begrudged her status. But—" she sighed "—it was about seven years ago that I was a finalist in her Zipit pageant. I didn't win, though, and I became disillusioned and then resentful. Still, I wanted to be like her—not only admired but powerful and in control."

"Did you suspect it was rigged in favor of white finalists?" He raised a hand to stop her response. "Allow me one admission. Among those in the Central Order who not only funded her management firm but also her pageant, some objected to her multiethnic policy. I, on the other hand, favored inclusion but Samuel Crown had a racist agenda and he nudged her in the other direction. It affected the outcome, I'm afraid. Pageant judges were coerced."

"I see," Easter said. "So I could have won the crown."

"Certainly, and you should have," he said. "One other thing before you go. Murph's status as a proxy must remain intact. Sorelle doesn't need replacing right away."

"Right away?"

"You didn't hear that from me." He winked. "No one is indispensable, least of all someone we know to be presumptuous."

"So we think alike," she said, her smile ingratiating.

"Easter." He spoke the name with an undertone of respect. "Did you know our ancestors were quite taken with your namesake, *Estarte*, goddess of fertility? Who knows? You, too, could someday be an icon. You and Patrick are essential to our cause. He must not fail in his surrogate role."

"He does have a certain savoir faire," she said. "Now I'd like to ask you something."

"Of course," he said.

She re-crossed her legs for comfort. "Patrick had a shot at fame with a primetime appearance on Wynn Traynor's show. I believe everything happens for a reason but I feel bad for him. He had a shot at it, but it was hijacked. Fame is an obsession with him. I wonder if he can achieve real fame with us on the Funtasy Channel."

Reggie went silent for a five-second count. "Yes, nothing happens by accident, does it? That also includes fame. I'm sorry his act was hijacked but his destiny lies in gene matching."

"Hmmm, destiny. Why do I intuit his act was sabotaged?"

"I like to think it was a fluke. You do realize our people own the rights to Wynn's show."

Eyes blinking fast, she said, "And you sent Sorelle to Sanctuary Beach, didn't you? I figured she wanted to lure Danny away from our pedigree people so he'd play football again. But she also wanted to find out who had the youth gene."

"Actually, she went covertly on her own," he said. "But we've reconciled since then."

Easter exhaled and uncrossed her legs. "Well, I suppose destiny has to be synchronized but I'm curious to know how you rein in a rebel like her."

He stole a glance at his watch. "It's been a pleasure chatting with you."

She stood and shouldered her purse before shaking his hand. "Same here, Reggie. I feel inspired just knowing you're on our side."

Bowing to her, he said, "Be sure to give my regards to Immanuel."

"I'll be happy to, but what about Patrick?"

"Not this time, dear. I hope you understand we must keep his ego in check."

"Yes, but he's an excellent courtier and he enjoys teaching the girls."

"Rest assured, his day will come." He rose and escorted her to the penthouse elevators. "But do remember you'll need Sorelle's assistance to make things happen. Agreed?"

"No problem." Easter forced a big smile before turning to jab an elevator button with her middle finger. "None at all."

FIFTY-ONE

I n her light waffle-weave pullover, reporter Ada Golden sat at a corner table at Ellie's where she ordered a small seafood dish from the menu.

Joining her, Patrick placed the same order for crab cakes. His gaze swept the room before asking a question. "So what's the scoop on the clinic?"

"Not a lot," she said. "Chad, the guy who works for Goat, was at the hospital when Tally passed this morning."

Patrick steeled himself to hear the details. "Blood clot?"

"Not sure, but cranial bleeding for certain."

Birdie Mae ambled over to the table, pulled a check presenter from her pocket, and poured coffee for him before moving on. "I got Tally's statement on video yesterday," Ada said. "I think the DA will bluff Chad into a confession. As for Goat, he's hobbling on crutches. Someone did a number on him."

Patrick's gaze slipped from the broad-shouldered reporter's ebony face to a group of regulars who arrived with Buzz. They settled in a far corner of the restaurant. Opposite Buzz's group, a man in a blue blazer sat alone, his body hunched over as he stared at the shoreline and ignored an iPhone chirping on his table.

In the next instant Patrick sensed the loner's identity. "See that guy in the blazer, the one nursing a cocktail?"

Ada angled her gaze toward him. 'Uh-huh. He looks out of place."

"He's Teddy Crown, a banker. Easier to identify with dorsal fins, if you get my drift. To him, emblot exists to stop Blacks from reproducing. He gave me a race-baiting video. His friends are in a secret supremacist clique. He knows I'm with the Sweethearts and the pedigree cause."

She lowered her gaze. "Easter says the cause is not racist, though."

"True, but not to him. He thinks America needs less color. The plan is genocide by neglect, so his people defunded genetic engineering grants with code word die-off."

She glanced in his direction. "It figures."

"He may have killed a scientist who found a hi-tech cure for emblot. Made it look like a suicide."

"Yes, it's next on my list to investigate."

"Did L.T. return your call?"

"No, but I cornered him last night. I expect he will turn on Goat like a Judas."

"Did he mention the organ cartel or its phony rehab facility?"

"No, but he said your daughter was like a breath of fresh air, and anyone who'd hurt a sweet girl like her ought to be put away for life."

She added a packet of sugar to her tea. "Patrick, I know how you feel about L.T., but I speak as a friend. You have to let it go. Moreau is remorseful. Besides, had he not used Angelina's testimonial on TV, you might still be looking for her. And his network would still be rounding up runaway teenagers."

"Took me more than a year to find her, Ada. I wasn't there when she needed me."

Ada squeezed his arm. "Don't dwell on it, y'hear?"

Patrick shook his head. "Yup. I reckon so, but I'll never forget it."

She squeezed harder. "Listen to me, okay? The way I see it, the feds think L.T. is their leverage with Goodnowe, but they're wrong."

"What leverage?"

"L.T. is refusing to cooperate with investigators. He plea-bargained with the FBI on conspiracy charges in the organ cartel case, even signed a statement that his testimony was not coerced. But it was. They also lied about the IRS, too, so I don't blame him for distrusting bureaucrats. I helped him with the negotiations back then but they deceived me as well."

"Sorry, Ada, but I can't bring myself to trust him. Years ago, here on the coast, he fled with all that condo money and left me to take the rap."

She sighed. "I've never told you this but when I was investigating the rehab scam, it was L.T.'s tips that kept me on track. If not for him, the cartel might still be harvesting organs in Georgia. I hope he's good for an encore."

Patrick shrugged. "What about Senator Blockton?"

She chuckled. "He resigned from Congress. Seems his grants bypassed scrutiny by the National Institute of Biotechnology."

He waited until she finished her meal before asking, "How about the girl he molested?"

Ada looked away. "I have friends, so she's safe. I'm curious, Patrick. Is acting a family tradition with you?"

Recognizing the diversion, he sipped the hot coffee. "Great-grandpa Landon Murph was fond of the stage. Still does small venues; buck dancing, juggling, same as vaudeville."

"Wait. You said *great*-grandpa. He's still alive?"

Patrick smiled. "No surprise. It's as if he adapts, like his cells change. And he's never been sick. Maybe he's the reason my blood has similar oxygen-carrying capacity. Doc Ronofski said geneticists don't, or won't, believe it."

"Why not?"

"Politics, Ada. Bioethicists fear gene matching will negate equality." He cocked his head and peered at her from the corner of his eye while trying to observe Teddy. "You leaving?"

"Uh-huh. Got work to do. You do, too."

"Right. We're workaholics. Stay safe, Ada."

As Teddy left his table to follow her, Patrick realized Ada would know what to do. But, curious about how she would deal with him, he tailed the banker at a distance.

On the boardwalk moments later, Ada wheeled about and thrust a microphone close to Teddy's face. "Hello, Mr. Crown. Care to explain your race-baiting video? You're into genocide, aren't you? Come on, man, speak up. The world is watching. Tell us about your pals and their racist ideology."

Teddy's expression resembled someone looking into the barrel of a loaded cannon. Recovering from the gotcha moment, he blurted, "Watch your step, woman, I speak for the world's badass bankers."

Stepping closer, Ada loomed over him. "You're no badass, pipsqueak, but go ahead, speak your feeble mind, or whatever is left of it."

Patrick squelched the impulse to laugh. The idea of racist demagogues having feeble minds had potential for a new skit.

HAVING ESCAPED ADA'S MICROPHONE, Teddy mumbled a stream of profanities and rushed to his car where he extracted a stash of amphetamines and pain killers from its glove compartment. Bottled water helped down the pills. After a short rest, and with nerves calmed, he opened the trunk of the car and fondled an AK-47, his favorite weapon.

No, now was not the time to execute his clandestine plan.

A Black reporter was not priority. First, he had to take care of an audacious counterfeit, the lone proxy man who threatened to rob Dan the Man of his glory as America's rightful hero.

AS AN OVERFLOW DINNER crowd spilled onto the porch at Ellie's before sundown, Patrick invited Cheryl for a walk along the beach. In the distance, clumps of panic grass, their tall spires jutting skyward, covered huge sand dunes.

Forty yards westward, Sorelle beckoned Patrick and his protégé to join her. As the pair drew near she addressed Cheryl. "Love your pink blouse. But pink becomes you, just as it did at my Zipit pageant last year."

Cheryl smiled. "Patrick's idea. He likes me in pale pink, says the color reminds him of—what was it, cotton candy?"

Sorelle's eyebrows arched. "Ahhh yes, county fair." Her voice rose in a theatrical flair. "But you guys now have the backing you need to do a TV show with more glitz. Oh yes! More color, more lights and costume changes. But I had to go along with Easter's pedigree agenda to get it done."

"Why compromise?" he said.

"Orders from headquarters," she answered. "But I still get to make my movie and audiences will draw their own conclusions about Danny's so-called divine origin."

The rising tide splashed his sandaled feet. "I see nothing divine about our having to deal with the Sweethearts' PR fallout. It's gone viral."

"Scandals can have a purpose, a glorious one," Sorelle said.

"But investigators might try linking Easter to Goat and his colossal fraud," he said.

Sorelle's tone shifted. "But her agreement was an oral one. Heads will roll but not hers. I'm still in control and I don't just pull strings, love, I yank them."

The surf splashed harder against his legs. "Does L.T. know pro football won't weaken Danny's supernatural mission?"

Sorelle clapped her hands. "Yes, and the hype helps to maintain that illusion. By the way, love, must I remind you that Teddy Crown is still a threat, especially to you. He dislikes me, true, but you he absolutely hates."

"And just how do I deal with that?"

"You don't. We have a remedy for psychopaths. Teddy will be, um...processed out."

"Processed out?" He side-glanced Cheryl before eyeing Sorelle. "Is that it?"

"For now," she said.

He propped his sunglasses on his head. "Nothing beats a stroll on the beach," he said.

Sorelle winked. "Not even cotton candy?"

His gaze slipped away from her. Sorelle remembered the county fair and the fluffy candy. But that was then. Eons ago. An infinity. Even her good-humored flippancy had lost its appeal.

He stepped into the saltwater surf, relishing its cleansing flow.

FIFTY-TWO

Teddy Crown turned away from the bureau mirror, repulsed by the image of himself. He opened a bottle of painkillers and downed quadruple the prescribed dosage. An empty decanter of cognac, only recently consumed, sat on an end table alongside an empty glass.

"You can share my pain meds if...." His voice faded after realizing the shapely woman who had lounged on his bed was no longer there. Her absence left him pained by betrayal. Finding easy access to the hotel veranda through a sliding glass door, he stared down at the Sanctuary Inn courtyard. Replete with cobblestones and ornamental trees, it lay only six stories below. Among its statuary, a lone figure sat on a concrete bench and stared back at him, unfazed.

He aimed the AK-47 at his most hated nemesis, but in Teddy's opioid haze the man appeared to smile in the crosshairs of the gun's scope.

"Can't allow you to make a fool of Danny," he said before squeezing off twenty rounds in rapid succession. But, like a shape-shifter, the target somehow avoided the bullets, yet it refused to depart the open courtyard.

Teddy fired another round. "How dare you taunt me, you bastard."

The stone-faced man stared back, unmoving, unspeaking, unworried—grinning.

Teddy aimed again, his hands unsteady. "Is that the only look you can manage, you contemptible idiot?" He pulled the trigger and laughed as the ricochet from slugs zinged off the bench. "Time now to die, you imposter! You have no right to Danny's women." His voice became a scream. "Noooooo right. Do you hear me? Noooooo *riiiiight*."

Distracted by the ornamental statuary of Adonis a few feet from his target, he frowned as it morphed into a bloated caricature. He reloaded the weapon and within seconds rained hollow-points that bounced off the statue and chipped its façade. A steady stream of water flowing from an urn on Adonis' shoulder formed a swirl of illusory crimson.

"At last you bleed." He blinked away the hallucination. Again he aimed. The quarry morphed into elusive shapes. A sound startled him. He turned to face two men in riot gear.

Loud commands bounced about in his head, the words fast becoming a frightful roar.

"Do you know who you're shouting orders to?" he said as a third man appeared, weapon at the ready and aimed his way. "Mr. Theodore Crown, esquire, son of the Imperial Master, that's who. You do not want to mess with me. Gun? No, I'm not putting it down, no matter what."

Cursing the men, he turned away and climbed over the guardrail, unmindful of the steep drop. The sensation of floating punctuated his fall.

Confident he would land on his feet and certain he could bound away with superhuman strength, he envisioned himself escaping his pursuers. But the courtyard sped upward too fast, its blinding mass of stone not the springboard he thought it to be. The assault rifle, his trusty and reliable friend, bounced off the flat stones inches from his distorted face. Blood gushed from his ears and nose and seeped from his cracked skull.

Like his life, the pain was gone, along with the dysgenic curse—all processed out.

WIDE AWAKE SHORTLY BEFORE DAWN, Patrick decided to revise a few skits in the mansion den. The situational humor he conjured with Cheryl and her colleagues only yesterday had real pizzazz.

But to maintain momentum might require a few new creations.

He imagined the ambience of Sanctuary Inn before daybreak could inspire new comedy skits.

He hoped to be free of interruptions as he arrived at its dining room. The room, quiet except for a server's casual greeting and a few early risers, would surely tease free his creative juices.

But he had not figured on seeing Sorelle. She sat alone spooning fruit over cereal. A folded copy of the *Sanctuary Sentinel* lay next to her breakfast plate.

He approached her table and lay his laptop on it. "Addicted to the news, are we?" he said.

She indicated a nearby chair. "Prepare to be surprised, love. As of yesterday, Sor' has an all-new fragrance. Matter of fact, I'm wearing it. Can you tell?"

He pulled out a chair opposite her. "Takes new perfume to thaw the ice queen, huh?"

"Is it that obvious?" she said. "I sprayed a little on my wrist."

He smiled, feigning approval. "From the aroma, I'd say your chemist spared no expense."

"By next week I'll have sampler displays in every boutique across Europe and America. But—" she turned a newspaper page "—other news beg discussing first. Your banker friend, the pathological pest, was found late yesterday in the hotel courtyard, dead by suicide."

"Whoa! The courtyard? Here?"

"Yes. Why are you surprised?"

"Maybe because, as you said earlier, he would be processed out?"

"Ah-hah, you remember. But speaking of news, my investigators informed me that Goat has a young nephew in Brazil who could be his protégé. He speaks several languages and travels extensively. He deals in fine art." A grin emerged. "Some broker sells them to private collectors."

His gaze strayed. "Selling stolen art might be a heritable thing."

"Oh, that again," she huffed. "Back to my investigator. He tailed

Sebastian and a certain senator to Goat's yacht at the marina. I wonder if Goat had to make good on Sebastian's investment."

"At your insistence, no doubt."

"You know me," she said, her smile beguiling. What if I told you all of Goat's computer files are now mine? If I choose to do so, I can bury him."

"You work fast," he said.

"I also paid an administrator at Bon Amite Hospital to wipe out Danny's original birth records."

"Let me guess. After that payment, nobody can ever claim you're his mother."

"Bravo! You'll have to admit I'm very resourceful."

Patrick confiscated a coffee cup from a nearby table and poured from her carafe. "And you think it matters? It doesn't, Sorelle. Danny is an incarnation. He's not even allowed a human mother."

She eyed him as if he needed a shrink. "By the way, the story you concocted with Nigel Pregnor for the tabloid may help the girls' image, but it played into a broader scheme by power brokers in New York." Diamond earrings glittered as she wagged her head. "True, you lampooned Goat. Sowing doubt or confusion, though, is the Central Order's specialty. Many people don't trust medical science. Genetic engineering is no exception. But what I want to know about are your trainees. You're sexually involved with each entertainer, aren't you?"

"Whoa! Are you wanting to start another scandal?"

"Reggie is now the Imperial Master. He admires your tabloid story but he told Easter to cool her heels. Again, the novice has no clue. But as luck would have it, you're a good fit for my talent portfolio. So remember, if the Order wants to deal with you, it has to go through me, not Easter."

"So what's happening to Moreau? Will he be indicted?"

She slowly munched her toast, as if calories could be measured by taste. "I'm sure they'll have to release him back into the wild. Oh, a fire destroyed the clinic and Chad is the suspected arsonist. All the hard evidence there is gone. How glorious is that?"

"But you have the evidence prosecutors need, don't you?"

"I'm not saying." She dabbed a linen napkin at the corners of her mouth. "And I'm not sharing, either. I'll use it any way I like. So there!

Meanwhile, I'm pitching *Star Harem* under a new title. I've renamed it *Treats*. One word—*Treats*. You like it?"

"It's okay."

"Just okay? *Treats* is also a metaphor. Get it?"

"Who wouldn't?" he said.

"Sebastian is helping me produce a docudrama. It'll show how those star-struck beauties were exploited by a conman, but Danny outsmarted him."

He poured more coffee. "You do know Sebastian was a party to denigrating the Sweethearts."

"Yes, but we would never let anything happen to Sebastian."

"We?"

"Yes, the Central Order chastises its own but we have each other's back."

Patrick's appetite slipped away. "You're a player, aren't you, like porno kingpin Sebastian, and you wanted me to think Easter was one of them."

She groaned as if dealing with an adolescent whiner. "Does it matter? Listen, we're flawed. All of us. You, too. You slept on the bus overnight with Easter at least twice this week, and don't deny it."

He shrugged away a nagging sense of guilt.

"Yet you have the unmitigated gall to accuse me of sleeping around," she said.

"Are you still blaming her for poaching your property?"

"Yes, but we came to terms. Want to hear more? Good. I bought Slack Creel's real estate for DiNago Diversified. But that's not all. I settled her debt with Creel Properties, so she *owes* me. Once again, I've dealt myself a winning hand. Ah, leverage. It's the one thing we both understand."

"Uh-huh, but she'll never give up on the pedigree promise."

"Admit it, Patrick, she's not the leader I am. She tried to use the girls as a bargaining chip and failed. Truth is, she doesn't know how to cover her bases."

"She'll learn."

"Only if you're always there to catch her when she falls." She wiggled her fingers. "Anyway, we have only a few hours together before I leave for New York. Let's not waste it talking about her."

He looked across the room, his voice apathetic. "Moving right along...."

She leaned toward him. "In the *Treats* script the leading man is a PI who—"

"I know, I know."

"Oh, and you also know, then, his lover is a former model. But get this; she manipulates mega-rich financiers into promoting gene matching. One helps her glorious ascension to the imperial throne."

"Let me guess. Reggie himself elevates you."

"Of course."

"So you'll endorse pedigree gene matching." He grinned. "After all, your son is the poster boy, totally in sync with its goals."

"My son? Can't let it go, can you? Yes, I rejected the pedigree program, but Danny morphed into this glorious spiritual man. It's value added. He is godlike, isn't he?"

"If you say so."

She rolled her eyes. "In *Treats*, moviegoers will know it's me because only I could dismantle a scam that big."

"Dismantle but not destroy," he said. "In your world, the super-rich get a pass."

"Patrick, life is not a movie. You don't destroy something that pervasive. It's like a tumor with tentacles around our social spine—too risky for surgery. The best you can do is make inroads, perhaps effect change in the way they do business, maybe even alter their mindset. David may kill Goliath, you see, but not the entire Philistine army."

Astounded over her insights, it occurred to him that Sorelle would always have the upper hand. She lived to manipulate friend and foe. Deceiving to gain leverage had become sport. "One last thing," he said. "Easter deserves credit for Danny's new re-up contract with the Marauders."

Chin resting on her fist, she studied his eyes. "You owe her, right?"

"No, Sorelle, *you* owe something."

"Like what?"

"Easter would never consent to letting Danny return to football without me convincing her that it's for the greater good. Believe me, persuading her took some doing."

"So it did. Are we ready to go up to my room?"

He frowned. "It's all one big farce, isn't it? Goat once said we all have our price."

She gave him a condescending look. "You haven't taken the high road yourself, Patrick. We all thrive on competition, not idealism." She stood to go. "Come with me, love."

"No, somebody is waiting to see me."

"Business or pleasure?"

He sighed. "It's been a rough ride with you, Sorelle, but it's nothing that another ride won't cure. At least with the Sweethearts, I'll draw a ride I can handle."

"You need me, Patrick," she said. "You know I'm indispensable to your career. Without me, you go nowhere in the entertainment industry."

"Maybe so, but I'm done with the wrong draws."

"Is this your way of saying goodbye?"

"It's as good a way as any," he said.

"Poor man, you still resent the fact they you're not Danny. And you're chapped that you can't beat the system. See, I know you better than you know yourself."

Wanting to appear unfazed, he opened his laptop. "Danny is just window dressing. Now, if you don't mind, I have work to do. Be good to yourself, Sorelle."

She stalked away, heels clicking on tile, not looking back.

FIFTY-THREE

From the hotel dining room, Patrick studied an article in the discarded *Sentinel*. Its report of an accident becoming a crime scene piqued his interest.

An incoming boater near Sanctuary Marina had tried to rescue two men from the brackish waters of Mobile Bay after they were abandoned by the yacht's owner. Investigators identified one of the men who fell from the deck of *LoveLord*, Sebastian Rubleau. He survived. The other man, Senator Blockton, could not be resuscitated. Both men had been suited for business, not a pleasure ride, and neither wore a flotation device.

Patrick pondered the news. Had Goat betrayed his colleagues to avoid paying a kickback?

One *Sentinel* journalist, citing an anonymous source, said Goodnowe's destination was Brazil, a country 'known for ignoring America's extradition treaty.' But a report from the Coast Guard stated the yacht was found burning in the gulf eighty miles from shore.

Goat's fate was not something Patrick wanted to dwell on at the moment.

Instead, memories of Easter Beaulieu at the Waldorf Astoria carried him back to a January night when he suggested humor was the great equalizer. It had proven to be much more. When combined with a slogan like *pedigree—a cause worth mating for*, it had a certain cachet. He had insinuated her recruits could be trained to eclipse the famous Globe Trotters.

Still, questions about gene matching's potential to change society on a grand scale needled him. But his musing was interrupted by a text message. It seemed to bode trouble.

I have powers far superior to yours and I will return in a different form. You won't see it coming. You are a pawn in this sovereignty game. It is our destiny to rule by divine right and dominate all things entrusted to our care. -RG.

Patrick read the message twice, knowing it was probably sent by Raul Goodnowe—RG—from a burner phone. Goat's bogus clairvoyance seemed a trifling annoyance. He deleted it.

CHERYL SAT in the shade of the veranda while writing in her diary during a morning break.

She smiled as her fingers tried to keep pace with thoughts she might compare to a harvester in the midst of unloading grain.

Freckles is hiding a serpentine surprise on the troupe's bus. It's digital moves look awesome. Her plan for slapstick fun is timed for maximum impact. After our target recovers, we girls will waylay him, even sweet-talk him into doing his Pony Xpress act. Following it, we have a much bigger surprise. I feel certain it's one he will long remember.

THINKING Easter would answer a question that still nagged him. Patrick complied with her request for a heart-to-heart talk at Ellie's.

Her hip-hugger jeans and shimmery crop top earned glances from Buzz Cassidy and his fellow admirers as she sashayed through the restaurant ahead of Patrick. She chose a booth that offered the best view of the beach, but out of earshot from Buzz and his buddies.

"It's a lot more pleasant here with the Labor Day gawkers gone," Easter said.

Patrick made a show of pulling a chair out for her. "It's perfect, but when will you clue me about our entertainment plans?" he said. "I'm excited about us adding some new material."

"Okay…" She paused as Birdie Mae placed iced tea on their table and offered a *howdy folks* greeting. With a sly wink, she plopped down extra wedges of lemon.

He spoke while Easter jabbed a straw at floating ice cubes in her tea. "Your verbal slugfest on the *Hotz* hit a home run with me, sweetie. "Dealing with Wynn's sarcasm wasn't easy."

"Right you are," she said. "Oh, the miniatures Larry found on our bus; could I see them, please?"

Patrick dug into his side pocket and slid the cameras across the table to her. "All yours," he said. "Slack Creel talked about rigging cameras on the bus a couple of months ago."

She stirred the ice cubes in her tea. "And I'm thinking somebody else leaned on Larry for that."

He took a deep breath. "Why do it for a huckster?"

"Because Mr. Goodnowe was helping our career as entertainers. But then Immanuel was not the stud he'd imagined. Hidden cameras didn't matter after that."

"Whoa!" he said. "It's still an invasion of privacy."

"True, but we can't afford to raise a stink about it, baby. We've seen enough PR fallout already." She gave him a sheepish look. "I trusted Larry never to give them to anybody."

Patrick glanced in Buzz's direction. "I never want a release of us making out. Okay?"

She smiled. "Okay, shy one."

Birdie Mae delivered his breakfast, made a face at Easter who devoured the raw pulp of a lemon wedge, and lumbered away toward Buzz and his pals.

Patrick scrunched his shoulders. "What about the fame we promised the Sweethearts?"

"I'm way ahead of you, comedy man."

"You always are."

She rattled the ice cubes and popped one into her mouth. "We'll take center stage at Marauders halftime shows, home games only. Our girls will share in the profits with a contract from all our other ventures, too. Anything else you wanna know?"

"Yeah. Sorelle padded your debt into the Creel deal." He sipped coffee before slicing into an omelet stuffed with crab and shrimp. "Now she can brag that she's one up on you."

"Y'know what, Patrick? I owe Sorelle nothing. Know why? Immanuel agreed to my terms."

"Favorable terms?"

"Yes, I'll share in his wealth. And someday I'll control his budget. Yeah, totally. Generosity is not an option, it's a law, and Immanuel has to honor the Scrolls. Also, Sorelle wouldn't want anybody blabbing about her real father. Your great-grandmother told me the truth about that. Eugenia is quite the clearinghouse, so you better believe that info is my leverage."

"Okay, what else?"

"Tomorrow we meet, Sorelle and me, with Tookie Ward. Immanuel will ink a billion dollar re-up with the champion Marauders. Good is happening, you know, thanks to a certain comedian finessing his ideas."

"Finessing?"

"I've seen how you work. You massage the mind. And you never quit on a good thing, do you?"

Patrick eased his hand up. "I had to make sure you got credit for Immanuel's new contract."

She slapped his upraised palm. "Yes. Teamwork made a dream work."

"Yeah, but had I not been sabotaged on the *Hotz* last year, all of this may not—"

"It was predestined, darling. With myself and Sorelle working on your brand, who wouldn't be surprised if Casanova Comic becomes a household name."

"Casanova two-point-o," he said as he pushed the plate of food toward her. "What else?"

"I'm having the girls sign a movie deal on Monday...with you. Sorelle says the script calls for a Casanova, one who becomes an amateur sleuth."

"Sorry. No can do."

"What?" She spread her arms wide. "Why not?"

"The visibility would be too much," he said. "I have a checkered past."

Excited, she jangled the multicolored charms on her wrist. "Listen, Patrick Murph. Enough of this hide-and-seek business. You have no problems that a few million won't mend."

"A few what? Million?"

"Yes. I negotiated a contract for you. Sorelle signed off on it." She raised her arms. "Ta-da! How does it feel landing a starring movie role? Feel like celebrating?"

He smiled. "I'm flabbergasted."

"Oh yes, we girls have a wine and cheese party planned for you on the bus." Taking his fork, she ate part of his breakfast. "Baby, you're destined to be America's newest matinee idol."

"Yeah, I can live with that, but who's the leading man in this *Treats* flick?"

"You'll co-star with Immanuel. When the movie's released, he'll go on a publicity tour. Then he'll play football. Go-go DiNago! It's a new day, darling. The nations are about to be shaken, just as the Scrolls predicted, and their treasures will come pouring in."

"Define treasures."

"One hint. It's the kind of wealth money can't buy. Think genetic assets."

Genetic assets. Patrick mulled over the words. "It's more than an innate defense against disease, isn't it? It has aesthetic value, too. Plus, pedigree could be considered a form of wealth."

"Eureka!" she said. "Does it remind you of DeSoto at Maubilla? He failed to see its true value."

"Okay, but that kind of wealth won't register in people's minds unless...."

She returned his breakfast unfinished. "Unless what?"

"I mean, good genes are valuable but the rich moguls might scheme to acquire—confiscate—the best of those assets, like my youth gene. Genetic dynasties could then become the norm."

"No-no," she said. "I won't allow a privileged few to be favored with top-tier genes. I can stop elitist bargaining like that from happening."

"But how? The rich hire lobbyists and loopholers and lots of other specialists."

"Our genetic riches are a power far beyond theirs," she said. "We'll use it as leverage when the time comes."

He pondered the idea. Even as the Central Order's tentacles wrapped around the world's social and economic spine, how could Easter leverage his youth gene?

"Wait," he said. "My great-grandmother used land as her leverage, but I valued my autonomy more than land. What does that tell you about some of us pedigree people? Especially prodigals."

"It tells me our choices shouldn't be dictated. After all, we're not a cult."

"But I'm an outcast," he said.

"But Eugenia has changed. She agrees selections should not be decided arbitrarily. The Scrolls say we give voice to our *choice*, remember? So, are you committed to the pedigree promise? And are you ready to share your genetic wealth?"

He chuckled. "It's hard not to when my gorgeous mentor's future depends on it."

FIFTY-FOUR

Her eyes softened as she watched him finish eating in the near-empty restaurant. "Aren't you amazed at how our lives have synchronized with the New Scrolls?"

"I'm even more amazed over your ability to intuit the future," he said.

"I do *read* the Scrolls, baby," Easter said. "Would it surprise you if a golden companion were in your future?"

"Golden?"

"Yes. The Scrolls even say a relative of yours is ageless. Do you realize how valuable Landon Murph's bicentenary genes are?"

Patrick chuckled. "Whoa, back up, he doesn't strike me as that old."

"Really? Do you know when he was born?"

"Well, they say he first saw the light of day during the hurricane of 1906."

"But there's no real record of his birth," she said. "Not even a notation in the family Bible."

"Now there's something I never knew." As his thoughts took shape, fantasy clashed with reality. "Okay, oversights happen. Or maybe an extra Bible is missing with his name in its registry."

"He could even be a triple centenarian," she said.

He gave her a suspicious look. "Is that how ageless is defined in the Scrolls?"

"If it means he has what you have, yes. And more."

"So the Central Order could target him, too."

"Well, we both know rich materialists will try cornering your youth gene, as if it's another elixir they can stock in their marvelous medicine wagon. But Dr. Ronofski says power brokers don't suspect your great-grandfather Landon has it."

"And they really don't know the youth gene's real value, either, do they?" he said.

"Well, being a Hernando DeSoto kind of capitalist, they think only of its potential Wall Street trading value. Of course, Reggie is the exception."

Shaking his head, he stood with arms raised in a sign of surrender. "I suppose we can deal with their schemes when the time comes."

"The time is now," she said. "We outflanked their first tactic but Reggie's not the only player."

He blinked the idea away. "Speaking of change, since you and Sorelle are sharing control of my acting career, tell me about your truce with her."

Easter rose and moved closer to him. "No formalities. It's like a mutual understanding."

He wanted to embrace her without an audience. "So when is our *Treats* shoot?"

She shadowed him across the expanse of tables and chairs. "Three months, give or take."

Ushering her outside, he stopped on the porch and held her hand. A stiff breeze swept over them, carrying with it a salty mist.

"You'll need to make one concession in the movie script," she said.

"Okay, let's hear it."

"Your character is more than a buffoon with a tune. He's quite impulsive. But he's also, shall we say...flawed, but in a way audiences can understand."

"Don't tell me he's a klutz. Does he stutter? I'm thinking he has to be likable. Right?"

"Um, yes, he's likable enough but moviegoers will be fascinated by his obsession."

"Obsession with what?"

She nibbled her lip. "Your character has a chronic sexual condition and his infidelity breaks the heroine's heart. Sorelle says that theme is realistic."

"Didn't see that one coming," he said. "Sounds like I'm being stereotyped."

She leaned against him. "Sorelle insists that you portray a connoisseur of trophies, the kind you mount—" she made air quotes "—'but not on a wall.' Her words, not mine. Sounds sort of funny, eh?"

"Yeah, but why blame a guy because he has an occasional testosterone rush?"

"Occasional?"

"Yeah, occasional." His grin gave way to a smile. "Okay, maybe a bit more than occasional."

She tugged his hand while descending the steps. "It'll come in handy with the Sweethearts."

"You know the girls mean a lot to me," he said. "I see them as real art, not sexy burlesque. My feelings for them run deep, too. Perhaps I'm just in awe of their talent, their beauty, their—"

She poked his midsection. "You know they're just as enamored of you as you are of them."

"Never thought admiring them would lead to this...this...."

"This what? Among us pedigrees, love is not only about making a better baby but nurturing the baby's mother, too, so confess your love and tell them how you feel."

He breathed deep and exhaled. "By the way, in our movie, is polygamy legal?"

"No, and that's another conflict that adds drama," she said. "And did you know we matriarchs are destined to control the pedigree cause? We girls have a lot to teach our paramour."

"You don't say."

"Yes, and the male primarily serves as seeder and courtier to his lovely wives."

Easter's easy laughter descended into a throaty purr while leading him along the boardwalk. "I'd like you to open up more and feel the vibes. And remember, make eye contact with them."

"Eye contact? Where have I heard that before?"

A SKY STREWN with wispy clouds and temps in the upper eighties lured Cheryl away from the steps of the mansion. With a digital camera slung over her shoulder, she strolled across the flagstone yard and settled in the gazebo where her latest impressions could be noted without distractions.

A reporter friend at the Buttcrack Beacon confided Goodnowe's yacht exploded far out in the gulf, but investigators found only the burned corpse of Chad on the vessel. He's the skipper who interned at the conman's clinic. Mysteries abound, yet I've seen every obstacle to our mission removed one by one. Almost. The Seeder must complete his purpose and fully regenerate his mates in the Pedigree Nation.

Looking up from her diary, she glimpsed Patrick and Easter walking from the beach toward the bus. Smiling, she checked the settings on her camera. "Surprise, surprise," she said to herself.

GLANCING back at Ellie's restaurant, Patrick imagined Buzz's fixation on Easter and her fluid moves as she sauntered along the boardwalk. The gadabout would not know her dream of a better genetic life or how much it appealed to the comedian's sensibilities, especially since Sorelle no longer controlled his love life or his sentiments about generosity.

With a hand low on Easter's back, he drew her closer. "A new skit hit me last night."

"Good, I hope it's a romantic one."

"Um, it's comedy, not romance, but—"

"Patrick, since when did you stop believing humor laced with romance is what we girls like?"

"Okay, so long as it's compatible with humor. So I'm watching a newbie on TV auditioning for a job. She points to a weather map and forecasts no rain. 'No chance,' she says. So imagine her reaction when thunder rumbles in the background—boom-boom-boom!"

Easter nudged him. "Don't forget to include romance."

"Sure thing," he said. "In my skit the girl—"

"Wait. What does she look like? Tall or short? Thin or plump?"

"I don't know. She's trying for weathergirl, not for Plumpkin Queen. Anyway, she rushes to a side window for a look-see. It's raining buckets. The camera follows her back to her desk. She meows like a cat, looking anxious and says, 'Well, at least we don't have to worry about a tornado out there.'"

Easter grinned. "So a twister comes roaring through, right?"

"Yep, right over the studio. She dives under a desk."

"Not if she's plump."

"Okay, she stuffs herself under a desk and timidly peeks out to face cameras and meows louder. Wide-eyed, she blurts, 'Well, okay, but at least we don't have an earthquake.'"

Easter laughed. "Don't tell me; the set falls apart."

"Uh-huh, a large weather map crashes to the floor. Blam-kinkle-shuuump-pop! She looks off-camera at the studio prop men, throws her earbuds at them, and yells, 'I've had it with you guys and your pranking me. *Meowww, meowww.*"

"What's with the meow?"

"I'm getting to that. She has a genetic flaw. We foreshadow it as—"

"Patrick, how is a meow romantic?"

"Whoa! Let's rewind. Under duress she thinks her meowing is normal."

"So how does that help her deal with the prop men who pulled the prank on her?"

"It doesn't."

"It should. Why not weaponize it?"

"But this is a skit where anything can happen."

"Okay, so how do we explain it to TV viewers?"

"Her parents have a recessive gene," he said. "They passed it along to her, so—"

"You'll need a voiceover. So when does romance make an entrance?"

"Romance? It's a skit about the cri du chat syndrome. She's mewing and it's a sexy sound and it happens at odd moments. Prop guys love it. In their prank, the illusions of bad weather trigger her need to meow louder. Funny, huh?"

She gently clawed his backside. "Ever heard two cats caterwauling?"

"Yeah, it's a god-awful noise at night."

"Okay, so why not give her a co-host, a weatherman? Let him have the same flaw. They attract each other, male and female, and really go at it, caterwauling to high heaven. The director tries but he can't stop them. They're both thunder and lightning and the prop guys' prank is backfiring on them."

"Yeah, that's slapstick-funny. They didn't see it coming. Ha! Neither did I. They'd find each other irresistible, wouldn't they? Like I do you."

She massaged his hip beneath his beltline as her voice softened. "Yeah, they'd get it on—on TV. But she has to be real silky-sultry, like *meowww*-m*eowww*."

He chuckled. "Hey, with that velvet voice you just nailed the weathergirl part."

Her hand slid inside his Dockers to caress his backside. "Speaking of cat 'n around, do you recall how your parents first discussed plural wives with you?"

"Not really. Why would they?"

"How could you not know you have brothers and sisters everywhere?"

"What're you saying, girl?"

She slowed her cadence. "Patrick, I'm saying your family tree is, shall we say, laden with fruit, like mine. Check out your siblings. You have forty-two sisters and fourteen brothers, all divided among one man's twelve wives."

"Whoa! Who has twelve wives?"

"Don't tell me you don't know about your father."

He tried to pull away but her hand kept him immobile. "Are you pranking me?"

"Get a clue, darling. He built lots of houses, all within the borders of his farm. Each house is occupied by a mother whose kids are your kin, your half-sisters and brothers."

"What? How is it you know more about my kinfolk than I do?"

"Because in the International Registry, pedigree families are listed, but in code."

"But you... I mean, you insisted I have a genetic test done. You knew everything about me long before we met on the *Hotz*. Who told you? Wait, I get it—Eugenia. Right?"

"Yes, her and the registry."

"You're kidding me," he said. "Wait. You didn't recruit me just for my coaching expertise, did you? You needed a seeder. So tell me, at what point did you know about my youth gene?"

She paused. "Some months after you came aboard, Doc Ronofski told me. Can you imagine how I felt? Then later I was overjoyed when Reverend Moreau suggested that I become your primary lover and groom you as Immanuel's proxy, even assist you in being my personal courtier."

"But somebody should have told me earlier."

"Why tell you? Eugenia said prodigals sometimes squander their birthright."

Groaning, he said, "Here we go again with the inheritance thing."

She smiled. "That's why she kept you out of the loop, so to speak. But now that the cat is out of the bag—*meow!*—it's time for you to do something about it. Something, well...generous."

"How could I not know my closest kin were polygamous?"

"Odd how we never see what we're not looking for, isn't it, baby?"

He studied her a moment. "I could've stayed and played by Eugenia's rules."

"Yes, but you didn't. Aren't you glad I brought you back into the fold? The way I see it, your redemption is providential. The girls agree. After all, it worked in your favor as well as ours."

He took a deep breath. "You know, all this time I've been afraid to tell Mom about you wanting me as a paramour for the girls. I'm guessing she knows about it, though; you did say it's providential."

Easter withdrew her hand. "Yes, all things work together for good."

Strolling unhurried away from the beach area, he considered what a providential future might mean. Who had started the polygamy trend in the Murph collective? Was Landon its leading progenitor? The realization hit him that he knew little about his ancestors.

Alongside Easter, he crossed the intersection at Peninsula Road and Bon View. Ahead of them and west of the mansion, a copse of palm trees shaded the Silver Eagle. As he veered toward the bus, a chorus of rowdy voices reached his ears. His gaze swung toward the mansion where Cheryl sauntered away from the gazebo to merge with the girls.

Spilling from the mansion, the girls romped like models in a *Sport-Scene* swimsuit issue, running through the spray of lawn sprinklers to reach the bus.

"Look, it's your surprise party," Easter said, pointing. "So act surprised."

He recognized a lone figure awaiting their arrival at the bus. "Freckles?" He did a double-take. "She's topless! C'mon, we have to put her on the bus."

Easter clenched his hand, forcing him to slow down. "Wait. Let's call her bluff."

"But she could be arrested if—"

"Then they'll have to arrest the entire team," Easter said.

On cue the girls paused five yards from the bus, twirled in place, and performed a shimmy-shake—topless—then did a samba dance, as if regaling oglers in a Rio de Janeiro carnival.

Declining to look toward the Sanctuary Research Institute where students had settled in, Patrick fist-bumped his forehead as the girls threw kisses toward him.

"Forget the good-girl image," he said while watching their provocative dance.

Easter pranced a few yards ahead of him before turning to backpedal, her cadence like a horse in dressage competition. An aura framed her head and the bronze highlights in her hair showed a brighter luster than he had witnessed in the past. Was it an illusion—the optics of light or heat reflecting off the sand to create a mirage—or did he simply want to accept it as one? He wasn't sure.

He hand-shaded his brow for a better view, but the light about her face had vanished. Catching up to her, he wanted to ask about the phenomenon but she quickly pulled him close to the bus. Behind the closed door of the bus, the Sweethearts hid from view.

"Hey, what's up?" he called to them.

"Remember to give the girls a Broadway smile," Easter said as the door opened in a hydraulic *whoosh*. Leaning in, she shouted, "Are we ready for our Casanova Comic?"

Easter jumped aside as the girls yelled in unison.

In the same moment Freckles thrust a large snake from the dark interior of the bus. It uncoiled in midair and hit him chest-high. He yelled and catapulted backward to land on his buttocks. Legs kicking and arms flailing, he soon recognized the snake as a replica of the python used earlier in Freckles' skit.

"Utopia to Houston," Freckles said into a microphone. "The buffoon has landed."

Laughing in boisterous celebration, the girls rushed from the bus and encircled him.

"Never have I seen you move that fast," Easter said. "Like you were shot from a cannon."

His adrenalin rush passed as the Sweethearts danced around him. Still on the ground, he realized the girls had not been bare-chested. Instead, Cheryl had recorded them in illusory flesh-toned bodysuits.

"Are you okay, baby?" Easter said. "You trained us to be spontaneous."

"What better stunt than this for a comedy show?" Anastasia said.

"Nothing beats slapstick," Vanessa said. "So consider yourself slapped, coach."

Back on his feet amid the girls' teasing, he accepted a round of hugs. "You girls want to be the best, uh-huh, but if y'all get any bester, don't know how I'll survive it."

Along with the group's dancing, he rhapsodized the nucleus of a rap song he had created for the Funtasy television show. "The sight of you makes me stronger longer. Together we can rejuvenate and regenerate, so rev up the rhythm and show 'em we're driven to enhance romance with an impromptu dance. Hear my desire for you, my fire for you...."

Corralling him, they urged him aboard the Silver Eagle.

Soon after entering the bus, he smiled as they drew ever closer, their whispered endearments invading his libido, irresistible in their appeal. All confided to wanting his acceptance and his love.

Pedigree now seemed to him more about love than clinical

science. Being grounded in a spirit of altruism, generous reproduction would always have the last word. And the godspot, that unique moment when multiple happenings coalesce for a perfect outcome, would not be a vain expectation. His destiny as a seeder seemed inevitable.

Was his and Easter's role in the pedigree cause truly inevitable? He was sure of it now. He was also sure close-up moments like these with the Sweethearts would intertwine with destiny to jump-start a new generation of better babies.

THE END

(If you enjoyed this book, please consider leaving a review)

Continue the Pedigree Nation series with Book 2, *Pedigree Persuasion*: https://books2read.com/Pedigree-Persuasion

Patrick Murph must take charge of the Pedigree Nation's expansion...

His romantic interest, Easter Beaulieu, pressures him to grow her cause at warp speed and save the world from genetic implosion...

But a new DOJ in Washington who despises the cause has other ideas...

Adding to the intrigue is Amelita Divoli who sports a beauty mark—a golden epidermal sheen. She seems destined to win the Zipit Beauty Fest, a pageant meant to enhance the pedigree movement's image...

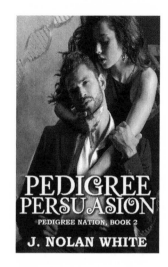

PEDIGREE PERSUASION

PEDIGREE NATION, BOOK 2

J. NOLAN WHITE

...until Patrick reveals she's a plant embedded by her billionaire sponsor to subvert the cause for his own sovereignty ambitions.

...one man

...one mutant gene

...one chance to save humanity

...until Attorney General Megan Meyers decides to bend the rules and build her creds for a presidential run by eradicating the pedigree cause.

Once again, Patrick must devise an ingenious strategy to beat an adversary at her own tyrannical game while saving America from its most dangerous despot.

TURN THE PAGE TO READ AN EXCERPT...

PEDIGREE PERSUASION
EXCERPT

"Be honest with me, Patrick." She tugged at a lock of hair near the tangle of hoop earrings, their glittery colors against her olive complexion clearly bohemian. "We're deeply in love, true, but does having the youth gene make you feel like maybe we'll never be the perfect match?"

"I'm serving as a seeder on behalf of a sports demigod who's hyped as the genetic messiah," he said. "What does that tell you?"

"No, I don't doubt your potency, baby, but do you have that extra surge of energy foretold in the sacred Scrolls?"

"You know I do, Easter, so why doubt yourself? I adore you."

"Because I just met the golden girl from South Africa and with her winning smile, she's sure to win the glamour thing in Vegas. Know what else she can do?"

He smiled. "Bite with her gold tooth?"

"She can steal your heart. Yeah, she's got charisma but also a genetic asset you won't believe. Ever seen anybody with a golden epidermal sheen? It's a rare mutation. Like rare as your youth gene."

Chuckling, he faked a look of surprise. "Next you're gonna say she has that, too, and we should meet up and make gold babies."

"Y'know, hon, for a comedian, your sense of timing could stand improving."

About the Author

J. Nolan White is a writer who was born in Baldwin County, Alabama. His interest in writing began at his hometown newspaper in Bay Minette but soon segued into editing three magazines, including ownership of *Genomics World*.

He has also won several short story contests and served as president of the Baldwin Writers Group for the last 10 years.

In 2015 he retired as editor of a fishing and hunting magazine —*Great Days Outdoors*—but still has an abiding interest in the environment and the wonders of nature. *Pedigree Promise* is his first novel.

Find out more about Nolan at https://books2read.com/Nolan-White

Made in the USA
Coppell, TX
31 December 2021

70443933R00229